STAR WARS

THE ESSENTIAL GUIDE TO ALIEN SPECIES

The
STAR.WARS ®
Library
Published by
Del Rey Books

STAR WARS®

THE ESSENTIAL GUIDE TO ALIEN SPECIES

TEXT BY

ANN MARGARET LEWIS

ORIGINAL ILLUSTRATIONS BY

R.K. POST

 THE RANDOM HOUSE PUBLISHING GROUP
NEW YORK

A Del Rey® Book
Published by The Random House Publishing Group

Copyright © 2001 by Lucasfilm Ltd. & ™.
All Rights Reserved. Used Under Authorization.

Published in the United States by Del Rey Books, an imprint of The Random House Publishing Group, a division of Random House, Inc., New York, and simultaneously in Canada by Random House of Canada Limited, Toronto.

Del Rey is a registered trademark and the Del Rey colophon is a trademark of Random House, Inc.

www.starwars.com
www.starwarskids.com
www.delreybooks.com

Library of Congress Catalog Card Number: 00-193267

ISBN 0-345-44220-2

Interior and cover design by Michaelis/Carpelis Design Associates, Inc.

Manufactured in the United States of America

First Edition: April 2001

9 8 7 6

Author's Acknowledgments

This book could never have happened if not for the help and support of so many people to whom I owe my gratitude:

Lucy Autrey Wilson, who gave me the opportunity.

Sue Rostoni, whose patience and sensibility were invaluable.

My editor, Steve Saffel, who believed in me, and his wife, Dana Hayward, who encouraged me.

All the Bantam and Del Rey *Star Wars* authors, whose imaginations made these creatures live in our minds. I would also especially like to remember the late novelist Brian Daley, who brought the magic of *Star Wars* to radio, and gave us an unforgettable series of Han Solo stories.

All the comic book artists and writers from Dark Horse and Marvel, who made these creatures incarnate in words and pictures. In particular I'd like to remember the late Archie Goodwin, who showed us how powerful comic book storytelling could be.

All the West End Games authors and designers, who created an incredible wealth of material.

Rich Handley and Daniel Wallace, my personal gurus of *Star Wars* wisdom. The depth of their knowledge is absolutely astounding. This book never would have been finished without their help. And Rich's wife, Jill, who let me crash in her back room after a long day of research. Also thanks to Jeff Boivin, Craig Carey, Helen Keier, and Pablo Hidalgo.

Lynda Chiarella, Leslie Danneberger, Bill Enger, Mark and Melea Fisher, Pat Grant, Brandy Hauman, Susan Irwin, Karen Jones, Kim Kindya, Valerie Meachum, Arwen Rosenbaum, Laura Sherman, and Kirk Taskila, who helped keep my interest in *Star Wars* alive.

My managers Kevin Dreyfuss and Andrew Leitch, who supported me in my creative endeavors when they didn't have to.

To all the creators at ILM and Lucasfilm, who with their incredible imaginations created many of these creatures out of clay, plastic, paint, and rubber, then made them dance on-screen.

My seven sisters and brothers, who now believe me when I say that *Star Wars* matters; and my mother, who never let me forget I have talent.

My husband, Joe, who made me dinner, did laundry, kept my computer working, and loved me throughout the whole process of writing this book, and continues to do so. I love you.

And to George Lucas, who through *Star Wars* inspired so many people from my generation to become creative professionals. Bless you.

Introduction

"Why do I sense we've picked up another pathetic life-form? . . ."
—OBI-WAN KENOBI

Star Wars takes place in "a galaxy far, far away"—a universe filled with wondrous worlds and fantastic heroes. To add depth and color to this ever-expanding myth, George Lucas, the designers at Industrial Light & Magic, and dozens of novelists, comic book writers, and game developers have created an entire universe of exotic aliens, many of which are included in this book.

Star Wars: The Essential Guide to Alien Species covers many of the most pivotal species in the *Star Wars* universe, selected because they met one or more of the following criteria: They appeared in at least one of the films; they were important to a major story line; or they were members of a species that begged for further exploration. While we've done our best to select as many as possible of the species readers may like to see, there are many that were not included. As with all of the *Essential Guides*, the goal was to provide a valuable and representative overview of the vastness of the *Star Wars* universe.

Since our view of each species is often based on only a few of its members— or perhaps even one key individual—readers may be deceived into thinking all the members of that species are identical. Of course, we know for a fact that this is never the case—that every group offers a full and amazing spectrum of diversity. So while each entry herein may note the shared characteristics exhibited by a given species, there will come events that lead any individual to "break the rules."

And to demonstrate how events may shape an individual, entries will also include a historical anecdote designed to reveal how that individual has been shaped by the course of history. Through these brief glimpses, we may glean new insights into the creatures that populate the highly diverse *Star Wars* galaxy.

In the course of your own investigations, may the Force be with you, and with all creatures great, small, wild, and wonderful.

Ann Margaret Lewis
Bronx, New York

The Story behind the Book

Much of the information included here was taken from the collection of the much-lauded Senior Anthropologist Mammon Hoole, a member of the Shi'ido species. The Shi'ido are able to change form at will, and utilizing this natural ability, Hoole has been able to study a great many alien species from the inside. And in a less covert fashion, he has solicited commentary from many prominent members of the galactic community, including explorers, adventurers, members of the military, representatives of the New Republic, and even of the Empire. The wealth of material he has amassed is truly mind-boggling.

During most of his years of study, Hoole has worked alone, taking on an occasional assistant or two. But when the planet Alderaan was destroyed, he was thrust into the role of surrogate parent when he adopted his orphaned niece and nephew, Tash and Zak Arranda. Hoole tried to continue his work as he had before, but the trio inadvertently angered key representatives of the Empire by foiling an important and destructive scientific experiment, and found themselves on the run. After a number of harrowing escapes, Hoole settled with his niece and nephew in a private home on a world whose location he has kept strictly secret.

At this home-based laboratory, Hoole shifted from field exploration to the assembling of the wealth of data he'd already gathered. Tash and Zak reached the age at which they began their own advanced education, and as the pressure of Imperial discovery eased, both were able to attend university. Left to his own devices, Hoole quickly compiled enough material to produce a general overview of the key species he had encountered in his travels. In-depth, technical data would be reserved for the advanced journals and texts.

More researcher than raconteur, Hoole enlisted the aid of a professional writer whose job it became to present the information in a form accessible to the general public. *The Essential Guide to Alien Species* was written and sent to a reputable galactic publisher on Coruscant. Recognizing the value of such a volume, the publisher snapped up the opportunity, leading to the edition you hold in your hands.

Senior Anthropologist Hoole wishes to acknowledge all those who have been kind enough to work with him over the years, and especially those who have shared material from their private journals, diaries, and letters. Everything that was provided has helped add new depth to this book and, as such, will provide insight into the nature of life in our galaxy.

About the Entries

Sentience Designation

Each species is designated as *sentient, semisentient,* or *nonsentient.* Usually this designation is based on a species' ability to reason, use tools, and communicate. A panel of multicultural scientists from the University of Coruscant approves the formal designation for each species only after a government-approved research team has conducted an extensive field study or has made some significant finding regarding the sentience of the species in question. The formal designations are defined as follows:

- **Sentient:** A species given the *sentient* designation is considered able to reason and understand abstract metaphysical or philosophical concepts and ideas, make and use tools, and communicate with written or spoken language. As most primitive tribal species receive this designation, it does not imply a species must be civilized to the point of space travel.
- **Semisentient:** The *semisentient* designation implies that a species has some reasoning ability but cannot grasp elevated or abstract concepts. In many cases, a semisentient group has not yet formed a written or spoken language. These species are considered to be moving up the evolutionary ladder—on their way to achieving sentience. Under the Empire, these species were not entitled to land ownership, but this prohibition is now being reconsidered in the senate of the New Republic.
- **Nonsentient:** A *nonsentient* species is one that does not reason at all and survives only via its natural instincts.

Relative Size of Adult

The average size of a member of a given species is provided here in meters.

Planet of Origin

Most alien species hearken back to a homeworld or system. Some, like the bantha, are found in many systems, and still others, like the Hutts, have transplanted themselves to a new home. The earliest location for a given species—often the planet of origin—will be listed here, and their present home will be likewise indicated.

Journal Entry

For each species, the body of the entry will offer the basics of appearance, historical background, general living habits, and notable elements of the species' culture. In each major entry, Senior Anthropologist Hoole has also selected a quote from his collection of anecdotal material, which will corroborate the data or offer some new insight into the species, as exemplified by an event involving a specific member or group of individuals from that species.

A General Time Line of Alien History

As native peoples gained sentience and headed for the stars, they charted trade routes, fought wars, formed alliances, and established galactic society as it is presently known. This time line of pivotal events from the history of alien species movement and development demonstrates the forming of the panorama of galactic history and culture.

Circa 5,000,000,000 Before the Battle of Yavin (B.B.Y.)

The galaxy is formed, many believe, by the gravitational collapse of an immense cloud of dust and gas spanning 100,000 light-years, made up of 400 billion stars. Around half of these have planets that could support some form of life. Ten percent of those developed life, and one in a thousand of these worlds developed sentient life (about 20 million forms of sentient life).

Circa 3,000,000 B.B.Y.

An asteroid strikes the planet Vinsoth, destroying most life on the planet. Surviving species evolve into the Chevin.

Circa 2,000,000 B.B.Y.

Wookiees begin to evolve on Kashyyyk, establishing dominance as climbers of the wroshyr trees.

Circa 100,000 B.B.Y.

An ancient people known as the Sith develops a unique culture, only to disappear. The dark Jedi later take the name Sith as their own.

Circa 27,500 B.B.Y.

The first human colonists arrive on Alderaan.

Circa 26,000 B.B.Y.

The ancient Nikto discover the M'dweshuu Nova and form a religion called the Cult of M'dweshuu, which dominates the entire culture.

The Verpine colonize the Roche asteroid field.

Circa 25,100 B.B.Y.

The Klatooinians, Vodrans, and Nikto sign the Treaty of Vontor, binding them to the Hutts as permanent slaves.

The Hutts defeat Xim the Despot and take over his criminal empire.

An unknown alien race introduces the earliest form of hyperdrive to the Corellians, who later release their own version.

Circa 25,000 B.B.Y.

Galactic exploration begins on a wider scale, establishing the Perlemian Trade Route and the Corellian Run trade routes.

Circa 15,000 B.B.Y.

The Aqualish (Aquala and Quara) fight a civil war, and an offworld exploratory vessel lands on their world. The two races unite to kill the visitors, while taking their ship intact.

The Hutts co-opt a planet named Evocar in the Y'Toub system, displace its citizens, and rename it Nal Hutta, or Glorious Jewel. They move their entire civilization to this world, abandoning their homeworld Varl.

Circa 10,000 B.B.Y.

The Gran begin their recorded history.

Under the rule of benevolent Queen Rana, Duros scientists develop interstellar flight. They begin to explore the galaxy and build space cities. They establish a colony on Neimoidia.

Circa 7,000 B.B.Y.

The Sith establish a lore library called Veeshas Tuwan on Arkania.

The Devaronians develop star travel.

Circa 5,000 B.B.Y.

Naga Sadow transforms the ancient Massassi and transports them to Yavin 4.

Circa 3,995 B.B.Y.

The Kanz Disorders begin, in which the Lorrdians are subjected by the Argazdans, who forbid them to speak with each other. They create a new language of facial tics, expressions, and hand gestures. They also become well-versed in reading body language.

Circa 3,600 B.B.Y.

The Jedi Knights free the Lorrdians from their slavery at the hands of the Argazdans. The Lorrdians later become vocal critics of slavery.

2,000 B.B.Y.

A humanoid race adopts the Bimm culture and is integrated into Bimm society.

1,000 B.B.Y.

The Gran found colonies on Hok and Malastare.

990 B.B.Y.

The Khommites decide that their species has reached perfection and start using cloning to propagate their species.

700 B.B.Y.

The Death Seed, a horrific plague of insects known as drochs, spreads through the galaxy. The populations of entire worlds are destroyed.

600 B.B.Y.

The first recorded domesticated rancors are reported on Dathomir.

490 B.B.Y.

The Arkanians perform brain-enhancement surgery on their simple-minded Yaka neighbors, increasing their intelligence.

The Corporate Sector is formed, encompassing dozens of unexplored worlds.

350 B.B.Y.

The Trade Federation is established. Neimoidians play pivotal roles in its formation and administration.

300 B.B.Y.

The Ho'Din exploit their homeworld, Moltok, for industrial purposes and nearly destroy their entire species.

The Bothans start to master intelligence gathering and begin exploiting it for political gain.

The Bith engage in a civil war destroying their planetary environment. Bith change their culture, repressing their emotions and preventing further wars.

280 B.B.Y.

The Ho'Din develop organic medicines to cure themselves of the parasitic organisms plaguing their species, allowing them to survive.

200 B.B.Y.

Dressellians are discovered by the Bothans, who, upon recognizing their potential, leave them to evolve without interference.

The human residents of Rydar II attempt to exterminate the Ranat species and fail when three Ranats stow away on a smuggling ship. When the ship crashes on the planet Aralia, the Ranats repopulate themselves on that world.

150 B.B.Y.

Bakura is discovered. The Bakur Mining Corporation begins to develop and mine the planet. They begin to research ways to save the native Kurtzen population from extinction. A few weeks later, a droid uprising on Bakura kills nearly 40 percent of the original colonists, establishing the Bakuran and Kurtzen distrust of droids and technology.

110 B.B.Y.

The Blood Carvers of Batorine join the Galactic Republic. Many relocate to Coruscant.

70 B.B.Y.

Followers of the H'kig religion settle on the planet Rishi and discover the avian Rishii species.

25 B.B.Y.

A group of Yuuzhan Vong, aliens from outside the galaxy, land on the obscure planet Bimmiel and begin surveying the surrounding sectors for the coming invasion.

Circa 22–19 B.B.Y.

Palpatine declares himself Emperor, bringing about the rise of "High Human Culture": the ideology that humans are inherently superior to aliens. Many aliens find their rights and freedoms restricted or revoked and face prejudice encouraged by the New Order.

19 B.B.Y.

The Empire enslaves the Wookiees and bombs their cities on Kashyyyk. The Trandoshans hunt those that escape the beleaguered world.

Caamas, a peaceful and noble world loved throughout the Empire, is completely ravaged by unknown attackers. Caamasi are relocated to refugee camps, one being on Alderaan.

When a space battle contaminates the world Honoghr, Darth Vader offers environmental aid to the Noghri people in return for their servitude. Vader then orders his staff to further contaminate the world to keep them enslaved.

Senior Anthropologist Mammon Hoole exiles himself from his homeworld, Sh'shuun, and begins his most famous studies of other species.

11 B.B.Y.

The Empire discovers the planet Maridun, home of the Amanin, and establishes bases. They later take the Amanin for slaves.

9 B.B.Y.

A "death wave" (only the fifth recorded in Chadra-Fan history) occurs on Chad as ocean floor quakes create massive tidal waves. Hundreds of thousands of Chadra-Fan are killed.

7 B.B.Y.

On the planet Falleen, scientists under Darth Vader's orders develop a biological weapon that accidentally infects the Falleen populace. To protect the remaining population from the virus, Darth Vader orders a bombardment of the planet. Over 200,000 Falleen die.

4 B.B.Y.

Lando Calrissian activates the Mindharp of Sharu and reawakens the ancient civilization of the Sharu.

3 B.B.Y.

Lando Calrissian assists the Oswaft of ThonBoka in gaining their freedom from an Imperial blockade that's causing them to starve.

2 B.B.Y.

Mon Mothma issues a Declaration of Rebellion, which is distributed by holo to thousands of galactic worlds who openly declare their allegiance to the Alliance. These worlds are quickly suppressed, but this shows a new light of hope to the oppressed species in the galaxy.

0 B.B.Y.

The world Alderaan is destroyed by the Death Star.

Firrerre is destroyed by Lord Hethrir, a student of Darth Vader. The Firrerreo people are either killed or enslaved.

4 After the Battle of Yavin (A.B.Y.)

The Ssi-ruuvi Imperium attacks at Bakura and is repelled.

7.5 (A.B.Y.)

Remnants of the Empire release, a deadly plague, the Krytos virus, that targets nonhumans on Coruscant.

9 A.B.Y.

The Noghri pledge their service to the Alliance and help to defeat Grand Admiral Thrawn.

11 A.B.Y.

Admiral Ackbar destroys the Vors' Cathedral of Winds in a ship accident, killing over 300 Vors.

12 A.B.Y.

A Khommite Jedi named Dorsk 81 sacrifices himself to save the Jedi academy on Yavin 4. His sacrifice spawns on Khomm a movement away from clone reproduction.

16 A.B.Y.

The Yevetha threaten the New Republic and are defeated.

17 A.B.Y.

The entire Pydyrian species is wiped out by explosive droids, planted by the warlord Kueller.

23–24 A.B.Y.

A radical political movement called the Diversity Alliance is formed, which spouts alien superiority and the genocide of the human species. After an attempt to infect worlds with a plague, the Diversity Alliance is disbanded.

25 A.B.Y.

The Yuuzhan Vong begin their conquest of the galaxy.

Table of Contents

STAR WARS®

THE ESSENTIAL GUIDE TO ALIEN SPECIES

Amanin [Amanaman]

a primitive tribal hunter-gatherer species, the Amanin, in some regions nicknamed Amanaman, are native to the planet Maridun, a world of large forests and grassy plains. They are tall, thin, yellow-and-green-skinned arboreal creatures who have long arms used to travel from branch to branch. On the ground they walk slowly, but are able to curl themselves into a ball and roll at speeds ranging from forty-five to fifty kilometers per hour.

When an Amanin tribe's population grows too large, the youth of that tribe cross the plains to find a new forest area to inhabit. They fight battles—called takitals—with the residing tribe over ownership rights to that land. Observing this, the Empire made a special agreement with one tribe's leader, called a lorekeeper because he records the history of the tribe. A short time after the Battle of Yavin, Senior Anthropologist Mammon Hoole recorded his experiences with a group of young Amanin, showing just what this agreement entailed.

> Adopting their form, and using my telepathic aura to mask myself so that my unfamiliar face or smell would not give me away, I secretly followed a group of about ten Amanin as they traveled through the blowing field of grass to the edge of the forest.
> My new companions took to the trees at once, swinging rapidly on their long arms from branch to branch. As they moved deeper into the woods, they grew tenser and more cautious. Suddenly, one Amanin spun around and glared at me, and I realized that I'd eased up on my telepathic

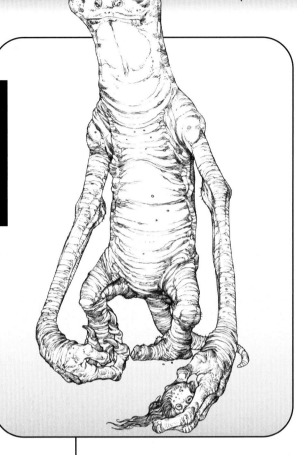

DESIGNATION
> **SENTIENT** <
PLANET OF ORIGIN
> **MARIDUN** <
HEIGHT OF AVERAGE ADULT
> **2-3 METERS** <

aura. Although I looked like them, I no longer smelled like them. The tribesman let out a high-pitched warning scream and lunged at me feetfirst, at which point I fled.
> After a few meters, I stumbled upon an entirely different cluster of Amanin. With a war screech, the leader of this second gang charged me. I found myself fleeing back the way I'd come, only to have the two groups meet somewhere in-between.
> What followed was a barbaric bloodbath. I slipped above the melee unnoticed. The invading group lost—outnumbered by the inhabiting tribe, who took their prisoners and the dead with them to their village.
> As night fell, a squad of Imperial stormtroopers arrived, led by two Amanin scouts. The victors were selling the prisoners into slav-

ery! As the stormtroopers took the prisoners away, the captured lorekeeper shouted, "You dishonor the takitals! You have no right!" A trooper struck him down with the butt of his rifle.

The Empire left Maridun not long after Hoole's entry was recorded. Though Jabba the Hutt took over the slave trade the Empire had established, the culture of the Amanin changed. Some youth began to move to the towns, and others adopted the use of blasters and additional weapons to conquer other tribes. Many lorekeepers moved to the cities in an attempt to win back their young people or to sell blessings and native memorabilia to offworlders.

Anzati

The Anzati are among the deadliest and most mysterious species in the galaxy. They appear human, save for two prehensile proboscises they keep coiled in pockets in each of their cheeks. Predators who mesmerize victims through a mild telepathic control, they uncoil these proboscises and insert them in the victim's nostrils to suck out the brain matter.

According to most reports, Anzati are loners who wander throughout the galaxy, returning to Anzat only to find mates and reproduce. They do not reproduce often, and an individual may live for many centuries. Youthful Anzati reach puberty at approximately one hundred years of age and leave Anzat to hunt for sustenance, which they call "soup."

Because Anzati are roamers, they are often considered a myth, and it has been difficult to determine the true location of their homeworld. Scientists who traveled to a world reputed to be Anzat have simply disappeared without a trace. Little has been documented concerning the species, and this account related by Yarna d'al' Gargan—a former slave dancer from the palace of Jabba the Hutt on Tatooine—is exemplary of the few recorded encounters with an Anzati.

> All the mysterious deaths—without marks or wounds—set the lowlies of the court on edge. A killer was loose in the walls, a murderer who destroyed without sense or logic.
> The day Jabba died I discovered the terror myself. A fellow approached me as I went to my quarters. His name was Dannik Jerriko, and he had been a quiet presence in the palace for several weeks. He addressed me in my own language, speaking in seductive tones. His eyes mesmerized me, holding me motionless. I suddenly sensed something wrong, and then I saw his tentacles—unfurling from his cheeks and dancing toward my face. I realized at that moment that he could only be an Anzati, the demon creature of myth. Although I would have been much stronger than he in a struggle, and my bulk would have crushed him, I could not fight back against his power. I felt his hunger.
> I was never more thankful for the stupid Gamorreans than I was at that moment. One stumbled upon us, and Jerriko melted into the darkness, leaving me my life.
> I knew then I had to quickly escape the palace, for I had seen the face of the unknown killer, and he would not let me live for long.

DESIGNATION
> **SENTIENT** <

PLANET OF ORIGIN
> **ANZAT** <

HEIGHT OF AVERAGE ADULT
> **1.7 METERS** <

Aqualish

ost anthropologists feel that the Aqualish carry a streak of anger and rage that hearkens to the early years of the species' evolution. They are known for hair-trigger tempers that flare without cause or reason.

Two races of Aqualish developed on Ando: the Quara, or fingered Aqualish, which evolved on the marshy islands of the world, and the Aquala, or finned Aqualish, which evolved in the vast seas. The Quara, however, represent only one-tenth of the population of Ando and are the victims of intense prejudice on the part of their evolutionary neighbors. These groups have been engaged in a race war that has lasted for generations.

Nonetheless, an unstable peace was accomplished when a spaceship from another planet landed on their world. Having never encountered extraterrestrial life, and fearing an invasion from the sky, the two groups banded together and directed their rage at the visitors, killing them without remorse. They kept the ship, however, and learned how to build more. Though they achieved spaceflight, they couldn't advance the technology. To this day, the Aqualish only steal technology and adapt it to their own purposes.

Upon achieving spaceflight, the Aqualish immediately began a course of conquest. The Old Republic quickly put a stop to it, and the Aqualish were demilitarized. However, they found other ways to make their presence recognized on a galactic scale—becoming tax collectors, repossession agents, and bounty hunters.

The following security police report from Bothawui shows how the slightest annoyance can set an Aqualish on an angry rampage.

> Officer Kras'ka Lo'lar
> Report 056.239
> I entered the restaurant and found the place trashed. Many of the patrons were under tables or running for the exits. A humanoid male, approximate 1.7 meters in height, with scarred features, seemed to be trying to calm a large Aqualish, who lunged forward with a punch that sent the humanoid flying. He landed on the floor next to me.
> I set my blaster on stun and fired at the Aqualish. It took two shots to take him down. He stumbled and fell to the floor.
> "Ponda!" The man cried suddenly, and he ran to the unconscious perpetrator's side.
> The man's horribly disfigured features showed an expression of disgust as he glared at me. "Why did you have to shoot him? He's an Aqualish. Small things upset him."

> "What 'small thing' set this off?"
> The marred man shrugged. "I'd just told him that he's going to have to wait to get his arm fixed. He didn't like that much."
> "His arm?" I looked more closely at the unconscious Aqualish and realized that he had only one real arm, and the other was a plastine prosthetic. He'd trashed the place single-handed!

DESIGNATION
> SENTIENT <
....
PLANET OF ORIGIN
> ANDO <
....
HEIGHT OF AVERAGE ADULT
> 1.7 METERS <
....

Arachnor

iant arachnids that reside in the humid macaab mushroom forests of Arzid, the arachnors feed primarily on the giant fungi that cover a large portion of the planet's surface, though they also consume the flesh of living creatures.

Macaab mushrooms contain several natural chemicals of interest, including a substance that can break through most of the mind-control implants that were used by the Empire. The fungi also contain chemical ingredients that, when ingested by an arachnor, cause the spider's webbing to become perhaps the stickiest and most inescapable of any known arachnid species in the galaxy.

Arachnors are extremely protective of their environment. Although they are nonsentient, they instinctively know how to frighten prey and direct them into their hidden webs. Once entrapped, a struggling victim becomes progressively more ensnared by the sticky material and literally wraps itself into a tight cocoon.

During the early days of the Empire, Senior Anthropologist Hoole visited Arzid with his assistant, a biologist named Chlar Kotchmin. Unfortunately the man did not survive his encounter with an arachnor, as Hoole writes.

> Kotchmin had moved ahead of me to study a trail left by the creature, when he suddenly slipped and tumbled down an incline, to land directly in a mass of webbing left by the spider. It immediately occurred to me, with a chill of horror, that the arachnor might have led us here purposely—to trap us. True to my suspicions, it crawled down from a large mushroom and wrapped my struggling friend in a stream of webbing, pinioning him in an airless shroud within a matter of seconds.

> Horrified, I leapt down the hill after him only to find myself face-to-face with the giant insect. It sprayed web at me, and I dodged, jumping toward the cocoon and drawing a blade to cut Chlar free. But the knife stuck to the web, and so did the sleeve of my tunic. I was firmly held in place!

> Doing my best to keep the rest of my body away from the web, I confused the arachnor enough to cause it to amble away—at least temporarily. I managed to remove my outer tunic, but realized then that I didn't have the proper tools to free my friend. By the time I rushed to the ship to get an energy slicer to cut him free, Chlar had suffocated.

> I am saddened by this occurrence. Kotchmin was an excellent researcher and an accomplished field scientist. I am only glad that I could return his body to his grieving family.

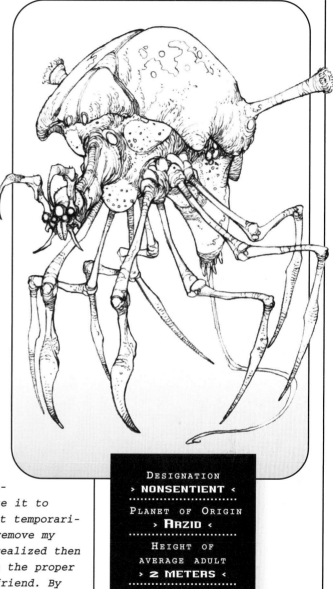

DESIGNATION
> **NONSENTIENT** <

PLANET OF ORIGIN
> **ARZID** <

HEIGHT OF AVERAGE ADULT
> **2 METERS** <

Arcona

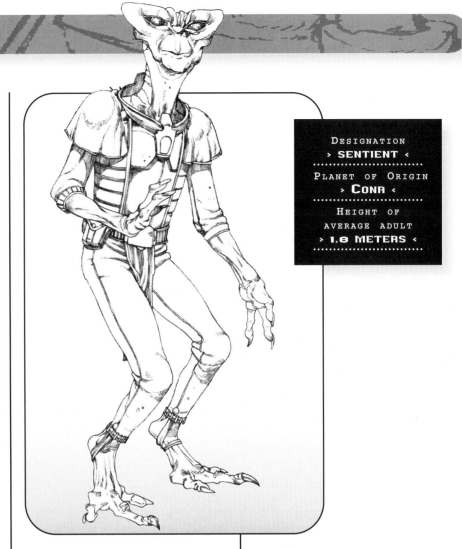

the Arcona are tall, reptilian humanoids, with triangular heads and bulbous sensory organs that sit between their two large, glittering eyes. They hail from the planet Cona, a hot, desert world with an atmosphere mixture of nitrogen, hydrogen, and ammonia. Everything the Arcona eat contains traces of ammonia from the planet's atmosphere. Offplanet, they constantly take supplements known as dactyl ammonia crystals to help rid their bodies of waste material. The Arcona have poor eyesight, and the central sensory organ is used to detect heat patterns emitted by other living creatures. Organs used for the sense of smell are located in their constantly flicking tongues.

Oxygen is rare on Cona, trapped in a layer of bedrock. Only certain plants access the oxygen to create water, and the Arcona have developed powerful talons that enable them to dig up the pods of these plants.

The planet is rich in precious metals. Several decades ago, prospectors came to Cona and learned that the natives are easily addicted to simple salt. Since salt is easy to transport, the prospectors started to trade salt for land. The Arcona have since enacted strict legislation to prohibit salt from reaching their world, but this has done little to stop its import.

Salt also causes failure in an Arcona's pancreatic organ, which changes ammonia into water. More visibly, it changes an Arcona's eye color from green to gold. For this reason, outside observers tend to think the natural Arcona eye color is gold.

Their society is largely communal, valuing the needs of the collective group over those of an individual. As a result, the Arcona lack a sense of individuality and rarely speak of themselves in first person, instead using the pronoun *we*.

DESIGNATION
> **SENTIENT** <

PLANET OF ORIGIN
> **CONA** <

HEIGHT OF AVERAGE ADULT
> **1.8 METERS** <

To the Arcona, the choice of a mate is taken with great care. Senior Anthropologist Hoole recounts his observations concerning community life and mate-choosing.

> *Every twenty days we traveled to the meeting at the Grand Nest. At one particular meeting, Nest Leader Kimar Walc announced that his son, Denn Walc, was days away from selecting a mate.*
> *Denn had been looking for almost five years, systematically scrutinizing available females, speaking and visiting with as many as he could, making lists of particular qualities. He showed me scores and scores of data files that he'd filled with information.*
> *The day after the meeting, Denn took me to meet the female he'd chosen. All of his painstaking deliberations had brought him to this one singular individual. He was shivering with excitement as we approached the entrance to her nest, but when she came out to greet us, his features reflected shock and horror.*
> *Her eyes were yellow. She'd become a salt addict in the short time since he had interviewed her. She was no longer suitable to hatch a brood.*

the Arkanians are a robust, extremely intelligent near-human people that inhabit the world of Arkania. They are differentiated from humans by their solid-white eyes, four-fingered, clawed hands, and impressive stamina. Their eyes act as infrared sensors, allowing most Arkanians to see well in all levels of light.

Arkania is rich in precious minerals—particularly diamonds. For this reason, the Arkanian culture flourished early from offworld contact. Arkanians became masters of cyborg technology and microcircuitry and took it upon themselves to "bestow" cyborg intelligence upon the feebleminded Yaka of a nearby world.

Many Arkanians protested this move, but their government, the Arkanian Dominion, approved the project. This caused a schism between the scientists who protested the action and those working for the Dominion, leading to a civil war. The Arkanian Renegades created the ultimate mercenary army, part droid and part organic, to overthrow the government, and while their coup failed, a few of the nearly invincible creations continued to live. They escaped to set up shop as bounty hunters. One of these cyborg warriors, known as Gorm the Dissolver, still haunts the spaceways.

The Arkanians were not always residents of Arkania, which was once a repository for ancient Sith knowledge. The following journal entry, written by Jedi historian Tionne, describes the knowledge she gained from a trip to Arkania, and an artifact she found there.

> Several Arkanian archaeologists guided me to sites they believed the Jedi had used, and I could sense the slightest trace of the power still there. Later, they showed me artifacts they'd found. These included a simple, nondescript cube small enough to fit in the palm of one's hand.
> They'd found a Holocron! Gently I placed the fragile instrument in my palm, activated it, and the holographic figure of a handsome Arkanian appeared.
> "Greetings, Jedi. I am Master Arca Jeth, on the world Arkania. This was once the home of great Sith knowledge, and I came here with my students to prepare for the possibility that the Sith might return.
> "Though we have done our best the darkness remains. Once it has touched something or someone, darkness grabs hold and never dies, although it can be subdued. This is what I have done here. And confident in its subjugation, some of my people have come to settle. As long as the light outweighs the darkness, life will prosper.
> "Seek balance, Jedi. Only in this will you avert tragedy, and only in this will you truly succeed."

DESIGNATION
> **SENTIENT** <

PLANET OF ORIGIN
> **ARKANIA** <

HEIGHT OF
AVERAGE ADULT
> **1.8 METERS** <

Askajian

isunderstood by the galactic populace at large, the Askajians were only recently brought into the galactic arena. They are peaceful and unsophisticated, preferring the life of home and children.

Due to their bulk, they are often dismissed as corpulent, unattractive humans. Actually, the species hoards water in epidermal sacs that help them survive long periods of time without additional moisture. When they are in less hostile environments, Askajians become far slimmer. They can expend up to 60 percent of their stored water without any detriment to their health.

Askajian females give birth to up to six children at a time. They refer to their children as cubs, and each female possesses six breasts with which they nurse. Askajians live in a primitive tribal culture with no real technology. Tribes often battle over watering holes or herding rights, and are led by chieftains, whose right to lead is determined by bloodline.

Dancers maintain a religious role as the keepers of a tribe's history and lore. One of the best-known Askajians is Yarna d'al' Gargan. This gentle, motherly Askajian was taken forcibly from her home to serve Jabba the Hutt as a slave. After Jabba's death, Yarna dictated the story of her first meeting with Jabba the Hutt to a New Republic reporter.

> We stood there before him, weak and bruised from our captors' brutality, my mate Nautag and I and our three remaining cublings. Jabba inspected us with glee, eyeing each and every one of us, wearing his horrible, permanent grin.
> "These slaves will serve me well," he said to Bib Fortuna. "Prepare them for their tasks and give the children to me."
> Nautag stepped in front of us. "No," he snarled. "My wife and cubs will not be slaves."
> Jabba's low, dark laugh echoed through the room. "Come then," he said. "Challenge me, if you dare."
> Bravely, Nautag charged, but Jabba's fist hit a control that opened the floor beneath my mate. As I watched, a huge creature devoured him in a matter of seconds.
> I let out a sorrowful wail as Jabba's guards wrenched my cubs from my arms. He ordered that I be brought closer.
> "You will dance for me. Continue to serve me faithfully and you will earn freedom for you and your children."
> I was dragged away, weeping hysterically. It was the last I was to see of my cubs for a year and a half. After that, Ugly One was to be my name, for no one but my fellow dancers ever asked me my real one.
> My name, Yarna, means "beautiful."

DESIGNATION
> SENTIENT <

PLANET OF ORIGIN
> ASKAJ <

HEIGHT OF AVERAGE ADULT
> 1.6 METERS <

Assembler (Kud'ar Mub'at)

there is only one example on record of a creature known as an Assembler—Kud'ar Mub'at, a master-mind who acted as a go-between for criminal organizations and potential employees.

The Assembler is a giant black spiderlike being, with a large, round body and six chitinous legs. He lives in a giant tubular-shaped web that drifts through space, and meets guests in his main chamber, adjusting the atmosphere there for each visitor. Woven into the web are bits of junk—space garbage, broken droids, etc. The web is part of the Assembler, connected to him by microscopic neurofibers that bring him nourishment. It allows him to communicate with his many "nodes"—individual arachnoid beings created from the web's essence, also connected to the web by neurofibers. Each node possesses only the marginal intelligence needed to do its job. A node named Lookout gazes through a single-lens eye to view the web exterior; the Calculator node interprets data; Identifier identifies objects or people; Signaler's glowing green eyes guide arriving ships into dock; and Docker and Handler secure ships against the web's entry port with their vacuum-adapted scaled tentacles. Listener is a tympanic membrane that picks up sounds around the web, and Balancesheet maintains the Assembler's finances. According to rumors, it is this last node that finally evolved to a point where it rebelled against its creator.

The most mysterious thing about this species is its origin. It was from the following recorded discussion with the bounty hunter Boba Fett, following Mub'at's death, that Imperial scientists discovered the most likely explanation of Mub'at's history.

> Scientist [name withheld]: Good afternoon, Fett. We're looking for information on Kud'ar Mub'at.
> Fett: You want information on Mub'at, I want ten thousand credits.
> Scientist: (pause) All right, Fett. Ten thousand credits. What can you tell us?
> Fett: They're arachnids that create and control their own environment through a web of neurofiber connections sending charges of electromagnetic energy. They consume anything that floats by them, including living beings, as long as they are not valuable. They create drones, called nodes, to carry out day-to-day affairs. These nodes are part of each Assembler, but separate from them.
> Scientist: How's that?

> Fett: Mub'at's species evolve from nodes—nodes from other Assemblers. Mub'at's own intelligence evolved as a node, and he killed the previous Assembler to take his place.
> Scientist: You have the facts to prove this?
> Fett: He consumes everything else, so why not his previous master?
> Scientist: I see. Is that all you have?
> Fett: Yes.
> Scientist: It's more than we've gotten from the others. [Hands Fett credit chit.] Thank you for your time, Fett.

DESIGNATION
> **SENTIENT** <
....
PLANET OF ORIGIN
> **UNKNOWN** <
....
HEIGHT OF AVERAGE ADULT
> **3 METERS** <
....

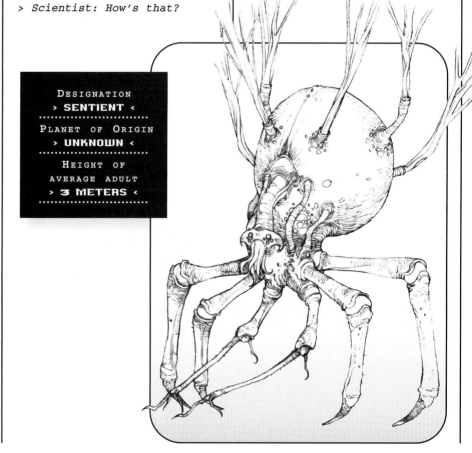

Bantha

herds of woolly banthas inhabit the desert wastes of Tatooine, as well as the grasslands and plains of other worlds throughout the galaxy. Since they can be found in most agricultural systems, it is believed that early space settlers transported them to these new worlds.

Generally used as beasts of burden, the tall, gentle creatures are intelligent and trustworthy. They are extremely strong, able to carry up to 500 kilograms of cargo or five passengers, including a driver. Because of the creatures' rocking gait, many first-time bantha riders complain of motion sickness.

Banthas are extremely adaptable, surviving comfortably in all sorts of climates, and able to go for weeks without food or water. The bantha's long, flexible tongue compensates for its short neck in feeding. From world to world, bantha subspecies vary in size, coloration, social grouping, behavior, and metabolic specifics. Depending on the location, their fur color may be off-white, tan, light brown, brown, or black.

In the wild, most bantha species fight only in defense of their herd and the young. When attacked, they usually flee. When trapped, or when young banthas must be defended, cows form a circle around their calves. They attack by lowering their heads and ramming their large spiral horns into the attacker.

Despite the creatures' usual passivity, some cultures use domesticated banthas as animals of war—spurring them to charge at foes and trample them underfoot. On Tatooine the woolly banthas have been left to roam free in the harsh desert climate, and the species has flourished. They are the transportation of choice of the native Tusken Raiders, who maintain a special relationship with their mounts, as Senior Anthropologist Hoole notes.

> Domesticated banthas make satisfactory beasts of burden. Wild banthas exhibit a kind of feral violence toward their captors. However, I was amazed to see that among the Sand People banthas act neither wild nor completely docile.
> Tusken children tend young banthas, but upon reaching adulthood, one Tusken and one bantha team up in a kind of deep emotional bonding, as if bantha and rider become extensions of the same being. When a Tusken is killed, the suddenly "widowed" bantha will fly into a vicious, suicidal frenzy; the same is true if a bantha mount is killed, leaving the rider alive.

> If a bantha is left without its Tusken companion, the Sand People wait until the beast tires of its rampage, then turn it out into the desert to survive alone. Likewise, when a bantha is killed, the bereaved Tusken wanders off into the desert on a vision quest. There, the Tusken must come to terms with the spirit of his bantha partner. If the bantha partner wishes to draft his companion into the afterlife, then the Tusken will die out on the sands. If, however, the bantha spirit

DESIGNATION
> **NONSENTIENT** <
PLANET OF ORIGIN
> **UNKNOWN** <
HEIGHT OF AVERAGE ADULT
> **2.5 METERS** <

guide is generous, he will lead the Tusken to another wild bantha, a riderless one, which the Tusken will take back to the tribe as a new companion. When such a Tusken returns, "reborn," he is much esteemed by the other Sand People.

Luke Skywalker, a native of Tatooine, recalled a singular encounter in which he and his friend Biggs Darklighter—both in their teens—observed how a Tusken bantha mourns its lost rider.

> It was just before Biggs left for the Academy. We were in the south range fixing a vaporator, when we both saw something ambling toward us. Once we could tell it was a bantha, we quickly started to pack up. We saw only one huge figure, but we knew that Sand People never traveled alone.
> As the creature neared, however, we realized that it had no rider. It was stumbling awkwardly, and as it got to about fifty meters away, it went down to its knees, then fell on its side.
> We'd never seen a bantha in that condition before, especially one that had the markings of a Tusken mount. As I got nearer, it didn't respond, though I could still see its chest rising and falling. When I knelt next to it, it moaned lightly and moved to get my scent, as if it were looking for something—or someone.
> It was then I remembered that when a Tusken Raider dies, his mount is sent out into the desert to die or to

find another bonding partner. This one had failed to find a new master.
> Biggs leaned over my shoulder and said, "I wonder if we can find a vet droid in Anchorhead."
> I shook my head, knowing somehow that no doctor was going to save this creature.

It was dying of grief. I reached out and touched its furry head above the eyes. Then, just like that—it stopped breathing, as if it simply didn't want to go on.

Barabel

arabels are a vicious, reptilian species that resides on the planet Barab I, a world of murky darkness due to its dim red dwarf sun. During the day, the intense heat and radiation from the red dwarf force all moving creatures below ground. Then, as evening arrives, the planet cools and creatures return to the surface to hunt.

Barabels are natural hunters who kill with strength and efficiency, and track prey using eyes that perceive infrared wavelengths. Their five-centimeter-long, razorlike teeth and huge claws are effective in rending flesh. They have black, armored hides that protect them from blaster bolts and basic melee weapons or bludgeons.

Barabels often work as bounty hunters and mercenaries. They are known for having an explosive temperament, but unlike other violent species, they have great intelligence and value wisdom. They have a gentle way with families and friends, but outsiders are met with belligerence.

When Barab I was liberated from Imperial rule, the Barabels almost started a war with an insectoid species known as the Verpine. They made arrangements, at one time, to sell frozen Verpine body parts to the Kubaz, who eat them as a delicacy.

Despite their vicious culture, the Barabels behave differently around Jedi. This is due to a dispute that the Jedi solved for them in their distant past. In an Old Republic security report, filed nearly twenty years before the Battle of Yavin, a security police officer noted this behavior.

> The incident had started when a group of about eight Dugs went into an establishment and insulted a table of six Barabels. By the time we arrived, it was a slaughter.

The largest Barabel charged my partner and lifted him over his head, to smash him to the floor. Just then, out of nowhere, a human wearing brown robes appeared. He activated a bright green lightsaber and spun the humming blade, making his presence known. Immediately, the Barabels dropped whoever or whatever they were holding and stood motionless.
> The man turned to the largest Barabel, deactivating his lightsaber. "You will have to make reparations for what happened here."
> The Barabel growled a little. "They started it, great Jedi. They insulted our people."
> The Jedi smiled slightly. "Dugs insult everybody. You know that. You shouldn't value their words."

> Hissing slightly, the Barabel replied, "You are wise, great Jedi."
> The Barabel turned to his fellows and together they moved to help the security police.
> I approached the Jedi and said, "That mind trick really works."
> He looked at me and shrugged. "I didn't use a mind trick. Barabels listen to Jedi. It's just the way they are."

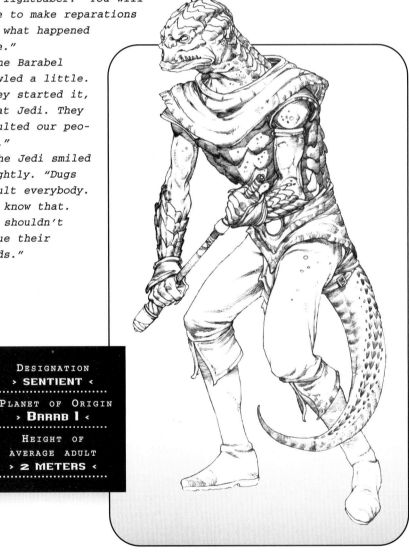

DESIGNATION
> SENTIENT <
....
PLANET OF ORIGIN
> BARAB I <
....
HEIGHT OF
AVERAGE ADULT
> 2 METERS <
....

Bimm

two species of Bimms inhabit the planet Bimmisaari: a small near-human species and another, furred, floppy-eared humanoid species. The two live side by side, sharing the same culture. Each refers to its own species and the other as Bimms.

It is believed that, in ancient times, the humanoid Bimms came to Bimmisaari from a nearby system and so admired the original Bimm society that they adopted it as their own. The original Bimms, being an open-minded, hospitable people, accepted the other species without question. However, they cannot interbreed, so when intermarriage happens between the species, the couples often adopt children.

The hospitable Bimms enjoy art, music, and telling stories. They like tales of heroism most of all, and listening to a Bimm story, one might think it fiction. But Bimms will take these hyperbolic tales very seriously. Of all heroes, Bimms hold Jedi in the highest regard.

They abhor physical confrontations and don't permit weapons in their cities. Their language is sung rather than spoken. And in an unexplained cultural tradition, Bimms are usually found wearing a special type of yellow clothing.

One of the Bimms' favorite activities is commerce, which they take seriously. Senior Anthropologist Hoole describes an experience in the open markets of Bimmisaari, where he'd taken on the form of a floppy-eared Bimm.

> I needed a new handheld bioanalysis device, as my old one had failed within the first weeks of my stay. I passed by several vendors until I came upon a floppy-eared Bimm with scientific equipment. The proprietor intoned, "What would be your pleasure?"
> "I seek a device for bio-analysis," I sang in response, proud of my diction.
> He smiled and held up a piece I recognized as top-of-the-line, manufactured by Bith engineers. "This is the finest I have," he piped cheerfully. "Two hundred credits."
> I hesitated a moment, then remembered that the prices were inflated so one might haggle. "It is a fitting device," I sang tenuously. "But would you consider one hundred credits?" This just a little less than what the piece was worth.
> "Not so, dear friend," he sang, bowing his head respectfully. "It would insult the workmanship. Perhaps one hundred fifty?"
> "One twenty-five would please me more, sir. Would you not consider it?"
> He cocked his head, and his eyes twinkled. "I would consider one thirty, although I do not wish to insult you."
> "No insult taken," I said. "I'll pay one thirty, and I compliment you on your bargaining."
> He bowed respectfully and so did I. I left feeling victorious.

DESIGNATION
> SENTIENT <

PLANET OF ORIGIN
> BIMMISAARI <

HEIGHT OF AVERAGE ADULT
> 1.1 METERS <

Bith

With elongated craniums that house supersized brains, the Bith are a highly evolved, humanoid species, the result of years of calculated breeding. The portions of their brains that control advanced reasoning are extremely well developed, while those portions controlling most instinctual behaviors—such as fear and aggression—are not.

Bith bodies have developed for handling complex physical work. Their five-fingered hands with opposable thumbs and small fingers make them well-suited for performing delicate tasks. Their large eyes allow them to perceive minuscule details. Because Bith do not sleep, they have no eyelids. Bith olfactory senses are located in folds of skin on their cheeks. Their sense of smell is extremely sensitive, allowing them to perceive the slightest chemical changes in the atmosphere around them.

Clak'dor VII has produced many complex thinkers and some of the most talented artists in the galaxy. The Bith have an aversion to conflict and are careful about expressing their emotions, partly due to the fact that the one time in history they allowed their emotions to get out of hand, it almost led to the destruction of their species.

Over three centuries before the Empire dawned, the Bith on Clak'dor VII were embroiled in heated competition, building stardrives to sell to other worlds, and the competitive drive led to full-scale war. One side attacked with a biological weapon that wiped out or degenerated most of the environment of the planet, while the other retaliated with chemical weapons that destroyed 90 percent of the population. The survivors built giant domed cities in which they've lived since that time.

As a result of this devastating war, Bith technology has not progressed for many years. Their own resources exhausted, they've come to rely on the goods and technology of other worlds. Their chief exports are their intellectual and artistic talents, and various agencies and companies galaxywide employ Bith as scientists, mathematicians, artisans, accountants, and musicians.

Bith rely on technology for most of their needs. They reproduce via artificial insemination arranged through reproduction centers, and over time they have lost the ability to reproduce naturally. Each prospective parent is matched with a mate possessing a suitable DNA pattern. Though couples may not live together, each parent is given children to rear in their respective homes.

As a testament to the value of Bith intellectual and musical artistry, Lady Sera Tharen of Corellia wrote in her book, *The Perfect Corellian Dinner Party*:

> *Having a Bith combo at your event is considered a mark of refinement. With their extraordinary intellects,* they can effortlessly maintain a vast repertoire of music—jizz, popular, ornate, and the classics. The mood and tone they set is just what you request; therefore they are ideal for occasions with light dinner conversation and dancing.
> Bith musicians are also consummate professionals. They do the job with an added bonus of excellence and are well worth the cost.

DESIGNATION
> **SENTIENT** <

PLANET OF ORIGIN
> **CLAK'DOR VII** <

HEIGHT OF AVERAGE ADULT
> **1.7 METERS** <

Blood Carver

blood Carvers are tall, thin humanoids with long, three-jointed arms and legs. Their skin is iridescent gold, and their small black eyes are accentuated by the two small pits in the flesh around them. Their small heads are mounted on high, thick necks, and their faces are narrow. The nose spreads across the face as two fleshy flaps, like a split shield, half hiding a wide, lipless mouth. These flaps, often called nose wings, are usually tattooed.

A Blood Carver's nose wings offer both the sense of smell and hearing, and both senses are supplemented by organs located in the pits behind the eyes. They may also indicate mood. When a Blood Carver is focused intently, the nostril flaps clap together in a wedge or blade shape; when the flaps spread wide, this indicates uncertainty, questioning, or respect. The Blood Carver's face color will also shift slightly, growing darker to indicate anger or lighter to indicate happiness.

Blood Carver society is feudal, led by a ruling class of tribal families, and they are not known to get involved in galactic politics. After Batorine was attacked by a species called the Lontars, most Blood Carvers moved to Coruscant, where they became famous as artisans who produced sculptures carved from the bright red wood of the blood tree indigenous to Batorine. However, to Blood Carvers, wealth is considered a sin of ego.

But the true art of the Blood Carvers is assassination—the carving away of unwanted persons. They train young warriors for an assassination corps that was at one time loosely affiliated with the Trade Federation. To fail in an assassination or to disobey orders may result in a warrior being "extended," or exiled. Also, their people believe that individuals who have failed will be excluded from the Art

DESIGNATION
> **SENTIENT** <

PLANET OF ORIGIN
> **BATORINE** <

HEIGHT OF
AVERAGE ADULT
> **2 METERS** <

Beyond Dying, their concept of the afterlife.

Blood Carvers show a unique response to compliments, as a disguised Senior Anthropologist Hoole discovered at a meeting of Blood Carver clans on Coruscant.

> The meeting seemed to be going well, when the clan leader presented his latest piece of sculpture for commentary. Suddenly, a young Blood Carver in the crowd remarked, "Beautiful!"
> Without hesitation, the clan leader swung out and punched the youth in the face. "You dishonor me!" the clan leader cried. He picked up a knife from the table and held it at the boy's throat.
> Stunned, I realized that the boy had uttered a compliment, when what the leader sought was criticism. "I was not thinking, I offer humility," the boy said.

> "Indeed." Disgusted, the leader stuck the knife back into the table. "Throw him outside and beat him."
> After the boy had been removed, the clan leader glared at the rest of us in the tent, his nose wings clapped in a dagger shape. "Only outsiders are so weak to offer praise. Learn not to be influenced by them."
> I said nothing else for the rest of the evening, fearing I might reveal myself as the sort of outsider they reviled.

othans are important players in the arena of galactic politics and are well known for their intelligence-gathering abilities. Before the Battle of Endor, two dozen of them sacrificed their lives to acquire the technical schematics for the second Death Star, as well as the revelation that the Emperor would inspect the station, thus rendering him vulnerable to a Rebel attack. Ever since that time, they've enjoyed a prestigious role in the New Republic.

Bothans are short, furry humanoids who express themselves with great eloquence and gentle ripplings in their fur that signify their emotional state. However, this latter trait can betray them when they are being duplicitous.

By their nature, Bothans are greedy for power, manipulative, and opportunistic, seeking the prestige that comes from controlling others. Wealth isn't as important as influence, and family clans constantly plot ways of gaining as much of it as possible. They seldom attack a competitor directly, usually waiting for rivals to do so, then finding ways to benefit from their efforts.

Bothans are also paranoid, and in their society, paranoia is well founded. Layer upon layer of schemes swirl around any clan, and those who associate with Bothans often find themselves unwittingly caught up in the web of politics.

The Bothan Council, made up of representatives from each of the clans, governs Bothawui as the primary law-making and law-enforcing body. The council elects one member to act as council chief, and all policies are decided by a majority vote, with the chief holding the tie-breaking vote. Each member of the council heads up several ministries and committees and appoints clan leaders to positions of importance.

DESIGNATION
> SENTIENT <

PLANET OF ORIGIN
> BOTHAWUI <

HEIGHT OF AVERAGE ADULT
> 1.5 METERS <

Spying is the Bothans' main industry. Everyone comes to Bothawui to get information, though information comes at a hefty price. The Bothan spynet, an underground system for buying and selling information, is as active under the New Republic as it was under the rule of the Empire. Leia Organa Solo noted her impressions of the Bothans in a private journal entry written at the beginning of the Yuuzhan Vong invasion, twenty-five years after the Battle of Yavin.

> During the war with the Empire we came to trust the Bothans as allies, but in later years we learned that, for them, there's always a hidden agenda. Because the Empire denied them power, they fought back in unity. If not for a common enemy, the Bothan clans would have been at each other's throats, competing to climb another rung on the ladder for control and influence.
> I do my best to keep free of prejudices when dealing with people, but with Borsk Fey'lya and his team, it's difficult. When we warned him of the Yuuzhan Vong, he accused me of being a traitor and making a play for power. He struck out at me, not realizing he was striking at his own survival.
> I realize that it's the way he was trained—to desire, to question, to challenge—but how can anything be accomplished without solidarity? How can we survive?
> Will this division and disruption continue? Will it end only when the New Republic is destroyed and conquered due to its lack of cohesiveness? And if that happens, will the Bothans be at the heart of it all?

Caamasi

In the languages of many cultures throughout the galaxy, the name *Caamasi* means "friend from afar" or "stranger to be trusted," and never did a people have a more appropriate title. The Caamasi are tall humanoids with golden down covering most of their bodies, purple fur around the eyes, and stripes extending around the back of their heads and shoulders. Their long hands have only three fingers, delicate and gentle.

The Caamasi are artistic, wise, and freethinking, and believe in peace through moral strength. According to Caamasi legend, the first Jedi Knights came to their planet ages ago in order to learn the moral use of the Force.

Caamasi are strict pacifists. Most are traders, diplomats, or scholars. All Caamasi can create lasting, vivid memories, called *memnii*, that are shared telepathically with others of their species. Clans will often intermarry simply to spread *memnii*, and the Caamasi can share a *memnis* with Jedi.

After the Clone Wars, Palpatine engineered the devastation of the planet Caamas. The heavy bombardment destroyed all vegetation, and most Caamasi were killed. A large Caamasi remnant community survived on Kerilt, though, and some later relocated to Susevfi. Refugees from Caamas went to several other worlds, one of them Alderaan.

It was a group of Bothans who helped Palpatine's agents sabotage Caamas's shield generators, allowing the sudden, violent attack to send firestorms raging across the world. A copy of the Caamas Document, detailing Bothan involvement in the tragedy, was discovered on Wayland and touched off a flood of demands for the Bothans to purchase an uninhabited world that would become home for the remaining refugees. Thus far, the Bothans have not fulfilled this demand.

The few remaining Caamasi, meanwhile, calmly and patiently await the time when they will have a new home. They continue to work side by side with the Bothans, offering a textbook example of forgiveness.

Senior Anthropologist Hoole notes how valuable the Caamasi were to the cause of peace in the galaxy.

> Before the rise of the Empire, I was invited to observe a Caamasi delegation as it settled a dispute between the Kubaz and the Verpine. The dispute was over the illegal activity of some Kubaz, who were hunting Verpine for food. Verpine, being insectoids, were considered a delicacy among the Kubaz elite. As a result of numerous deaths, the Verpine wanted to prosecute the government of Kubindi for attempted genocide.

> The Caamasi, through calm, gentle explanation, cajoled the Verpine into accepting the Kubaz promise to tighten their internal policing measures (under the watchful eye of the Republic), the tough prosecution of the murderers, and their government's sincerest apology.

> What would have taken regular negotiators weeks took only two days.

Chadra-Fan

Small and nimble, the Chadra-Fan are rodentlike beings whose senses have proved to be among the most acute in the known galaxy. In addition to the standard range of senses, Chadra-Fan employ infrared vision and pick up even the slightest of olfactory changes. This helps in finding mates, as the Chadra-Fan males and females project a pheromone aura. Unfortunately, with these pheromones they may project extremes such as fear and anger, and this often leads to confusion—or worse. Otherwise, they communicate verbally in high squeaking tones, the interpretation of which depends on a keen sense of hearing.

Their home planet Chad is three-quarters water, covered by chaotic seas, marshes, and bogs and prone to perpetual flooding. Therefore, Chadra-Fan have an intense fear of water and of drowning. The world's weather is caused by its bizarre elliptical orbit, which has confused scientists for many years as to whether it occupies the third or fourth position in the star system. On Chad, the bayous are the species' primary habitat. In recent history, tidal waves swept across their communities three or four times a year, so they sleep in swaying, open-walled structures that hang from the cyperill trees high above the water.

Chadra-Fan seek companionship. Left alone, they die of loneliness within a period of weeks. They never travel alone, preferring even the companionship of complete strangers. Senior Anthropologist Hoole observed the Chadra-Fan and wrote:

> Wanting to observe the natives in their natural state, I presented myself as a lone survivor of a destroyed village. They eagerly welcomed me, gave me a place to sleep, and even arranged a job for me working with the local ocean ranchers.

> On the first day, the ocean ranchers were guiding a new herd of bildogs and proops up from the sea for slaughter. I made a couple of friends, Kimsh and Shusk, who instructed me on what to do on our barge. As we traveled, though, the crew suddenly became agitated, sniffing the air and rushing around the deck as if preparing for disaster. It was a storm. Our herd dived beneath the surface, to resurface when the winds were gone.

> As the worst of the storm struck, the barge pitched to port, and Kimsh fell over the side. Shusk was with two other crewmates, struggling against the wind. He was beginning to lose his grip, as well.

> There was no sense in maintaining my charade. I changed my form and size to that of a Wookiee, directing my mass into my muscles. With a grunt, I pushed my friends to the deck, then lay above them, holding them down with my long arms so that the wind could not carry them away. It took tremendous concentration to maintain my form—all of the crewmates were radiating overwhelming fear.

> After half an hour, the winds subsided. Aching, I helped my crewmates to their feet, then explained my whole reason for being there, apologizing profusely for deceiving them.

> Shusk smiled, and his pheromones expressed his calm. He said, "Hoole, why didn't you just come as yourself and ask us questions? We'll tell you anything you want to know. We talk to anybody."

DESIGNATION
> SENTIENT <

PLANET OF ORIGIN
> CHAD <

HEIGHT OF AVERAGE ADULT
> 1 METER <

Chevin

The Chevin are a technologically advanced, carnivorous, migratory pachydermoid species that inhabits Vinsoth, a temperate planet covered mainly by grassy plains, with arctic regions and occasional patches of desert. Chevin have thick, wrinkled gray skin that keeps their body temperature even, allowing them to adapt to each environment.

Chevin stand on thick legs that support their large, bulky frames. Their large heads, from which a trunk-like snout drops to the ground, allow them to forage while watching for predators. Though slow, Chevin are good hunters, circling their prey until it stumbles into their high-tech, hidden traps.

Their cultural goal is to acquire money, power, and status by any means necessary. The galaxy has come to know them as smugglers, gamblers, blackmailers, and gunrunners. They are also slavers, exploiting the humanoid Chev species, with whom they share their world.

Although the Chevin are more than capable of using weapons of destruction, they are more likely to hire someone else to fight for them, or force their slaves to do so. They acquired their initial technical knowledge from offplanet sources and adapted it to their own needs.

As a migratory species, they travel their world in large community platform vehicles. Wealthier groups use repulsorlift vehicles, while others employ land vehicles with wheels. Slaves are forced to walk from campsite to campsite as the Chevin search for new areas for hunting the backshin—their primary source for meat.

Following the Battle of Endor, Ephant Mon, former assistant to Jabba the Hutt, broke from his upbringing and launched a movement to integrate the slave population into free Chevin society. The source of his rebellion is revealed in this memoir:

> When I left Vinsoth many years ago, I joined a crowd of criminals in order to further my own ends. I used others, manipulated them, and ultimately ended up serving them. My most trusted friend was a Hutt crimelord, and he discarded me as he would a piece of trash.

> Then I met the Jedi—a condemned man. But instead of seeking my assistance, he tried to help me. He said, "Escape yourself. Find your true life again." When Jabba rejected me, I realized the Jedi was right. I found myself yearning for the blue skies, the blowing grass. And so I came home.

> Upon my return, my family welcomed me, fed me, clothed me, and gave me my own personal slave. I accepted the young Chev, but it occurred to me that he was acting to me as I had acted to Jabba. From being a servant, I knew what it meant to be a slave.

> We are the slaves, to our own laziness, to our own comforts. We are nothing more than parasites, feeding on the lives of our fellows. This must stop.

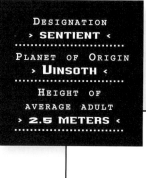

DESIGNATION
> SENTIENT <
....
PLANET OF ORIGIN
> VINSOTH <
....
HEIGHT OF
AVERAGE ADULT
> 2.5 METERS <

Chiss

little is known of the Chiss, a humanoid species from the Unknown Regions, other than the fact that Grand Admiral Thrawn was one of them. Thrawn, whose real name was Mitth'raw'nuruodo, revealed almost nothing about his species. However, agents of the New Republic, after conducting analyses of surrendered Imperial logs, found a few points of interest.

Exhibiting blue skin, jet-black hair, and glowing red eyes, the Chiss generally command attention in a crowd of regular humanoids. Their skin and eye color, it is believed, are due to a chemical reaction they experience in an oxygen atmosphere.

The Chiss are an attractive, intelligent, and extremely private species, so protective of their society that they have managed to keep their existence largely secret from the rest of the galaxy. Scientists believe they bypass the adolescent stage of life and advance quickly to full maturity. They are highly evolved, taking great interest in arts and science, and maintain a powerful military. In many accounts, they are described as pensive—contemplative, deliberate, and calculating—studying situations from every viewpoint. They often consider all the alternatives, even what might have occurred if something had been done differently.

When attacked, the Chiss fight with calm, intelligent, well-planned strategies. They are an honorable species, however, and in the event of war, they always wait for their opponents to strike first. This is such a moral imperative that they exiled Thrawn when he called for a preemptive strike against an enemy.

Despite this rejection, Thrawn was protective of his people, and he never revealed their whereabouts. No other recorded encounters with the Chiss

exist, although they are reputed to have driven back the Ssi-ruuk, a military threat considered by many to be as fearsome as the Nagai and the Yevetha. There have also been reports of a major encounter between the Chiss and the Yuuzhan Vong during the battle at Garqi.

One of the most interesting Imperial logs concerning the Chiss was recorded by Palpatine himself, noting his first meeting with Thrawn.

> The alien Captain Voss Parck brought to me is interesting, not because of his appearance—which reveals the physical limitations of his race—but because of the brain that clearly lies behind those glowing red eyes. This one is constantly thinking, analyzing, strategizing. He showed no fear, but was curious, studying me in turn.

> He is well trained. He expressed no anger when I demonstrated my distaste at his presence. I was subtle about it, of course, as subtlety is more likely to insult such an intellect. I was hoping to spur him to anger, and I failed.
> I am intrigued, to say the least. And I could see that he was as intrigued with me. I could sense that he did recognize me as a threat, but wasn't fearful of harm. He simply studied me as a potential opponent.
> I am amused. I believe I will watch his new career with interest.

DESIGNATION
> SENTIENT <

PLANET OF ORIGIN
> UNKNOWN SYSTEM <
IN THE UNKNOWN REGIONS

HEIGHT OF
AVERAGE ADULT
> 1.7 METERS <

the four-armed Codru-Ji reside on the planet Munto Codru, a world largely ignored by most galactic species. It lacks major exports, and industry is limited to those that keep the world running. Hence, it stays out of the spotlight, allowing the Codru-Ji to pursue life on their own terms.

Adults appear simply to be attractive humans with four arms. In reality, however, the Codru-Ji are born as canines, at which point they are called wyrwulves. This young six-legged canine creature is treated with great love and affection by its family and is given rudimentary guidance in how to survive and behave. When the wyrwulf reaches puberty, it cocoons itself in a blue chrysalis. After a few weeks, it emerges as a fully developed Codru-Ji child.

Senior Anthropologist Hoole, in his personal journal, mentions an incident involving a Codru-Ji child, which caused him great embarrassment.

> It was my first encounter with the Codru-Ji, and I had little time to do background research. I had been invited to the governor's home for dinner, and as I entered their home, the governor and his mate greeted me warmly. We started toward their sitting room, when suddenly, a large, six-legged canine creature romped down the hallway and pounced on me, knocking me to the ground.
> "Please!" I cried instinctively, "Get this mangy beast off of me!"
> The creature immediately jumped off, lay down next to me, and began to whine.
> "My son," the governor said coolly, "is not a mangy beast, Hoole."

> I scrambled to my feet. "I—uh," I stammered. "I'm sorry, sir, I didn't realize—" It then occurred to me that a customary gesture was necessary. Recalling one of the few research articles on Codru-Ji customs I'd read, I immediately grew two more arms, placed two on my head, two on my stomach, and bowed low to them all. "Please forgive my error."
> The governor nodded and actually smiled. "I think we can forgive you this time, Hoole. Give Rikki a scratch behind the ears and I'm sure he'll forgive you, too."
> I did just that, and the wyrwulf licked my fingers. Wiping the saliva on my pants, I said, "Shall we proceed to our meeting, sir?"
> "Yes, we shall," the governor said, although his mate still wore a cool look on her face.

Isolated at the rim of the galaxy, the Munto Codru political system developed without outside influence.

It is a largely mysterious system beset by political struggle, wherein coups occur frequently. There is a tradition of "ritual kidnapping," in which the children or loved ones of the opposition are taken. Once an agreement is made and ransoms are paid, the abductees are returned without incident.

Scientists believe the Codru-Ji are descendants of a highly developed ancient race that once inhabited their world and built huge, ornately carved stone palaces. Although the Codru-Ji maintain these structures and use them as provincial capitols, they believe them to be haunted and prefer to avoid them.

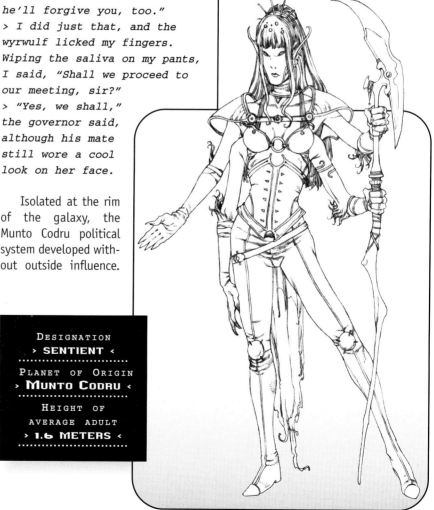

DESIGNATION
> SENTIENT <

PLANET OF ORIGIN
> MUNTO CODRU <

HEIGHT OF AVERAGE ADULT
> 1.6 METERS <

the Coway are cave dwellers indigenous to the planet Circarpous V, known to the locals as Mimban, which they share with Mimbanites, a similar, town-dwelling people. A muddy, swamp-laden planet, Mimban is largely forest covered. It also has a wealth of dolovite, a mineral useful for technology development. Hence, the Empire set up mining facilities in archaic temples left behind by an extinct race.

The Coway spend most of their time underground, so when the Empire arrived on their world, the Coway avoided them by moving deeper under the surface. Unfortunately, the Imperial mining operation infringed on that space, causing the Coway to rebel with unpredictable spurts of violence.

Coway are covered with fine gray down. They are bipedal humanoids, with small eyes and large eyelids, and infrared vision that allows them to see in the dark. Their digestive system utilizes strong amino acids for digesting uncooked meats, lichens, and fungus that would be poisonous to humans.

A primitive tribal species, with no sense of technology or advanced learning, they worship a warrior god named Canu, who, according to holy writings, demands strength from his people. The males of the species are dominant and maintain order through brute force. Coway are suspicious of all intruders and will attack outsiders or challenge them to contests.

Before the Battle of Yavin, Han Solo and Chewbacca encountered the Coway and were forced to fight for their lives as part of Coway tradition. Solo recorded:

> Bwahl the Hutt had a line on some ancient artifacts that he wanted to sell, and to pick them up for him we had

DESIGNATION
> SENTIENT <
PLANET OF ORIGIN
> MIMBAN <
(CIRCARPOUS V)
HEIGHT OF
AVERAGE ADULT
> 1.6 METERS <

to go to this mud planet out in the middle of nowhere.
There, we met a big goon named Jake, ugly, dressed in a dirty miner suit.
> I gave him the money, and apparently it wasn't the amount Bwahl had agreed to pay. So all of sudden we were surrounded by this group of natives. They attacked with hatchets, spears, and knives. I took a couple out with my blaster, but Jake got wounded in the first two seconds.
> Chewie charged through these guys, tossing natives around right and left. Suddenly, everything stopped. The natives dropped their weapons, and one—probably the chief—offered Chewie a spear! Chewie took it, and the chief socked

him across the jaw. Chewie roared, then decked him. After that, the chief and all the natives bowed low, then turned and disappeared into the cave.
> My guess is they'd never seen a Wookiee before, and they're hoping they never see one again.

Despite their cultural differences, the Mimbanites and the Coway speak similar languages. Because of Coway cave drawings and Mimbanite pictographs that are similar to those in the Temple of Pomojema on Mimban, there is believed to be a connection among the Coway, the Mimbanites, and the temple.

ecause the Devaronian males, with their reddish skin, sharp teeth, and horns, resemble images of malicious beings from other cultures, many species perceive them as evil. Although Devaronians are *not* evil, the New Republic has not accepted Devaron as a member world.

The two Devaronian sexes differ physically. They evolved, originally, from creatures that used their horns to defend themselves from predators. While the females of the species lost their horns through evolution, the males did not. Also, the males have sharp incisors used for hunting and rending flesh, whereas the females have the blunt teeth of omnivores.

Devaronian males are known to be extremely irresponsible. Devaronian females, on the other hand, are extraordinarily straightforward and ambitious, running businesses and participating in local politics. Males are not permitted to hold public office. Females rarely leave their world unless for some work-related reason. Males, on the other hand, exhibit an irrepressible wanderlust and are found in most spaceports, serving as wandering merchants, bounty hunters, galactic traders, and explorers. Once they leave Devaron, they rarely ever return. Strangely, however, Devaronian males always send money they earn to their wives and offspring. The truth is, the females prefer the financial support to the actual presence of the males.

When the male Devaronians developed stardrive capabilities, the females took advantage of it by setting up trade with other systems. Their world has therefore become wealthy, with females running the economic and political systems.

The Devish people maintain one tradition that has kept them from gaining membership in the New Republic. The Devish form of capital

DESIGNATION
> **SENTIENT** <

PLANET OF ORIGIN
> **DEVARON** <

HEIGHT OF
AVERAGE ADULT
> **1.6 METERS** <

punishment is considered cruel and unusual. Mika'sai'Malloc, the daughter of Kardu'sai'Malloc, the Butcher of Montellian Serat, described in her personal journal her father's execution.

> We stood at the Judgment Field outside the demolished ancient city of Montellian Serat—the city my father had destroyed. The pit of ravenous quarra had been prepared the moment we heard that he had been captured. The creatures were more than ready.
> My mother wanted nothing to do with him. The rest of our family had come, though—some to mourn, others to rejoice. I watched as they brought him forward to the pit. As he neared the edge, the hungry quarra began to growl eagerly, smelling his fear.
> "The Butcher of Montellian Serat!" the herald cried. The throng of ten thousand Devish voices rose in a cheer as the guards pushed him forward into the pit.
> The quarra bit into him before he even met the ground. He struggled a bit at first, then relaxed and arched his neck so the quarra would tear out his throat.
> At least he knew how to die honorably.

Dewback

herbivores, the dewbacks are nonsentient reptiles that inhabit the desert wastelands of the planet Tatooine. This species was domesticated long before the Empire took its place on the water-barren world, where they are used by moisture farmers as beasts of burden and by desert stormtroopers as patrol animals. Though sluggish in the cool of the night, the cold-blooded dewbacks can be urged to bursts of great speed, loping in the daytime heat.

Dewbacks are relatively large beasts, ranging between 1.3 to 2 meters in height, and 2 to 3 meters in length. Their scales are generally gray and brown or a dull red and blue, though they are known to change color with their environment.

Their name comes from the dew that gathers on their bodies during their nighttime rest. Dewbacks, which live in small groups of two to five animals, lick the dew off each other's backs for moisture. They are comfortable in the desert and are often seen digging through sand dunes in search of small animals, brush, or moisture. Every year, they return to the Jundland Wastes, where they engage for several days in a mating ritual. After this, the females fill thousands of nests with eggs. All the dewbacks then wander back into the desert. Interestingly enough, their mating season begins just as the krayt dragon mating season ends, thus timing the egg laying in such a way as to protect the eggs from destruction. The two lizard species have chosen the same location for their mating ground due to the fact that the sand in that area remains at the ideal temperature for incubating eggs.

A half year after being laid, dewback eggs hatch, and the young, without any guidance from adults, make their way into the desert. It is inter-esting to note that dewbacks will not breed in captivity. Owners of domesticated dewbacks must release them during mating season, allowing them to go to the Jundland Wastes. In most cases, domesticated dewbacks return to their rightful owners.

While many dewbacks are domesticated, most remain in the wild. Those that are domesticated are generally used as patrol animals, because they are well suited to the high temperatures and blowing sands. They are also faster and more agile than the bantha, the beast used most often by the Tusken Raiders. At full run, dewbacks have been able to pace landspeeders for short distances, and local patrols have come to find them more reliable than landspeeders because of their ability to continue moving through the fiercest sandstorms.

In the wild, Tusken Raiders hunt dewbacks for their meat and their hides. They use the dewback's leathery skin for boots, pouches, belts, tents, and other gear. Krayt dragons also hunt dewbacks, as they are relatively easy prey. Dewbacks will fight only if threatened, and even then, they usually attempt to run away from any threat larger than themselves.

As a boy, Luke Skywalker's friend Windy owned a pet dewback. Luke wrote of his experience with the creature in this journal entry dated nineteen years after the Battle of Endor, relating to his fourteen-year-old nephew, Jacen Solo, who was fond of keeping pets at the Jedi academy on Yavin 4.

> Jacen came to me with an interesting problem. He had a small rock lizard he had captured near the river, and he had been having difficulty keeping it in its cage. It

DESIGNATION
> **NONSENTIENT** <

PLANET OF ORIGIN
> **TATOOINE** <

HEIGHT OF AVERAGE ADULT
> **1.8 METERS** <

came close to hurting itself several times, just trying to get free. No matter how hard Jacen tried to calm it through the Force, it tried to escape.

> This situation reminded me of a pet dewback named Huey.

> Dewbacks are much larger than rock lizards, of course, but like this little creature, Huey was gentle and happy being around almost anyone who loved him. Windy and I took care of him, rode him, and played with him, and Huey helped around the farm, moving equipment. At night Huey stayed on the terrace, where he was happy to sleep in the cool air.

> Windy told me how he woke up early one morning, jolted awake by a loud banging sound, and found Huey ramming his head against the gate to the terrace exit. He wanted out. He had never wanted out before, especially at this time in the morning. Windy's father woke up, too, and when he saw how upset Huey was, he told Windy he had to let him go.

> "Let him go?" Windy said. "What do you mean? He's our pet. He's happy here."

> "I hate to tell you this," Windy's father said, "but I think Huey needs to go into the Wastes to find a mate. It's about that time of year."

> Windy wasn't happy about that at all. "He's still a baby, Dad. He might not know to come back."

> "He has to leave, or he'll go crazy. He's already denting the gate, and he'll knock it down in a second. I'm going to let him out. If he can, he'll come back."

> "How do you know?"

> Windy's dad did his best to explain. "You and Luke have been a good friend to him. He loves you both."

> So Windy watched as his father opened the gate and let Huey loose.

> Huey did come back several weeks later, but two weeks after that a krayt dragon killed him when Windy and I were out trying to prove our independence.

> I told Jacen this story and suggested that he try letting his rock lizard go. He wasn't happy, but he said he'd give it a try.

> His rock lizard did come back, carrying a sack of eggs in its mouth. He, or rather, she, went right into the cage and put the egg sack next to the heat rock where they'd be warm. Nature, like the Force, must be allowed to go in its own direction for the best results.

Dianoga

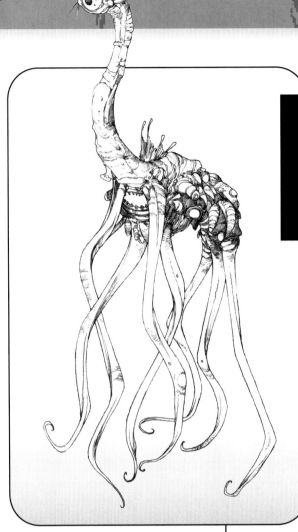

the scavenger known as the dianoga is an amphibious, squidlike creature that makes its home wherever refuse collects in water environments. Each dianoga possesses a single eyestalk that extends out of the water like a periscope, which it uses to scan its environment, and each individual boasts seven tentacles with which to move and gather food. Should any of these tentacles be severed, the damaged limb will grow back.

It is believed that the creatures originated on the planet Vodran, crawling into the waste containment tanks of spacefaring vessels, where they bred. At spaceports, they migrated to other ships and dispersed themselves throughout the galaxy. Now dianoga can be found in most warm, watery collections of waste in almost every known spaceport and large ship. Since these creatures actually feed on and digest waste products, most vessel commanders will allow a dianoga to remain in their ship's waste system. They rarely damage the inner workings of the system, preferring to rest peacefully along the bottom of a tank and feed.

Dianoga are self-fertilizing hermaphrodites, not requiring others of their species to reproduce. When they do reproduce, the young go through a microscopic larval stage, and they create small colonies. Once the population becomes too great for an environment, dianoga leave that colony and migrate to a new, uninhabited space. Even on large ships dianoga can be tolerated in colonies of only three or less, after which the creatures begin to hamper the workings of the waste system through sheer weight of numbers.

These creatures are shy and peaceful and will usually turn aggressive only if starved or panicked. They rarely

hunt living beings, although they are curious and tend to check each new object they encounter, living or otherwise, testing for edibility. Some cultures have developed ways to eat dianoga, though; most popular is the dish known as dianoga pie.

In a personal journal entry dated around the Battle of Hoth, Luke Skywalker remarked on his own experiences with the creatures.

> I was working with Dack on one of the transports, when we started fiddling with the waste system. I went down to open up one of the chambers. As I did, the giant red eyestalk of a dianoga popped out

DESIGNATION
> NONSENTIENT <
PLANET OF ORIGIN
> VODRAN <
HEIGHT OF AVERAGE ADULT
> 10 METERS <

to glare at me. He was probably annoyed because I was letting in the cold air.
> I was a little surprised. I didn't think they could survive in such cold weather. Dack laughed and said they can survive just about anywhere; they just like nice warm waste dumps.
> I first ran into one of these creatures on the Death Star. Leia, Han, and I had ended up in a trash compactor, and the dianoga must have found me interesting. He pulled me under the garbage-filled water, and I almost drowned. That experience left me a little skittish.
> Anyway, the transport commander and the engineer decided to let this dianoga stay. He was the only one so far, so he wouldn't do any damage. If he got troublesome or reproduced later on, the commander said he'd have the pros take care of him.

Dinko

known for its volatile temperament, this vicious, caninelike creature inhabits the forested areas of Proxima Dibal, where it preys on smaller woodland creatures. Being somewhat small themselves, dinkos consider anyone or anything they encounter as a threat. They are mostly blind and can detect only movement, so they attack almost any motion they perceive.

But any opponent that thinks a dinko's size makes it easy prey is mistaken, as dinkos have several means of defending themselves. Their sharp teeth and razor-sharp claws make them particularly dangerous in normal combat, and they have a scent-spraying ability that repels any potential attacker with its virulent, almost toxic odor. But contrary to popular belief, the dinko's scent is generally not used for defense, but as a signal establishing dominance in mating.

Dinkos are stubborn creatures. They fight with extreme hostility to defend their cubs and territory, and when locked in a fight, they do not yield. Once a dinko latches on with its extremely strong jaws, it will kill its prey simply by holding on until the creature suffocates.

Dinkos are largely extinct, due to a personal vendetta launched against them by a certain Corporate Sector crimelord known as Ploovo Two-For-One. Ploovo was viciously attacked by one of these creatures, and thereafter established a bounty for any dinko killed.

In a personal log entry, Captain Han Solo spoke of his own experience with a dinko, which is believed to explain the reasons behind Ploovo's vendetta.

> Ploovo, that scum, deserved everything he got for betraying us to the Espos.

> It was a stretch of luck to even find a dinko. Most pet shops don't carry them, because they're just too vicious. I knew no one would really want a dinko as a pet, but some people have been known to breed them for fighting. That's where I found out about dinkos in the first place. I won a couple of credits on a scrappy little creature called Fang. Of course, the animals they use in dinko fighting are de-scented. No one would want to be near one otherwise.
> The dinko I found hadn't been descented. That made the deal all the more rewarding.
> Ploovo, of course, thought the box I brought him was his payment. Oh, I paid him what he wanted all right, then gave him a little extra.
> When Ploovo reached into the box, the little guy, bless its smelly little heart, latched on to Ploovo's thumb and squirted its scent all over his nice new suit. It was great and it was just the distraction Chewie and I needed to escape from the Espos.
> Too bad I couldn't keep the creature. It was quite a useful little runt.

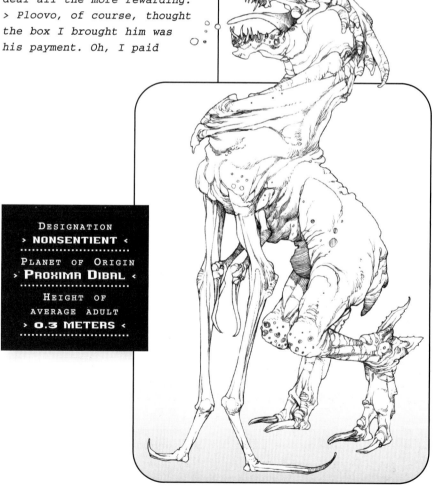

DESIGNATION
> NONSENTIENT <

PLANET OF ORIGIN
> PROXIMA DIBAL <

HEIGHT OF AVERAGE ADULT
> 0.3 METERS <

the Drall are small, furry, bipedal creatures native to the planet Drall in the Corellian system. They have large, black eyes and a gentle countenance and are an intelligent, highly dignified species.

Methodical and levelheaded, Drall are most known as excellent scholars and scientists. They are, by nature, abstract thinkers—preferring to develop new scientific theories rather than put them into practice. Therefore, despite the advanced nature of their scholarly pursuits, they often trail behind the galaxy in technological achievement and usually implement technologies that have been developed elsewhere.

Drall society is clan-based and hierarchical, with no elected head of state. Powerful family groups run the government. The head of each family is generally the eldest female, who holds the title of duchess. Upon the death of a title holder, her title and holdings are transferred to the female of the next generation who shows the levelheadedness and leadership skills necessary for the role.

Most Drall hold positions that involve processing medicinal agriculture—Drall's primary industry. Although Drall are rarely seen elsewhere in the galaxy, offplanet corporations have hired Drall to serve as scientific researchers.

The Drall people love to gossip. It's something of a cultural tradition, as exemplified in an employment file entry from Kirk Takill, manager of medical research at the New Republic Medical Institute on Corellia.

> Darkin, the new researcher from Drall, is diligent, accurate, and polite. About the only criticism I have is that he talks too much.
> He feels it's necessary to give daily updates on his family business. For example, his younger brother is an engineer here on Corellia, and Darkin announces every promotion, every commendation his brother receives. He also gives reports on his younger sister, his father, his mother, and his grandmother on a daily basis.
> What makes it worse is that he's curious about our families, too. He would ask me and the other employees too many personal questions, so I finally had to break it to him that we humans prefer to keep our family life private.
> Darkin was upset about this. He apologized, explaining that not many Drall leave home. I told him to keep the family talk to a minimum, and he agreed. Turns out, though, that many of Darkin's human coworkers had gotten used to listening to his daily reports. When he stopped giving them, they started asking him for updates. He now holds court in the lunchroom, surrounded by everyone who wants to listen.

DESIGNATION
> SENTIENT <

PLANET OF ORIGIN
> DRALL <

HEIGHT OF AVERAGE ADULT
> 1 METER <

Dressellian

dressellians are fiercely independent people who inhabit the world of Dressel. Their species is humanoid, although they do boast a singularly wrinkled appearance.

This stiff-necked species values individual freedom over all else, and they have difficulty working in groups. They are often critical of others, particularly offworlders. Despite this, in the threat of Imperial domination, the Dressellians came together to form a fierce, freedom-fighting force, determined to live as they chose, on their own terms.

The Dressellians aren't technologically advanced, although since the end of the Galactic Civil War, more and more offworlders have filtered technology to them. During the war, Dressellians fought with simple black-powdered, slug-firing weapons. The Bothan underground made contact with the Dressellians and supplied them with some energy weapons, though transporting weapons proved dangerous, and very few made it to their intended recipients.

Today, the government of Dressel consists of large communal states that rule via direct democracy, each with elected leaders who moderate elaborate group discussions. This system survived covertly despite the Empire's best efforts to squash it. The state leaders became, in fact, the leadership of the Dressellian underground movement. Although they are now part of the structure of the New Republic, Dressellians largely prefer to keep to themselves. Their representatives often choose not to attend senatorial sessions, except when their war colleagues, the Bothans, coax them to be present for a particularly important vote.

A Dressellian individual named Orrimaarko was instrumental to the Alliance's victory at Endor and, following that battle, in his transmission to General Crix Madine, exemplified the Dressellian mind-set toward the rest of the galaxy.

> Many times it has been stated that one goal of the Alliance is integration of the member species. I respect that, and so I fight for it, but too often I've found myself ridiculed behind my back. There have been times when I have been made to feel that I was working alongside people who were no different from the Imperials, the prejudice ran so deep.
> Can you explain to me why so many commanders at the Battle of Endor were human? Ackbar had to lead, of course, because of his knowledge of Imperial tactics and his access to ships and firepower. But when it came to choosing the leader for the shuttle team, I felt I was the best candidate because of my espionage experience. Instead, Han Solo, a man who barely graduated the Imperial Academy, was elevated to the level of general and given the command. I submit to you that I would have had that shield down faster and more efficiently. I only hope that in the future the best person for the job is chosen based on skill rather than on what is most popular or convenient.

DESIGNATION
> **SENTIENT** <
....
PLANET OF ORIGIN
> **DRESSEL** <
....
HEIGHT OF
AVERAGE ADULT
> **1.8 METERS** <
....

Droch

drochs are insects and the source of the mysterious Death Seed plague, a horrifying pestilence that has gripped shipping lanes and ports on very rare, but notable, occasions.

This purple-brown, chitin-shelled, multilegged creature burrows under the skin and drinks life from its victims while they sleep—or sometimes when they're awake, if the insect is hungry enough. Small and agile, drochs can slip unseen onto ships and kill whole crews, leaving "death ships" drifting in space. Their rapid reproductive rate allows them to infiltrate an entire city population in a matter of only a few days.

Drochs are actually harmless on their homeworld Nam Chorios. A species known as Grissmaths originally established the world as a prison colony some 750 years before the Galactic Civil War, then planted the drochs to kill off the political prisoners they had imprisoned there. However, the crystalline landscape reflected the sun's radiation in such a way that it killed the weakest insects and weakened the others. In addition, the world is strong with the Force. Its life-giving nature canceled out the droch's life-draining abilities. Hence the drochs were unable to extract enough life from the prisoners who lived there. At best, they merely inflicted annoying insect bites and drained victims of energy for a short time, then were absorbed into the body a mere twenty minutes after they burrowed under a victim's skin.

Daylight kills drochs; therefore, the darkness of space proved to be their favorite breeding ground. For this reason they tried to escape Nam Chorios on any ships that visited there. On the rare occasions that they succeeded, the consequences proved to be tragic.

Drochs do not begin life as sentients, but while absorbing life from a

DESIGNATION
> NONSENTIENT/
SENTIENT <
....
PLANET OF ORIGIN
> NAM CHORIOS <
....
LENGTH OF
AVERAGE ADULT
> .005 METERS <

victim, they also absorb intelligence. The larger ones, called captain drochs, absorb life through the smaller ones without ever having to touch the victims, and the more life they drink, the more intelligent they become. One captain droch is reported to have mutated, growing to human size. This droch, named Dzym, lived to be about 250 years old and controlled his underlings long enough to reach populated space, until Princess Leia Organa Solo and Luke Skywalker stopped him.

Today drochs are trapped on Nam Chorios. The crystalline formations on the planet, called tsils, possess their own sentience and do not allow any ship larger than a single-person fighter to land on the world. The New Republic heavily enforces this regulation.

An Imperial officer at the Ord Mantell spaceport, Lieutenant Wynn Barezz, reported what was found on a security recording taken from an armed cargo ship that had been infected by the Death Seed plague.

> It began about an hour and a half into the trip, when a crewmember reported trouble with a shipmate. The captain sent the copilot to investigate, and after about twenty minutes the copilot hadn't returned. The pilot could be seen starting to set her controls on autopilot, when a shadow moved across the floor. Moments later she jumped as if bitten by an insect, after which she began to convulse horribly. She fell from her chair, and the rest of the recording is of her dead body lying on the ground. The ship arrived in port set on autopilot and was immediately placed in quarantine.

drovians are tall, corpulent beings from the planet Nim Drovis, who have divided into two separate, distinct tribes: the Gopso'o and the Drovians. While both have the same physical attributes, they have been at war for centuries.

The technologically advanced Drovians are solidly built, with bottom-heavy physiques that are supported by thick, trunklike legs. All of their limbs end in three sharp pincers. Despite their powerful physical attributes, nearly all of the Drovians are addicted to zwil, a narcotic that was first introduced by offworld traders. Zwil was a cake-flavoring agent common to Algarine cuisine, but Drovians are able to absorb it into their systems, sucking on zwil-coated fist-sized plugs that they place in their membrane-lined breathing tubes. The narcotic is particularly fragrant, a flavorful combination of cinnamon and vanilla.

The world of Nim Drovis is a harsh, jungle rain-forest environment that breeds acid-producing molds that can eat through the skin of an unsuspecting victim. Those Drovians and Gopso'o who do not fight in the war actively seek to exterminate the mold, attacking the plant-based pestilence with acid- and flame-throwing weapons.

Drovians and Gopso'o have been fighting so long, they've forgotten their reasons for fighting. It is believed that the original argument was over the grammatical construction of the word *truth*: one side believed it should be plural and the other singular.

Ism Oolos, a Ho'Din physician assigned to the New Republic Medcenter on Nim Drovis, wrote of the Gopso'o–Drovian hatred in his personal journal.

> I made the mistake of asking a Drovian the reason for

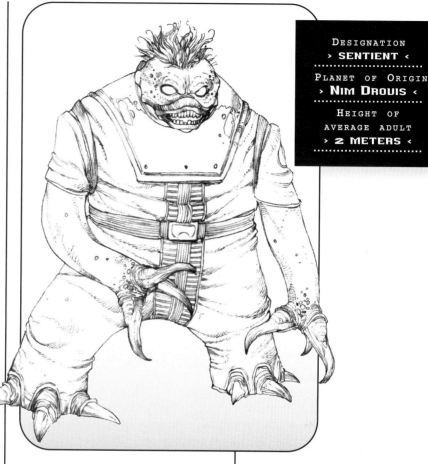

DESIGNATION
> **SENTIENT** <

PLANET OF ORIGIN
> **NIM DROVIS** <

HEIGHT OF
AVERAGE ADULT
> **2 METERS** <

their animosity against the Gopso'o. The Drovian, whose temperament I'd normally describe as "agreeable," thrust me against the wall, pressing his sharp pincers hard into my chest.
> "My mother was killed by a Gopso'o," he snarled in my face. "She was beaten to a pulp and hurled into a mass of fungus that burned her body so badly, we didn't even recognize her when we found her. Then, a Gopso'o fragged my younger brother with a flamethrower. He accidentally ran into a squad of fungus killers, and they decided to kill him instead."

> "Bu-but why did this all start in the first place?" I stammered.
> "Who cares? I have all the reason I need, and so does everybody else. They're killers, you hear? Murderers." He let me go and pointed his pincer at my nose. "Take it from me, Wormhead. You're an outsider. Keep your nose in your own business."

Dug

ugs are a vicious, bullying species that hails from the planet Malastare—one of the mainstay planets of the Old Republic. They inhabit the lush western continent, while another immigrant species known as the Gran dominates the eastern continent. Eight thousand years ago, the Old Republic set up an outpost in the eastern continent because Malastare is positioned along the Hydian Way trade route, and the Gran followed soon after to set up their own settlements. The Gran view their Dug neighbors as subservient laborers, incapable of ruling themselves. As a result, the Gran represented Malastare to the Republic Senate instead of the world's native species, leading to a long-standing antagonism between the two groups.

The Dugs' physiology puts them at the extreme fringes of the humanoid classification. Their skin hangs loosely over their skeleton, and inflates during mating calls. Their ears jut backward like fins, and customary beads dangle from an extra flap of skin near the ears. The center of gravity for their skeletal structure is thrust so high on their torsos that they literally walk on their upper limbs, while their lower limbs function for fine manipulation. Their unusual physique may have developed due to the world's high gravity.

Dugs can travel quickly across land and move swiftly through trees by leaping and swinging. Many of their buildings are towers, and interiors are made with open platforms. Most other species find them impassable. Although the Dugs are a technologically advanced species and can construct complex structures, many prefer to live in tree thorps—primitive villages—deep in the unsettled wilderness.

Dugs are most known for their foul

DESIGNATION
> SENTIENT <

PLANET OF ORIGIN
> MALASTARE <

HEIGHT OF AVERAGE ADULT
> 1 METER <

tempers. Derogatory and insolent, they are violent when contested. Their reflexes are extremely quick, and so they are experts at Podracing, a dangerous sport that has been declared illegal in most parts of the galaxy for years.

Dugs have been to war with many species, among them the Gran and the ZeHethbra, a species with colonies in the Malastare system. As a result, the Republic demilitarized the Dugs, leaving them extremely bitter. They consider themselves warriors, and being denied armaments has made them even more vicious and brutal, as was confirmed in a log entry recorded by Lord Darth Vader during the early years of the Empire, while the fledgling government was tightening its hold on the Malastare system.

> *Motivating the Dugs to fight is not difficult, for at the core of their beings are knots of unfocused rage.*

However, that rage is not centered in the true warrior's drive of hatred, but in insecurity. They are valueless, and they know this. That is why they will always be defeated.
> *Despite this, we could easily direct their bitterness against the remaining Gran senatorial representation. I conducted interrogations with several Dugs and found them easy to manipulate, hungry for attention, and anxious to achieve a higher status. One insulted me in an attempt to gain a higher footing in our discussion. He demonstrated venomous spirit, though breaking him was so simple it was disappointing.*

Duros

along with the Corellians, the Duros are among the oldest space-faring peoples in the galaxy. Their entire society evolved around spaceflight, and they helped blaze the hyperspace routes for trade throughout the galaxy.

Duros are tall humanoids with blue skin, large red eyes, slit mouths, and no noses. Their sense of smell is conducted through glands beneath their eyes. Other than this, they have no outward physical peculiarity that makes them appear different from standard humanoids.

Since Duros culture is centered on space travel, a majority of the Duros population lives in six space-station cities that orbit their planet. Thousands of years ago, the world was lush and fertile. After the Duros discovered space travel and left to live on the space stations, they neglected the planet, leaving it to fall to ruin. The Empire finished the job, destroying the environment with pollution from its mining operations.

The Duros are technologically advanced and build a great many of the galaxy's space-faring vessels in their shipyards. In fact, the shipbuilding industry dominates their economy and serves as the world's government. Those who wish to participate in the government purchase shares of stock in the corporation.

Culturally, the Duros' longing for the skies has led many of their youths to become pilots and join starship crews. They gravitate to spaceports, from which they start their new journeys. To a Duros, the joy is not in where one goes, but in getting there, and they spend a lot of their time just "getting there."

Although one would characterize the Duros species as quiet, they are also friendly, even-tempered, and love to tell stories. There is one way to

DESIGNATION
> **SENTIENT** <

PLANET OF ORIGIN
> **DURO** <

HEIGHT OF AVERAGE ADULT
> **1.7 METERS** <

upset a Duros, as a Duros pilot stated emphatically in this letter to a local HoloNet news organization.

> Recently I applied for a job with a shipping company, and they asked me if I was applying for an accounting position. "Accounting?" I repeated. "Why would I want to do that? I'm a pilot!"
> "Really?" The woman looked surprised and apologetic. "Oh, well, pardon me." She reached under the desk and handed me an application pad. "It's just that I'd never met a

Neimoidian commercial pilot before."
> Neimoidian?! I was incensed, and I tossed the app-pad down on the desk and walked out.
> How in space can someone confuse us with that slimy, spineless, no-good people? Our eyes are a nice, deep blood-red, not dark pink like theirs! Our skin is bluish green, not greenish blue. We have a more defined jawline, and our lips are much more prominent. And at least we take care of our offspring.
> There needs to be cultural education, so our proud, space-faring people will not be confused with a bunch of spineless cowards.

Despite the protests of the Duros, Neimoidians *are* actually their genetic offspring, having descended from ancient Duros colonists.

Short, furry bipeds, the Eloms live in the desert caves of the planet Elom. They share the world with the Elomin, a species who live above ground.

With tough skin hidden beneath thick, oily fur, and fat layers designed to trap moisture in their bodies, Eloms are specially evolved to live in their harsh desert environment. Their hands and feet have hard-tipped, hooked claws, optimal for digging. Two prehensile toes on each foot can be used to grip extra tools. Because they live in caves lit only by phosphorescent crystals, they have excellent night vision, but their small, dark eyes cannot tolerate bright light.

Two hard, sharp tusks protrude from an Elom's mouth, and they have thick jowls for holding extra food. They are herbivores and primarily feed on hard-shell rockmelons and crystalweeds.

Their Elomin neighbors discovered the Eloms during a mining accident. Elomin had been mining for lommite, an element used in manufacturing transparisteel. After this accidental first meeting, the Old Republic designated the Eloms a sentient species and gave them the rights to the lands they already inhabited.

This amused the Eloms. A peaceful, unsophisticated people, with a strong sense of community, they continued living as they had for centuries, and accepted the Elomin as part of that community. The Elomin, however, felt the Eloms did not fit within their "ordered" view of the universe, and so the two species remained separate until the Empire took over the mining operation and enslaved the Elomin. The young Eloms decided to fight to free their world, and freed many Elomin slaves, bringing them to cities safe in the underground labyrinth.

Since the world was liberated, the two species have become more integrated, and many young Eloms have left to seek their fortunes among the stars. Those Eloms who leave are ambitious and intelligent, but also lonely and ignorant of the ways of the galaxy. Usually they fall in with the wrong crowd. Unfortunately, many have become criminals. One such Elom was Kav Dryfus, who died in an Imperial prison. Before he did, though, he recorded his memories of fighting the Empire alongside the Elomin.

> When the Empire came, one of the Elomin we assisted was Ryannar N'on Dikasterar, whom I'd met many years ago. He did not recognize me at first. But as recognition dawned, he said, "I'm sorry, you know."
> "For what?" I asked.
> "I thought you people were demons of chaos. I realize now that order sent you to protect us."
> I laughed. They could be so silly with the "order and chaos" stuff. "That's good," I said. "And there's no reason to be sorry. Let's go to work."
> He agreed, and together we went to free more of his people. It was then I was captured. But I am at peace because he is free. Maybe we'll work together again someday. He's a decent guy, after all.

DESIGNATION
> SENTIENT <

PLANET OF ORIGIN
> ELOM <

HEIGHT OF AVERAGE ADULT
> 1.4 METERS <

Elomin

DESIGNATION
> SENTIENT <
....
PLANET OF ORIGIN
> ELOM <
....
HEIGHT OF
AVERAGE ADULT
> 1.6 METERS <
....

elomin are tall, thin humanoids with pointed ears and four small horns topping their heads. They share the cold, barren planet Elom with another species known as the Eloms, who live in underground caves. When Old Republic scouts arrived on Elom about one hundred years before the dawn of Imperial rule, the Elomin were a relatively primitive people who employed slug-throwing weapons and combustion engines. Contact with the Old Republic influenced their technological development, and soon they had starships, repulsorlift vehicles, and high-end mining equipment. They allowed a shipbuilding corporation to come to their world to mine lommite, an element used in making transparisteel for starships.

Culturally, the Elomin aspire to find or create order in all things. Originally they had no concept that another, completely different species might share their world. Even when an expedition force uncovered cave formations in the distant desert region, and the caverns showed evidence of being inhabited, the Elomin refused to accept the implications and omitted these findings from their reports. Only when a group of Elomin came face-to-face with Eloms in a mining accident were they finally forced to accept the existence of their neighbors.

Elomin art reflects order in that it is repetitive and mathematically structured. Their architecture is predictable and ordered, as are their cities. Nothing they build or create is left to chance. Because they seek order, the Elomin have some difficulty dealing with other species, whom they view as perpetrators of chaos. Old Republic representatives discovered that the Elomin had difficulty working in integrated space crews, but that they excelled at navigation and piloting duties, viewing the universe as a logical, organized puzzle and endeavoring to find the pieces and bring them to their logical places.

Ryannar N'on Dikasterar was the Elomin who first discovered the Elom, and he reported his observations to his superior, Mine Director Donatellinsar R'a Pereriansa.

> Fate has cursed us and order is scoffing at us, Director. Today the mine collapsed, as did society as we know it.
> We were opening a new tunnel when it collapsed on the crew, trapping many of the miners in the rubble. We began digging furiously, hoping to save their lives. As we worked, the wall of dirt, gravel, and rock opened up, indicating that someone was working from the other side. Eagerly, we dug faster, and after clearing a larger hole we looked through and found...others. They were huge, hairy, tusked, and putrid smelling. Foul beasts, damned of chaos.

> One, named Kav Dryfus, led us to the injured miners and offered to help transport them, leaning to assist one man. I shoved the creature away, so he backed off and continued to watch us from a distance.

Under Imperial rule, Elomin were forced to work as slaves in lommite mines, and despite the prejudice they had endured, the Eloms, who had not been discovered by the Empire, helped some Elomin escape. Now that the New Republic has liberated Elom, the two species have begun to create a more integrated society.

the energy spider, or "spice spider," is a giant arachnoid creature that tunnels its way under the alkali flats of Kessel, spinning webs throughout the rock, which, when mined, is the addictive substance known as glitterstim spice. This spice grants the user some telepathic ability. The Empire used it for interrogation, and claimed all the substance on Kessel as Imperial property. For this reason, and due to the fact that it is destroyed in direct light, smuggling glitterstim became very profitable.

The arachnoids that create the spice usually possess more than ten legs, although the number of limbs will depend on the age of the creature. Their legs are thin and hard like crystal, shiny and translucent. Their bodies are filled with tiny pinpricks of light, and they have multiple mouths and thousands of glittering eyes, which see only in the dark.

Energy spiders feed primarily on creatures known colloquially as bogeys, phosphorescent nonsentients that float through the black tunnels feeding on lichens and other underground fungus. These creatures can pass through rock, but cannot pass through the glitterstim web. They are thus trapped for the spider's meal. It is the bogey's phosphorescence that lends the blue photoactive nature to the black glitterstim strands the spider produces. The web material is also crystalline and extremely sharp. If not handled properly, it can cut deep into tender flesh.

These spiders will eat other beings, a fate that has befallen many Kessel slaves who disappeared in the mines. Nien Nunb, a Sullustan who fought for the Alliance in the Battle of Endor, now owns the mines. He previously shared ownership with Lando Calrissian, and under their control, slavery was ended. Tightly regulated, the spice is available

DESIGNATION
> NONSENTIENT <
....
PLANET OF ORIGIN
> KESSEL <
....
HEIGHT OF
AVERAGE ADULT
> 2 METERS <
....

in limited quantities for medicinal purposes, though it is still smuggled onto the black market.

The mine staff only recently discovered the energy spiders. For many years prior to that, the spice's origin remained a mystery. Because the invasion of their environment has caused their population to decrease by the thousands, the spiders have been designated a protected species. Special infrared gates have been built to limit the spiders' contact with the miners.

A former mine administrator, Moruth Doole, reported the effect the spiders had on the spice trade.

> There have been more interruptions in the operations here, as slaves have been disappearing all over the place. Reports have been coming in about a giant spider, and I can't afford to send my guards down there to hunt such a creature; guards are costly. But I can't afford to keep having slaves taken, either; that slows production. > Whatever this thing is, it moves fast and takes many victims with it as it travels through the tunnels. I've stopped personal inspections out of fear of the beast. Perhaps spraying insecticide will work.

ewoks are small, furry sentients who inhabit the forest moon of Endor, a world circling a gas giant near an area of the galaxy known as Wild Space. While Imperial propaganda depicted them as having been wiped out after the Battle of Endor, the species lives on in its wooded home, a lush environment alive with thick vegetation and myriad forms of wildlife. The moon's low axial tilt and its regular orbit around the gas giant create an extraordinarily temperate climate. Trees 300 meters tall cover the moon and are central to the landscape. For this reason, they are central to Ewok culture and religion.

Though Ewoks suffer from limited eyesight, these small creatures have an excellent sense of smell that more than compensates. They are excellent hunters, and being omnivores, they also gather food from the many plants around them. As they forage and hunt, they are extremely alert and may be easily startled. Many carnivorous creatures inhabit the forest, and Ewoks must always be prepared for an attack. Some researchers have noted that they seem to possess a sixth sense: they seem to know danger is coming far in advance of visible evidence. It has been likened to the Jedi Force talent, although only a few Ewoks have shown the ability to manipulate this mysterious power.

Ewoks are curious, good-natured creatures who enjoy community, family, and friendship. Music and dancing are part of their everyday life. In fact, they use music to communicate with other villages via loud, rhythmic drumbeats. News echoes through the ancient trees—imbuing their environment with an aura of extranatural life.

Though their culture is rich, Ewoks are primitive, wearing only hoods adorned with bones and feathers, which act as decoration and indicate position within the community. However, they learn quickly, and when exposed to technology, they often adapt to it quite well—after an initial bout of jitters. Few have yet ventured into space, and when they do, it is only by tagging along with star pilots or New Republic crews. They have developed no technology of their own beyond standard woodworking tools and rudimentary weapons.

The language of this species is quite expressive and can be learned and spoken by other species. Because the verbal nuances are similar, Ewoks can also learn to speak several other languages. And through their exposure

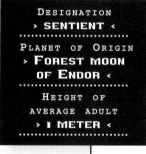

DESIGNATION
> SENTIENT <

PLANET OF ORIGIN
> FOREST MOON OF ENDOR <

HEIGHT OF AVERAGE ADULT
> 1 METER <

to more and more offworlders since the Battle of Endor, many Ewoks have taken to speaking to visitors in a variant called Ewokese-Basic.

Ewoks live in tribal clusters centered in villages built of mud, thatch, and wood, suspended fifteen to thirty meters above the forest floor. Intricate walkways serve to join together residences and village squares, and stairs, rope ladders, and swinging vines help the Ewoks to get quickly from the forest floor to their homes in the trees. Because of their small size, the Ewoks are frequently hunted by the giant Gorax and the fearsome Duloks, so they are often timid about venturing into new territory or leaving their villages unguarded.

The Ewok people are fierce fighters, brave, suspicious, cautious, and

loyal to their tribes. This is also evidenced in their religion, which emphasizes the importance of home, family, and the trees that are considered their "guardians." The trees, they believe, are intelligent, long-lived beings who watch over them, and in a reciprocal manner they must watch over the trees. This was one of the main reasons they helped the Rebels fight the Empire, since they felt that the Empire posed a threat to every aspect of their environment.

War is not common among the Ewoks, however. Although they live in tribes and remain fiercely loyal to them, Ewoks will greet outsiders with warmth as long as they act with honor and respect. They will even accept others into their tribe if the visitors demonstrate a familial loyalty to the tribe.

Because their religion is so important to Ewok society, the village shaman governs a tribe side by side with the ruling chieftain. The shaman interprets signs to guide the chieftain in his decisions. Their belief system includes references to a living energy—like the Force—that feeds the trees and likewise feeds and guides the Ewoks.

This belief was evident in the wedding vows of Princess Kneesaa a Jari Kintaka and Wicket Wystri Warrick, spoken during a ceremony that also served as Kneesaa's induction as the new chief of Bright Tree Village, upon the death of Chief Chirpa.

> [Transliterated from Ewokese]
> Wicket: Today I hold the spear held by Chirpa and our esteemed ancestral leaders. And today I take a wife, the lovely Kneesaa.
> Kneesaa: Today I take the hand of Wicket, my handsome husband. Today I listen to the wisdom of the trees who guided us to love and live in their shade.
> Wicket: Like the trees, we will live in peace and stand tall against the great winds.
> Kneesaa: Like the limbs of the trees, our lives will intertwine, making us inseparable.
> Wicket: We will grow in wisdom together.
> Kneesaa: And we will bear new leaves and branches, nurturing our seedlings in our shade.
> Wicket: So it has been from the beginning of time.
> Kneesaa: And so it will be till the end.
> Wicket: Forever.
> Kneesaa: Forever.

Falleen

DESIGNATION
> SENTIENT <

PLANET OF ORIGIN
> FALLEEN <

HEIGHT OF AVERAGE ADULT
> 1.7 METERS <

alleen are reptilian humanoids that occupy the Falleen star system. They are a handsome species exotic in appearance with scaled, gray-green skin and a spiny, sharp ridge that extends down the center of each individual's back. This ridge is indicative of their reptilian nature, as is their ability to change skin color. Female Falleen look slightly different from their male counterparts, in that the spinal ridge is smaller, their skin is lighter, and the ability to change color is somewhat more limited than in the male counterpart.

Unlike most reptilian species, Falleen grow hair. The females like to wear it long and adorn it with combs and beads. The males wear their hair tied up in a single braid or topknot. In recent years, some females have taken to wearing topknots, in an effort to attain the same elevated status as is enjoyed by the males.

This species is considered aesthetically pleasing by most humanoids. Although their physique is perceived as well defined and attractive, the widespread acceptance they enjoy is not solely based upon appearance. They, like the Zeltrons, can exude pheromones at will, and these chemicals are used to control the perceptions of others—perceptions that the Falleen frequently manipulate to their advantage. The Falleen are also a long-lived species, living 250 standard years on the average. Some healthy individuals have been known to live 400 years.

Falleen pheromones are so powerful that they can produce an almost hypnotic effect, and the manipulations often take on lustful overtones. In the following log recording made by Han Solo's copilot Chewbacca, before the destruction of Prince Xizor's castle on Coruscant, Chewbacca notes Princess Leia Organa's reaction to Xizor's Falleen pheromones.

> [Translated from Wookiee by C-3PO]
> I knew I had to get Leia out of there. Being within a meter of Xizor made her almost lose complete control. The chemical reaction was so powerful that even a woman of her strength and fortitude, who fights against the Empire without faltering, falls victim to his wiles, despite the fact that he is of a different species.
> I'm glad I helped her escape before she was lured into doing something she'd later regret.

What also makes the Falleen attractive is the aura of mystery in which they have wrapped themselves. They are not a talkative species and tend to be pensive. They do not show emotion in public, and they maintain a great deal of control over their physiology. Culturally, they remain stoic and shun outward signs of passion and anger. They experience emotion, but simply don't show it. As a result, the Falleen regard beings who do show their emotions to be inferior.

They also have harnessed the ability to control their skin color and have learned to use it as a covert weapon, reverting from their normal shades of gray-green to red or orange, for example, in order to exude an essence of confidence or mastery. They use their pheromones to enhance the effect and further make a subject susceptible to suggestion.

Pheromones may also be used between Falleen as communication tools, although they always suspect duplicity and remain disciplined in order to resist suggestions that may be imposed upon them by others.

While the Falleen have employed space travel technology for generations, they rarely venture to the stars. Because they consider the Falleen system to be the bastion of the galaxy's greatest culture, they prefer to manage their own affairs on their homeworld, rather than deal with offworlders. Their music, sculpture, art, and architecture provide a source of great pride for them, although they rarely share them with offworlders.

Falleen society is feudal, with noble houses ruling lower classes of artisans, technical workers, general workers, and slaves. Monarch rulers govern their kingdoms, caring more for internal political intrigues and the display of their wealth, rather than wasting resources in waging war against one another. These kings maintain commerce with one other and occasionally argue over boundaries, although the boundary disputes are never taken to extremes.

Young Falleen nobles will sometimes spend part of their adolescent years on what is called a pilgrimage, a tour of the galaxy that allows them to experience all it has to offer. Most of them return to employ what they've learned when the time comes for them to ascend to the throne.

One prominent Falleen was Xizor, whose entire family was killed at the hands of the Empire. Darth Vader had ordered a biological weapons lab to be built in Xizor's home city, and when a lab accident contaminated the area, Vader ordered that the city and its 200,000 inhabitants be burned to ashes. From that point on, Xizor retained a deep desire for revenge against the Dark Lord. He rose to lead the Black Sun crime syndicate on

Coruscant, plotted to kill Vader and take his place, and ultimately planned to usurp the Emperor. His ambitions, however, led to his death at the hands of Vader, the man he hated most, when Xizor overstepped his bounds and threatened Vader's son, Luke Skywalker.

The dual disaster of biological contamination and a brutal orbital strike to "cleanse" the infected city convinced the Falleen to remove themselves from all involvement in galactic affairs. For this reason, even under the rule of the New Republic, the Falleen are rarely ever seen traveling outside their system, and they have shown no desire to join the new galactic government.

Fia

the Fia live on the unstable, rocky world Galantos that rests in the Farlax sector outside the Koornacht Cluster. They are a small people with wide, bell-shaped legs and webbed fingers and toes, perfectly adapted for living in their strange environment.

New Republic geologists have long studied the planet Galantos, considered odd because its rocky landscape is interspersed with lakes and oceans of pale-green organic gelatin, a spongy material that provides life-giving nutrients for all life on Galantos. The land masses are prone to groundquakes, creating an unstable living surface for inhabitants. The Fian physique is perfectly suited, however, to the constantly shifting planet surface.

Stone and metal ores are plentiful in the rocky regions, and the Fia use these materials to construct their buildings. Since the gelatinous lakes and oceans cause the planet surface to roll and shift during large storms, the architecture is designed to withstand this stress.

Because of their environment, the Fia have become a very patient people, to the point of outright obstinancy. While their universe shifts around them, they remain steadfast. An example of this was apparent when they applied for membership in the New Republic. Threatened by the Yevetha, a bullying, xenophobic species, Councilor Jobath of the Fia went to see Leia Organa Solo on Coruscant and literally camped outside her residence for days until his petition for help would be heard.

Following the Fian acceptance into the New Republic, the Bothan New Republic official Borsk Fey'lya visited Galantos. His report showed how deeply the Fian attitudes affected him.

> My Dear Council Members,
> It is with great disappointment that I must ask for my recall from Galantos. Try as I might, I cannot relate to the Fia on an official level.
> They are driving me insane!
> Every five-minute conversation takes fifteen minutes. Every point is ploddingly deliberated, especially the minor ones, in excruciating detail. It's not that they avoid any given topic, but they are willing to take all the time necessary to address every trivial bit of minutiae, and do so correctly. I tell them, "That is what addenda are for," and they reply, "Why would we need an addendum if we do it right the first time?"
> I cannot perform here. Send someone with more patience, although I can't think of anyone who would be able to endure these people.
> Respectfully,
> Councilor Borsk Fey'lya

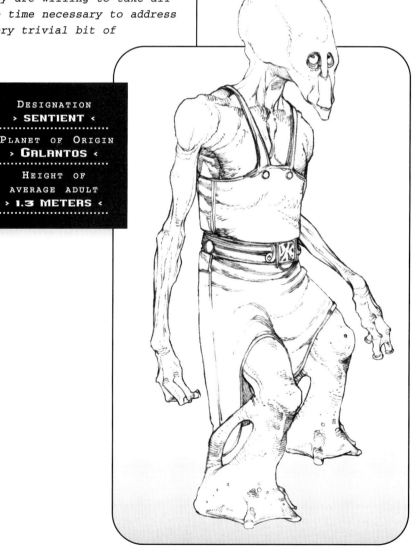

DESIGNATION	**> SENTIENT <**
PLANET OF ORIGIN	**> GALANTOS <**
HEIGHT OF AVERAGE ADULT	**> 1.3 METERS <**

Firrerreo

DESIGNATION
> SENTIENT <

PLANET OF ORIGIN
> FIRRERRE <

HEIGHT OF
AVERAGE ADULT
> 1.6 METERS <

Firrerreos are members of one of the rarest species in the known galaxy, as only a few thousand of them still exist. They are near-human, with multicolored hair worn long and open. The only other oddity they exhibit is present in their eyes, which have nictitating membranes that protect them against large bursts of light, as well as from flying debris. The species is also able to heal unusually quickly.

At one time, the Firrerreo culture was founded in a rigid clan-based system. Clan rulers ran the world, and only members of the most favorable clans were allowed to leave. Among these were Hethrir and Rillao, two Force-sensitive individuals who were handpicked by Darth Vader to be his students. Vader had learned a valuable cultural secret, namely, that when a Firrerreo's name is spoken, the Firrerreo is compelled to obey the speaker.

Hethrir proved an apt pupil, so the Dark Lord named him Imperial Procurator of Justice. In his zeal to please his master, Hethrir ordered the extermination and enslavement of his own people. Thousands of adults were placed onto passenger freighters, while the Imperial Starcrash Brigade released an incurable virus into the planet's atmosphere. Millions of men, women, and children died in agony as the contagion ate its way through their bodies. Firrerre became a dead world and was quarantined. On the ships, Hethrir ordered that the survivors be placed in suspended animation, to be sold off in shiploads to slavers.

The following recording made by Rillao explains the situation of her people.

> I cannot call him my mate any longer. Even if I wanted to call him by name to insult his status, it would taste foul upon my lips. Inside me I carry his child, but he will never know its name. For he is without honor for what he has done.
> My people now will wander without a home, asleep in suspended animation. Without his knowledge, I will go with them to guard them. I will do my best to see that he does not find us.

Rillao later gave birth to their son, Tigris, and Hethrir did track her down, unfortunately. He imprisoned her in a torture web on one of the slave ships and took his son with him.

Ten years after the Battle of Endor, Princess Leia Organa found Rillao and freed her, then awakened one of the other sleeping Firrerreos. Though the ship had no lightspeed capability, the two Firrerreos remained with the sleeping prisoners, and Leia departed. However, she sent a New Republic vessel to find the freighters and awaken the passengers. After some deliberation, the New Republic then made arrangements with the natives of Belderone. In exchange for helping the natives rebuild after Imperial destruction, the Firrerreo survivors would be given citizenship on that world.

The natives of Belderone showed some resistance, because Rillao had been, at one point, a servant of Darth Vader. However, a Belderonian named Flint convinced his people through an emotional appeal to accept the wayward Firrerreos as their neighbors.

Gamorreans are large, green-skinned, porcine creatures from the planet Gamorr, who are known for their brutal strength and warrior nature. They are bulky beings with short snouts, jowls, and tusks, and the males have horns on their heads. Members of this species communicate with one another through a series of grunts and other guttural sounds—a complex language that suits their war-like sensibility. Although they can understand offworld languages, the structure of the Gamorrean voice box makes it impossible for them to pronounce words in any language other than their own.

The Gamorrean clan-based culture is centered on war and the preparation for war. In their society, males are taught the arts of battle and weaponry from the time they are children. As adolescents, males go immediately into battle. Females, on the other hand, take care of all the other necessities of life; they hunt, fish, weave, make weapons, and run businesses. They also form the clan's governing body as the Council of Matrons. These women make the decisions of when to go to war and against whom.

The campaigning season, or war season as it is sometimes called, begins in early spring and runs through late autumn on Gamorr. During these months, the males of the clans make war upon each other—attacking each other's tribal homes and bringing back the spoils to please their females. The males that are the most successful and the most valiant win the right to choose any females they want as mates. Often, those males who do not succeed are killed in battle, and this becomes the culture's own form of natural selection.

Gamorrean males take great pleasure in slaughter and brutality. It is for this reason, as well as for their brute strength, that they make ideal mercenaries and bounty hunters. They are so enthusiastic about violence that they are even willing to be slaves if it gives them more opportunity to fight.

Although they work as hired muscle for many offworld employers, two stipulations must be met before they will agree to do so. Han Solo was once employed by Jabba the Hutt in a negotiation to hire a group of Gamorreans, and his log account of the negotiation details these stipulations.

> Chewie and I were accompanied by a group of Jabba's Nikto, who provided us with extra muscle on this job. Despite

that, we ran into quite a bit of difficulty with the Gamorreans. While they agreed to the terms of the contract, they demanded that I sign it in blood and fight one of them before they would actually come to Tatooine.
> Actually, Chewie was happy to take on the bruiser they'd chosen, but I realized that if he did, they'd think they were working for us and not for Jabba. I was pretty sure Jabba would be less than pleased at that, so I

DESIGNATION
> SENTIENT <

PLANET OF ORIGIN
> GAMORR <

HEIGHT OF AVERAGE ADULT
> 1.7 METERS <

informed them they would have to go to Tatooine to meet their employer. They were a little upset and picked a fight with the Nikto. It was quite a mess, and Jabba ended up short a few goons.

> In the end, I finally managed to calm them down and convince them to fly to Tatooine with me. The food Jabba had sent along provided incentive, but I knew that when we arrived, they'd be expecting to fight the man in charge.

> Jabba's powerful, though, and I figure he can take out one of these guys. And if he can't, hopefully there'll be someone else who wants to hire a fast ship and a slick Corellian pilot sometime soon.

When they fight, Gamorreans prefer traditional weapons such as swords, battle-axes, and heavy maces. They have learned to use blasters over the years, but high-tech weapons are considered in bad taste and aren't used in battles on Gamorr. Still, Gamorreans employed as merce-

naries often carry imported weapons and are well versed in their use.

They often use the money they earn to buy more and more technologically advanced weaponry. They have employed space travel and have even colonized another world, called Pzob. On the whole, however, Gamorreans prefer the simple tools.

While the Gamorrean people aren't known for having a soft, sensitive side, they exhibit an unusual attitude when it comes to their morrts. Morrts are furry parasites that feed on blood and other biological materials. They attach themselves to a Gamorrean's body and remain there for years at a time. Gamorreans look upon them lovingly as pets, and prestigious Gamorreans are often seen with twenty or more attached to their bodies at one time.

gands inhabit a world also known as Gand. They are a short, humanoid species identified in part by their hands with three fingers and their durable exoskeleton. The Gand physiology remains largely a mystery to xenobiologists—nearly a dozen different physical varieties exist within the same species. The world's ecology is extremely inhospitable for other humanoid species because of the giant ammonia clouds that fill the atmosphere. Gands, however, do not breathe as humans do.

Most Gands do not breathe at all. They produce gases in their bodies by ingesting food and passing waste gases through their powerful exoskeletons. Some Gands, though, do breathe, but they take in only ammonia, and when offplanet, these Gands must wear a special suit outfitted with a breathing apparatus that supplies them with the gas in specifically regulated amounts. Scientists do not know if this Gand race is an older variation of the nonbreathing variety, or if it is simply another coexisting race. And as Gands do not readily share information about themselves, it is unlikely that any new information will become available in the near future.

For most of the Gand species, only a minimal amount of sleep is required to keep them functioning normally. As this is common throughout the Gand varieties, scientists believe this may be a result of culture rather than breeding.

The planet Gand's most notable export is the skills of its findsmen. Findsmen are religious hunters who locate their prey by divining omens sent to them in the course of arcane rituals. While many offworlders disavow the power of the findsmen's rituals, their accuracy can be unsettling to the casual observer. Some findsmen sects require that their pupils go

DESIGNATION
> **SENTIENT** <

PLANET OF ORIGIN
> **GAND** <

HEIGHT OF
AVERAGE ADULT
> **1.6 METERS** <

through chemical baths or genetic tampering to cause knoblike growths to appear on their chitinous exoskeletons. Findsmen use these four-to-five-centimeter growths as weapons in hand-to-hand combat. Throughout the galaxy, findsmen are hired as security advisers, bodyguards, bounty hunters, investigators, and assassins.

The Gands are considered by most offworlders to be the most humble of people. This is because Gand culture demands that an individual's identity be earned. Thus, Gands are soft-spoken and polite. They refer to themselves only in the third person, and then, depending on what status they've earned, they may or may not refer to themselves by name. A Gand who has reached only the first level of status would refer to himself as simply "Gand." Once a Gand achieves a major accomplishment in life, either at home

or abroad, that individual may use the family name. Only when a Gand has become a master of some skill or achieved high praise or recognition may she finally use her first name.

Gands rarely refer to themselves in first person. Only those who have accomplished the greatest feats of heroism or who have completed extremely difficult tasks may use self-identifying pronouns such as *I* or *me*. Doing so presumes that one is so great that everyone knows one's name.

If Gands believe they have acted wrongly, they feel it reduces any accomplishments they have made in their lives. When this happens, they use "name reduction" to show penitence. For example, a Gand who previously has earned the right to the family name might revert to the use of "Gand." There have been very few cases of Gands who have committed such unspeakable acts that they actually leave the society entirely. When this happens, they must discard their culture, and their culture discards them. After this, they may refer to themselves any way they wish.

A criminal psychiatrist named Gawynn Karastee analyzed one such Gand who was incarcerated in a penal facility on Coruscant.

> *The Gand known as Zuckuss is clearly schizophrenic and exhibits multiple personality disorder. In my presence, he has displayed two distinct personalities, one being the lawful, moral, and traditional findsman one would expect when encountering a Gand. He is confident, refers to himself in the third person, and discusses with absolute gravity the nature of his work in religious and philosophical terms.*
> *The other personality is amoral, untraditional, and extremely violent. He exhibits signs of extreme insecurity and refers to himself in the first person, speaking in a dialect similar to that of many Corellian humans. He indicates that he is no longer a member of Gand society and is no longer bound by its rules. He rarely refers to religion at all, avoiding the topic by changing the subject.*
> *Through my interviews with Zuckuss, I've come to find that he is suffering from extreme guilt related to his role as a findsman. It seems to me that his primary personality is the one that is insecure, and he's trying to make up for his failings by*

exhibiting signs of the confident findsman figure. The insecure personality surfaces more often, stating that he "just didn't cut it." The extreme pressure of some situation drove him over the edge, causing him to flee home. There have been reports that for many Gands, failure to become a findsman is reason enough to abandon their culture. To make up for his own failure, Zuckuss's findsman personality surfaces when he is feeling most insecure.
> *Zuckuss is dangerous to himself and others.*

Non-Gands are rarely, if ever, welcomed on the planet Gand. Offworlders usually get no closer than one of the orbiting space stations. If they are allowed on the surface, they must remain in a specified area called the Alien Quarters, centered in the spaceports. The very few who have been allowed into the culture itself have done so under the sponsorship of jan-wuine—a person of greatness—or the ruetsavii—the ruling councils. A sponsored non-Gand would be accepted into society as hinwuine—a being of standing. Scientists have tried to interview some of the hinwuine, but have failed.

Gank

Often referred to as Gank Killers, Ganks are a mysterious species with a bloodthirsty nature. They reside primarily on the Hutt moon called Nar Shaddaa. Although they have taken up residence there, it is most likely not their native home.

Relatively little is known about the Ganks. They are fur-covered, carnivorous bipeds. Their square yellow faces are twisted into permanent snarls, topped by cruel, beady eyes. They have massive shoulders and arms as thick as tree trunks. They are militaristic creatures who enjoy battle and who usually take jobs as mercenaries, bounty hunters, guards, or assassins. They are primarily employed by the Hutts, who use them in numbers sufficient to form an army of sorts.

Rarely ever seen alone, Ganks work in packs. In fact, they work so well as a group, it has been hypothesized that they possess a rudimentary sort of telepathic ability that allows them to keep in constant communication with one another. Technologically advanced, they wear high-tech battle armor in combat. For many years, no one knew what a Gank actually looked like, as they were almost never seen without the armor that covers them completely from head to foot.

Galactic scientists have not been able to get close enough to the Ganks to ask them questions about their civilization, or even if they have any centralized form of leadership. Most who have gotten within speaking distance have been killed. However, an entry from Senior Anthropologist Hoole's notes indicates that they do communicate—through implants.

> It was not a good situation. I was being chased by Ganks. No need to explain why. I just infringed on a Hutt's good graces, and he was taking it out on me.
> The only way to avoid them was to join them, so I rounded a corner and changed form. As they passed, I jumped into their midst, following them through the passageways.
> It didn't take them long to figure out they'd lost me. When they did, they immediately grouped together to discuss what to do next. But they didn't talk aloud. I watched in fascination as they communed silently, yet their communication couldn't be telepathic; if it was, I'd have been able to sense it. It had to be mechanical in some way.
> It was then that one of the Ganks turned to face me. He had realized that I was not a part of their collective! Immediately I turned to run, changing as I did into a large Rishii avian. They fired after me and singed my wing, so as soon as I could I slid into a crack between two buildings and made myself the color of the brick, attempting to blend in. Only in doing this did I lose them.

DESIGNATION
> SENTIENT <

PLANET OF ORIGIN
> UNKNOWN <

HEIGHT OF AVERAGE ADULT
> 1.6 METERS <

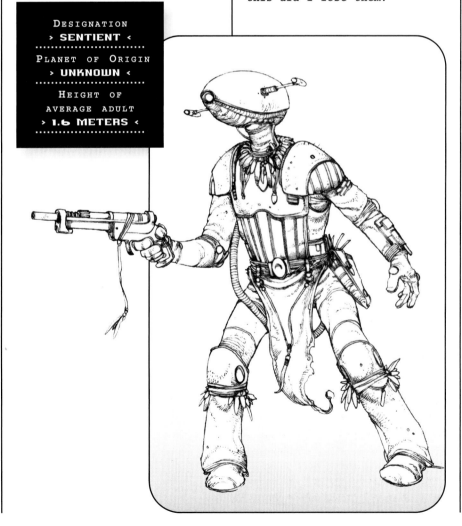

the Givin are a humanoid race who look like animated skeletons, because their skeletons are indeed on the outside of their bodies. Their appendages are long, thin, and tubular, and they have large, triangular eye sockets and frowning mouths that give the impression that they are in constant pain. The outer skeleton actually acts like an organic vacuum suit composed of impermeable bone plates connected by flexible membranes. They do not breathe in the traditional sense, and they produce energy from stored fats.

Givin culture is centered on mathematics. It is the main course of study for young people, who compete to get into monasteries, where the focus of their efforts is to mathematically solve the meaning of life. The Givin planetary governor is selected through contests involving the calculation of multidimensional differentials. All political decisions are made according to the guidelines of null-modal probability.

The Given are also fine shipbuilders, and their ability to survive in a vacuum has proven to be very useful. They regard species who are not able to survive in a vacuum as inferior, and are most comfortable associating with Duros and Verpine—both shipbuilding species. Givin, however, design some of the fastest ships in the galaxy. In their ships, only the sleeping quarters are pressurized, and the computers are used only for data storage. They do not have navigational computers, since Givin calculate navigational vectors in their heads.

Because their planet, Yag'Dhul, has three moons, all with irregular orbits, severe tidal effects frequently wreak havoc and leave parts of the world without atmosphere. The Givin evolved to withstand these environmental problems, and their understanding of mathematics helps them predict the severe weather patterns.

Givin traditionally greet one another with a simple quadratic equation. However, New Republic Councilor Leia Organa Solo noted that they greet outsiders quite differently.

DESIGNATION
> **SENTIENT** <

PLANET OF ORIGIN
> **YAG'DHUL** <

HEIGHT OF AVERAGE ADULT
> **1.8 METERS** <

> The Givin delegation wanted to meet Luke because their people had disagreements with Jedi during the time of the Old Republic. When we met them, Pol SulliVaan, the Givin ambassador, stepped forward and recited what sounded like a long math problem.
> I was stunned. I'd forgotten this quirk in Givin culture, and I wasn't prepared. I'm not terrible at math, but I do need to be in the right frame of mind for it. And this wasn't the traditional quadratic formula with which I understood they greet each other.
> So I just stood gaping like an idiot. I had no idea what to say! Suddenly an image flashed in my mind—a picture of a simple stream of mathematical terminology. I glanced at my brother and saw the slight curl of a smile on the edge of his lips.
> The image held in my mind, and taking Luke's telepathic hint, I recited what I saw.
> Ambassador SulliVaan nodded. "It is a pleasure to meet you, Councilor Organa Solo, and you, Master Skywalker."
> As we walked to the conference room, Luke winked at me.

Gotal

otals are members of a tall, bipedal species native to Antar 4, a moon that orbits the gas giant called Antar in the Prindaar system. The world is rich with mineral deposits, and over 60 percent of the planet is covered by water, with extreme tidal variations. Antar 4's night and day cycle is erratic because of the reflective nature of the planet. At times, the entire moon is bathed in light, and at others, the entire moon is plunged into darkness. Because of this, native species rely heavily on senses other than sight.

Gray-brown, coarse skin protects their faces from extreme temperatures, and red-tinted eyes allow them to see shapes in pitch-darkness. Flat noses protrude only a centimeter or so from their face, and they have sharp incisors for chewing game meat. Shaggy gray fur covers their bodies.

For the Gotal, two cone-shaped horns on their heads make up for what they lack in hearing and sight. A Gotal's cones can detect changes in magnetic fields, infrared emanations, energy waves, neutrino bombardment, and practically every other form of electrical emission. It is said that they can even detect the Force, although that has yet to be proven. With their cones, Gotals can sense another creature up to ten meters away. By sensing a person's electromagnetic aura, they can determine mood, awareness, health, and strength.

Because Gotals can read others so well, they are also extremely polite and sensitive. They speak aloud only to convey abstract ideas—never to express emotion. Because the cones emanate their emotional disposition, they exhibit no vocal inflection, so other races mistakenly perceive Gotals as nonemotional.

A Gotal's cone sensitivity makes them function well as mates and par-

ents. Love at first sight is extremely common for Gotals, and when they mate, it is usually for life. They produce children almost immediately and enjoy their progeny. For the first year of life, Gotal offspring have difficulty filtering out nonessential information, so the overwhelming amount of "noise" often makes children irritable. They are fully mature at age twelve. Although technologically advanced, Gotals avoid droids because they emit electromagnetic radiation, which interferes with their cones.

Predne Balu, an Imperial security officer on Tatooine, reported a unique problem with Gotals as represented in his coworker, Feltipern Trevagg, a tax collector in Mos Eisley.

> Feltipern Trevagg was one of the few Gotals on Tatooine, and he refused to listen to anybody who wasn't of his own species. That was mainly why he died.

> Trevagg caught sight of a female alien with a cone and fell for her instantly. But she was an H'nemthe. I could see he was getting all hot and bothered and tried to warn him, but he wasn't about to listen to me. Stubborn, that's what he was—and arrogant. He thought he was so much better than me that he didn't need to listen.

> Well, he's dead now, slaughtered in the H'nemthe mating ritual. Arrogance and stubbornness are what got Feltipern killed.

Gran

The Gran are tan-skinned humanoids. Three eyestalks hold large black eyes, and small horns rest at the back of the skull. With their keen eyesight they can discern more colors than most humanoid species, including those at the infrared end of the spectrum. Through their perception, they particularly enjoy the visual arts, and they often decorate their architecture in bright, vibrant colors.

The Gran originally evolved from ungulate herbivores. Each Gran has two stomachs and they chew their food slowly. For a Gran, a meal can take most of a day, and they might not need to eat for two or three days afterwards.

To keep Gran society on an even keel, every individual is trained for a specific job that best suits his or her talents within the guidelines of a rigid career quota system. When Gran first left their world Kinyen to colonize other worlds, including Malastare, great gaps opened in the delicately balanced society. For this reason, Gran politicians eventually refused to allow anyone to leave the world without permission and forbade offworlders from visiting the planet's civilized centers. After the Empire fell, the New Republic initiated contact with the Gran, and their society has opened up once more. The Gran are pacifists, and the only battles they have ever truly fought have been against the Dug natives on Malastare.

Polite and agreeable, Gran maintain a patient outlook and like to converse, observing emotions in members of their own species through subtle changes in body heat and skin color. Gran need to be with someone for companionship. Left alone, a Gran will go insane or die of loneliness. When two Gran mate, it is for life. If one member of a couple dies, the other generally follows within a few days. When Gran leave Kinyen for trade, they usually travel in groups. A solitary Gran is usually a criminal, for in their society, the most severe punishment is exile.

Senior Anthropologist Hoole wrote about the mental state of one such Gran, whom he observed at a murder trial.

> The accused, a young Gran named Ree-Yees, dressed in black, looked anxious and manic as the high councilor pronounced his sentence.
> "Ree-Yees," she said. "For the crime of murder, you are immediately and eternally banished from Kinyen and Malastare. You are not to be seen in contact with other Gran, or your sentence will be death."
> Desperate, Ree-Yees jumped over the railing and lunged at the councilor, grabbing her by the cape roughly. "I'm already going mad!" he cried. "Please don't send me away to be alone!"
> The guards roughly pulled him away, and she said impatiently, "That's it! Get him out of my courtroom and off Kinyen. This court is adjourned!"
> As the guards led him away, the Gran wailed as if his spirit was dying.

DESIGNATION
> SENTIENT <
....
PLANET OF ORIGIN
> KINYEN <
....
HEIGHT OF
AVERAGE ADULT
> 1.6 METERS <
....

Gundark

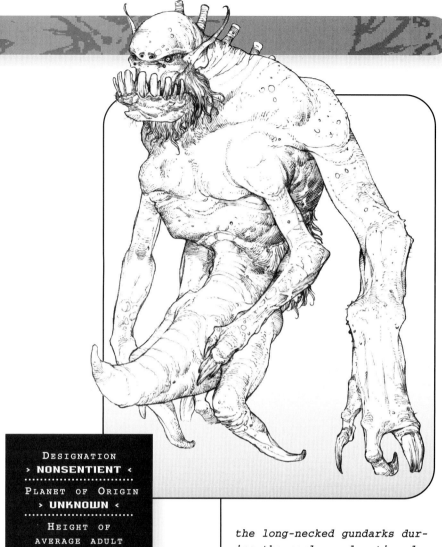

gundarks are large, bipedal, furry anthropoids, each with four arms and large ears. They are very strong—able to rip healthy hundred-year-old trees out of the ground. They have very short tempers and are known to attack without provocation.

This creature is found throughout the galaxy on worlds that are generally temperate. They prefer warm climates, building their nests in hollowed-out trees or caves. Scientists have only speculated how this creature managed to populate so many worlds, but as with the bantha, they believe traders and other space travelers transported this creature to different systems. Unlike banthas, which were used for farming and pack labor, gundarks were transported for sport—game hunting or gundark fighting, the latter having been banned for years now in many systems.

Like most primates, gundarks are born one at a time. When they are born, they have only two arms and small ears. During puberty, the youthful gundark sprouts two more arms, their ears grow to match the width of their heads, and their strength reaches its maximum potential. Thus the phrase "strong enough to pull the ears off a gundark."

Gundarks are omnivores and show enough intelligence to use rocks as simple tools for cracking open nuts and hard fruits. Their lives center around the gathering of food for their community, and there are definite hierarchical roles within a gundark society. Females fulfill the role of hunter-gatherers, and the males are the home protectors. The males will attack any creature coming within scent distance of the nest, and they do so with great ferocity.

Gundarks have keen eyesight and hearing, and their sense of smell is especially powerful. An adult gundark

DESIGNATION
> **NONSENTIENT** <

PLANET OF ORIGIN
> **UNKNOWN** <

HEIGHT OF
AVERAGE ADULT
> **1.5 METERS** <

can smell an intruder up to a hundred meters away, allowing them to get ready to attack while the intruder moves into range.

There is one other species called gundark—the long-necked gundarks of Kharzet III. These creatures are not true gundarks, however, as they are quadrupeds with long, flexible necks. The reason for having two very different species with the same name was explained in a zoological textbook published by Coruscant University Press.

> *A young human scientist named Kin Kimdyara mislabeled the long-necked gundarks during the early exploration days of the Old Republic. It was the young man's habit to classify creatures in his field notes by comparing them to creatures already known, with the intention of renaming them after he had returned to his lab. He named these creatures gundarks because of their foul temper, likening their immediate, hostile reaction to that of primate gundarks.*

> *Kimdyara died only days after recording his initial observations, without having opportunity to rename the quadrupeds. The name has therefore stuck, having fallen into common usage.*

the Gungans of Naboo are bipedal amphibians who live primarily in cities beneath Naboo's great bodies of water. They are predominantly tall and thin, with long, expressive ears and a bill-like mouth. Their skeletal frame is made of cartilage, making them more flexible for underwater movement. When they are swimming, their nostrils seal, nictitating membranes cover their eyes, and their eyestalks partially retract into their skull, making underwater travel easy for them. They also have tough skin on and around their heads, allowing them to burrow through sand and gravel. Their well-padded kneecaps and powerful legs allow them to swim quickly.

This species is omnivorous, although most of the meat they eat is obtained from sea life, and they have large teeth for cracking open shellfish.

Gungan culture centers on their environment and the other living things that populate it. They are particularly linked to the creatures known as kaadu, which are used as battle mounts for their Grand Army. Gungans believe the kaadu are joined with them in a way that no other creatures are. Gungans treat kaadu as family and mourn them like family when they are lost. The Gungan people domesticated the kaadu thousands of years ago, and when Gungans moved to their underwater cities, they brought the kaadu with them. Kaadu are the mainstay of the Gungan militias, or militiagung, and entire schools are devoted to teaching Gungans to ride and live in harmony with these creatures, since it is considered essential for growth.

In battle, Gungans who ride kaadu often wield the most authority and prove to be the most effective leaders. Kaadu are given to Gungan officers amid great ceremony, and officers never abandon their steeds unless the

DESIGNATION
> SENTIENT <

PLANET OF ORIGIN
> NABOO <

HEIGHT OF AVERAGE ADULT
> 1.9 METERS <

animal dies or is retired due to age. In a like manner, kaadu exhibit profound love and loyalty for their owners.

Gungan society and government have been built upon treaties made by the many different settlements and clans. While the members of the clans exhibit different outward biological features, they remain the same in terms of their fundamental physiology. The two primary tribal races within Gungan society are the Otolla, which are the most numerous, and the Ankura, a heavier race that does not exhibit the long ears, eyestalks, or bills. Scientists believe that while these two different clans share common ancestry, the Ankura have lived on land longer than the Otolla and have since evolved to appear as a more land-based form.

Early in their history, the Gungans fought off unknown invaders to their

world and did so by assembling the first Grand Army. After throwing off the mysterious invaders, the Gungans maintained the militiagung and Grand Army as a means of defending against any foe, including their world's ever-present sea monsters.

Today, to form the army, all Gungan cities and communities must agree to unite. Made up of the combined might of the militiagung, they wear leather and metal headgear and marginal body army, and carry small circular shields. Their main long-range weapons are plasmic energy balls. Gungan generals and officers transmit their orders via horns, wild and emphatic gestures, and piercing whistles.

The Gungans are a simple but proud people who bristle at any attempt to conquer them. They are technologically advanced, although they prefer organically based technology over mechanically based advancements, which they believe conflict with the balance of nature. They use hydrostatic fields to maintain bubble domes over their underwater cities and use biotechnology to build their underwater ships, force fields, and weapons—but other than that, Gungans live pretty much as they did thousands of years ago. They have not traveled offplanet, nor have they shown any interest in doing so.

Gungans are not tolerant of troublemakers, and their sentencing for criminals is often severe, as evidenced in a proclamation made by Boss Nass, a leader of the Gungan population, dealing with a repeat offender.

> *Mesa standin' before you today to make 'nouncement that all da Gungans musta be obey. No one is to be makin' trouble. Makin' trouble is like to ruin a life, hurt one, or to takes from them.*
> *Because o' dis, mesa makin' nocomeback law to punish one named Bar Ras. Bar Ras take tools from neighbor's placin' work, and when da neighbor come to him to get tools back, Bar Ras pounded him. For this, Bar Ras may nocomeback to da city. No Gungan issa to speak wit him or see him. He come back, hissen to be pounded t'death.*
> *Be gone wit him.*

Once a Gungan has been cast out, it may be difficult for him to return to society, and even if he does so, he may find that massive peer pressure will make life quite uncomfortable until his offenses have faded from memory.

The modern Gungan language is a combination of pure Gungan language—used only for religious ceremonies and formal occasions—and Basic. Hence, it has come to be called Gungan Basic. This is more than a pidgin form of Basic; it is actually a complex language in its own right, containing original nouns, verbs, and phrases that occur only in that language.

Gungans came to speak their version of Basic, called Gunganese, through their contact with Naboo colonists. Instead of learning Basic as it was spoken by the Naboo, they created their own form of it as a kind of knowledgeable protest to the Naboo's unwanted presence on their world. In a way, they rejected the Naboo, yet were able to communicate with them. And as the original Naboo colonists were warlike and caused many conflicts with the Gungans, the language did serve to help create and maintain an unsteady peace in the long term.

Hawk-bat

Scientists believe the evolution of the hawk-bats of Coruscant may be related as much to their artificial environment as to the designs of nature. They are a reptavian species, part reptile and part bird, with ruby eyes and leathery wings that span nearly 1.5 meters. They have strong talons for gripping prey and a sharp beak ideal for rending flesh. They have keen eyesight, and with their sonar cry they are able to locate prey even in pitch-darkness. Scientists theorize that their large wingspan and eyesight developed because life in Coruscant's artificial environment required they be able to see from great distances and in near-absolute darkness to locate prey in the lowest levels of the planetary city, then fly at great speeds to capture it. In the lowest levels anthropologists have found hawk-bat fossils from ten millennia ago that show a very different type of bird with smaller wings and normal avian eyes.

Hawk-bats are extremely territorial and make their nests on ledges and tucked away in crevices within the sprawling artificial canyons of Coruscant. Hawk-bat eggs are considered a delicacy, and because they are so rare and expensive, only the finest restaurants serve them. Emperor Palpatine kept a flock of hawk-bats on the palace grounds so that he could have hawk-bat eggs at his leisure. When people sought to try this delicacy for themselves, the creatures were hunted almost to extinction.

The New Republic, however, enacted legislation against the hunting of hawk-bats or their eggs. After twenty years of allowing the population to return to its original size, the New Republic once again allowed the sale of hawk-bat eggs, but only from birds kept in captivity. Wild hawk-bats are allowed to remain untouched in their natural environment.

DESIGNATION
> **NONSENTIENT** <
....
PLANET OF ORIGIN
> **CORUSCANT** <
....
HEIGHT OF
AVERAGE ADULT
> **1 METER** <
....

A number of cookbooks have been published on the subject, and Chef Handree Braman, an Ortolan whose restaurant, the CardSafe, is one of the most lauded on Coruscant, wrote one of the most famous.

> Hawk-bats are delicate creatures who need to be treated well. They must be fed regularly on fresh grains and fruit and allowed to fly about a large nest area. If they are kept in small cages or fed leftovers from other meals, they become tough and gamy.

> These creatures are best prepared at temperatures of 1,000 degrees for no more than twenty minutes. Most recipes call for hot grills, as their hide is very tough. The high temperatures allow the creature to cook all the way through, while their skin holds in the natural juices. This causes the meat to fall right off the bone, making for the tenderest meal.

H'nemthe

the H'nemthe, from a planet of the same name, are a bipedal species with blue-gray skin, double rows of cheekbones, a gently curved nose, four conelets on the skull, and three fingers on each hand. They are omnivores, primarily feeding on fruits and vegetables and occasional wild game.

Because their cones can be used to sense heat differences in their environment and emotional differences in other creatures, H'nemthe are efficient hunters. For this reason, scientists have speculated that their cones serve a similar purpose as those of a Gotal. The two species are unrelated biologically, but both come from worlds where lunar orbits cause extreme weather patterns. In both cases, these cones help them locate food and analyze their environment.

H'nemthe society is very structured and is based on the fulfillment of spiritual awareness through the searching for true love and the creation of life. The population breakdown makes finding true love quite difficult, however: there are twenty males for every female.

This ratio developed as a balance for the traditional H'nemthe mating ritual. After mating, the female disembowels the male with her razor-sharp tongue. As a result, mating is infrequent and is done only in cases of true love. The male considers it the culmination of spiritual fulfillment, as he goes on to the netherworld to guide his coming child. The woman is fulfilled in that she brings a new life into the world.

A great H'nemthe philosopher wrote the following passage on the mystery of this tradition.

> It is, to outsiders, a cultural contradiction, but even they know the truth though they deny it. All life must come from death, just as all life must lead to death. It is the way of the universe.
> For death is not true death but a change in form. Just as in science, elements will change when acted on by other elements, so, too, do we physical beings change form when acted upon by the force of the universe—love. With that power, our element shifts to another place where we gain eternal knowledge, and the ability to guide the generations that follow.

> Love is the catalyst in the vast experiment of life in this universe, and it cannot be denied.

Because there are so few females, they are protected by law. Virgin females are rarely, if ever, allowed to leave the planet and are not allowed to eat anything but vegetables and fruit to make sure they do not taste flesh until they taste that of their mate. As a result, H'nemthe females are often found to be very naive.

DESIGNATION
> SENTIENT <

PLANET OF ORIGIN
> H'NEMTHE <

HEIGHT OF
AVERAGE ADULT
> 1.7 METERS <

Ho'Din

the name *Ho'Din* means "walking flower," and few other species so intently focus on plant life and the health of their environment. In fact, the Ho'Din body coloration and head of snakelike tresses of red and violet cause them to look like the wuppa flower native to their world.

Although the Ho'Din believe they evolved from plants, they are actually cold-blooded, oxygen-breathing reptiles possessing two large dark eyes and lipless mouths. Because they are cold-blooded, Ho'Din live in warm rain forests, in tree villages and homes literally grown from the plants, and a cold spell will send the Ho'Din immediately into hibernation. Their "hair" serves as thermographic receptors, with which they monitor ambient temperature. Their four-fingered hands, with ridged suction pads, are indicative of their reptile lineage, as is the light webbing between their fingers and toes. Very conscious of how they look, Ho'Din often trim this webbing.

Ho'Din children are born blind and bald. After a few days of life they gain sight, but their hair does not grow until they reach the age of seven. At that point, it appears as green sprouts and grows one centimeter a year until they reach the age of thirty—the age of sexual maturity.

According to their religion—called [Dinante Fli'R]—Ho'Din primal ancestors were plants. Because the Ho'Din committed sins against [Dinegia], the normally passive force of nature, [Dinegia] changed the Ho'Din into animals. By being respectful to plants, the Ho'Din believe they will complete [Flik'a kirki], or virtuous circle of nature, and be reborn as plants. They deposit their dead on the forest floor as a gift to the soil, and they celebrate harvests as a sign of [Dinegia]'s forgiveness. Also, Ho'Din reproduce only

DESIGNATION
> **SENTIENT** <
....
PLANET OF ORIGIN
> **MOLTOK** <
....
HEIGHT OF AVERAGE ADULT
> **3 METERS** <
....

within the auspices of a religious ceremony that symbolizes the manner in which insects fertilize plants. Another Ho'Din religious tradition is to speak in rhyme—a means of showing environmental harmony—although many youthful Ho'Din have dispensed with the practice.

The Ho'Din are master botanists, who revile technology and limit its use. Ho'Din religious leaders, focused on keeping the planet's environment untouched and remaining self-sufficient, run the planetary government of Moltok. The Ho'Din import little from offworld traders, and medical exports make Moltok a rich world.

In the following passage, a Ho'Din named Baji, who spent time on Yavin 4 acting as a healer, describes his unique cultural reaction to an ecological disaster on a world called Barenth—a place he had visited to research healing remedies.

The ancient laboratory around me crumbled
The ground shook and the buildings tumbled.
Quickly I rescued plants and seeds
Unique specimens for my research needs.
Later I returned for an investigation
And found the grounds and plants filled with radiant contamination.
I mourned my plant brothers and knew what was right:
I would stay here and heal this place for the rest of my life.

Howlrunner

howlrunners are the most dangerous animals native to the planet Kamar just outside the Corporate Sector. This species is mostly canine; however, they offer an unusually unsettling appearance in that a howlrunner's head looks like a human skull. This is actually a cartilage and bone layer that covers the flesh underneath. Scientists believe that this cartilage layer developed over thousands of years of evolution, as howlrunners tend to burrow and tunnel through rocky ground to create their dens. They can live in any terrain, however, and often migrate in giant packs searching for new hunting grounds.

Howlrunners are carnivores, and they hunt with great cunning and skill. Their name derives from the terrifying howling sound they make when tracking down prey. Because they hunt in packs, this sound often frightens and disorients the hunted creatures, making them easier to track.

Howlrunner packs work as a team to kill larger herd creatures. Usually they prefer to hide in the brush or grass to spring upon unwary prey. If their hunt leads to a chase, howlrunners will tirelessly follow their victim until it collapses in exhaustion.

Because of their popularity as big game, howlrunners have become an endangered species. Hunters come to Kamar in the hopes of capturing or killing howlrunners for their famous skulls. Howlrunners have also been captured for fighting contests—a sport that has been made illegal in most sectors.

In a HoloNet interview with Incom Corporation, engineer Jo Ewsli explains his reason for choosing *Howlrunner* as the name for a ship he designed.

> I was on Kamar several years ago and witnessed a pack of howlrunners chasing down their prey. They ripped it apart, not necessarily because they outpowered their prey, but because they were quicker and more agile than their opponent. They took small nips out of the creature until it finally fell.

> In the same sense, this ship is tough and quick, and the two forward lasers look like fangs. It's meant for hit-and-run inner-atmosphere missions or quick missions to close in on a large target.

> These ships pack more punch than an outside observer would think, so they can be very pesky and very vicious. Like the howlrunners themselves, they'll take you out when you're not paying attention.

DESIGNATION
> **NONSENTIENT** <

PLANET OF ORIGIN
> **KAMAR** <

HEIGHT OF AVERAGE ADULT
> **1 METER** <

Hssiss [Dark Side Dragon]

While this creature is found primarily on Ambria, it has been seen on other worlds where masters of the dark side of the Force once lived. Old Republic files dating back several millennia have proved these creatures to have existed back during the time of the ancient Jedi. Little else is known about their origin.

The Jedi named Tionne, one of Master Luke Skywalker's pupils, was able to locate most of the available information on these mysterious beasts. After encountering one on a research trip to the planet Vjun, she wrote the following in her notes, now published and available through the Jedi academy on Yavin 4.

> I did not sense its presence right away, although I could sense that something was wrong. It was able to cloak itself from my perception. But it apparently knew I was near, for as I grew closer to the still, dark lake, it rose from the water and lunged at me, bristling with the dark side.

> It was a large, green-gray reptile, about two meters long, with a double row of spikes running down its back from its head to its tail. Its fangs, which protruded from its top and bottom jaw, were nearly seven centimeters in length.

> I battled it, and eventually killed it, lopping its head from its shoulders with my lightsaber. I didn't leave the battle unscathed, as its sharp claws had ripped across my back. The wound became infected very quickly, despite the fact that I treated it with antivenoms. Only a Jedi

healing trance cleared away the infection. In this, I deduced that both their claws and their teeth could inflict a poisonous touch of the dark side.

> Later, I was able to find out about this creature through the Emperor's discarded files in the Imperial Palace. They are called hssiss, or dark side dragons, once encountered by Nomi Sunrider in Lake Natth during her training on Ambria. Apparently, many sorcerers of

the dark side kept packs of these creatures with them at all times for protection. High Prophet Jedgar utilized hssiss to mute the signal of his power from suspicious Jedi, and the Sith are said to have used them to the same effect in ancient times.

> The dragons also have some limited intelligence and can use dark side energy to confuse or distract an opponent.

DESIGNATION
> **SEMISENTIENT** <

PLANET OF ORIGIN
> **AMBRIA** <

HEIGHT OF AVERAGE ADULT
> **2 METERS** <

Hutt

Hutts are large gastropods that presently inhabit the world of Nal Hutta in the Y'Toub system, the center of an area of the galaxy known as Hutt Space. Each Hutt has a thick body with a long, muscular tail and small arms protruding from the upper torso.

Physiologically, the Hutts are an anomaly. Like sea mammals, their nostrils close and their large lungs enable them to stay underwater for hours at a time. Like worms, they are hermaphrodites, with both male and female reproductive organs. Like marsupial mammals, they bear their young one at a time and nourish them for a time in a brood pouch.

Despite this, scientists generally classify them as gastropods because of the way they move—slithering around like giant slugs. They have no skeleton to speak of, merely an internal mantle that supports and shapes their heads. Their mouths open so wide they can swallow just about anything. They also have extremely tough skin that protects them against heat and chemical burns, and their mucus and sweat make the surface of their skin slippery.

Hutts are among the longest-living species in the galaxy, with a maximum recorded life span of 1,000 years. During such a lifetime, they can grow in size and weight to over 1,500 kilograms. Because they are so long-lived, Hutts rarely reproduce, though they possess healthy sexual appetites. Infant Hutts are extremely small and blind, and they move to a parent's pouch, where they remain for around fifty years. When they finally leave the pouch, they have matured to the intellectual level of a ten-year-old human. As they move toward adulthood, they gain in corpulence, a trait considered a sign of power and prestige. The bigger a Hutt is, the more power it acquires, both among peers and non-Hutt species.

This is exemplified in the case of Jabba the Hutt, who, as described in a log entry written by Han Solo, made a leap both in size and in rank during the time Solo knew him.

> When we first met, I actually kind of liked Jabba, and he seemed to like me. I've always wondered if this was because of where he was in his life. I think it was the fact that he still liked me that he came in person to meet me at Mos Eisley.
> Actually, that was the last personable conversation we had, and I know I must have crushed his ego. The next time I saw him, his power had grown to match his size.

Plus, he hated me.
> With Hutts, size has a lot to do with attitude. After his growth spurt, Jabba changed. Oh, he was angry during our encounter at Mos Eisley, but once he really became the big boss, so to speak, he became obsessed with getting even.
> I wonder; if Jabba hadn't grown so much, would he have let me out of the carbonite, given me a tongue-lashing, and then let me go?

The Hutt species is very egocentric. On their world, they consider themselves the center of the universe and are likened unto gods, predominantly by the Klatooinians and, to a lesser degree, the Nikto. A Hutt's success in life is in direct proportion to

DESIGNATION
> SENTIENT <

PLANET OF ORIGIN
> NAL HUTTA <
(BY WAY OF VARL)

HEIGHT OF AVERAGE ADULT
> 4 METERS <

its ego, and a Hutt's ego can be tremendous. They are experts at manipulating others and getting them to do their bidding.

Before inhabiting Nal Hutta, the Hutts evolved on Varl, a temperate forest world with two suns, which they worshipped as gods. In Hutt religious beliefs, one of the sun gods, called Evona, was pulled into a black hole. When this happened, the other planets in the system collided and crushed each other into asteroids that bombarded the planet Varl. The second sun god, named Ardos, collapsed itself into a white dwarf out of grief over losing its mate.

Because the Hutts survived the destruction of their original system, they believe that they have actually become greater than the gods they once worshipped. There is no absolute scientific substantiation for the Hutts' religious tale, however, and most scientists tend to believe another story, frequently told by spacers and traders throughout the galaxy. This story indicates that the Hutts destroyed their own planet in a civil war, the likes of which has not been witnessed anywhere in the known galaxy.

Nal Hutta is ruled by a council made up of the eldest members of the Clans of the Ancients. These clans are families that can trace their ancestry back to their days on Varl. The means by which this council makes decisions is a mystery, in that the Hutts will not allow outsiders to observe the governmental proceedings. Hutts all over the galaxy—even those on the farthest outskirts—abide by the decisions of this council.

For Hutts, blood is always thicker than slime. A Hutt's clan is paramount, and most decisions are focused on how they will affect the prosperity and the position of one's clan. Ancestral fortunes, passed on from generation to generation, have allowed Hutt clans to control some of the richest holdings in the galaxy. The clans control criminal empires, called kajidics, that are sometimes even more powerful than the council of the clans. Kajidics that are most powerful monetarily control the politics of Hutt society.

The Hutts, in general, are not builders, manufacturers, or inventors. They are businesspeople who connect someone who needs something with someone else who can fulfill that need. They are the galaxy's brokers, making deals and manipulating the economy with calculated, strategic power plays. Their kajidics are secretive and vast, and a majority of the transactions made in the galactic business world will likely have a Hutt connected to them in one way or another.

Ishi Tib

shi Tib are green, amphibious beings from the planet Tibrin, a world of wide oceans and coral reefs. Their skin is rough and leathery, and they have yellow eyes set in two eye-stalks, which come off their heads at an angle and allow them to see at wide angles in the dim light under the ocean surface. Each Ishi Tib has two pouch-like cheeks and a large beak with two nostrils. Their nostrils allow their strong sense of smell to function efficiently both in water and on land, and with their gills they can breathe underwater. The beak is sharp and powerful, giving them the ability to crack open tough shellfish. Their bodies are thick and muscular, with two-fingered, stubby hands and flat, finlike feet.

Their water-based physiology yields a unique disadvantage. Every thirty hours, an Ishi Tib must immerse himself in a saltwater solution like that of his native oceans. If he does not, his gills and skin will dry out and crack open, and he will die of internal and external bleeding.

Ishi Tib are patient, quiet, and calculating. They are excellent planners, capable of maintaining organizational control over large, complex projects. Though they rarely leave home, they are considered desirable employees, acting as tacticians, executives, accountants, and project managers. Being a tenacious people, they are not satisfied with leaving any job unfinished.

The Ishi Tib evolved from large, bony fish that escaped from predators by jumping up onto the air-exposed portions of the Tibrin coral reefs. Today, the Ishi Tib cities are built upon, or even grown out of, this very same coral. They grow edible seaweed and breed fish and crustaceans for food in underwater corrals.

Ishi Tib society is centered on communities, or schools, of no more than 10,000 individuals. Representatives elected to one-year terms govern these school communities in accordance with ecological law. There is no marriage, and reproduction is decided based upon the needs of the school and resources available to support an addition to the population. Fertilized eggs are laid in hatcheries in a sandbar area near the coral reef, and the school, as a community, raises the children. As a result, no Ishi Tib knows who her relatives really are.

Despite their subdued nature, they retain a primal ruthless streak, and some unscrupulous members of society have exploited this behavior, as a journal entry written by Senior Anthropologist Hoole illustrates.

> It was the first time I had to deal with Jabba the Hutt. Eager to fan his own ego, he allowed me to stay around his court, taking notes for my studies.
> Jabba employed several Ishi Tib. They were a pleasant group to be around, and I found myself admiring their peacefulness and intelligence. One day I realized why he employed them, when his servants brought in a human who had apparently killed one of the Ishi Tib. They demanded vengeance, and Jabba was glad to oblige.
> The Ishi Tib ripped the man apart. They went completely out of control, rending the human's limbs and consuming his flesh in front of all present.

DESIGNATION
> SENTIENT <

PLANET OF ORIGIN
> TIBRIN <

HEIGHT OF AVERAGE ADULT
> 1.7 METERS <

Ithorian

ithorians are a mammalian species that, until its destruction, inhabited the planet Ithor in the Ottega system. They are often referred to as Hammerheads, because their head curves forward like a common hand tool. The only other trait that differentiates them from standard mammals is that each Ithorian has two mouths, which rest on either side of the neck. With these, they speak in stereo, and their native language is based upon this ability, which other species find impossible to reproduce. For this reason, most Ithorians learn to speak Basic.

Twenty-five years after the Battle of Yavin, a ruthless species called the Yuuzhan Vong ravaged their world and killed much of the population. Prior to this, Ithor was a lush, tropical world where technology and nature existed together in harmony. The environmentally focused Ithorians lived in floating cities called herd ships, where all individuals are required to support the greater common good. These floating cities traveled above the surface of the planet without touching down, in order to do as little damage to the planet as possible. Each herd ship had many levels, and they were the centers for commerce, culture, and industry. Every five years the herd ships gathered at an event called the Meet, where Ithorians celebrated, debated, and voted on planetary issues. Presently, smaller Meets are held in space, for those few remaining communities not able to return to Ithor.

All Ithorian ships mimic the environment of their planet with indoor jungles, artificial storms, humid atmosphere, vegetation, and wildlife. The Ithorians like to travel to other worlds in caravans to trade merchandise.

Ithorians are peaceful herbivores, and for every plant an Ithorian individual consumes, they plant two more

DESIGNATION
> **SENTIENT** <
PLANET OF ORIGIN
> **ITHOR** <
HEIGHT OF AVERAGE ADULT
> **2 METERS** <

in the effort to keep their environment thriving. When visiting another world, they are sensitive about disturbing that planet's ecology.

Despite their peaceful nature, they developed powerful deflector shields and weaponry, which they use to protect their own world and ships. A few Ithorians have been so driven by their desire to create peace that they have acted violently, or have come up with elaborate schemes to eliminate violence all together.

In the following private journal entry, an Ithorian named Zorneth makes a startling confession.

> I was working with another botanist, a human named Klorr Vilia, who had developed a very special herb that I knew would serve my interests. While working with the herb, Klorr tasted it and suddenly devolved into a mindless creature with no thoughts but joy and peace.
> Seeing this, I immediately

began cultivating the herb, which I called savorium. I laced herds of wooly thookahs with the herb so those who ate them would immediately become peaceful. I planned on spreading it throughout the galaxy, making all peoples peace-loving and harmless. What more could any Ithorian want?
> Sadly, the mindless Vilia sacrificed himself to destroy the plants he'd helped me create, ruining my plans. I fail to understand why he did this. How could he not want to bless others with the same bliss that he enjoyed?

Ixlls are members of a flying mammalian species that inhabited the moon Da Soocha V, once home to the New Republic's Pinnacle Base. When that moon was destroyed by an Imperial attack, this species was wiped out, except for about a hundred of them who left the world with the evacuating New Republic personnel. The New Republic has temporarily relocated the species to one of the uninhabited moons of Endor, neighboring the Ewok homeworld, and has made strides in integrating the species into their new environment.

Often described as "balls of fur with wings," the Ixlls are soft creatures with round bodies, pointed ears, large eyes, and a long tail. They often wear hoods to keep their faces warm, and pouches are used to carry small objects. Like most mammals, they bear live young and will have two or three at a time. A mother will sit atop her newborns for a week or two to keep them warm and fed, until they have grown to where their eyes are open and they are able to move about.

Ixlls communicate in high-pitched tweets and whistles. Their language can, in fact, confuse an astromech droid, whose programming can be affected by the similarity in sounds. These high-pitched signals are also used as natural sonar, which augments their normal vision.

Ixlls once lived in warrens atop the column formations of Da Soocha V, and on their new world they've found similar high trees and rock formations upon which to make their nests. Evolved from omnivorous predators, they eat small insects and vegetation. They maintain a well-developed, peaceful, albeit feudal, society, and are skillful with their hands, able to make simple, elegant items such as leather bags and ornaments. They learn very quickly about technology,

and on Da Soocha V many had even mastered an understanding of repulsorlift technology and starship engines. One of the few forms of weaponry they've developed is exploding stones, black powder grenades that they carry in pouches they wear around their necks.

This small species is friendly, trusting, and helpful. They are also playful and like to "borrow" small objects. This habit caused troubles at the Pinnacle Base, as was reported by Wedge Antilles.

> *The Ixlls are unwittingly driving our technicians crazy.*

> *One of our guys sets a tool down and it disappears. He goes to pick up a hydrospanner and it's gone. Ixlls have been found raiding the food rations, inside X-wing cockpits messing with controls, digging in tool cabinets, even in personal footlockers.*
> *Though this may be endearing, it's slowing down work on the overhaul of much-needed fighters. We may have to put up some sort of barrier to keep them out of the base. It might be our only way to keep us operational.*

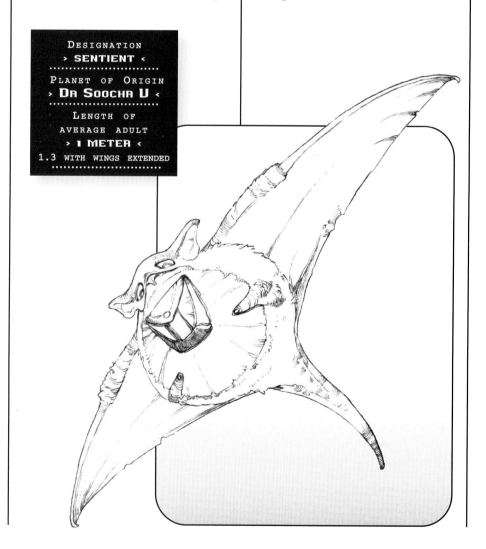

DESIGNATION
> **SENTIENT** <

PLANET OF ORIGIN
> **DA SOOCHA V** <

LENGTH OF
AVERAGE ADULT
> **1 METER** <
1.3 WITH WINGS EXTENDED

jawas are a small, rodentlike people who live on Tatooine, the harsh desert world that is the home planet of Luke Skywalker. Under their full-body robes they are small, gaunt creatures, with shrunken faces and yellow eyes.

Each Jawa is about a meter tall, with tiny flexible hands and feet. Though they may have evolved from rodents, scientists believe they progressed to stand upright by reaching for lichens and fungi that grow on underground cave walls—caves that once housed rare natural springs around which their society initially developed.

These springs eventually dried up, and the Jawas adapted to their changing environment with sheer ingenuity. To protect themselves from the fierce double suns of their world, they started wearing coarse, homespun cloaks with large hoods under which only yellow, glowing eyes remain visible.

Most human races have noted that Jawas give off a strong, distinct odor. This is the combined result of a mysterious solution in which they dip their clothes to retain body moisture, and the fact that they do not bathe often in their water-bereft environment. Jawa individuals often use scent to discern one another's health and emotional state.

For their own nourishment, Jawas acquire water by inserting long, thin hoses down the stems of the funnel flower, a flora native to Tatooine, and siphoning off the liquid. Their diet is made up primarily of hubba gourd, a fruit difficult for humans to digest, the name of which translates to mean "the staff of life."

To make their living, Jawas salvage, repair, and resell junk they find in the desert. Sometimes they even "find" items that haven't been lost, or haven't been locked down. Jawas are

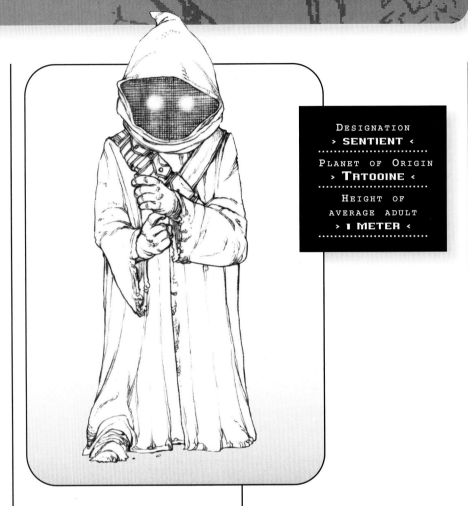

DESIGNATION
> SENTIENT <

PLANET OF ORIGIN
> TATOOINE <

HEIGHT OF
AVERAGE ADULT
> 1 METER <

proficient at repairing equipment. For junk that is unsalvageable, they have high-powered solar smelters that melt it down into salable ingots.

Jawa society is divided into clans or tribes. Once a year, all the Jawa clans meet at a giant swap meet in the great basin of the Dune Sea, where they trade items, share stories, and even barter sons and daughters as "marriage merchandise." The trading of family members in marriage is considered a good business practice, as it ensures the diversity of their family bloodlines.

The Jawa culture is centered on family. They take great pride in their clans and lineage, and in fact, their language includes forty-three different terms to describe relationship, lineage, and bloodline. Clans keep close

track of these relationships, recording lineages with extreme detail. The clans travel together in large vehicles known as sandcrawlers, nuclear-fusion-powered ore-hauling vehicles abandoned by unknown contractors during the reign of the Old Republic. Each crawler carries up to 300 Jawas and acts as a fully equipped repair shop, allowing the Jawas to perform skilled repairs as they make their journey across the desert wastes.

While a great many of the Jawas travel constantly, looking for salvage, the remainder stay behind in clan fortresses built from large chunks of wrecked spacecraft. Master repair experts live in the fortresses, where they perform advanced salvage repairs that exceed the capacity of the sandcrawler shops. These elaborate fortifications are often subjected to attacks by Tusken Raiders, who kill Jawas in order to take their scavenged treasures and water. This contributes greatly to the Jawas' cautious, even paranoid nature. But their best offense is their defense—the stability of the fortresses they build. Jawas are not inherently fighters. Because of their size, they'll often run away when confronted. When cornered, however, Jawas have proven themselves to be capable users of the weapons they scavenge from the desert sands.

The most prominent member of each clan is the shaman, a female who, the clan believes, has the ability to predict the future. The shamans also perform elaborate spells, hexes, and blessings to protect the tribe and to provide for the wellness of its members. Each shaman takes on a student during her tenure, training her to take the shaman's place when she dies.

Because of her position of influence, the shaman controls most clan decisions regarding defenses, travel, and day-to-day life. She does not travel in the sandcrawler, but remains at the fortress, where she can be more effectively protected.

In as-yet-unpublished notes from his second visit to Tatooine, Senior Anthropologist Hoole mentions the loyalty Jawas show to their shaman.

> *As Sand People raged violently through the fortress, killing Jawas and plundering the keep, I joined a group of Jawas as they ran to the dwelling of the shaman. We surrounded the house made of scrap metal that had been fused together, brandishing old-model blasters, slug throwers, and sharp spears of metal. As the Tusken Raiders came at them, they stood*

their ground, many of them losing their lives bravely to protect the shaman within.
> *Despite their stature, they put on a valiant defense and managed to keep the Tusken Raiders from entering the shaman's abode. Out of the nearly fifteen who defended the house, only three of us survived after the Sand People took their leave—with many of the clan's valuables. But because much of the clan was away in the sandcrawler, and the shaman was alive, the clan would survive to rebuild their home.*
> *That night while they pieced together their lives, they sang songs of victory and mourning.*

Jenet

the Jenet are a tall, rodentlike species that live on the planet Garban. They are argumentative creatures with pale pink skin and red eyes. White fuzz covers their thin bodies, and their ears end in points. Long whiskers jut out from each side of their rodentlike noses.

Jenet are scavengers with keen eyesight, strong senses of smell and hearing, and a digestive system that enables them to consume just about any organic material. With their long, lanky legs, they are quick runners and can jump, swim, and climb with great proficiency. Their bodies are also very flexible, enabling them to slip through openings no bigger than twelve centimeters, by dislocating their limbs and separating their cranial plates.

One of the most remarkable qualities a Jenet will exhibit is its memory. They have photographic recall and can quote even the most trivial facts and events. This often makes them irritable and petty, and any minor insult, any miscalculated statement, may cause a Jenet to hold a grudge for a lifetime.

When a Jenet is introduced or discussed by another, a complete history of that Jenet's accomplishments or misdeeds will be included as part of his or her spoken name. This catalog of events indicates the rank they hold in society and determines if they are worthy of another Jenet's cooperation. Status is constantly being adjusted due to an individual's deeds, though in order for an accomplishment to raise an individual's status, two other Jenet must witness the event. To avoid presenting fraudulent credentials, they are not allowed to introduce themselves. Two Jenet, working together side by side, may never learn each other's names if no one is there to introduce them.

In bearing their young, Jenet have

DESIGNATION
> SENTIENT <

PLANET OF ORIGIN
> GARBAN <

HEIGHT OF AVERAGE ADULT
> 1.4 METERS <

short gestation periods of around ninety days and usually deliver litters of four to six offspring. These mature quickly, are able to walk and forage in just two months, and are fully developed after one year. Unfortunately, because of their quick birth rate, isolated populations often suffer from inbreeding.

Jenet possess few technological skills, although they have achieved hyperspace travel, which most believe they acquired through scavenging. They all contribute to the Community Heap—a pile of scavenged materials kept by a community, administered by their government, that often includes discarded food, broken tools, and household goods.

A premier and a Council of 127 run the Garban planetary government, employing millions of Jenet whose job it is to remember everything about as many citizens as possible. And the Jenet hold another, more devious position in certain circles of galactic society, as is demonstrated in this descrip-

tion offered by Bwahl, a Hutt of some renown.

> The Jenet my servant Lotkha brought me is actually quite useful. I've taken to calling him Jen, which he's come to tolerate without argument. Of course, he accepts the unwanted title because he fears me.
> In any event, his memory has proven profitable. I keep him present at all my meetings, and he remembers the proceedings in astounding detail. He watches for responses I cannot watch and reports them to me. Through him, I learn their weaknesses, their fears, and their needs. These Jenet make efficient, vindictive spies, who are judicial with the knowledge they retain.

Kitonak

esilient and steadfast, the Kitonaks live on Kirdo III, a barren desert world that is even bleaker than the infamous Tatooine. They are built for their environment, with leathery hides that cover them completely—including all their bodily orifices—and can withstand extraordinarily harsh abrasion. They have eyes, ears, and a mouth, all of which are nearly invisible in the folds of their skin. This skin layer protects them from the 400-kilometer-per-hour winds that whip across the white sandy surface.

Kitonaks possess two trunklike legs and two strong, pudgy arms, which end in equally pudgy, surprisingly nimble fingers. Their legs, and their almost pointed shape, allow them to plant themselves firmly in the sand to wait out a windstorm.

And waiting is inherent to the Kitonaks. They are one of the most patient species in the galaxy. Kitonaks are *so* patient that they annoy other species with their plodding, methodical mannerisms. They rarely do anything quickly, and this includes breathing and eating. Each Kitonak possesses an extra set of lungs that enables it to store oxygen for a good three or four hours, and their stored fat allows them to go without food for weeks, providing that they do not overexert themselves.

Their culture is a simple, primitive one, with no advanced technology. They live in small tribal groups that migrate around the desert following herds of chooba, their primary source of food. Their method of hunting is most indicative of their slow-paced way of life, in that it involves standing motionless and mimicking a sulfaro plant—the chooba's favorite dish. They wait while the chooba climbs to the top of their head, looking for the "plant's" meaty interior, at which

point they swallow the chooba whole. One of these creatures can provide a Kitonak enough nourishment to last for an entire standard month.

The Kitonaks' unique physiology also enables them to move while prone. They can slither across the sand and can burrow through the dunes. Standing, they "walk" by contracting and stretching their feet, rather than by moving their legs. Though this requires a great deal of time for them to get anywhere, the Kitonaks tend to feel they have absolutely no reason to hurry. Ironically, their feet contain their olfactory organs, allowing them to smell prey through the sands, rather than having to deal with the rough winds that swirl around their heads.

Because the Kitonaks have no natural foes, they fear only two things: quicksand and caves. Should one of them fall victim to quicksand, their patience often allows them to float and breathe until help comes. The problem is that help isn't often very speedy.

Caves, however, are considered gateways to the underworld. In their society many tales have been told of Kitonaks who have entered caves and have not returned. For this reason, they will avoid entering caves at any cost.

Kitonaks get most of their education from stories. Every evening there is a "telling of the story," which lasts for several hours. Each tribe member

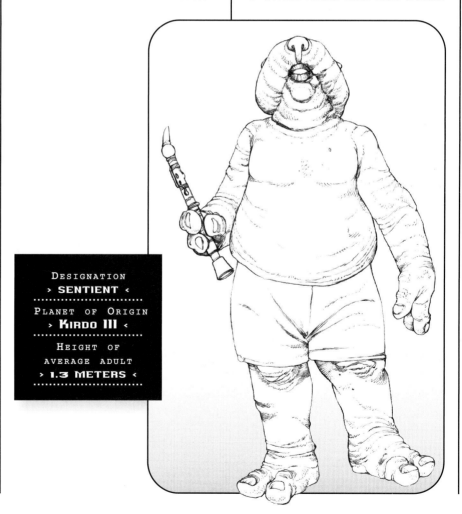

DESIGNATION
> **SENTIENT** <
....
PLANET OF ORIGIN
> **KIRDO III** <
....
HEIGHT OF
AVERAGE ADULT
> **1.3 METERS** <
....

takes a turn adding new twists to the shared plot. This tradition is meant to instruct the young on the value of patience, but it also relates a good deal of information about the world in which they live. A full story may actually last several nights, but each night is carefully planned to end an episode in the tale.

Reproduction is centered on the rainfall, which occurs only once in a decade. This rainfall, when it comes, lasts several days, creates vast lakes, and turns the dry riverbeds into flowing rivers. When this happens, Kitonaks begin their Great Celebration of Life, in which they dive into the river and conduct a mating ritual called the Dance of Love. After this, they emerge downstream, and some of the females will emerge with newborn children. This occurs because the Kitonak gestation period equals the period of time between rainfalls. Females fertilized during the previous celebration are the ones that give birth during the current one.

Kitonaks also mature fully in nine years, just in time to take part in the next celebration. After each celebration, if their tribe has grown too large, some go to find another tribe that has fewer members. These solitary Kitonaks will often hollow out chidinka plants to make a chidinkalu, a pipe instrument with which they play songs to attract a new tribe. Unfortunately, slave traders have kidnapped some of these young, wandering Kitonaks for exploitation by the Empire. As slaves they did not last long, because other species had no patience for their slow, tenacious personalities.

Yet the Kitonak temperament inspires very different reactions in other individuals, as evidenced in this quote from the diary of singer Sy Snootles as she writes about her fellow band member Droopy McCool.

> What a dear, dear fellow, his handsome eyes hidden behind those lustrously soft folds of flesh, his steadfast posture—unmoving against even the harshest of circumstances.
> He would sit and listen to me without interrupting as I would spill my anxious thoughts for hours, and when I was finished he would gently calm my fears. His patience was unending. No one else I know could have made us all put up with Max Rebo the way he did.
> He exhibited grace and had such an accepting attitude that he was the glue that kept us together as a group. When Droopy disappeared not long after our gig at Jabba's palace, the band split up, and I truly believe this was largely due to the void he left.

Klatooinian

the Klatooinians have been in the service of the Hutts for nearly 25,000 years. They are a caninelike species that long ago evolved into a sentient race, with brown or greenish coarse skin and doglike faces featuring dark eyes and heavy brows.

These beings have proved to be extremely loyal as foot soldiers, displaying tenacity, fierceness, and unwavering devotion. The Hutts—always opportunists—exploited their loyalty by tricking them into cosigning a contract that placed them, the Nikto, and the Vodrans into Hutt servitude for an indefinite period of time.

And time is pivotal to understanding Klatooinian culture. In the middle of Klatooine's Derelkoos Desert, a natural fissure cutting into the world's crust allows liquid wintrium to seep out and touch the dry desert air. This led a large glass "sculpture" to form, looking like a giant waterspout frozen in time. Originally called the Fountain of the Ancients, this phenomenon is a religious symbol of patience, fortitude, and "Strength with Age." Because they feel all must remain as it was at the time of the ancients, the Klatooinians allow no technology within a kilometer of the fountain, preserving it as an unchanging symbol upon which they can base their faith in an ever-changing world.

This overriding reverence for time is at the center of Klatooinian religious belief, so it was natural that the Klatooinians were in awe of the Hutts, who revealed that they live to an age of over 1,000 years. In fact, the Klatooinians have come to believe that the Hutts *were* the Ancients, and so they feel it is right to serve them.

As young children, Klatooinians spend their first decade being indoctrinated in a schooling that drains them of all individuality, then they are

DESIGNATION
> SENTIENT <

PLANET OF ORIGIN
> KLATOOINE <

HEIGHT OF
AVERAGE ADULT
> 1.8 METERS <

sold into servitude in the cities or towns under Hutt rule. However, many young Klatooinians escaped to help the Rebellion, while others hid in the Klatooinian wilderness. Nonetheless, even under New Republic rule, the Klatooinian government still lives in fear of their Hutt lords.

Klatooine is ruled by the Council of Elders, which resides in a palace built around the Fountain, now called the Fountain of the Hutt Ancients. The following excerpt from a letter to the Council of Elders from a youthful Klatooinian shows how the patience of the people is becoming frayed under the weight of the contract they signed millennia ago.

> As you sit in a structure near the Fountain of Ancients, you are nothing but a pack of cowards, trembling in your fine robes woven from the silk of a Hutt's slime. We rot under the tails of the Hutt masters, crawling on our bellies to eat dust like the most cowardly of lizards.
> Some of us refuse to believe that the Hutts are our Ancients. Our ignorant forefathers had no idea who they were dealing with when they met the Hutts. But we know now.
> We will not lay down our arms. We will continue to resist them, and though we die, we do so knowing that our freedom can soon be won. If we rebel, we will become a liability to the Hutts. They will abandon the contract and free us.

Kowakian Monkey-Lizard

kowakian monkey-lizards are a playful, reptilian species living on the Outer Rim world Kowak. Considered by many a silly-looking species, they have long, floppy ears, beaklike noses, and wild, yellow eyes. While this small reptile may look as if it might be easy prey for any larger predator, its nimble body, prehensile tail, acute hearing, and sharp eyesight make it hard to catch. In addition, the monkey-lizard's brown skin will actually change its tint in different environments, making it virtually invisible to pursuing predators.

Monkey-lizards live primarily in tree nests and enjoy swinging through the verdant rain forests of their homeworld. They feed on insects, worms, and small rodents, eating frequently as their tiny, energetic bodies require a great deal of nourishment.

At first encounter, one might perceive a monkey-lizard to be non-sentient, because of its strange, spastic behavior. But they are intelligent, with a developed sense of humor. They can learn to speak in most languages, yet communicate only when they feel like it.

These creatures are seldom, if ever, seen off their native world. On rare occasions, they manage to sneak onto visiting ships, winding up in the strangest places. Senior Anthropologist Hoole reported in his notes that he saw one in the court of Jabba the Hutt.

While intelligent, monkey-lizards appear to be on the brink of further evolution. They maintain no structured society, although they do exhibit hierarchical boundaries within a group of nests. Leadership appears to fall to the oldest female, and each monkey-lizard in a nesting group is assigned a specific role. One will be a food gatherer, while another will maintain the nest, while yet another will scout for predators.

A group of University of Coruscant zoologists visited Kowak and registered this report.

> At first the monkey-lizards seemed reticent and skittish about our presence. We kept our distance, watching them through macrobinoculars for a time, slowly moving our encampment closer to their nesting place.
> After a week, they began to visit our camp, inspecting our equipment, looking in our tents. We began to share some of our food with them and allowed them to move around our camp at will.
> That's when everything broke loose.

> It started with the snake they put in my sleeping bag. It actually bit me and caused my leg to swell up to twice its normal size. Then, they took to pulling apart our delicate equipment, eating all our food, hiding in our tents, and placing containers of water on top of branches, where they would spill on us.
> Further study was rendered impossible. We had no choice but to pack up and leave.

DESIGNATION
> **SENTIENT** <

PLANET OF ORIGIN
> **KOWAK** <

HEIGHT OF AVERAGE ADULT
> **0.7 METERS** <

Krayt Dragon

krayt dragons are large, vicious, carnivorous reptiles that inhabit the mountainous regions of Tatooine's Jundland Wastes. They are, without question, the most ferocious creatures on Tatooine, and they are considered by many the most vicious in the Outer Rim.

Like most reptiles, krayt dragons are cold-blooded, and they shed their yellow-brown skin on a yearly basis. Unlike other lizards, however, they continue to grow throughout their lifetimes and do not weaken with age. An average krayt dragon can grow to be nearly five meters in length and weigh about 2,000 kilograms. A krayt dragon can live to be one hundred standard years old.

Krayt dragons walk on four squat legs, at the ends of which are four-toed claws with sharp nails that can shred durasteel. Their sense of smell is activated by the flickering of their forked tongues, which, like most snakes and reptiles, collect the smell for their nostrils.

Despite their ferocity, krayt dragons are often sought by big-game hunters. Although hunting such creatures may not seem wise, the krayt dragon's gizzard often holds an incredibly valuable and beautiful dragon pearl. One pearl would easily make a person independently wealthy; hence many foolhardy hunters try to obtain this treasure. Not many such fortune-seekers have returned.

High summer in the Jundland Wastes is the krayt dragon mating season, and the mountains ring with their bellowed cries. Most intelligent beings refuse to venture into the Wastes at this time, but those who do are mindful of that sound, because a dragon in a mating frenzy will kill everything it can reach.

Luke Skywalker, the Jedi Master, wrote about his first experience with a

DESIGNATION
> NONSENTIENT <

PLANET OF ORIGIN
> TATOOINE <

LENGTH OF
AVERAGE ADULT
> 5 METERS <

krayt dragon and how the creature killed his friend's pet dewback.

> I grew up on a moisture farm not far from the Jundland Wastes. We had to be careful not to attract the attention of krayt dragons or Tusken Raiders. Sometimes you can't help it though. I came nose-to-nose with a krayt dragon when I was just thirteen.

> My friend Windy and I decided to take our pet dewback Huey out for a ride. We thought we'd prove how independent we were, but ended up in a sandstorm. The dewback panicked because he smelled something, and bolted into a cave. We found him,

but unfortunately a krayt dragon found us there and attacked. Only his head and shoulder fit through the cave entrance, but he picked up Huey in his jaws.

> He had us trapped and was banging against the entrance of the cave, when something distracted him. He turned away, and when I peeked out again, the dragon was sleeping. A few moments later Obi-Wan Kenobi showed up and guided us out of the cave and to safe shelter.

> Looking back now, I believe he must have put the dragon to sleep. There's no other way it could have happened.

Kubaz

tall and gaunt, with a long trunk for a nose, the Kubaz are a humanoid species of the planet Kubindi. They have green-black skin, and bristly black hair grows from the tops of their pointy heads. They have four broad, stubby fingers on each hand and two large toes on each foot. They often wear goggles on their eyes when visiting worlds in systems with a yellow or red sun.

The planet Kubindi orbits a powerful blue giant star known for its extraordinary solar flares. As a result, it is an arid world with erratic weather patterns and is often victimized by large bursts of radiation from the star. At one time, the solar flares were so powerful, they burned away all edible plant life. What remained was polluted, and appetizing only to the native insect population. Because of this, the Kubaz resorted to eating the insects, which were the only edible food source left on the planet.

Over thousands of years, their culture, business, finance, and space and computer technology grew entirely out of the production and sale of insects, and Kubaz physiology adapted completely to accommodate their insect diet. Their snoutlike, flexible trunks evolved as a perfect means of sucking insects out of hives. Kubaz insect banquets are a highlight of culture, as the food is considered a delicacy. While a Kubaz will not be insulted if a guest does not wish to partake in the insect meal, they would conclude that the guest simply lacks refinement and good taste.

Kubaz are particularly skilled at establishing networks of business associates and information suppliers, at "knowing someone who knows someone," and they use this to their advantage. They are also extremely talented at observation and at reading intentions. These natural traits make

DESIGNATION
> SENTIENT <

PLANET OF ORIGIN
> KUBINDI <

**HEIGHT OF
AVERAGE ADULT**
> 1.8 METERS <

them excellent spies.

One such spy is a Kubaz named Garindan, who usually worked in the backwater world of Tatooine. In this report to the Imperial prefect of Tatooine, Garindan showed his skillful ability to follow a trail.

> I was aware that something was up when Port Officer Feltipern Trevagg started spending a lot of time around the marketplace. He was definitely hunting something—not unusual for a Gotal. This behavior started around the time that the notice was received about the possibility of Jedi being present on Tatooine. That had to be his goal, for surely the Empire would reward him handsomely for the capture of a Jedi. No doubt his cones could sense their power! So to find the Jedi, all I had to do was follow the Gotal.

> Trevagg hooked up with a young H'nemthe female, and I just hoped he would live long enough for me to find the Jedi. He took the young lady into the cantina and perked up when a dusty old man came into the place, followed by a youth. I knew this had to be the Jedi, and when the old man brandished a lightsaber, I had my confirmation.

> So I followed him as he and his entourage made their way to Docking Bay 94, from whence I contacted the sandtroopers. The rest, as we say, is history.

Kurtzen

a mild-mannered, peaceful, clan-oriented people, the Kurtzen are white-skinned humanoids who make up 5 percent of Bakura's total population. They number only 4.3 million, but their population is growing slowly, thanks to the timely intervention by the Bakur Mining Corporation. Only a scant twenty years before the Battle of Endor, the Kurtzen were a primitive species, dying from a genetic dead end caused by the limited gene pool of their small population.

The Kurtzen were originally a nomadic people who traveled from camp to camp following herds of ungulate species for food. Their culture revolves around their mystical tradition of focusing the power of life into objects, trinkets, and totems, which are carried around at all times for good fortune. For this reason, one might find Kurtzen wearing several pouches on their broad, leathery belts. In fact, their wardrobe is focused on the goal of drawing energy from the outside to the inner self. This is why Kurtzen prefer to dress in neutral-colored, sleeveless robes. The cut of the fabric, the open color, and the open arms are a welcoming gesture to the universal power of life. Researchers believe the Kurtzen started these traditions in the hope of encouraging wellness when more and more of them started becoming sick.

On his visit to Bakura, Senior Anthropologist Hoole discovered how the Kurtzen use their totems and trinkets.

> As I watched the Kurtzen healing ceremony, I was enthralled by the use of music, color, and imagery. The subject was a teenage boy who had apparently developed a lung condition. The shaman prayed over him, while the other Kurtzen circled his body and chanted. The boy seemed mesmerized. His eyes were wide open and glazed as he stared straight ahead.
> Suddenly, the shaman took one of the boy's totems, which he had been wearing around his neck, and held it up. The boy stood up and, throwing his head back, swallowed the small, beaded object, string and all. I was certain something so large would cause him to choke, or would get stuck in his digestive tract. But according to the shaman, they do this all the time, and with the passing of the totem, so, too, passes the disease.
> When the totem reappeared the next day, the boy's family celebrated. And remarkably, within a few days the boy was feeling better.

The Bakur Mining Corporation encountered the Kurtzen after establishing their first facility for constructing turbolifts, and offered them medical and technological aid, which the Kurtzen eagerly accepted. The Kurtzen have adopted Bakuran technology, and the Bakur Mining Corporation helped find a cure for the Kurtzen genetic defect.

Now, instead of roaming the surface of Bakura, the Kurtzen inhabit the Kishh district of the continent of Braad. They maintain limited control of the region, subject to Bakuran laws. Under Imperial rule, they were ineligible to vote on Imperial matters, but now that Bakura has joined the New Republic, the Kurtzen have obtained a full spectrum of rights.

DESIGNATION
> SENTIENT <
....
PLANET OF ORIGIN
> BAKURA <
....
HEIGHT OF
AVERAGE ADULT
> 1.5 METERS <
....

Lorrdian

While the Lorrdians are actually a genetically human race, their culture makes them worthy of note. Because of their history, these humans have developed a unique ability.

During a period of Lorrdian history known as the Kanz Disorders, a species called the Argazdans subjugated the Lorrdians and barred them from communicating with one another. However, the Lorrdians devised a type of sign language consisting of subtle hand gestures, body postures, and facial tics and expressions. They also taught themselves to read the body language of others as one would read an open book.

This new language became more than just a simple means of communication, however. It led to a new way of life, and it helped the Lorrdians overthrow their masters by enabling them to form a guerrilla force and keep the different divisions of their army completely informed of one anothers' activities.

Today Lorrdian culture continuously celebrates and improves this language. Each generation teaches the system to the next, finding new ways to elaborate upon what they now call "kinetic communication." All Lorrdians are taught how to carefully interpret movements, gestures, and mannerisms, and they are so good at reading body language that they can tell a person's mood and intentions within a matter of seconds. With more time, they can identify cultural background, homeworld, occupation, and class.

Lorrdians are also famous for being the best vocal and physical mimics. Because of their perceptive powers, they can imitate almost any being's voice or mannerisms, within the restrictions of their physical ability. In his journal, Senior Anthropologist Hoole, a mimic himself, noted an example of their skill.

DESIGNATION
> SENTIENT <

PLANET OF ORIGIN
> LORRD <

HEIGHT OF AVERAGE ADULT
> 1.6 METERS <

> I don't know if I should be jealous of them or admire them.
> I was visiting Lorrd with my niece and nephew principally to study this unique ability. While we stayed at the governor's home, Tash and Zak collaborated with the governor's son Kal to play a joke on me. I was walking through the house when I heard Tash's voice calling for me from upstairs. Concerned, I ran up the stairs to find out what was going on. When I entered the room from whence I had heard the voice, her voice suddenly emanated from the room I'd just left downstairs, and it was moving away—out the front door of the house.

I ran down the stairs and out the front door to find Tash, Zak, and Kal laughing hysterically on the front lawn.
> I was both relieved and angry. Considering all the trouble we'd been through, Tash and Zak should have known better than to raise a false alarm. I sent them to their separate rooms.
> Although I was upset, I realized how easily I was fooled. This boy had re-created Tash's voice so easily that he had tricked the trickster. And if a child could do that, what could the adults do?

Massassi

the Massassi people are now extinct, but they were once residents of the world Yavin 4, later home to a Rebel base and subsequently the location of the Jedi academy. The Jedi known as Tionne, in conducting research on Jedi history, found records dating back 4,000 years that describe the Massassi people as warrior slaves to the Dark Lords of the Sith Naga Sadow and Exar Kun.

The Massassi people were red-skinned, yellow-eyed humanoids who led simple, primitive lives on an unknown world in the Sith Empire. Naga Sadow enslaved them, then, after he fled to Yavin 4, altered them through dark side sorcery. They became large, sharp-clawed creatures with finlike growths coming from their heads and backs. They were easily angered, strong, and ruthless.

In their new forms, they were for the most part mindless, carrying out the commands of their new master. They still maintained their own culture, with priests and elders, while constructing the massive temples on Yavin 4 for their Sith master. Those temples are now used to house the Jedi academy.

Very little has been found that describes the actual lifestyle, culture, belief systems, or biology of the original Massassi. Archaeologists and linguists are still studying the hieroglyphs in the Massassi temples to learn their language and perhaps understand more about this mysterious people. Meanwhile, Tionne discovered the fate of the Massassi and learned the identity of the dreaded Massassi night beast, a creature that attacked the Rebel base on Yavin 4 after the battle with the first Death Star. She described her discoveries in the following report, submitted nearly nine years after the Battle of Endor.

> According to the Jedi Holocron, Exar Kun destroyed all the Massassi in a ritual designed to free him from his physical form and make him an all-powerful spirit that the ancient Jedi would be unable to destroy. Apparently, Kun chose one warrior to remain alive, on the off chance that things went awry.

> The name of this warrior was Kalgrath. Kun altered Kalgrath, turning him into a large, green, monstrous version of his previous form, and put him into a deep sleep until such a time that the temple would need protection.

> The presence of the Rebel forces caused a stirring that either woke the beast by itself, or woke Exar Kun's spirit who woke the beast. Whatever the case, the creature was eager to find his own people.

> Not knowing that all the Massassi had been killed, and believing they had left Yavin 4, Luke Skywalker unwittingly sent Kalgrath off in a ship to the former location of the ancient Sith Empire to find the remaining members of his people.

> I have been able to track the creature to the deserted world Ziost, at which point the trail ends. A group of researchers there noted dark shadows lurking about their camp, and I have been promised that if the creature is found, we will be notified.

DESIGNATION
> **SENTIENT** <
....
PLANET OF ORIGIN
> **YAVIN 4** <
BY WAY OF THE SITH EMPIRE
....
HEIGHT OF
AVERAGE ADULT
> **1.9 METERS** <
....

Melodie

Melodies are amphibious humanoids who dwell in the caverns and deep mountain lakes of the equatorial mountains of Yavin 8. Like many amphibians, they have two distinct phases of life: water-dwelling and land-dwelling. Melodies, however, hatch on dry land from eggs, then move to water as adults.

Melodie children are small humanoids with yellow eyes and humanlike hair. They breathe via conventional lungs that have the capacity to retain air, allowing them to remain underwater for long periods of time. The hands of the young are slightly webbed.

Adults, known as elders, look much like their younger counterparts from the torso upward, but they have long tails instead of legs, striped with blue, green, purple, pink, and orange. They breathe through gills, taking oxygen from the water. Middle-aged adults can still survive in the open air for limited periods, but the elderly cannot surface at all.

Melodies make the transition from one form to the other when they reach maturity in about their twentieth year. This "changing ceremony" takes place in shallow underground pools coated in special algae that allow the Melodies to continue breathing throughout their transition. The algae cannot grow in deep water, forcing the Melodies to dwell in less-defendable pools for several days or weeks.

While changing, the Melodies are defenseless. Therefore, the as-yet-unchanged children guard them while the metamorphosis takes place. Predators such as the purella spider know the changing season and often attack. Children drive off as many attackers as they can, but many Melodies—adults and children—do not survive. Once the transformation is complete, the children take the new

DESIGNATION
> SENTIENT <
....
PLANET OF ORIGIN
> YAVIN 8 <
....
HEIGHT OF
AVERAGE ADULT
> 1.5 METERS <
....

elders to deeper lakes within the mountains, where there is a great celebration.

Children live in land settlements surrounding the area where the elders live. Younger adults surface to teach children how to provide for themselves, protect the settlements, and care for the very young. Older children also act as teachers and guard the eggs. They go foraging for plants that they grind into paste for newly hatched infants to eat.

A peaceful, primitive people, they avoid the outside world. A few children Melodies have left home in order to study at the Jedi academy on Yavin 4. One such Melodie was a friend to Anakin Solo, and he wrote about her in his personal journal.

> My friend Lyric had to go through her change. It was a strange experience, but Tahiri and I were happy to be there for her and to help protect her from avrils, raiths, and the purella.
> Lyric started to change while she was still on land. The small pink webs between her fingers grew longer to connect her fingers together completely. When this happened, we put her in the changing pool. She floated on top of the algae for a second, and then sank beneath the surface. When I went underneath the water, using a trico filter, I found that her legs had fused together into a single tail. At first it frightened me, but she assured me that she was all right.

Mimbanite

imbanites are humanoids with small, thin bodies, green skin, wild green and red hair, and large eyes. They live in the towns and civilized areas of the rain-forest world known in some circles as Mimban and in others as Circarpous V.

After the Battle of Yavin, Princess Leia Organa and her brother Luke Skywalker found themselves on this world, which was being mined by the Empire. Because of certain physical limitations, the Empire did not use the Mimbanites as slave labor, so they lived by begging and scavenging scraps from garbage heaps.

The Mimbanites, or Greenies, as the local human population refers to them, are genetic cousins to the Coway, a strong, violent species who live in the caves of Mimban. While the two peoples look similar, they are worlds apart in terms of cultural behavior. Scientists believe that several millennia ago the Mimbanites left the Coway tribe to strike out on their own, only to be subjugated by other races.

There is assumed to be a connection between the Coway, the Mimbanites, and the Temple of Pomojema on Mimban, due to the Coway cave markings and Mimbanite pictographs that are similar to images found in the temple. Since the dawn of the New Republic, scientific teams have studied the temple and the languages of the Coway and Mimbanites to determine the historical link between these peoples and the long-dead race that constructed this awesome structure, now in ruins.

In this journal entry, Luke Skywalker writes about the Mimbanites.

> These people were so abused and malnourished, they had absolutely no fighting spirit. The miners literally beat them up for amusement. I remember one giant thug dumping his drink on the floor of the local bar, just so one of these poor, degraded beings could lick it up.
> Strangely enough, the Mimbanites are related to the Coway, another indigenous group on Mimban. But the two have absolutely nothing in common besides a basic physical resemblance. While the Coway will fight without

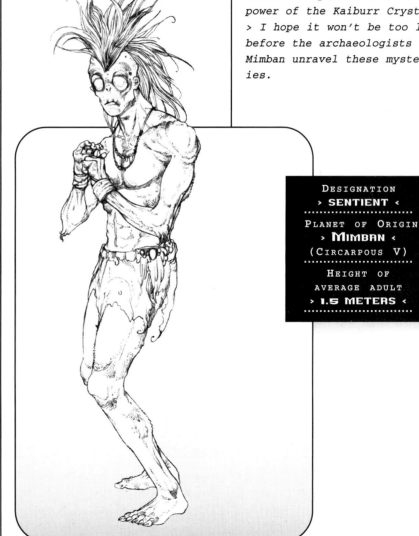

provocation, the Mimbanites are completely lacking aggression.
> The gap between these two groups is so wide I wonder what could have caused them to develop differently. Were the Mimbanites so beaten down by the Empire that they became as they are, or is their lack of self-esteem more historical and deep-rooted than that? Is it somehow connected to the ancient civilization that built the ancient temple and used the power of the Kaiburr Crystal?
> I hope it won't be too long before the archaeologists on Mimban unravel these mysteries.

DESIGNATION
> **SENTIENT** <

PLANET OF ORIGIN
> **MIMBAN** <
(CIRCARPOUS V)

HEIGHT OF
AVERAGE ADULT
> **1.5 METERS** <

the Mon Calamari are an idealistic, noble people whom many considered the heart of the Rebel Alliance, and who are now a cornerstone of the New Republic. A positive, forward-thinking species with goals of justice and fairness, they have established themselves as leaders and proponents of galactic harmony.

Often called Mon Cals, they are an amphibious species with salmon-colored skin, webbed hands, high, domed heads, and huge, fishlike eyes. Mon Calamari are equally at home in water and on land, and are able to breathe in both environments.

Development of Mon Cal science began with simple fish farming and kelp cultivation on their mostly water-covered world. Their scientific and technological advancement progressed slowly because it was difficult to get metal from the planet. This problem was later solved by their neighbor species, the Quarren, who lived among the greatest depths of Mon Calamari's oceans. Thus began the Mon Calamari's symbiotic relationship with the Quarren, who mined minerals found only at those depths.

Soft-spoken and gentle, the Mon Calamari are generally peaceful and even-tempered, with a remarkable capacity for intense concentration. Mon Cals are also legendary for determination and dedication that border on obstinacy. Once they have made a decision, they are not easily swayed from it. One such racial decision was the quest to reach "the islands in the galactic ocean"—the stars.

The Mon Calamari and Quarren live in multilevel cities that float on the surface of their vast oceans. The Mon Cals live on the upper levels of the twenty-to-thirty-story structures, as they prefer more sunlight, while the Quarren live in the lower levels, where there is more comforting darkness.

DESIGNATION
> **SENTIENT** <

PLANET OF ORIGIN
> **MON CALAMARI** <

HEIGHT OF AVERAGE ADULT
> **1.7 METERS** <

These cities are the centers for civilized culture, and their repertoire of art, music, and literature is impressive.

Mon Calamari technological talents are so well honed that they can engineer starships or structures for most environments. A good example was the Rebel Alliance Echo Base on Hoth, which the Alliance expanded from an existing installation constructed by a Mon Calamari smuggler named Salmakk. As this following communiqué from an Alliance Intelligence operative indicates, the base was extremely well designed.

> *Preparations at Echo Base proceeded exceedingly well,*

despite the fact that we had to deal with some stragglers left over from Salmakk's operation. The place is in excellent condition. The shield blast doors, the way the walls were constructed from the natural environment of rock and ice, the sheer mastery of high-tech structural engineering it took to develop this place boggles the mind. I know our engineers can add a great deal to it; it was designed to be expanded.
> *We've even found an appropriate place for the ion can-*

nons. Salmakk already had pedestals ready; he just hadn't put them into use yet. So I'd say we'd be ready to move within two standard weeks.

When the Mon Calamari reached space they began building their incredibly complex starships, which are frequently the vessels of choice for the New Republic. Each of these ships is unique in design, and other species who serve on Mon Cal ships find it difficult to access computer interfaces, which are geared to Mon Calamari physiology and to specific movements the Mon Cals make in utilizing the command chairs. In addition, display monitors are geared to the Mon Cal vision spectrum and seem warped and distorted to non-Mon Cals.

The Empire took notice of the Mon Calamari when the need for slave labor dramatically increased. With the assistance of some disgruntled Quarren who deactivated the planet's protective shield, the Empire conquered the Mon Calamari. Both the Quarren and the Mon Cals were put to hard labor, but

the Mon Cals began a movement of passive resistance. In order to squash their resistance, the Empire destroyed three Mon Cal floating cities.

It was then that this peaceful species put aside their pacifist ways and fought back against their taskmasters. In the beginning they used simple kitchen implements, hand tools, and any other weapons they could find. They and their Quarren comrades—with the aid of the Rebellion—drove the Empire from their world. Mon Calamari then became the first world to officially throw its support behind the Rebel Alliance.

To this day, there is still some friction between the Quarren and the Mon Calamari, exacerbated by the Quarren's initial betrayal. The Quarren do not truly understand the Mon Cal need for constant growth and their desire to search the stars for truth. They feel the truth is available right at home, in the ocean. In addition, the Quarren are no longer satisfied with their original arrangement with the Mon Cals, since the raw materials they provided to the Mon Calamari brought the wrath of the Empire down upon them.

Despite this friction, Mon Calamari society continues to function. They have a highly efficient government set up very much like the Republic Senate. Quarren and Mon Cals are equally represented in this body, and because of the Mon Calamari's peace-loving nature, they continue to work toward harmony with their Quarren associates.

Small, avian people native to the planet Mrlsst, the Mrlssi have blue-feathered skin and bright-colored plumes for hair. They have large eyes that give them extraordinary vision effective over great distances, and three-fingered talons with sharp claws. Their faces, though covered in flesh, are reminiscent of their avian ancestors.

Known for their intelligence and creativity, the Mrlssi have centered their entire culture on education. Some of the galaxy's finest universities are on Mrlsst, and these schools are the basis of financial well-being for most of the cities on the planet. The Mrlssi are especially renowned for achievements in physics and the technological sciences and for their desire to share their knowledge with other people. They are a highly cultured people who appreciate the finest in art, literature, and music. They often consider creations from other cultures to be vulgar.

So dependent are they on their educational resources that they will go to great lengths to profit from their scientific discoveries—sometimes too far, Wedge Antilles reports in a journal entry.

> The Phantom Project was just that, a phantom. It didn't exist.
> President Keela apologized profusely when the truth came out. He really didn't know it was a fake, or he wouldn't have hooked the Empire and the New Republic into engaging in a bidding war. Apparently the academy on Mrlsst has become a hotbed of political one-upmanship, and the Phantom Project was just a ploy to obtain money and prestige.
> In the end, Mrlsst paid for

DESIGNATION
> SENTIENT <
....
PLANET OF ORIGIN
> MRLSST <
....
HEIGHT OF AVERAGE ADULT
> 1.3 METERS <
....

their mistake when they were bombed by the Empire. We discovered, meanwhile, that Rorax Falken, another brilliant mathematician, had developed a gravitic polarizing device. We used it to destroy Loka Hask's Imperial ship before it caused too much damage.

Despite this potential for duplicity, people from all over the galaxy come to study on Mrlsst, and in general the Mrlssi have proved to be excellent teachers and mentors. They expect the best from their students, and when a student has trouble, the Mrlssi educators will do everything in their power to help that student learn. Such efforts have placed them in the forefront of research into various learning disabilities, and they have developed successful treatment and training for dealing with certain brain disorders.

Physiologically, the Mrlssi are very much like their avian ancestors. They eat small rodents and reptiles such as wuorls, as well as insects and various vegetation. Unfortunately, from spending so many years on the ground, they have lost their wings. While some Mrlssi bemoan the loss of their ancient heritage, most feel the cost is insignificant in comparison to the knowledge they've gained and advancements they've made.

Myneyrsh

the Myneyrshi are one of two species native to the forest world called Wayland. They are tall, thin, bipedal humanoids with four arms and a smooth layer of shiny crystal covering their bodies, which makes them look as if they are made of glass. New Republic scientists have theorized that this layer is a result of a chemical reaction to the moisture and oxygen in the air.

The Myneyrshi are a primitive people who, despite their contact with humans, have not advanced technologically. They rely on bows and arrows as their prime weapons, and many use spears and knives, as well. Domesticated animals provide transportation and rudimentary agriculture. Myneyrshi appear to be actively defiant of technology, because it is seen as representative of their Imperial conquerors. Their shamans have declared technological devices to be "items of shame," and most Myneyrshi will not go near them.

Most of Myneyrsh life is centered on ritualistic behavior. They have rituals for waking, eating, and sleeping. One such ritual, witnessed by Luke Skywalker and his brother-in-law Han Solo, is the offering of a fowl as *satnachakka*, or a peace offering. While the bird is elevated on a spire, no conflict, physical or otherwise, may occur. Another is a presentation of a ritual staff, a gesture of unity and friendship.

These people are excellent hunters and trackers and can move through the forest almost without sound. Their awareness of their environment is extremely responsive, and Skywalker likened their perception skills to those of Force-sensitives.

The Myneyrshi are strong-willed, with enough spiritual mettle to combat the mental manipulations of the dark Jedi clone Joruus C'baoth, who had forced them to cohabitate with

DESIGNATION
> SENTIENT <
....
PLANET OF ORIGIN
> WAYLAND <
....
HEIGHT OF
AVERAGE ADULT
> 1.9 METERS <

their old enemies, the Psadans. While C'baoth attempted to mentally manipulate the Myneyrshi, they resisted his rule long enough to form an alliance with their enemies.

Like their Psadan neighbors, the Myneyrsh people hold their history in a long oral tradition. The following is a transcription of a portion of the Myneyrsh oral history that describes their enslavement to C'baoth:

> In the time of the coming of the rains, so came the Dark Man, speaking fire and throwing lightning from his fingers. Strong he was in will and power, and though the Myneyrshi were strong, our warriors could not defeat him.
> The Dark Man pulled us from our green-roofed homes and made us serve him with the outsider peoples and our enemies the Psadans. The Psadans

were as we, unable to have their warriors fight the Dark Man. Our peoples suffered, but we grew angry and turned against him. We made the Psadans our family. Together, we said. Together we fight the Dark Man.
> And so we were freed, by uniting. Forever will we be one with our Psadan family. No more will we make war against one another, for together we are stronger people.

Mynock

Silicon-based life-forms, mynocks are large, mantalike creatures that are the bane of starship captains across the galaxy. They live on energy, particularly stellar energy or electromagnetic energy.

While many have speculated that these creatures originated in the system of Ord Mynock, the beasts' true planet of origin is unknown. It is even possible they evolved in the vacuum of space, as most planetary environments prove fatal to them.

They are not intelligent creatures, resembling in their biological makeup microscopic, oxygen-based organisms. They have few organs and reproduce by splitting, as do most one-celled organisms.

Because they thrive on stellar energy, mynocks ride the stellar winds to capture particles emitted by stars. Their black, leathery skin absorbs electromagnetic radiation efficiently. Once they've consumed enough energy, mynocks will land on asteroids and attach themselves via their suction-cup-like mouths, to feed on silicon and other materials. They do this in order to produce the extra mass required for replication. When it has absorbed enough mass, a mynock splits into two, then the two mynocks launch themselves into space again.

Mynocks are extremely protective of their territory, however temporary it may be. They are known to attack in large numbers when cornered, when their territory is violated, or when they are otherwise physically threatened.

Mynocks are also the main food staple for the giant space slugs that often inhabit asteroid fields. For this reason, some spaceports will try to keep at least one space slug on hand to cut down on the mynock population.

Constantly thirsting for energy, mynocks will often attach themselves to passing starships. In this desperate journal entry, Tonaa Rikstnns, a maintenance worker at the Sluis Van shipyards, writes about how badly mynocks can terrorize a spaceport.

> The mynock problem is getting so troublesome the maintenance crews can't keep up with it. The creatures chew on a ship's power cables and suck out power through the ion ports. Of course, we end up eating the cost of these repairs.

> Our department is too understaffed to deal with this issue, and it's getting so bad that pilots are taking their ships elsewhere for repairs!

> I'm going to recommend that we populate our asteroid shipyard with a couple of space slugs to see if that will help cut back the mynock population.

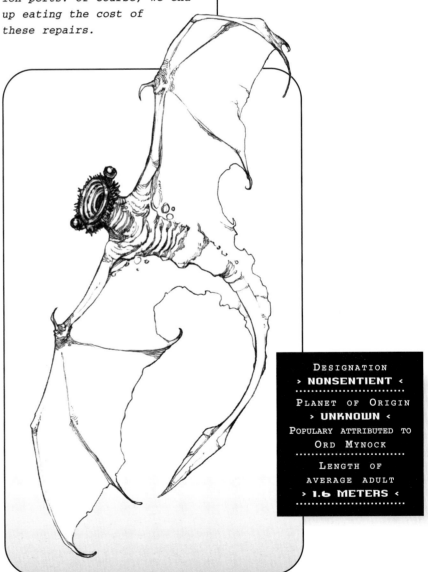

DESIGNATION
> **NONSENTIENT** <
....
PLANET OF ORIGIN
> **UNKNOWN** <
POPULARY ATTRIBUTED TO
ORD MYNOCK
....
LENGTH OF
AVERAGE ADULT
> **1.6 METERS** <
....

Neek

neeks are tiny, skittish, reptilian herbivores from the planet Ambria. Since they are so small, they are usually food for predators, particularly their larger cousins the hssiss. Their primary means of defense against such predators is their short sleep cycle. The average neek will sleep only one or two hours at a time, so that at least a quarter of the population of any flock remains awake at all times.

These lizards have a unique skeletal structure. Unlike some reptiles, they walk on their hind legs, and their forelegs are smaller and used as arms. They have tiny fingers that enable them to pluck vegetation. The long tail gives them extraordinary balance and acts as a stabilizer as they run at speeds nearing sixty kilometers per hour.

Neeks have pleasant temperaments, but are extremely paranoid and easy to startle. They gather in flocks, like birds, banding together for protection and companionship. They take easily to sapient companionship, and some people have been known to keep neeks as pets, though the neeks remain true to their wild roots. Those who do keep neeks do so because of their perceptive skills. Their large eyes dilate, allowing them to absorb light waves more effectively and view their surroundings in complete detail, even in low light. They also have auditory receptors on their necks that capture sound waves.

Famed ancient explorer Jith Bavion writes of neeks.

> A neek is an explorer's best friend. They've been invaluable to us in our trek into new territories.
> To cite an example, on a planet in the Outer Rim, we had ventured deep into a rain forest looking for signs of intelligent life. As I walked, I carried one neek on my shoulder, and when we entered a clearing near a set of caves, he became very agitated and even bit me as I tried to calm him. We had two other neeks with us, and they were acting the same way.
> We quickly readied our weapons, just in time to protect ourselves from the large, dragonlike creature that emerged from the cave. We easily dispatched the beast, but had we not been ready we would have lost team members for certain.
> I made it a point to treat the little fellows with some sweet berries that evening. They deserved it for all they'd done.

DESIGNATION
> **NONSENTIENT** <
....
PLANET OF ORIGIN
> **AMBRIA** <
....
HEIGHT OF
AVERAGE ADULT
> **0.3 METERS** <
....

Neimoidian

eimoidians are actually descendants of ancient Duros colonists who settled Neimoidia, so they exhibit many physical attributes of their ancestors. However, they have slight facial and body differences that distinguish them, due to their 25,000 years of development in a different environment. Their jawlines are lower, and their bodies are thinner and longer because the gravity on Neimoidia is greater than that of the average Duros floating city. In addition, while Duros have blue-purple skin with bright red eyes, the Neimoidians have green-gray skin and dark red or pink eyes. These color differences have been attributed to specific chemicals in Neimoidia's atmosphere.

Though Neimoidians are a reptilian species, they hatch from eggs and grow through a grub stage like many insects. From birth, the grubs are raised in communal hives and have access to limited amounts of food. As a result many die, but those who live learn to hoard their food. By the time they leave the hives at age seven, they are extremely fearful of death and very, very greedy.

It is for this reason that they are a race of merchants, and definitely not warriors. Before fighting in a battle where there exists a possibility of injury or dying, Neimoidians will surrender or turn and run. With the Trade Federation, they amassed an army of droids and droid ships to fight for them and serve their technological needs.

Neimoidians are usually seen wearing flowing robes and impressive headgear, every element of which has some special significance and indicates an individual's status. They are obsessed with influence, and their ability to handle funds was crucial in their rise to the top of the Trade Federation, a commercial regulatory

DESIGNATION
> SENTIENT <

PLANET OF ORIGIN
> NEIMOIDIA <

HEIGHT OF AVERAGE ADULT
> 2 METERS <

body especially prevalent during the latter years of the Old Republic.

After centuries of running the Trade Federation, their control of the organization subsided when the Republic began taxing the trade routes they'd established. This crushed the Neimoidians, and their delicate financial control of their organization began to crumble. After the particularly humiliating defeat of a trade blockade of the planet Naboo, the Neimoidian reputation began an ever-downward spiral.

Bereft of power and position, the Neimoidians have considered every possibility for regaining their status. In his "Encyclical on Historical Greatness," Neimoidian leader Chal Haan writes of the Neimoidians' most recent attempt.

> It is when one is brought low that one must consider starting over, and to do this we must look where we began.

> Duro. A forgotten land, a forgotten culture, but one of greatness, honor, and respect. Long ago we abandoned this glorious past. The Duros are leaders, explorers, and adventurers. These are our people, and we must rebuild ourselves in their image. We must embrace our Duros heritage, and in doing so we will once again achieve glory.
> Neimoidia is our home, but Duro is our heart and our blood. Let every son and daughter of Neimoidia lift their head high and proclaim, "I am Duros," for in this is truth, dignity, and prestige.

nerfs, once native to the peaceful world of Alderaan, are four-legged, herbivorous ungulates. Since these creatures are raised on other worlds besides Alderaan, the species survived their homeworld's destruction.

These are rangy creatures with curving dull horns and long but scanty fur that covers their muscular bodies. They have clawlike hooves and tufted tails. Because they chew their cuds, they tend to build up a great deal of saliva in their mouths, causing them to expectorate a great deal.

Although domesticated, nerfs are known for being temperamental and foul-smelling. If they are in disagreement with their handler's wishes, they will sit down or kick angrily at their often-hapless masters. Most nerf herders are patient, simple people who live outdoors and tend to travel with their creatures as they migrate about the grassy plains to feed.

Princess Leia Organa Solo talks about nerfs in this account of a particularly embarrassing moment at an animal fair during her childhood.

> I remember how much the pen stank as we neared the nerf. I didn't want to get close to it, but my father calmly led me up next to the enclosure. A nerf herder was in there with the beast, cleaning its stall.
> The nerf turned its head to look at me, and spat. A giant glob of brown nerf saliva landed right on my dress. I was horrified.
> The nerf herder started laughing, and I was outraged. "Why are you laughing?" I demanded. "What's so funny?"
> "You are. Don't you know that nerfs spit? That's why the line is there, so people can stay outta spittin' distance."
> I stomped away to the concession stand to get something with which to clean my dress. After a halfhearted apology, my father chuckled about the encounter the rest of our trip.
> To this day I have a great deal of trouble eating nerf. I think about that smelly animal, and the thought of eating it still makes my stomach turn.

Nevertheless, nerf meat is considered some of the most delicious in the known galaxy. In addition, their fur is quite popular, and their hides make excellent leather goods.

DESIGNATION
> **NONSENTIENT** <

PLANET OF ORIGIN
> **ALDERAAN** <

HEIGHT OF AVERAGE ADULT
> **1.3 METERS** <

also called Ryyk, the Neti are a plant-based species that scientists once believed evolved on the planet Myrkr. Now extinct, they had gray, barklike skin, several branchlike appendages that acted as arms, and rootlike appendages that acted as feet. Their hair was a bush of vegetable "fur"—usually brown or blackish green—that rested atop their massive trunks.

Like most plants, the Neti gained sustenance from photosynthesis and procreated by producing seeds. However, their seeds were produced only once every hundred years, and then in very small numbers.

Neti were a long-lived species, with lives spanning several millennia. They were a calm, quiet, methodical species and were known to plant themselves in one spot and remain motionless for centuries, simply to observe their environment. One such Neti was the Jedi Master Ood Bnar, who fought in the ancient Sith War and subsequently resided, motionless, on the planet Ossus, only to awaken 4,000 years later and save Luke Skywalker from a deadly enemy.

One of the most fascinating features of the Neti was their ability to grow, shrink, or manipulate the shapes of their bodies at will. They showed the ability to take an almost humanoid form, or to grow into an enormous, solid trunk within moments.

Luke Skywalker studied literature relating to these creatures. Some writings put forth the hypothesis that due to their plant nature, the Neti were extremely sensitive to the Force. If it could be proven that they are linked to the planet Myrkr—a planet that has yielded the Force-blocking ysalamiri and the Force-sensitive vornskrs—it would strongly indicate a connection to the Force. The Jedi historian Tionne found materials to refute this theory,

DESIGNATION
> SENTIENT <

PLANET OF ORIGIN
> RYYK <

HEIGHT OF AVERAGE ADULT
> 2–5 METERS <

however, in Bodo Baas's Jedi Holocron taken from the Emperor. She relates this information in her notes.

> Ood Bnar was apparently of a species called Neti that were native to the planet Ryyk, which was destroyed by a supernova not long before the Sith War, about 4,000 years ago.
> Ood survived the cataclysm because he was on Ossus teaching students. According to Baas's Holocron, Ood was the only Neti not on Ryyk when it was destroyed. Only fragments of their culture still exist, which would explain how some documents have mistaken the name of

their homeworld for that of their race.
> Alone in the universe, Ood threw himself into teaching and preserving the traditions and knowledge of the Jedi on Ossus. When the Sith War began, he planted himself above a cache of lightsabers in an effort to keep them safe from the Sith invaders, and only roused himself 4,000 years later to sacrifice his life for the Ysanna Jedi named Jem.

Nikto

Of all the creatures in service to the Hutts, the Nikto are the species most identified with their masters. They are fierce people, and probably the most dangerous species to work as the Hutts' enforcers and warriors. They are a fearless and humorless people.

The Nikto are a reptilian species consisting of five different races, each displaying unique cosmetic features. These different races evolved due to an intense amount of stellar radiation bombarding their planet from a dying star known as M'dweshuu. Although these different races exhibit superficial differences, they are genetically compatible and can interbreed. However, 93 percent of children born of mixed parentage maintain the characteristics of only one parent and pass those specific characteristics on to their children, whereas only 7 percent show signs of mixed breeding. In *The University of Sambra Guide to Intelligent Life*, Tem Ellis writes of a special prejudice Nikto exhibit.

> On Nar Shaddaa, there was one young Nikto who showed characteristics of two of the Nikto races. His name was Rych Ha'andeelay.
> This young Nikto showed scars on his arms and legs, where he had been slashed with a knife, and burn scars on his arms. He was an outcast, unable to secure solid work among his own people. For this reason, he gladly took the opportunity to work as a soldier for the Hutts.
> "If I die for them," he said, "at least I will die with honor, and perhaps someone will remember me fondly. If not, I die at home, an outcast."

DESIGNATION
> SENTIENT <
....
PLANET OF ORIGIN
> KINTAN <
....
HEIGHT OF AVERAGE ADULT
> 1.8 METERS <

All Nikto have obsidian black eyes, which are protected by transparent membranes when they are underwater and during Kintan's windstorms. They all have leathery, reptilian skin and sport various horns or spikes.

The Kajain'sa'Nikto, or Red Nikto, come from the Wannschok, or Endless Wastes—the desert region of Kintan. They exhibit a series of ridges on the forehead, with eight horns ringing the eyes, and two horns on the chin. The nose is concealed beneath moving flaps of skin that hang above the mouth. To breathe, they expand the permeable membrane above the mouth, preventing them from inhaling blowing sand, grit, and other contaminants from their desert environment. They also have a pair of breathing membranes that rest on either side of their neck, protected by thin breathing pipes. These also filter out contaminants and capture exhaled water vapor to keep it recycling into their system, allowing them to go for longer periods of time without drinking.

The Kadas'sa'Nikto, or Green Nikto, originated in the forested and coastal regions of Kintan. This race has green-gray skin with visible scales and small horns surrounding the eyes. Green Nikto have visible noses, which are sensitive enough to allow them to pick up the scent of other creatures in a forest or jungle environment. They have long claws that enable them to climb trees.

Mountain Nikto, usually called the Esral'sa'Nikto, are blue-gray in color and have pronounced facial fins that expand from their cheeks. Like the Kajain'sa'Nikto, they have flaps of skin that cover the nose, with permeable membranes above the mouth. Their long fins are lined with small vibrating hairs that enhance hearing. By fully expanding their fins, they can disperse excess heat, and by flattening the fins against their skulls, they insulate themselves against the cold. They also have expanding and contracting neck cavities that disperse or trap heat and recycle moisture in their systems. They have small recessed claws.

The Pale Nikto, or Gluss'sa'Nikto, are white or gray and populate the Gluss'elta Islands, a chain of a dozen islands. These Nikto have ridges of small horns surrounding their eyes, like Kadas'sa'Nikto, but they also have small fins similar to the large fins of the Esral'sa'Nikto.

Finally, the M'shento'su'Nikto, or Southern Nikto, have white, yellow, or orange skin. They do not have horns or fins, but possess a multitude of breather tubes on the back of their skulls, which tend to be much longer than the standard breather tubes. These act as primitive ultrasonic sensory tubes. Scientists believe the extermination of natural predators on Kintan slowed the full development of these organs in other Nikto.

It was because the Nikto races frequently banded together to protect themselves from predators that they eventually became a unified people. The stellar radiation had caused horrific monsters to evolve on their world, and their constant threat caused the Nikto to develop tools of defense, cities with high protective walls, and military strategies. They literally fought themselves to the top of the food chain, burning down forests and swamps to force the most dangerous creatures into extinction. But by doing so, they turned their world into a barren wasteland.

When Nikto astronomers discovered the star M'dweshuu, a strange

cult arose worshipping it with blood sacrifices to appease the spirit of the celestial body. The Cult of M'dweshuu spread quickly across the world, killing thousands of Nikto who did not bow to the cult's beliefs.

After this group ruled Kintan for thirty years, the Hutts visited the planet and witnessed the cult in action. They were interested in taking the star system for themselves, and had already enlisted the Nikto's neighbors, the Klatooinians and the Vodrans, as servants. Churabba the Hutt saw that the cult was suppressing a very disgruntled people. To turn the Nikto to her side, she bombarded the cult's stronghold from space, wiping it out completely. The grateful Nikto people, regarding her as savior, joined the pact that required them—along with the Klatooinians and the Vodrans—to serve the Hutts.

This cult rose again, about 1,000 years before the Battle of Yavin, and temporarily pushed the Hutts off Kintan, but the Hutts sent armies of mercenaries to squash the rebellion. Since then, the Nikto have remained in the service of the Hutts, but not without the occasional unrest.

Because Hutts feel they cannot trust their servants, the Nikto have no real government of their own. They are ruled by an attaché of the Hutt Clans of the Ancients, and this attaché speaks for them on every political level.

Noghri

noghri are hairless, gray-skinned bipeds native to the mostly barren planet Honoghr. They are strong and sinewy creatures, with extraordinarily quick reflexes and inherent agility. They are not tall, but their small size often belies their ruthless and effective skills.

These people are compact killing machines, built to hunt and destroy. They are predators with teeth-filled jaws, large, quick-moving eyes, and an extremely keen sense of smell. This sense of smell is *so* refined that a Noghri can identify a person's bloodline by their scent.

Noghri society is clan oriented, and families often cluster together, creating singular villages. Each clan has a dynast, or clan leader, usually one of the oldest female members, who makes the ultimate decision on all clan affairs. Each clan has a dukha, or community building, within which all major events are held. All village life revolves around this one central meeting place.

The planet Honoghr is a sparse, barren world, with a rapid yearly rotation. Its environmental problems began with a space battle between two Dreadnaughts sometime before the Battle of Yavin. This battle poisoned Honoghr's atmosphere, killing much of the planet's life. After this happened, Lord Darth Vader came to Honoghr and convinced the Noghri that only he and the Empire could repair their damaged environment. In return, he asked that they serve him as assassins and bodyguards. Lord Vader himself related the usefulness of the Noghri to the Imperial cause.

> These small creatures would be a great asset, a useful resource. They are a proud race, despite their size, and they move quietly—so much so that had I not the power of the Force, they would easily have been able to catch me off guard. Their use of weaponry is impressive, and once given, their loyalty is unshakable. With their ability at tracking and their stealth, they will prove useful as bodyguards and assassins.
> I have made arrangements to keep their world subdued for the foreseeable future with continued contamination in the guise of environmental assistance, and already they have shown themselves indebted to me.

The Noghri, who were at the time of Vader's intervention a peaceful agrarian people, felt they had no choice but to agree to Lord Vader's solution. Bound by their word of honor, they served Vader and later Grand Admiral Thrawn, who enlisted the Noghri to be his servants when he announced to them that he was Vader's successor.

It was not long after, as the New Republic was struggling to combat Thrawn's brilliant battle plans, that Princess Leia Organa Solo came to the Noghri to ask them to work with her in

DESIGNATION
> SENTIENT <
....
PLANET OF ORIGIN
> HONOGHR <
....
HEIGHT OF
AVERAGE ADULT
> 1.4 METERS <
....

overthrowing Thrawn. Because of her scent, they recognized her immediately as the daughter of Vader, but refused to help her because of their pledge to Thrawn. They finally agreed to betray him, however, when Leia showed them that the "help" the Empire was giving them was not curing their destroyed world, but poisoning it further, with the goal of keeping them enslaved.

The Noghri were enraged and vowed revenge on Thrawn and the Empire that had maintained the deception for so long. Because they were still trusted by Thrawn, they were able to get close enough to kill him. Then, out of loyalty to Leia, and because of her attempts to truly repair the Honoghr environment, they decided to serve her as personal bodyguards.

Before destroying Thrawn, however, some Noghri began to take their world's environmental woes into their own hands, in an attempt to begin the rebuilding the Empire had always promised. They built what they called "the future," a Hidden Valley near a river, located under a series of cliff walls and visible only from directly above. This place is an agricultural oasis on an otherwise nearly dead world, proving that their environment could be recovered, with the proper care.

In a report she wrote after these events, Leia Organa Solo discusses another discovery she made regarding Vader's first contact with the Noghri.

> One element of the dynast's story gave me pause, and that was the timing of events. She stated that my father had come to Honoghr two generations earlier. When I did the math at the time, I decided it had to be about forty-four standard years, but later I realized that was impossible! If that were the case, my father would have been only six years old!

> After speaking with the environmental team that we had assigned to work with the Noghri, I found that the world's rotation is less than half a standard year, which is much shorter than we originally thought. With all the proper calculations, that means Vader came to Honoghr only twenty-eight years ago. I had made the mistake in thinking that a Noghri generation is twenty years long, when it is less than half that.

the Ortolans, from the ice planet Orto, are short, pudgy bipeds with trunklike noses and beady black eyes. They have floppy ears, small mouths, and hands sporting four chubby fingers and not-quite-opposable thumbs with suction capabilities for manipulating tools. Their bodies are covered with a thick, baggy hide, blanketed with fur that resembles soft velvet.

The Ortolan's trunk possesses an incredible scenting ability, allowing them to smell food up to two kilometers away. It also has extremely sensitive tympanic organs that channel low-wavelength sounds up to their eustachian tubes in their ears. When this input is added to the sounds registered by the normal ears, which are also extremely sensitive, an Ortolan can pick up the entire range from subsonic to ultrasonic sound waves. In fact, much of their language is carried out at these extreme frequencies, so that to observers from other species, they seem to be almost mute, save for the rare times they decide to communicate at normal levels. Their trunks also may be used to generate sound, particularly at the subsonic range.

Food is the most important thing in an Ortolan's life because it is so scarce on their world. The planet Orto is a frozen wasteland that cannot sustain a growing season long enough for solid crops, and most must be grown near the equator for appropriate temperature and water.

Due to this challenging environment, a heavy layer of blubber serves as insulation and provides an auxiliary energy supply for an Ortolan in times when food becomes scarce. Otherwise they eat at every possible opportunity.

Ortolans have few children, and as they are completely developed at birth, parents raise them only to the

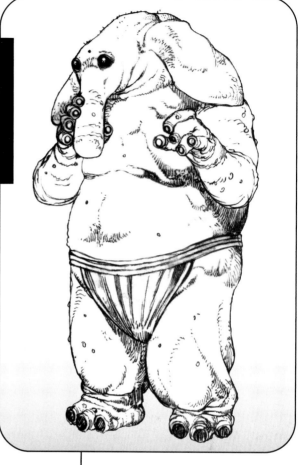

DESIGNATION
> SENTIENT <
....
PLANET OF ORIGIN
> ORTO <
....
HEIGHT OF
AVERAGE ADULT
> 1.4 METERS <
....

age of seven, after which—to help conserve the family's supplies—many are simply thrown out of the house to fend for themselves, unless the child exhibits a talent that's particularly valuable.

Because of their highly developed hearing, the Ortolans' favorite form of entertainment is music. Concerts on Orto feature all levels of sound, from subsonic to ultrasonic. These performances are usually held in food bars and are extremely loud to drown out the sounds of food vendors and eating.

As is revealed in this entry from the memoirs of Sy Snootles, because of their peculiar obsessions, Ortolans are not the best businessmen.

> I could have killed Max—the little blue dope—and I'm a pacifist! All he had to do is look at the size of my mouth and my body to see that I don't eat much. Droopy wasn't happy either. He eats only once a month!

> Jabba was going to pay us in food! But any boss worth working for pays the band and gives them a meal on top of it! I was wrong to let Max run our business affairs. After this fiasco, I vowed to leave and take Droopy with me. If that fool Rebo wants to work for food, then he should just have a solo career.

magestic, dignified, and beautiful, the Oswaft of ThonBoka are, strangely enough, often mistaken for spacecraft. They are intelligent, manta-ray-like creatures that are 500 to 1,000 meters in length and can grow to be a kilometer in diameter. They live in a sack-shaped nebula known as ThonBoka, which is filled with gases, organic molecules, carapace creatures, and interstellar plankton upon which the Oswaft feed. Huge, powerful wings balance their sleek, muscle-covered dorsal surface, and tentaclelike ribbons hang from their ventral sides. Their entire bodies exhibit a glasslike transparency that flashes with inner color.

The Oswaft are long-lived, with documented life spans ranging into the thousands of years. They appear extremely patient and seem to lack any curiosity concerning the galaxy outside their environment. They rarely leave their habitat. Their culture is slow, regimented, and deliberate.

Oswaft feed continuously on molecules and chemicals of the nebula as they move, and they fabricate precious gemstones and other raw materials from chemicals and waste products. In open space, where there are no gases or nutrients to feed them, the Oswaft will starve to death. It is this characteristic that placed them in danger of their lives three years before the Battle of Yavin.

The ThonBoka nebula, a strange formation of stars and special astronomical phenomena, can be entered from only one side. Three blue-white stars in the center of the nebula surround the Cave of Elders, the only architectural structure in ThonBoka, where the Oswaft ruling Council of Elders meets. This cave is made entirely of precious gems and is a scaled-down replica of the ThonBoka nebula itself.

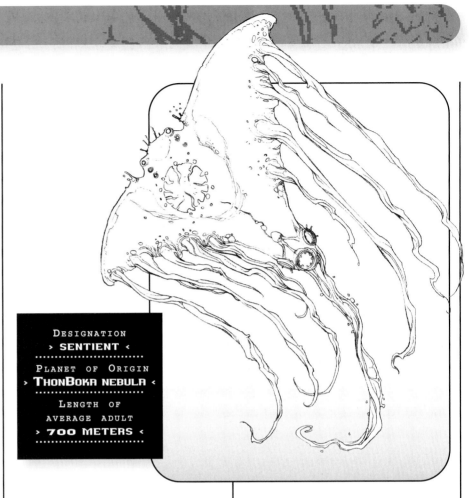

DESIGNATION
> SENTIENT <

PLANET OF ORIGIN
> ThonBoka NEBULA <

LENGTH OF AVERAGE ADULT
> 700 METERS <

Upon discovering the Oswaft, the Emperor viewed as a threat their ability to jump through hyperspace unaided, and sent the Imperial Navy to blockade the entrance to the ThonBoka, intent on preventing the flow of the nutrients and slowly starving its inhabitants. One Oswaft, named Lehesu, escaped and made contact with Lando Calrissian, who agreed to help. Lando ran the Imperial blockade and helped the besieged Oswaft elders fight back against their jailers by having them create "phantom images" of themselves—exuding through their pores waste products that formed the shape of their bodies. The Empire fired weapons at these images, and accidentally fired on ships of their own fleet. Thus the blockade was shattered.

The Oswaft exhibit other remarkable abilities, including a telepathic form of communication that uses electromagnetic pulses similar to those employed in regular ship transmission technology. Lando Calrissian noted:

> *The Oswaft's telepathic ability is so strong that, when used to its full potential, it could be a powerful weapon. The electromagnetic pulses they use to transmit images and pictures as language can overload most ships' internal systems. During the battle with the Centrality fleet at ThonBoka, I encouraged the Oswaft to simply "shout" at the enemy ships. The intensity of the signals destroyed several enemy vessels almost instantly.*

Pa'lowick

Shy, slender-limbed amphibians from the planet Lowick, Pa'lowick have plump, rounded bodies and long, froglike arms and legs. Their skin is very smooth and exhibits a pattern of greens, browns, and yellows, allowing them to easily blend in with their natural, equatorial rain-forest environment. The most distinguishing Pa'lowick attribute is a thin, tubelike trunk, which sprouts from the center of each individual's face, ending in almost incongruous humanlike lips. Some Pa'lowick possess a second mouth, with tusks resting just beneath their trunk. Youthful Pa'lowick retain this extra mouth through young adulthood, at which time it disappears, absorbed into their facial skin.

The second mouth helps the youthful Pa'lowick gain more nutrition during its growing years, as the trunks take in only a limited amount of food at a time. Adults require a lesser amount of food and energy, and so the extra mouth disappears. The tusks, which fall off at the same time the mouth is absorbed, provide young Pa'lowick an extra means of defending themselves.

Pa'lowick bodies are made for their marshy home on Lowick. Their long legs allow them to move easily through the still, murky waters, hunting for fish, reptiles, and waterfowl. Their snouts are perfect for eating giant marlello duck eggs, which they puncture with their tongues to suck the yolk through their tubelike mouths. Their eyes, which rest at the end of two stalks sprouting from their foreheads, allow them to hide underwater while keeping an eye out for predators.

Pa'lowick reproduce by laying eggs, and the female will guard the eggs in her home until they hatch. They live in roofed, hutlike nests made of dried mud, reeds, and grass. Children are raised and educated within their largely agrarian communities, which are run along a feudal system of noble families. A rather primitive people, they use only minimal technology provided by traders and prospectors. Miners looking for valuable Lowickan firegems discovered the species only ten years before the Battle of Endor.

One Pa'lowick who has made a name for herself is Sy Snootles, the renowned lead singer of the Max Rebo band. In her journal, she writes of her people.

> In my culture, vocal music is a sacred tradition, and it is the one thing that has kept me alive all this time. If I couldn't sing, what would I have done? All of us in the band have the same history—all of us were kidnapped from our homes, and all of us survived through our music. Perhaps that's what made us so close—except when Max annoyed us, of course.
> In any event, it was because Jabba liked my voice that he provided me with enough water to bathe twice a day so I would be properly hydrated. He wanted my voice in top shape. Jabba hinted once that he and I might share the bathwater together, since he, too, preferred to rest in water. I'm glad I escaped the palace before that could happen. I couldn't have stood the shame.

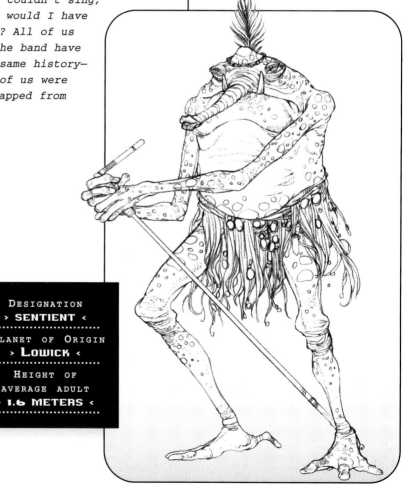

DESIGNATION
> SENTIENT <

PLANET OF ORIGIN
> LOWICK <

HEIGHT OF AVERAGE ADULT
> 1.6 METERS <

Phindian

The Phindians are tall, thin, mournful-looking beings with dark skin that sometimes exhibits white splotches. White circles surround yellow or gold eyes. Phindians have long, flexible arms that hang below their knees.

Phindians are most known for their contrary cultural attitude. They tend to be sarcastic, or exaggerate to an extreme. This is part of their normal social pattern, and most offworlders find it annoying, as Phindians will often avoid getting to the point of a discussion simply because they like to talk.

The planet Phindar was, at the time of the Old Republic, ruled by a powerful criminal organization simply called the Syndicat. This organization, also run by Phindians, controlled the food and supplies that were delivered to the populace. By controlling these goods, they controlled the people. In addition, anyone who rebelled or protested was "renewed"—they had their memories wiped as if they were simple droids. These people were then sent to other worlds and cut loose, so that members of the Syndicat could bet on how they would survive.

Through the efforts of Obi-Wan Kenobi and his Jedi Master, Qui-Gon Jinn, this Syndicat was eventually overthrown. The two Jedi aided the people in regaining control over their supplies and food, so that they could control and rebuild their own society. Then, for the first time in several hundred years, they held a democratic election and selected a government.

Phindians are a technologically advanced people and were using new technologies and flying starships long before the Syndicat took control of their world. It was this technical mastery that helped their scientists invent the mind-wiping devices used on many of their own people. The scientists

DESIGNATION
> **SENTIENT** <

PLANET OF ORIGIN
> **PHINDAR** <

HEIGHT OF AVERAGE ADULT
> **1.7 METERS** <

were forced to do their work under duress, and when they finished, their Syndicat masters showed their gratitude by having the scientists' minds wiped. This technology has since been made illegal on their world.

The Phindian people show great affection for family and friends. Their ritual for parting is described in the following entry from Senior Anthropologist Hoole's notes, nearly fifty years before the Battle of Yavin.

> As I stood at the ramp to my ship, my friend Karke came to me and squeezed me three times, encircling my body completely with her long arms. Each hug symbolizes an emotion in parting: sadness that the parting must happen, joy that the friendship continues, and hope that the parties will see each other again.
> I was honored that my friend gave me such an exclusively Phindian gesture, and I hugged her three times back. I've promised to write her often. She smirked and said sarcastically that I was getting too sentimental, so I'd better get out of there.

Pho Ph'eahian

The Pho Ph'eahians of Pho Ph'eah are a bipedal, humanlike species with four arms and bright blue fur. Because of their color, they stand out in a crowd, and as they are a gregarious species, they often enjoy being the center of attention.

Their homeworld Pho Ph'eah offers standard gravity and diverse terrains. What makes it unique is that it receives little light from its star. Geothermal forces warm the planet when it is in the "dark" portion of its orbit. The Pho Ph'eahians' fur acts as an extra thermal layer, locking heat in their bodies and trapping moisture in their circulatory systems.

They are a mountain-dwelling people, and their arms suit them for climbing up rocky cliffs in search of food. Pho Ph'eahians are omnivorous. They eat the small animals that roam their mountain homeland, as well as vegetables that are grown in large farms. Their agriculture is extremely high tech, and they pride themselves on inventing new methods of food production.

Few Pho Ph'eahians travel off their world, but when they do, their cheerful disposition and outgoing personalities make them crowd pleasers and natural entertainers.

When the Old Republic first made contact with the Pho Ph'eahians thousands of years ago, they had already developed nuclear fusion and limited in-system space flight. Since then, they have made technology their prime industry, developing new stardrives, weapons, and other high-tech exports. Pho Ph'eahians are often employed as mechanics and engineers in spaceports—particularly in the Corporate Sector—and are paid very well for their services.

In the following log entry recorded by Han Solo, he tells of one other unique characteristic exhibited by Pho Ph'eahians.

> One time, while some Pho Ph'eahians helped us fix the Millennium Falcon, Chewie and I discovered something really weird about them. They're clean. I mean really clean. We had two Pho Ph'eahian mechanics helping us, and both were hung up on keeping their hands free of grime. They constantly wiped off their hands—all four of them—and kept using my 'fresher to wash up. They kept towels hooked to their belts as they worked, and every once in a while, they'd pull a fresh one from their packs.

> I finally got up the nerve to ask them about it, and the head guy Garv answered cheerylike, "Our bodies are sacred manifestations of our spirit, you see? While we can get dirty in our work, we cannot let it rest too long on our skin or it will stain our soul."

> So, it was a religious thing. Realizing this, I warned them that if they kept using the 'fresher on the Falcon to wash up, they'd have to refill my water tanks when they were done. They laughed—like they always do—and said they'd be happy to do it.

> Weird guys. Really, really weird.

DESIGNATION
> SENTIENT <

PLANET OF ORIGIN
> PHO PH'ERH <

HEIGHT OF AVERAGE ADULT
> 1.7 METERS <

Piranha-beetle

iranha-beetles of Yavin 4 are extraordinarily dangerous swarming insects that literally eat the flesh off their prey. They are iridescent, blue creatures about three centimeters long, with wings and extremely sharp mandibles.

These insects live at the top of large trees in hives that they construct from their saliva and chewed vegetation. Like most hive-based insects, they have a queen that administrates the reproductive and nutritional needs of the hive. She emits the signal that instructs a group of beetles to swarm and find food, which is brought back to the hive for the entire group. The swarm will charge through the forest and attack any creature it finds.

Only one person has ever been known to survive a full attack from a swarm of piranha-beetles. Bevel Lemelisk, one of the Death Star's chief designers, described the unenviable experience.

> The Emperor was not pleased when the Death Star was destroyed, and I was chosen to suffer as an example.
> As I stood in a cage, he released the piranha-beetles through holes in the floor. One bit me, then at the smell of blood the others swarmed over me. Mandibles with serrated razor edges cut into my flesh, slicing through the skin on my thighs, chest, and cheeks. Thousands and thousands more swarmed at me. They buzzed in my ears, tearing at my eyes, blinding me.
> I screamed and begged, but the Emperor laughed at my pain. After I was blinded, I could feel the pain for an hour or so afterwards, then—
> I woke up, whole, in a new body. The Emperor had found me important enough to clone me, giving me the warning that he'd find a more interesting way to kill me next time, if I failed him again.

When the Alliance set up its base on Yavin 4, before their battle with the first Death Star, a group of hapless scouts accidentally stumbled upon a nest of these creatures. Concerned that the piranha-beetles could swarm into the base, they sprayed insecticide around the base perimeter to keep them at bay.

This practice continued when Luke Skywalker established his Jedi academy at the same location. But after exposure to the insecticide made some of the younger students ill, he used the Force to imprint a sense of "distaste" and "disorientation" to the academy area. The intangible Force ward, as it came to be called, confuses the beetles and turns them around so that they return to the forest.

DESIGNATION
> NONSENTIENT <
....
PLANET OF ORIGIN
> YAVIN 4 <
....
LENGTH OF
AVERAGE ADULT
> .03 METERS <
....

Priapulin

Priapulins are nonviolent amphibious gastropods that, unlike many such creatures, possess a rudimentary skeletal structure. Their spine is made up of five knobby notochords—cartilage-type growths—arranged around their four-meter-long, tubular bodies. When in confined quarters, they usually fold themselves in an S-like curve designed to take up less space.

At the top of a Priapulin's body are three pairs of rimmed, deep purple eyes that allow the Priapulin to see in all directions at once. Protruding along the body are long, flexible spines in varying shapes—tiny hooks, spatulas, and thorny balls. These act as digits used for manipulating tools. The underside of the Priapulin's form and lower tail, or foot, is covered with a brush of thick bristles that constantly rub against each other.

An aquatic species, they need to be in water almost constantly and can die quickly in arid environments. They even tell time in terms of the tidal shifts of their world; one tidal hour equals ten galactic standard hours. Priapulins speak Basic in smooth whispers, producing tones by rubbing their bristles together near their breathing vents, and so manage to convey the most subtle of emotions. Their native language is not understandable to—or pronounceable by—most outsiders.

The Priapulins long ago took to space, despite their need to remain in moist environments. They created unique spacecraft designed to suit their needs, filling the craft with living food and sealing the outer hull to hold a cycling system of water pools.

There is no competition in their culture. As on their world, the system of teamwork they maintain among their spaceship crews is distinctly symbiotic. An example of this type of symbiotic cooperation is the relationship Priapulins maintain with small creatures called food-kin, who provide their nourishment. These creatures are small and hard-shelled and possess many claws. They are proud to fulfill their role as food, and once a Priapulin consumes them, their offspring remain inside the Priapulin's body. After a time, the Priapulin gives birth to, and cares for, the food-kin's babies, who in turn act as food, and so on.

Though they are pacifists, during the time of the Empire some Priapulins resorted to piracy. One such Priapulin was Charza Kwinn, a pilot from the days of the Old Republic, who wrote in this personal log entry:

> After raiding the stores of the Imperial freighter vessel I'd conquered, I sat down with my food-kin to share what I'd gained through my efforts. They were clicking their claws in joy over the food I had acquired for them, but I found myself feeling very sad as I watched them eat.

> Once I was a proud pilot, shuttling Jedi Knights and dignitaries throughout the well-traveled spaceways. Now I hide in shadows and attack those who would prey on us. Once I would say I was a peaceful being, who had no interest in harming another living being. Now I prey on the Imperial humans, as they would prey upon others. Will I have a soul when I am done?

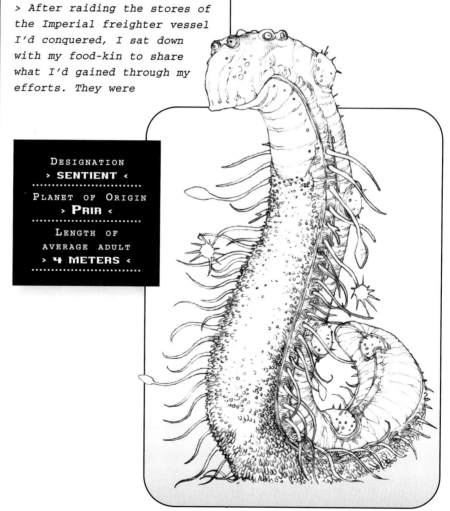

DESIGNATION
> SENTIENT <

PLANET OF ORIGIN
> PRIA <

LENGTH OF AVERAGE ADULT
> 4 METERS <

Psadans are short, stocky, bipedal humanoids who share the world Wayland with their less combative neighbors, the Myneyrshi. Because thick, stonelike scales cover their bodies, and irregular, lumpy plates form a sort of shell over their backs, scientists believe the Psadans evolved from hard-shelled mammals. This hard shell starts at the forehead, covers the head, then trails down the back to midwaist. The front torso is covered by smaller, tightly packed plates. This shell protects them from predators and, in combat, makes them extremely hard to kill. They can withstand a blaster bolt with only mild damage. The shells do have some nerve endings, however, so a Psadan whose shell has been cracked or damaged does experience pain.

Like the Myneyrshi, the Psadans are primitive, possessing and utilizing little technology. They fight with clubs, spears, and knives, and while they have warred with the Myneyrshi for centuries, they found common ground when the humans came and subjugated them. The clone Jedi Master Joruus C'baoth, acting as a self-proclaimed guardian, forced the two species to live together and ruled them through intimidation and abuse.

This is a strong-willed people with a strict religious belief system in which they worship nature. When they kill an animal for food, all parts of the animal are used. Their clothes, weapons, tools, homes, and utensils are all taken from various animal parts. Their neighbors, the Myneyrshi, maintain similar traditions, so when the two species banded together to fight the Empire, they found they had more in common than they had previously believed.

Because the Psadans are an obstinate people, Joruus C'baoth had great difficulty controlling them, as he indicated in his writings.

> Today I found a Psadan fighting with one of the humans. After forcing them both to their knees, I demanded that they reconcile. The Psadan smiled, nodded, then turned to the human and spit on him.
> The fight started again so furiously that I had to strike them both with lightning to get them to stop. I've had them thrown into solitary confinement booths for two weeks. But even then, the Psadan defies me, refusing to eat as long as he is confined.

DESIGNATION
> **SENTIENT** <

PLANET OF ORIGIN
> **WAYLAND** <

HEIGHT OF
AVERAGE ADULT
> **1.5 METERS** <

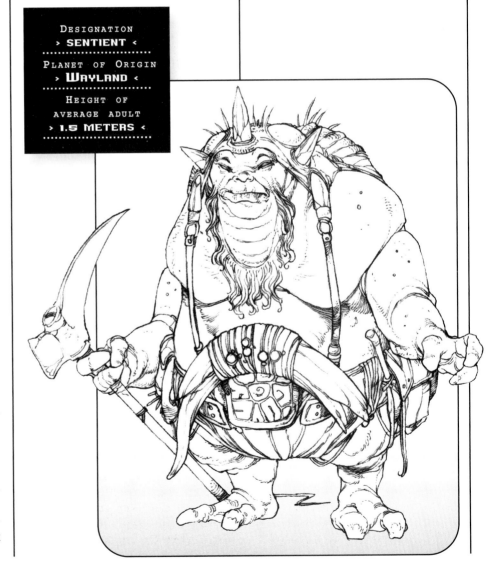

Pterosaur

Pterosaurs are large, carnivorous reptiles that soar through the skies of the planet Ammuud in the Corporate Sector. Their bony skeletons create an almost gliderlike frame upon which their skin, tough and leather-like, is stretched. They have two extra appendages that serve as legs, and a long tail that gives them balance as they glide through the air. They can stand upright on their hind legs and use their tail for additional support when they need to.

These creatures lay eggs in nests perched in high trees and on mountain cliffs on Ammuud, far away from enemies. They have keen eyesight that enables them to see prey from a kilometer above. They are predators, feeding mainly on small reptiles and land mammals. Upon seeing prey, they fold their wings inward and dive toward the creature, clamping it in their claws or strong beak.

Like most reptiles, pterosaurs are cold-blooded. They thrive in the warmer, more humid areas of Ammuud's surface. During cooler evening hours they tend to sleep and huddle against one another for warmth.

The royal families of Ammuud have kept some pterosaurs in captivity for racing and riding purposes. During the ancient times of Ammuud this was one of the primary forms of entertainment. As the people of Ammuud have plunged into clan-focused wars, these activities are now infrequent.

In this log entry, dated before the Battle of Yavin, the noted Tynnan executive named Odumin observed that these creatures apparently make good hang gliders.

> It was one of the most brilliant things I'd ever seen.
> In [Han] Solo's absence,

Chewbacca chose to place a sky-scan sensor on a ridge above where the Millennium Falcon was placed, so he'd spot attackers coming in from out of our view in the valley below. A herd of grazers was milling peacefully near the Falcon, *and while the Wookiee set up the equipment, the creatures were spooked by pterosaurs. I was trapped with the ship, and Chewie was stuck on the hill above, with the raging herd rumbling toward him.*
> *A couple of pterosaurs spotted Chewbacca and decided to attack. He shot them with his bowcaster, then, taking the tripod he'd used to set up the equipment, he placed the carcass of a pterosaur over it. He spread two of the tripod's legs to maximum length and curled the leading edge of the wings over them, fixing the wings in place with clamps. He then fixed a*

bracing member from the equipment as a king post.
> *He worked quickly, as the stampeding grazers neared. Just as I thought there was no hope, he finished his work and held up—something that looked like a hang glider. He launched himself from the cliff and aimed for the* Falcon *and freedom.*

DESIGNATION
> **NONSENTIENT** <

PLANET OF ORIGIN
> **AMMUUD** <

LENGTH OF AVERAGE ADULT
> **2 METERS** <

urella spiders are native to Yavin 8, the eighth moon orbiting the gas giant Yavin. Yavin 8 is also home to the Melodies, the native humanoid amphibian species, who are occasionally the victims of the purellas' clever hunting techniques.

The purella spiders are large, red arachnids that feed on Melodies and the local rodents known as raiths. Each spider has eight double-jointed legs and huge mandibles that they use for rending their prey into small pieces. Their orange glowing eyes allow them to see in the dark.

Purellas are somewhat sentient, able to determine strategy and to patiently hunt their prey. They can sense the presence of nearing creatures, and Melodies have reported that a spider can even telepathically enhance a victim's fear. It's as if the purella prefers the taste of a victim that is afraid. Normally, a purella will drop onto an intended victim and attack first with a bite of venom that will instantly immobilize the hapless target. The four barbed pincers that line its mouth are venomous, and while the bite causes the victim to become paralyzed, the mind remains active.

Like the arachnors of Arzid, purellas spin webs that are extremely strong and sticky. There's no escaping from this web once a victim is ensnared. This same web acts as a type of alarm system, picking up the slightest tremors of movement from nearby tunnels and alerting the purella to the presence of potential prey. Anakin Solo once encountered a purella on Yavin 8, and he wrote about it in his daily student journal.

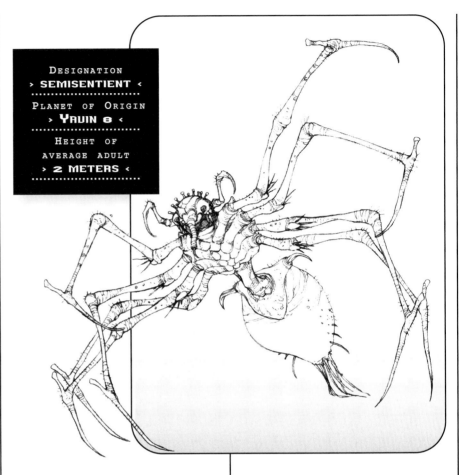

DESIGNATION
> SEMISENTIENT <
....
PLANET OF ORIGIN
> YAVIN 8 <
....
HEIGHT OF
AVERAGE ADULT
> 2 METERS <

> When we went to Yavin 8, Lyric, Tahiri, and I struck out on our own to investigate some interesting hieroglyphs in the caves. It didn't turn out to be a good idea, though, because we were attacked by a purella.
> Unfortunately, it managed to corner us and strike us with its sharp pincers, leaving us temporarily paralyzed. Then it put us in its web, where we couldn't move. I was worried that it was going to eat us, and then I got an idea as I watched it move across the web. When it walked across the gooey strands, it was careful not to let the bristles on its skin touch the web. It was worried about getting caught in its own sticky goo!

> By the time I'd realized this, the poison that paralyzed us had begun to wear off. So Tahiri and I worked together to bounce the web, pushing harder and harder and using the Force to help us, creating waves in the web to knock the purella off balance.
> It worked. The spider stumbled, rolled on its back, and was stuck in her own web. That bought Tahiri time to get her multitool to cut us free.

Pydyrian

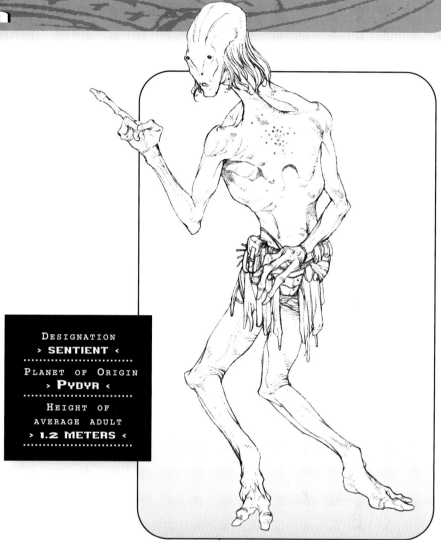

the Pydyrians were once a proud, wealthy race until the Almanian warlord known as Kueller destroyed them. Only a small number of them survived, consisting of those who were considered useful to Kueller in his campaign to acquire riches and power. Before their destruction, the Pydyrian people were highly advanced in the sciences, particularly in medicine. They were the ones who first developed the healing stick, a device that is kept in most standard med kits, used for mending minor injuries.

Pydyrians are small people who scientists believe evolved from flightless birds. They possess thin, long faces and slender arms and legs, with three fingers on each hand and three toes on each foot. What links them to their bird ancestry is their legs, which bend backwards rather than forward like most other humanoid races.

The wealth of Pydyr's populace—before its destruction—was legendary. The world yielded valuable seafah jewels, with which they decorated their homes and businesses. Their cities were built primarily of mudbrick adorned with frescoes and seafah jewel mosaics. Pydyrians used droids for all menial tasks, spending most of their lives in perfect luxury. Droids cleaned streets and buildings, cooked meals, taught classes, and generally kept Pydyrian society functioning.

Over a period of time, Kueller had all droids supplied to Pydyr fitted with explosives. At a predetermined time, every droid found in the cities and homes of Pydyr exploded, and 1.5 million Pydyrians were killed instantly. Kueller sold the jeweled houses and possessions to disreputable art dealers, keeping only a thousand Pydyrians alive because they were trained as seafah jewelers. Meanwhile, he continued to harvest Pydyr's natural wealth

DESIGNATION
> **SENTIENT** <
....
PLANET OF ORIGIN
> **PYDYR** <
....
HEIGHT OF AVERAGE ADULT
> **1.2 METERS** <
....

until Luke Skywalker and his friends stopped him.

Pydyr's naïveté was the crux of Kueller's plan. In this report, the Pydyrian minister of security addressed his fellow council members before the tragedy.

> I cannot help feeling that our esteemed council is making a mistake. Again they cut back on defense and security spending, while plunging more money into medical development and local businesses.
> Though this is laudable in and of itself, the truth of the matter is that we are cutting back on much-needed security measures. In addition, our military languishes, suffering from a lack of staff and equipment, as we delude ourselves with the belief that New Republic forces can get here to save us in time in the eventuality that we are attacked.
> Ours is a wealthy world, and one day someone is going to see us as a victim just begging to be robbed. We are literally inviting them into our coffers, along with our homes and families.

Qom Jha and Qom Qae

Qom Jha and Qom Qae are two peoples native to the Nirauan system and who share the same genetic background. They appear as a cross between the mynock and the bat, as is evidenced by their leathery wings, small snouts, and rows of tiny sharp teeth. They have sharp talons on their feet, allowing them to perch on small outcroppings of rock and branches. The Qom Jha like to perch upside down on stalactites like bats, while Qom Qae will perch upright on cliffs or rocks. They both possess large eyes, but each has different vision abilities, due primarily to their environments. The Qom Jha can see better in darkened spaces, whereas the Qom Qae can see better and for great distances in bright light.

The larger, darker-skinned Qom Jha live in the caves of Nirauan, while the smaller, brown-skinned Qom Qae live in cliff nestings in the open air. These two clans are greatly at odds, each claiming to have been wronged by the other in the past. Despite their differences, they banded together to help Luke Skywalker and Mara Jade infiltrate the Hand of Thrawn, an Imperial stronghold on their world.

Each clan of the Qom Jha and Qom Qae is led by a Bargainer, one of the elders of the group. Only the Bargainer is able to speak for the good of an entire clan, and their rulings are obeyed without question. If a member of the tribe disobeys a Bargainer's orders, that individual is punished severely or even exiled.

These species are marginally Force-sensitive and can communicate almost telepathically. They read surface thoughts and feelings and can determine the intentions of an intruder who may approach their nesting. It was this last ability that made them aware that the human settlers in the Imperial fortress were not their

DESIGNATION
> SENTIENT <

PLANET OF ORIGIN
> NIRAUAN <

LENGTH OF
AVERAGE ADULT
> 1 METER <

friends, and compelled them to aid Skywalker.

In a log entry recorded after his experiences at the Hand of Thrawn, Luke Skywalker notes the Qom Jha and Qom Qae, and their form of communication.

> What was most interesting is how I found I could communicate with them. They would speak aloud through a series of chirping sounds, and at the same time project "packets" of information and images at their intended recipients—almost certainly through the Force. To my ears it sounded like gibberish, but my mind understood. Mara had a little difficulty understanding, but then it does take some getting used to. The longer she was around them, the more she understood.
> I've encountered other creatures now who can influence or make use of the Force: for example, the ysalamiri and the vornskrs. Unlike these, however, the Qom Jha and Qom Qae are sentient. I've told Leia about them, hoping that when the cleanup crews and New Republic Intelligence teams go to Nirauan, we'll establish formal contact with them.

he cautious amphibious creatures known as the Quarren share the world Mon Calamari with the forward-thinking Mon Calamari species. The Quarren possess leathery orange skin, turquoise eyes, and suction-cupped fingers. Since four tentacles sprout from the lower half of their faces, they have earned the not-so-flattering nickname Squid Heads, by which they are known to outsiders.

While the Mon Calamari are dreamers and idealists, the Quarren are more practical and conservative. They've made a place for themselves in the galaxy acting as accountants and business managers. Despite this, not many leave their home planet, as they prefer their peaceful ocean life to the vastness of the star-studded void.

The two species share a common native tongue, but while the Mon Calamari have almost completely stopped using the language in favor of Basic, the Quarren continue to speak their own language regularly, unless they find themselves dealing with outsiders.

Through years of contact that was sometimes filled with conflict, the Mon Calamari built a political friendship with the Quarren. The Mon Calamari encouraged the Quarren to work with them in pursuing dreams of space and advanced science. While the Mon Calamari provided the ideas, the Quarren provided the raw materials, then worked with tools and technology they helped the Mon Calamari to create. Together they built impressive ships ideal for deep space travel and their impressive floating cities that dominate the Mon Calamari oceans.

These giant cities extend far below the surface of the water and serve as centers of learning, culture, and government. In contrast to the Mon Calamari people, who prefer more daylight and live in the upper levels of the cities, the Quarren live in the lowest levels of each metropolis, in the cool security of the deep. This fits with their cultural identity as a pragmatic people, unwilling to trust or embrace the new idea or lofty concept. Their literature reveals a people who do not dream of brighter tomorrows, but hold fast to remembered yesterdays. In this, they feel they belong in the sea, not in space.

And yet, many Quarren have followed their neighbors offplanet. As they benefited from the discoveries and achievements of the Mon Calamari, they have grown dependent upon them. This dependency often has caused friction between the two peoples, and may have prompted the Quarren to betray their ocean partners the day the Imperial fleet arrived.

On that day, Mon Calamari's planetary defense systems failed to protect them from invasion. Rumors persist that the Quarren aided the Imperials by sabotaging the protective network. Regardless, the planet was overrun.

The Empire enslaved both the Quarren and the Mon Calamari and forced them to work in labor camps. In this, the two species found a unifying cause and cooperated in a plan of passive resistance. The Empire retaliated by destroying whole cities, filling the ocean with the blood of both species. This served only to incite these peaceful peoples to rise up in rage, and using only primitive utensils, hand tools, and sheer force of will, they drove their Imperial taskmasters off of their world.

Today, Quarren and Mon

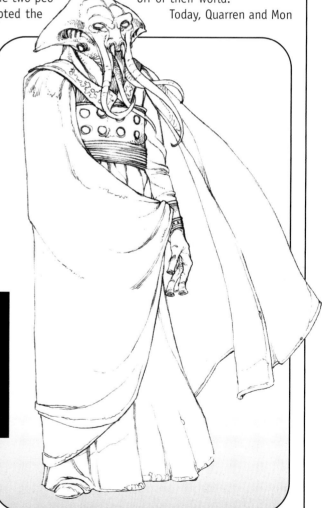

DESIGNATION
> SENTIENT <
....
PLANET OF ORIGIN
> MON CALAMARI <
....
HEIGHT OF
AVERAGE ADULT
> 1.7 METERS <
....

Calamari live in peace with each other, although there still is some trace of lingering resentment. However, one sign that healing is occurring between the two peoples is that more inter-species romances are being recorded, such as the ill-fated relationship involving two Rogue Squadron pilots: Ibtisam, a Mon Calamari, and Nrin Vakil, a Quarren. Ibtisam was killed in action, shot down in an Imperial ambush, and at the memorial service on Mon Calamari, Nrin gave a moving eulogy.

> Ibtisam was my friend and my love. We started out not liking each other much, but it didn't take us long to come together in friendship as colleagues and fellow sol-diers.
> It grew beyond that, of course. I quickly began to recognize her beauty. She was attractive in appearance, in heart, in thought, and in deed. I was proud that she'd come from my world, proud that as children we shared the same oceans, and overjoyed that we discovered we had so many things in common, so many things we valued that were the same.
> She died a hero. She died my friend. She died my love. She died knowing she sacri-ficed herself for the Republic of her heart, but also the people of her homeworld, one unified and inseparable popu-lation inhabiting this great world of ours.
> She died for all of us here, Mon Calamari and Quarren. She had learned, as I did, the strength and value of the other. She and I were

so proud to stand side by side, representing our world in the greatest group of sol-diers and pilots this galaxy has ever known. Holding hands in love, we reached across a chasm that had separated our peoples for centuries, but was really only a few centimeters wide.
> To honor her memory, I call upon each of you to reach out today to someone who is the other. Realize that the

ocean you think separates us is really only a puddle. We are one people of Mon Calamari. For Ibtisam's sake, we should be proud of that, and we should also be joyful that we have each other to lean on and to count on when the oceans are turbulent.

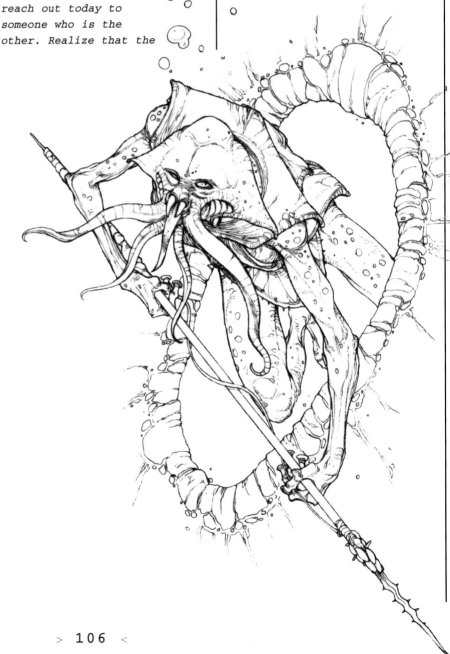

Ranat

ranats of Aralia are rodents that actually evolved on the world Rydar II, near their current home Aralia. Unfortunately, they tended to kidnap human infants for food, so the Rydarian people killed every Ranat on Rydar, with the exception of three who stowed away on a merchant ship. That ship later crashed on Aralia—after the Ranats had devoured the crew—and those three gave birth to the beginnings of a population that now numbers into the millions.

The Ranats are small and have thin, muscular, fur-covered bodies that are slightly flat, making them capable of squeezing through very small openings. Their fur runs dirty yellow to a dark, rusty brown, and their tails are scaled and hairless. They have pale yellow noses, black whiskers, small, round, black eyes, and naked pink ears. A Ranat's most notable feature is the incisors that jut up from the bottom jaw like a pair of sharp knives.

In the period following Imperial rule, an entrepreneur named Hayzo Trebors, believing Aralia unpopulated, decided to build an amusement park there. As construction began, workers discovered the Ranats. The project ended in disaster, and resulted in the Ranats' original misdesignation as semisentient, as this journal entry written by Trebors reveals.

> We hoped that the agreement Governor Targan of Rydar II and I made for the development of Aralia would be a lucrative one for all parties, and we jumped right in, starting construction without hesitation.
> Then my construction manager came to me concerning the rodent problem. I hired pest controllers, but these ferocious rodents organized armies

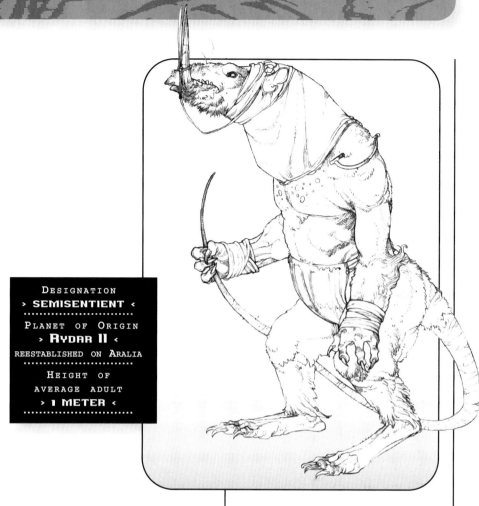

DESIGNATION
> SEMISENTIENT <
....
PLANET OF ORIGIN
> RYDAR II <
REESTABLISHED ON ARALIA
....
HEIGHT OF
AVERAGE ADULT
> 1 METER <
....

and exterminated my exterminators. The union wasn't happy.
> Then I got an idea. If these smelly critters were formally declared, by an Imperial government official, to be only semisentient, they would have no claims to the land, and we could wipe them out using the most extreme measures available to us.

Because Ranats have been proved to possess language, their semisentient designation is being reconsidered by the New Republic. Though they use no advanced technology, they are intelligent and will often collect pieces of technology for entertainment value.

Most Ranat populations use their incisors and claws to tunnel under the jungle soil to build their sprawling underground towns. Because their incisors grow as much as one centimeter in a standard hour, Ranats must gnaw constantly to keep them at a reasonable length.

At least twice a year, female Ranats mate with as many males as possible. About 120 days later, each female bears three to six young, then moves them into the town nursery, where all mothers care for the children of the town. As soon as an infant is capable of a firm grip, it is allowed to wander to the world above. Children reach adulthood in three years, and Ranats live only until they reach twenty years of age. Because they reproduce so frequently, however, their population shows no signs of decreasing.

ancors are huge creatures that are found on several worlds throughout the galaxy. There are several different varieties of rancors, but all have relatively the same physiology and temperament. Their homeworld is unknown, but most research points to their origin on Dathomir. How they managed to spread to so many different systems is still a mystery, but most scientists believe they were taken to some worlds by sentient species who used these massive creatures as battle mounts or beasts of burden.

Standing on two trunklike legs, upward of ten meters tall, rancors provide an intimidating sight to those who face them. Their hides are often a combination of gray, green, and brown in color, and they exhibit glistening black eyes and huge fangs. Their long, somewhat slender arms are out of proportion when compared with the rest of their muscular bodies. They have long, sharp claws on their fingers and toes.

Rancors are fearsome fighters. Their fists can smash prey flat, while their massive jaws enable them to swallow human-sized morsels whole. Their thick, powerful hides make them highly resistant to blasters and other handheld energy weapons. Even melee weapons cannot puncture their tough layers of skin.

Despite their fierce fighting abilities, the rancors actually prove to be inherently benign when they are well fed and allowed to live alongside their own kind. They can be domesticated and trained for riding or to haul goods, as in the case of the Witches of Dathomir, who also trained them to perform construction labor.

Rancors are a hard-to-classify species, exhibiting characteristics of both mammals and reptiles. Like mammals, rancors give birth to live young rather than lay eggs. Like reptiles, rancors do not suckle their young, but

like mammals, they do care for their young. Babies are always born in pairs, and the twins cling to their mother's back and belly. The mother is gentle with her relatively small three-meter-tall children—showing a gentle, loving nature that is often incongruous with her fearsome appearance. Once grown, rancors are solitary creatures that come together only to mate.

Jabba the Hutt's palace rancor-keeper named Malakili revealed the strong bond that many humans are able to form with these creatures.

> Today my rancor died. Jabba wouldn't let me feed him properly, and mistreated him by making him fight all sorts of creatures. Jabba let him be fed only when Jabba was angry with someone. While that occurred frequently, it wasn't every day, and the animal needed regular nourishment. Jabba insisted that the rancor

should remain hungry so he could make a good show.
> That was just not right.
> Jabba totally misjudged the creature's nature, because of its appearance. They are really sweet and gentle creatures, especially when fed. My rancor saved me from the Sand People. He even played fetch! Is that the behavior of a monster?
> Now Jabba's dead—killed by an ally of the Jedi that killed my rancor. Serves him right.

DESIGNATION
> NONSENTIENT <
....
PLANET OF ORIGIN
> UNKNOWN <
....
HEIGHT OF
AVERAGE ADULT
> 10 METERS <
....

Rishii

an avian species, the Rishii live in the mountains of the planet Rishi. They are a primitive, tribal people with an accepting and agreeable attitude toward outsiders. This species has a pair of large, feathered wings that enable them to fly at great speeds. Their wings are attached to their humanlike arms and hands, which end in nimble fingers that make the Rishii dexterous tool-users, though they haven't advanced much beyond working simple utensils made of bone, wood, and stone.

These bird-people are excellent hunters because their senses are extremely sharp, particularly those of sight and hearing. The weapon of choice is a sling, because it can be used while the hunter is perched or in flight. The Rishii can also swoop down from great heights to clutch small rodents and mammals in their talon-like fingers.

The Rishii have little interest in modern technology. Those items that have been traded to them have become nest liners and perch decorations. The Rishii have been intrigued, however, by the "shiny rocks"—that is, spaceships—that allow other beings to fly like they do.

Family groups live together in open-air nests built on cliff perches. Members of each tribe live and work together peacefully, and families are determined to respect members of other tribes who visit their nesting place. Because all offworlders are strange to them, they have an equal acceptance of humans and other aliens who have settled in the hot, humid lowlands, though they don't understand why anyone would want to live there.

The Rishii exhibit a special talent for learning languages. They mimic others and are able to reproduce the words perfectly, no matter what the language. The results can yield odd responses, as in the case of a student studying the Rishii.

> As the professor and I neared a couple of Rishii perched on branches, they eyed us curiously.
> "Hello," I said clearly, bowing my head slightly.
> "Hello," the Rishii said in return, bowing his head.
> "What is your name?" I asked.
> "What is your name?"
> "No," I said more sternly. "What is your name?"
> "No. What is your name?"
> I sighed. "Do you live around here?"
> "Do you live around here?"
> "Can you tell me about your people?"
> "Can you tell me about your people?"
> "That's it," I said, frustrated. "This is impossible! How do you communicate with these things?"
> "That's it. This is impossible! How do you communicate with these things?"
> "Shut up!"
> "Shut up!"
> I rolled my eyes and sighed, and the Rishii imitated my gestures. Aggravated beyond belief, I marched back to camp, hearing the professor chuckling behind me.

DESIGNATION
> SENTIENT <

PLANET OF ORIGIN
> RISHI <

HEIGHT OF AVERAGE ADULT
> 1.6 METERS <

Rodian

the Rodians are humanoids who are renowned as hunters. They possess multifaceted eyes, thin, tapering snouts, and green, scaly skin. Their long, thin fingers have suction cups at the ends, and a ridged spine crests at the tops of their skulls, evidence of their unique reptilian ancestry.

Early in their history, the rock-climbing lizards who were the Rodians' defenseless ancestors developed tools and weapons in their quest for survival. They concentrated on honing their hunting skills for acquiring food, and because they focused on hunting game, they never developed agricultural skills. The act of hunting became an ingrained part of their culture. Rodians sought honors from society—especially the Grand Protector, the leader of their civilization—in recognition for their hunting skills. For this reason, the Rodian people are, to this day, obsessed with the hunt and with the violence that results.

Their original targets were predators native to Rodia, but after a time, all predators that the Rodians hunted became extinct. When this happened, the Rodians began to hunt one another. To engender large-scale slaughter, they found or manufactured excuses for wars and nearly fought themselves to extinction, laying waste to their environment. For this reason, they now have to import much of their food and many other resources from off-planet.

Though extinction at one time seemed inevitable, a brilliant Grand Protector named Harido Kavila developed one of the Rodians' greatest cultural gifts to the galaxy. He developed Rodian theater and, with it, helped stop his species from destroying itself.

Since Rodians romanticize violence, drama was a good way to expiate the people's violent tendencies

DESIGNATION
> SENTIENT <
....
PLANET OF ORIGIN
> RODIA <
....
HEIGHT OF
AVERAGE ADULT
> 1.6 METERS <
....

without requiring them to inflict harm upon one another. Their dramatic efforts developed gradually, and the early works were little more than staged fights. But Rodian dramatists quickly realized that the effect of drama was magnified if the fights were presented as elements of an even greater story. Soon the complexity of Rodian stories grew, and they came to be as good as the choreographed violence.

Rodian drama has come to be highly regarded throughout the galaxy, for although it is violent, it deals with motivations and situations that provoke strong emotional responses in audiences. In addition, these dramas show the realistic effects of violence, so that non-Rodians—and even Rodians themselves, if the drama is well written—are struck by the moral impact of each performance.

Rodians are also renowned as brilliant weapons makers, and most Rodians work in the vast factories that manufacture their famous products, such as top-of-the-line blasters. This is their main export, and it fits well with their legendary talents as hunters—talents that they also offer for profit.

Those who continue to hunt and who sell their talents often make a great deal of money and gain widespread fame on their homeworld and beyond. Bounty hunting has become an honored profession for Rodians. Prizes are awarded annually for Best Shot, for deceased catches; Longest Trail, awarded for persistence; Most Notorious Capture; Quickest Catch; and Most Difficult Hunt.

Because hunting is treated as a challenge and a contest, when Rodians leave home to participate in bounty hunting, they find it irrelevant that they may be participating in a law enforcement activity, rather than sport. Rodian bounty hunters often "pad" catches, allowing their quarry to commit a number of additional crimes, substantially raising the value of the final kill or capture, and bringing them more status back home. They often freelance or work under contract to crimelords and other disreputable figures.

Despite their hunting prowess, Rodians are often viewed as cowards by members of other species. This is because they are generally unwilling to take risks or put themselves in danger to bring in quarry. For this reason, they often use the biggest and most destructive weaponry available to complete a commission. In addition, since they usually receive prizes when returning home with a kill, they may charge less to their employers if they are permitted to keep the remains of the victim. They charge exorbitant fees for bringing in live quarry because it often increases risk, and usually the Rodian will conveniently "forget" that part of a bounty agreement during the hunt.

All Rodians exude a peculiar scent that most non-Rodians find repugnant. These transcripts, of HoloNet nightclub entertainer Joon Odovrera's final performance, address this very trait.

> *So a Rodian walks into a bar. [pause] Everyone leaves. [rim shot]*
> *No, seriously, folks, have you ever smelled one of these guys? I swear they have the odor of animal droppings on the bottom of your boot. They say it's a kind of mating hormone, but I tell you what,*

that's a smell only a mother could love. [pause] Maybe that's why they're so inbred. [rimshot]
> *But really, folks, I shouldn't rip on our Rodian friends like that. They've contributed a lot with their drama, haven't they? [clapping in audience] And how! Great theater. Only, they have to hand out aroma inhalers at the door. Can you imagine the smell of Rodians under the heat lamps and greasy makeup? I've heard of full-sensory immersion theater but this is ridiculous. [laughter]*

> *We got any Rodians in the room tonight? No? Trust me, you'd know if they were here. You'd all be crowded on one side of the room...*

Besides being seen as solitary bounty hunters or as actors, Rodians are rarely seen off Rodia. This is because most Rodians believe that life is dangerous enough without having to cope with the potential of open combat with one of their own.

Ronto

rontos are huge, gentle pack animals used as common beasts of burden by the Jawas on Tatooine. They are known for both their loyalty and their strength, and a single ronto can carry hundreds of kilograms of equipment. Though large enough to frighten off most attackers, including Tusken Raiders, they are also skittish and easily spooked, especially when brought into more congested urban areas.

Much like the native Tatooine dewbacks that are also used as beasts of burden, rontos are easy to train and often become quite fond of their masters. These mammals exhibit a superb sense of smell—they can detect a krayt dragon as much as a kilometer away—and their two sets of ears provide a superb sense of hearing, as well. They have poor vision, however, and because of that, sudden movement often takes them by surprise.

Rontos need plenty of water, but their thin, leathery skin easily sheds excess heat, allowing them to function well in desert surroundings. Despite their usefulness, however, they are rarely exported, because offworlders feel their skittishness makes them unreliable.

During mating season, female rontos give off a powerful, musky scent. While attractive to male rontos, it is repulsive to most other species, and females in heat have to be isolated. Many have likened it to the scent that Rodians exude.

This can lead to unusual difficulties, as recorded in the following security report filed by Trooper Davin Felth of the Imperial forces on Tatooine.

> Five full-grown, excited rontos had surrounded one small, skinny Rodian and were butting and rubbing against him like they were in love.

He was terrified and kept trying to get away, but just as he would try to make his break, they'd move their bodies in front of him and nudge him between them like a ball.
> The Jawa ronto owners were frantic, but the situation was clearly out of their control. They'd grab hold of the rontos' reins, only to be tossed around like scrap in the wind. After a few minutes of assessing the situation, we decided to fire a few shots under the feet of the rontos, to frighten them off. It worked for the most part, but the Rodian got butted by one of the rontos and was knocked unconscious.
> We woke the Rodian up after a few minutes with smelling salts—though his body smelled a lot stronger than the salts, so we were surprised when they did the trick.

DESIGNATION
> **NONSENTIENT** <

PLANET OF ORIGIN
> **TATOOINE** <

HEIGHT OF AVERAGE ADULT
> **4.25 METERS** <

Ruurian

insectoids, the Ruurians are a caterpillarlike species, each slightly more than a meter long, with bands of vivid reddish brown decorating their furlike skin. Eight pairs of short limbs extend from their bodies, each with four flexible digits. Feathery antennae emerge from their heads, and multifaceted red eyes, a tiny mouth, and small nostrils complete their facial features.

Ruurians are known in the Corporate Sector for their scholarly achievements. They have a special talent for learning languages and are often employed in diplomatic or educational fields throughout the sector and the galaxy at large.

There are four Ruurian life stages: egg, larva, pupa, and chroma-wing. The larval Ruurians, the form of this species that is best known throughout the galaxy, are concerned with matters related to all aspects of day-to-day life on Ruuria. They hatch from eggs fully aware and capable, and so they run the government, fulfill educational responsibilities, perform manufacturing and business functions, and contribute to the running of their homes. They do all this from the moment of their birth.

After many years in the larval stage, each Ruurian forms a chrysalis—the pupa stage—and later emerges as a chroma-wing. The chroma-wing is concerned only with mating. When this happens, the entire household dynamic changes, as Senior Anthropologist Hoole notes in his journal.

> I was honored to be present when the huge, shiny, pouch-like pupa burst open, revealing the male Ruurian in his new butterflylike chroma-wing form. As he emerged, he looked desperate, and his face was flushed.

DESIGNATION
> SENTIENT <
PLANET OF ORIGIN
> RUURIA <
HEIGHT OF AVERAGE ADULT
> 1.1 METERS <

> Immediately, the larval Ruurians of the family guided the new chroma-wing to a room where his mate was waiting patiently, and they left them alone as they prepared a feast and a comfortable nesting place for the couple.
> Winged Ruurians are no longer required to perform any function other than mating, eating, and sleeping. The other Ruurians explained that the larva the couple produces will care for them in every way.

Ruurian society consists of 143 clan-based colonies. The role each Ruurian will play in society is largely dependent upon what stage of life each has achieved.

the creature known as the Sarlacc is a mystery to modern zoology, as few scientists have been able to get close enough to a specimen to study it. One of the largest recorded examples of the species rests in the Great Pit of Carkoon in the Tatooine Dune Sea, although others have been spotted on various worlds. Luke Skywalker's personal experience with the Tatooine creature, along with the stories recorded by his companions on that mission, have been well documented.

What scientists do know is that the Sarlacc is a massive, omnivorous creature that superficially seems more like a plant than a reptile or mammal. Some evidence exists to indicate that the creature reproduces via plantlike spores, but fortunately very, very few take root.

From the mouth of its sandy pit, the Sarlacc looks like a great hooked beak with a snakelike head coiling from its center, surrounded by a number of writhing, grasping tentacles. This is only the mouth of the creature; soundings have proved that the enormous body of the Sarlacc is buried deep beneath the surface. It uses its tentacles to snag prey and drag it down to the grasping, reptilian mouth. These tentacles have been known to reach a full four meters beyond the pit to grab unsuspecting creatures.

Sarlaccs don't travel from their pits, further lending to the belief that they are plant based.

The mature Sarlacc, however, does have mobile tentacles and legs but has adapted its legs as anchor roots. Scientists currently believe the Sarlacc is an animal, much like sponges and anemones are animals. Because it lives in the middle of the desert, the Sarlacc does not feed often, but because of its highly efficient digestive system, it doesn't need to. Its body preserves food for incredibly long periods of time, digesting it slowly and storing it until the Sarlacc needs nourishment. Unfortunately, the victim often remains alive for much of the time, in part sustained by the Sarlacc's internal nutrients.

One of the prevailing rumors about the Sarlacc is that the creature is mildly telepathic and actually gains knowledge and sentience from victims as it consumes them, sometimes over thousands of years, depending on the species of the meal. Some data Senior Anthropologist Hoole secured from the bounty hunter Boba Fett have confirmed this.

> Fett's helmet recorder was running, apparently, during a period in which he was trapped inside the creature. When I sat down to study the tape, I was horrified. Not only was it clear to me that the Sarlacc was sentient, but it enjoyed torturing those it was digesting. Fett's actions and responses plainly indicated that the creature manipulated the thoughts of its victims, and even kept their intelligence stored in its memories so it could savor their pain at another time.
> The recordings also showed a more anemonelike physical structure than most scientists have believed, and the secretion of some digestive enzyme that might be the cause of their hallucinogenic power over their victims. This theory was supported by the fact that Fett could plainly be seen reacting to stimuli that were not there.

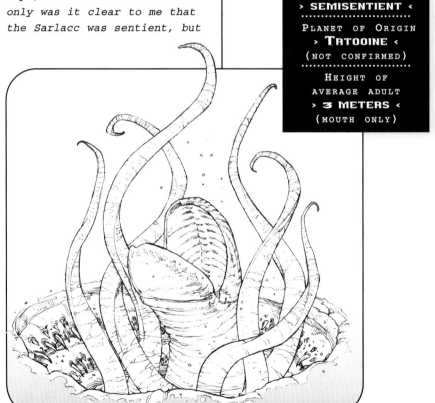

DESIGNATION
> SEMISENTIENT <

PLANET OF ORIGIN
> TATOOINE <
(NOT CONFIRMED)

HEIGHT OF AVERAGE ADULT
> 3 METERS <
(MOUTH ONLY)

Selonians are furry, bipedal mammals native to Selonia in the Corellian system. They are taller than most humans, with slightly shorter arms and legs. They have long bodies and are comfortable walking on two legs or four. They have retractable claws at the ends of their pawlike hands, which give them the ability to dig and climb efficiently. They have tails about a half meter long that counterbalance their bodies when they are walking upright. Their bodies are covered with glossy short hair that is usually brown or black, and they have long, pointed faces with bristly whiskers and sharp teeth.

Selonians are thoroughly grounded, serious-minded people, primarily concerned with the safety of their family dens and their people as a whole. In their society, the needs of the entire group are more important than those of an individual. Because Selonians believe their individual actions might affect the entire den, they refuse to lie, and consider it as terrible a crime as murder.

Den dwellings are constructed underground. The den groups consist of one fertile female, called the queen, a few fertile males, and a large number of sterile females. The den members focus on protecting the fertile female from harm and keeping their home safe. Within the den, there are sub-groupings called septs—offspring fathered by the same fertile male. A queen can be pregnant up to five times a year, each time giving birth to five or more children. Sterile females take care of the queen and the males, who, at best, are treated like prize breeding stock.

Select Selonians are trained to deal with humans and other aliens. While Selonians appear outgoing, friendly, and charitable, most have no interests beyond the den.

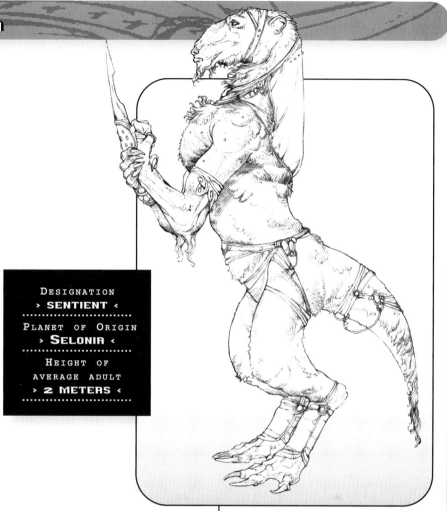

DESIGNATION
> **SENTIENT** <

PLANET OF ORIGIN
> **SELONIA** <

HEIGHT OF
AVERAGE ADULT
> **2 METERS** <

Selonians have mastered ship-building technology, and they construct ships that carry them within their own star system. Since they have no desire to travel beyond the boundaries of Corellia, their ships do not have hyperdrive capabilities.

Though rare, cultural changes do occur in Selonian society. Recently, a few breed males have attempted to start a movement for "breeders' rights," and their literature seeks to explain the motivation for what could be considered deviant behavior.

> *Everyone wants to be valued in this life. Everyone wants to make a difference. But the breed males in the dens of Selonia are valued for only one thing—their genes—while the queen rules all.*

> *We who hold this place in society want more of our lives than being locked in our dens all day, the queens expecting us to perform at a moment's notice. We can do much more and contribute much more if we are able to participate in society as the nonbreeder females do.*

> *Many people argue that we have everything we could possibly want. We are fed, clothed, and housed. But one thing we do not have is dignity. And like any sentient being, we are worthy of it.*

Shi'ido

Until recently, little was known about the mysterious species known as the Shi'ido. Hailing from the planet Lao-mon, or Sh'shuun in Shi'ido, they are a species rarely seen around the galaxy. Senior Anthropologist Hoole, after years of writing and researching other species, has released the most comprehensive—albeit brief—information relating to his own people.

In natural form, Shi'ido are humanoid, with pale skin. They are born with the ability to mimic the form of any species that is approximately the same mass as themselves. Younger members of the species can manage only to take the form of other humanoids. This physical limitation disappears when an individual reaches the age of around 150 years, allowing older Shi'ido to shift and enlarge their shape to mimic larger and more complex beings. Hoole, for example, notes that he has in his later years taken the shapes of a Whaladon and a Hutt. If a Shi'ido attempts a form that is beyond the normal limits, however, he may be forced to stay in that form until his body can recover, which can be several weeks.

Shi'ido physiology is extremely flexible, yet their thin bones are dense, allowing support even in the most awkward mass configurations. Their physiology includes a series of tendons that can release and reattach themselves in different formations. They also have a great deal of hidden fleshy mass that they can access and use to enlarge their shapes.

Shi'ido transformations are made complete by the use of telepathic suggestions they impose upon their viewers, painting the image of what they want the observers to see. This helps cover over any inaccuracies in the Shi'ido's transformation, but it is extremely difficult to maintain. Older Shi'ido often have greater mastery over this talent.

Shi'ido are long-lived. Some of the oldest members of the species are 500 years old. This longevity has led to their tremendous interest in learning about the universe, though they'd rather not have the universe learn about them, as Hoole revealed.

> One might say we're a private people who are always nosing around in other people's business. That's why we've gained a reputation for being spies, thieves, and criminals, although I would state with utmost sincerity that most Shi'ido are merely curious, seeking to study various peoples by living with them. We generally have no interest in harming or steal-ing from others.
> We maintain a democratic government that prefers to remain autonomous in the galaxy at large. We are so private that when scout ships come to our world, we've been known to take the shapes of rocks, trees, and other terrain, or to attack in the shapes of ferocious creatures, to confuse or frighten away visitors.
> If my people want to be found, they'll take the first step in contacting the New Republic.

DESIGNATION
> **SENTIENT** <

PLANET OF ORIGIN
> **LAO-MON** <
(SH'SHUUN)

HEIGHT OF AVERAGE ADULT
> **1.8 METERS** <

Shistavanen

The Shistavanens, often called Shistavanen Wolfmen, are hairy, canine bipeds from the Uvena system. Like most canine-based species, they have high-set doglike ears and muzzles, sharp teeth, and sharp claws on their hands and feet. They can walk on four legs as well as two.

Because of their canine ancestry, Shistavanens are excellent hunters and trackers. They can follow prey with ease, using heightened senses to navigate crowded urban streets or desolate desert plains. Their sense of sight is so highly developed that they can see in near-absolute darkness. They move quickly and possess remarkable endurance.

Shistavanen society is based on an isolationist ideal. They do not like outsiders visiting Uvena Prime or meddling in their affairs. While they haven't banned outsiders from coming to their world, their open prejudice toward non-Shistavanens is made clear by their restrictive laws and trade rules.

As a result of their xenophobic society, most Shistavanens are not talkative. While on other worlds, they remain most often by themselves or with others of their own kind. There is a small minority, however, who are actually outgoing. These few are frequently hired as scouts, bounty hunters, or security guards.

While Shistavanens are suspicious of other species, so other species are openly afraid of Shistavanens, as is apparent in this journal entry written by a Shistavanen student at the University of Coruscant.

> My parents, Tagg and Nira Sivrak, sacrificed a great deal to send me offplanet to go to school. Studying cartography has been my dream, ever since my uncle showed his great heroism as a pilot for the Rebel Alliance.
> But...they don't like me here. Everyone is afraid of me, and they run away if they see me coming. No one wants to talk to me. Even my professors! Our people have been so private for so long that others react only to my appearance, and refuse to look beyond it. To them, I seem a constant threat.
> Perhaps our people are right to remain apart. Among others, we are only misunderstood.

Uvena Prime is a self-sufficient world, and the Shistavanens have even colonized all the unpopulated worlds in the Uvena system to prevent strangers from doing so. Most of the population is at hyperspace-level technology, though some pockets of civilization remain at a lower level because of their isolationist ideology.

DESIGNATION
> SENTIENT <

PLANET OF ORIGIN
> UVENA PRIME <

HEIGHT OF AVERAGE ADULT
> 1.8 METERS <

Slashrat

Slashrats are vicious, carnivorous rodents native to the planet Bimmiel. They have long snouts that taper back into a wedge-shaped skull that is entirely covered in chitin or keratin, like human fingernails. This chitin is thick, however, and polished smooth by the slashrat's burrowing through sand. Each of these creatures possesses short, powerful limbs that end in razor-sharp claws that are ideally designed for digging. Its gray fur is like down, except for a fringe at the back of the skull. Its long, flat tail, covered with keratin scales, moves in side-to-side undulations, which help propel the slashrat's supple body through the sand. The tail is also employed as a weapon. It whips about ruthlessly, and its sharp edge can easily slice through human skin.

These creatures are reputed to move very, very quickly, gathering speeds in excess of forty kilometers per hour, even when tunneling through dense sand dunes.

According to observer Jedi Corran Horn, slashrats "smell like rotting ronto meat mixed with sour ale and cigarra." This powerful odor, called killscent, is exuded when they are attacking prey, to communicate to others of their kind that food is nearby. A group of slashrats will close in upon the prey, herding the victim toward a designated kill site.

Slashrats also have an uncanny sense of smell that guides them through sand when they are tracking prey. Eyesight rarely enters the picture; everywhere they go is determined by what they smell. The scent of dead members of their own species, for instance, will communicate danger and cause them to keep a distance. However, slashrats will often ignore this scent if it is accompanied by kill scent, indicating food.

Trista Orlanis, a graduate student

DESIGNATION
> NON-SENTIENT <

PLANET OF ORIGIN
> BIMMIEL <

LENGTH OF
AVERAGE ADULT
> 1.2 METERS <

at the University of Agamar and one of the New Republic researchers who first encountered slashrats, speculated about the ecological origins of this mysterious species.

> As the planet Bimmiel nears the sun, it warms up naturally and the ice caps begin to melt. The resulting moisture triggers an abundance of plant growth. The heat also brings the shwpi out of hibernation. Shwpi are herbivores, and they live to eat, multiply, and eat more. They don't digest most of the seeds they consume, so they excrete them, sheathing the seeds with organic fertilizers.
> Certain other animals, such as the slashrats, cannot tolerate the heat, so they retreat toward the polar regions, leaving the shwpi population to increase. During this period, the shwpi have the tendency to overgraze the environment.
> As the planet begins to move away from the sun, the surface cools, which frees the other species to sweep back into the equatorial areas. The predators, most notably the slashrats, then hunt the shwpi constantly and, in doing so, seem the major proponents of ecological balance.

In addition, the overgrazing of the shwpi leads to soil erosion and the perpetual drifting sands that are the ideal environment for slashrats to proliferate, creating an almost symbiotic relationship between the two species and their environment.

Sluissi

the Sluissi are reptilian creatures inhabiting the Sluis Van system. The upper half of a Sluissi's body is much like a humanoid's, with two arms and four-fingered hands, the fourth being an opposable digit. The bottom half of the body is like that of a snake—with a long singular tail. The Sluissi have round black eyes and a long, swooping hoodlike fold of skin on the back of the head. Their arms have extra, winglike extensions of skin that apparently help them move when they are flat on the ground. They have forked tongues, which, as with most reptiles, are used for their sense of smell.

The Sluissi are a technologically advanced species renowned for the ability to repair and maintain starships. They have been active members of galactic society since the early days of the Old Republic, when they established major shipyards throughout the Sluis sector, including the Sluis Van space facility itself. They run efficient, respectable operations where ship captains can find the finest repair expertise to be had.

The Sluissi people, however, are known to be extremely methodical and almost painstakingly slow at their work. To them, their work is art, and great art takes time. Hence, they do their jobs extremely well. They love to tinker, and a Sluissi technician can improve engine efficiency, power output, and system response in even the oldest, most worn-out ships. In a like manner, Sluissi are extremely patient and easygoing. Nothing ever seems to excite them. They are industrious and remain calm in the face of adversity, characteristics that make them highly prized members of ship crews and repair crews all across the galaxy.

Despite this, their philosophies can try the patience of even the most forgiving client. Wedge Antilles wrote of them.

> Over the past couple of years we've enjoyed the fine work the technicians of Sluis Van have provided in maintaining our X-wings. The slowness of their work, however, has caused us more than a little frustration. While they are certainly to be commended for their talents, they need to be encouraged to carry out their duties a little faster. My pilots end up sitting around for so long they lose their edge as they wait for our ships to get fixed.
> Nonetheless, the thoroughness of the Sluissi work cannot be beat. I remember waiting an extra day for one of our ships, as the Sluissi worker forced his body up into the cramped engine compartment to get at the hardest-to-reach spots, evaluating every single part for efficiency. It paid off when he showed us a melted power conduit, one we'd never thought of changing. My pilot could have been stuck floating helpless without power, had the Sluissi not been so meticulous.

DESIGNATION
> SENTIENT <

PLANET OF ORIGIN
> SLUIS URN <

HEIGHT OF
AVERAGE ADULT
> 1.7 METERS <

Space Slug

Space slugs are large, toothed, silicon-based gastropods that survive in the cold vacuum of space, feeding on stellar energy emissions, minerals from asteroids, and small vacuum-breathing creatures like mynocks. They primarily inhabit asteroid fields, where food is plentiful.

Most space slugs measure approximately ten meters in length, but there have been tales of slugs so large that they are able to swallow small spaceships whole. The mynocks that the adults might swallow are more likely to become internal parasites, rather than nourishment.

These creatures travel between asteroids by pushing off one rock and gliding to another. To do this, they use a highly developed, genetically endowed spatial sense that allows them to calculate the trajectory and speed of every moving body in their area. This primal sense helps them target food, as well.

Like some gastropods, space slugs reproduce asexually. Upon reaching a certain size, a slug has sufficient mass to reproduce through fission. The slug splits into two smaller slugs. Instantly after birth, the new slugs inherently know how to survive on their own. They usually separate to seek out their own territories. Occasionally, however, the biological reaction that triggers the fission process does not occur, and the single space slug continues to grow throughout its life to a prodigious size.

Space slugs are prized by sentients for their organs and body parts, which industrial manufacturers use to produce special lubricants and fibers. Some space stations and shipyards also keep young space slugs on hand to reduce the mynock population, though in such instances their size is carefully regulated.

DESIGNATION
> NONSENTIENT <

PLANET OF ORIGIN
> UNKNOWN <

LENGTH OF AVERAGE ADULT
> 10 METERS <

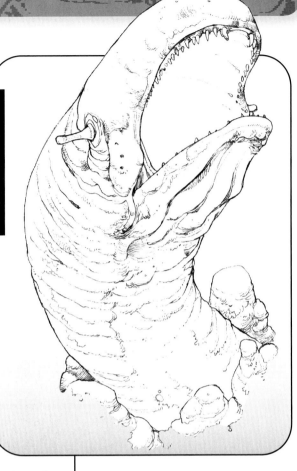

The following reply from Gamgalon the Krish, a noted game hunter, to a HoloNet ad shows the value attributed to these creatures, and the difficulty in capturing and keeping them.

> I am responding to your ad for a healthy space slug to be shipped to your locale. I have managed to come upon one in an asteroid field outside the Hoth system. I should be able to get it for you in a couple of weeks' time.
> The creature is 900 meters long. To extricate it from its present lair, we'll need to hire a Corellian towing ship and two Bith industrial power winches. We'll also need a tank of sedative to knock the creature unconscious.
> In addition, you'll need to lace your asteroids with katrium on a regular basis, which will make the space slug sterile and lock it at its present size. You don't want this one to get any larger. You should also set up energy fields around your sensitive base areas to keep it from making appearances where it's not wanted.
> Depending upon how difficult it is to extricate the creature from its asteroid home, I may ask a little more in addition to your advertised bounty of 100,000 credits.

ew Republic representatives first encountered the Ssi-ruuk during the conflict at Bakura directly after the Battle of Endor. Ssi-ruuk are a warlike, warm-blooded reptilian species that communicates through a language made up of a series of musical tweets and whistles. An adult Ssi-ruu can range in size from 1.9 to 2.2 meters tall, and their physical strength can match that of a typical adult Wookiee. They have strong tails, three digits on their claws, and a sharp beak and talons for rending prey. They are carnivorous.

Members of this species possess a keen sense of smell, made more potent by the two forked "tongues" that flicker from their nostrils. They tend to rely on smell more than on their eyesight, which is extremely sensitive to light, requiring them to have three lids that protect each Ssi-ruu's vision from any sudden burst of illumination. Their heightened sense of smell actually allows them to read the emotional states of their associates through changes in scent. At the same time they find the scent of other species distasteful.

Though fearsome, this species as a whole has one great fear. They shrink from battle on a personal level. Most Ssi-ruuk will not engage another species in combat when they are not on their own homeworld Lwhekk. This avoidance is based on the religious belief that if a Ssi-ruu dies on a world other than one that is properly consecrated, the Ssi-ruu's spirit will wander aimlessly throughout the galaxy for all eternity.

Ssi-ruuvi society is a clan-based hierarchy, and each clan is designated by the color of their scales. The highest-ranking group is the blue-scaled clan (designating the rulers and leaders). Other clan colors are the gold scales (religious), red-brown scales

(military), and the green scales (workers). Most Ssi-ruuk are of this last caste, which is the lowest caste to still receive esteem and honor. The clans strictly avoid interbreeding with one another, as the products of such unions, determined by their brown scales, are outcasts, the lowest caste of all.

An absolute ruler—called the Shreeftut—controls the Ssi-ruuvi government. Two councils advise this monarch: the Elders' Council and the Conclave. The Elders' Council is made up of the most respected citizens of the Outer Rim Ssi-ruuk homeworld. Words from an elder are considered as

important as those from the monarch himself. The Conclave is a group of spiritual leaders who guide the Shreeftut in setting and enforcing laws that adhere to and complement their religion.

The Ssi-ruuk initially left their home system to search for new energy resources. While they have not developed fusion technology used by most space-faring species in this galaxy, they developed instead a process called entenchment, wherein living creatures' life energies are technologically drawn from their bodies and shifted into a droid, ship, or other piece of technology to give it power. They later discovered that humans and some other sentient species tend to have more life energy than their usual source, their servant race known as the P'w'eck. In fact, Force-using humans are considered best of all, since such

DESIGNATION
> SENTIENT <

PLANET OF ORIGIN
> LWHEKK <

HEIGHT OF
AVERAGE ADULT
> 2 METERS <

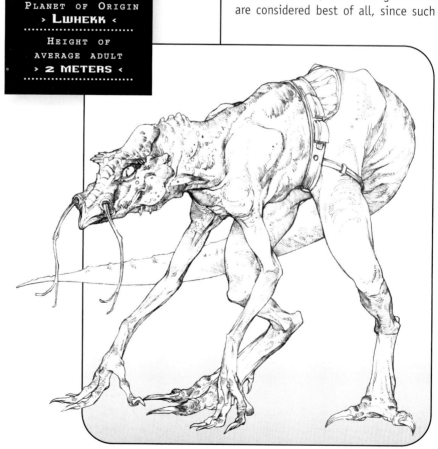

individuals can draw life energy from other creatures into themselves, thereby expanding an entechment to have a broader area of effect.

The Jedi were discovered by a group of Ssi-ruuk at Bakura, and they sought to capture one of the most powerful Force-users, who they felt would serve their energy needs for many years to come. Their choice was Luke Skywalker, who was indeed captured but later escaped them at great peril.

In a military debriefing following the incidents at Bakura, Commander Skywalker had this to say about the Ssi-ruuk:

> The Ssi-ruuk are extremely xenophobic, although they didn't seem so much afraid of other species as disgusted by them. They looked upon other species as nerfs ready for slaughter. And they did so with a religious zeal that would make them a threat to all other forms of sentient life.
> During my escape, I found that they were unable to fight opponents head-on. Instead, they sent their servants, the P'w'eck, to fight for them.
> The entechment process I witnessed is horrifying and painful for the victims, and I personally sensed the fear and anguish of the victims after they were enteched. For the most part the consciousness of a living person still continues, imprisoned in a mechanical form. It was horrible to watch. And to make it worse, the Ssi-ruuk seemed to think they were doing their victims a favor.

Adding further to this species' reputed threatening nature, Senior Anthropologist Hoole's journal notes:

> There are no Imperial records of contact with this species. There are some Old Republic references to a reptilian species on the Outer Rim, but these are sketchy reports at best.
> Recently I was able to obtain a copy of the Ssi-ruuk's recorded message to the people of Bakura, demanding their surrender. A human named Dev Sibwarra gave it, and he appeared to be under some sort of mind control. Since this youth had not been enteched—he would not have been in his own body, otherwise—one would suspect that they use other sentients as slaves, as well as, prior to, or in addition to, enteching them.
> Master Skywalker informed me that the slave mind control can be broken for victims of the Ssi-ruuk, but the entechment process is sadly permanent.

Sullustan

Sullustans are jowled, round-eared humanoids with large, round, black eyes. They inhabit subterranean caverns beneath the surface of Sullust, a volcanic planet with an inhospitable atmosphere that is filled with black clouds of volcanic ash, dust, and toxic fumes.

The Sullustans prefer to remain in their cool, humid cave environment, and go to the surface for only short periods of time. They must don environment suits for long excursions, and on the surface they face the threat of dangerous predators. Many of Sullust's creatures are extremely tough to kill, and Sullustans do their best to avoid them.

Sullustan physiology is well adapted to their underground environment. Their eyes see well in dim light, and their oversized ears make them extremely sensitive to even the faintest sounds. Their language, which sounds to most species like rapid chatter, includes extremely subtle sound fluctuations that only Sullustans can reproduce and perceive. Because of their skilled hearing, they love music and produce fine musical compositions.

Any Sullustan born with a hearing impairment experiences extreme difficulty, as is noted in this account from Dr. Rachael Tikaris, a noted specialist in prosthetic medicine.

> Despair is not the
Sullustan way, but from what
I understand, a deaf Sullustan
usually does not live very
long. This is often because
predators victimize them, but
also may be because they take
their own lives.
> The subject I was working
with, Din Tinray, was like a
prisoner, dependent on others
to watch her, guard her, and

translate for her. She was, I
could see, an embarrassment
and a burden to her parents.
At family gatherings she was
ignored because she could not
communicate well with her relatives.
> I eventually managed to re-
create a Sullustan ear. After
her implant surgery, Din was
a completely different person—
and became a valuable member
of her society.

All Sullustans also exhibit an enhanced sense of direction; without this natural ability, they wouldn't be able to dwell in the labyrinthine passages. It makes them some of the best navigators and pilots.

The Sullustan people have turned their underground environment into a near paradise, and their passageways

lead to beautiful underground cities. Sullust is home to the SoroSuub Corporation, a leading mineral-processing company that maintains energy, space mining, food-packaging, and technology-producing divisions throughout the galaxy. Almost 50 percent of the Sullustan population works for SoroSuub. During the rule of the Empire, SoroSuub proclaimed its loyalty. They dissolved the legal government of Sullust and took control of the entire world. Many Sullustans supported the Alliance and left Sullust quickly to help in that cause. When the Empire fell, the leadership of SoroSuub tried to escape, but were captured and imprisoned. A new board of directors took control of SoroSuub, and the people returned to their original, democratic form of government.

DESIGNATION
> SENTIENT <

PLANET OF ORIGIN
> SULLUST <

HEIGHT OF
AVERAGE ADULT
> 1.5 METERS <

Talz

The Talz are a tall, strong species from Alzoc III, a frigid world covered with fields of snow and ice. Until recently, these sentients were virtually unknown except in specific scientific circles.

Made for their environment, Talz are covered from head to foot with thick, white fur, and their extremely large hands sport sharp-clawed talons that are used for digging through frozen ice and snow. Their fur also protects them from the cold, as does an extra layer of blubber lying beneath their hair. Their four eyes—two large and two small—are used for seeing at different times of day. The small eyes are used for daylight vision, as the bright sunlight reflecting off the snow can be almost blinding. The larger eyes are used during moonless nights, hence their ability to see in the dark. When one set of eyes is being used, the other set remains closed. In addition, a small, tubelike snout takes in enough oxygen despite the exceptionally cold air.

The Talz are a quiet, gentle species who are tireless in their work, which is done with simple handmade tools. Their society is clan based, and they keep supplies plentiful through a sophisticated system that distributes resources for the benefit of all Talz communities.

Alzoc III is a world wealthy with natural resources, and during Imperial rule the Talz labored as slaves in ore mines. Under the New Republic, the Talz have assumed ownership of their mines and have begun to develop a system of trade with offworlders. Despite this, they are still wary of their trading partners and rarely, if ever, leave their world and venture out into the galaxy.

Although they have the characteristics of humanoids, the Talz reproduce by bearing their young singularly in a larval "sac," or external womb, in which the unborn infant develops. These larval sacs are carefully guarded and kept warm by the parents. The Talz emerges from the sac as a full-size individual with the mind of an infant.

The Talz named Muftak writes of this in his personal story, told in an autobiographical novel called *Sands in Winter*. There he relates the story of how his larval sack was accidentally loaded onto an Imperial freighter and taken to the distant world Tatooine.

> When I emerged newly born, I had no idea who or what I was. I couldn't even communicate to find out. I wandered, learning to speak the language and listening to people until I gained knowledge on everyone but myself. I became a paid gossip, passing information about others. It was a living, but my own nature remained a mystery.
> Some time later, when I learned of my Talz heritage, I learned that when we Talz leave our larval sacs, we must be educated for several years to become a true adult. It's sad that I missed out on that education. I could have really used it.

DESIGNATION
> SENTIENT <

PLANET OF ORIGIN
> Alzoc III <

HEIGHT OF AVERAGE ADULT
> 2.1 METERS <

Tauntaun

cy Hoth has an environment that has yielded few indigenous life-forms, but one of its most populous is the tauntaun. Used by Rebel Alliance personnel as beasts of burden during their stay on Hoth, tauntauns are tall, sturdy creatures with inherently difficult attitudes.

Tauntauns have remarkably cold-resistant bodies. Their blood is extremely thick, and their inner organs are packed close inside their skeletons to keep them safe from cold. A thick layer of fat acts as insulation under the tauntaun's oily pelt. Each beast has four nostrils, a large pair on the upper portion of the muzzle and a smaller pair directly beneath them. The larger pair conducts oxygen to the bloodstream during physical exertion. When the blizzard winds blow, or the tauntauns lie down for the night, the large pair seals to keep snow out, and the second pair takes over the responsibility of keeping a minimal amount of oxygen flowing to the lungs.

Tauntauns are omnivorous, but feed mostly on a type of fungus that grows beneath the frost layer. They exude waste products and oils through special ducts on their skin, giving them a foul odor. To match their smell, they are ornery creatures, spitting and gurgling in protest when forced to do something they really don't want to do. Their ill temperament is most likely due to their inhospitable environment, which is enough to give anyone a bad temper.

The females of the species are the most cantankerous, because they outnumber the males and are always in competition for mates. For this reason, many domesticated tauntauns are spayed. They have curved horns on the sides of their heads with which they battle other females. Their most effective weapon, however, is their spitting. To disable their opponents, they spit with surprising accuracy, often aiming for the eyes. The gooey saliva is not deadly, but any liquid freezes instantly in a blizzard environment, and the effect can be lethal.

Because of their foul tempers, the Rebel Alliance had some initial difficulty training them as mounts. General Carlist Rieekan, however, discovered a good way to get through their obstinance to have them perform well in this regard.

> First, because these beasts feel they always need to compete, we needed to eliminate competition. Therefore the wranglers made sure to bring in only females to be trained as mounts. Being all one gender, they had no males to fight over in the group. While they were still a little testy, they weren't combative with one another, and that's what made the difference.
> After this, we kept them warm and fed and gave them pieces of mook fruit every time they performed correctly. They adapted quickly to our needs and proved valuable scouting transportation while the speeders were still being adapted to the cold.

DESIGNATION
> **NONSENTIENT** <

PLANET OF ORIGIN
> **HOTH** <

HEIGHT OF
AVERAGE ADULT
> **1.8 METERS** <

Taurill

taurill are small, industrious, semi-intelligent simian creatures with grayish brown fur and large, curious brown eyes. They have two pairs of muscular arms that end in dexterous fingers. Their two legs are flexible enough to be used as a third set of arms.

From initial observation, one might think the taurill to be nervous or paranoid. They are constantly shifting position, blinking their eyes, and staring rapid-fire in all directions. The truth is, these creatures are actually searching for new information to feed their hive mind.

A hive mind is a single organism made up of thousands of bodies that share one collective consciousness. Each individual taurill is merely a set of eyes, ears, and hands that acts on behalf of the Overmind. As a result, taurill are considered semisentient; individuals do not possess independent thought, and their behavior is not motivated by higher emotional or philosophical concepts.

However, taurill have, in many cases, proven to be effective workers and laborers. By instructing only one or two taurill, a person can set an entire group to carrying out a task in unified force. These creatures are rarely seen alone; when separated from the group, an individual will eventually stop moving completely, and may simply die of starvation and dehydration. Thus, it appears that proximity is necessary for a taurill to remain in touch with its companions.

When she was chief of state, Leia Organa Solo reported an encounter with Durga the Hutt that involved a group of taurill.

> As he floated in on his repulsorsled, my breath caught in my throat. Dozens and dozens of hairy creatures were swarming over Durga and his retainers. They were called taurill, semi-intelligent creatures that Durga employed as workers and pets.

> We plunged into our discussion, where Durga proposed an alliance between the New Republic and the Hutts. As we reached the crux of Durga's proposal, one of our guards began slapping at a couple of the taurill who were being a particular nuisance. One grabbed his gun and pressed the firing stud, frying another taurill who was hanging on the end.

> The group of a hundred taurill in the reception chamber burst into simultaneous action, chittering and screeching, heading out the door, into the air ducts, hiding behind the chairs and around the corners. Finally one of Durga's retainers recalled them by using a synthesizer that created a humming musical tone.

> I believe this incident was orchestrated by Durga to distract us from his real purpose for being on Coruscant, which was to break into the computers. We found the tampering quite easily once we knew what to look for. The taurill were his means to an end.

DESIGNATION
> SEMISENTIENT <

PLANET OF ORIGIN
> UNKNOWN <

HEIGHT OF
AVERAGE ADULT
> 1.2 METERS <

Thernbee

Covered in white fur, the thernbees are large, four-legged creatures that inhabit the wilds of Almania. The thernbee has a smallish face with short ears, a pink nose, a huge pink mouth, and large blue eyes. As its broad shoulders are nearly a meter and a half across, a thernbee is large enough to dwarf any human. It also has a powerful tail that can be used to toss a large human male several meters.

One of the strangest things about these creatures is that some of their white hair falls out with each and every movement. Their coats are often patchy, with pink skin showing through. Scientists believe that industrialization on their planet introduced a chemical into the environment that causes an unavoidable allergic reaction on the part of the creatures.

Thernbees are a playful species—sometimes to a sadistic degree—and they are usually omnivorous. When hunting down a small creature, the thernbee will toy with it by crushing one bone at a time to give the prey the illusion that escape is possible. In addition, its saliva contains a form of anesthetic that saps the victim's will to fight.

During the battle with the warlord known as Kueller, thirteen years after the Battle of Endor, Luke Skywalker came upon one of these creatures. Through his experience with the thernbee, he discovered that they are actually psychic, though in a primitive fashion. They can read the emotions of other creatures and often try to communicate their own feelings to others. For this reason, New Republic scientists have classified these creatures as semisentient.

In this request to his sister Leia Organa Solo, who was chief of state at the time, Luke makes his recommen-

DESIGNATION
> SEMISENTIENT <

PLANET OF ORIGIN
> ALMANIA <

HEIGHT OF AVERAGE ADULT
> 2.7 METERS <

dations concerning the fate of the thernbees.

> I believe that the thernbees of Almania are intelligent in a rudimentary way and do deserve some protection from the government of the New Republic. Kueller has greatly damaged their environment, so many of them are starving.
> I'm proposing that we begin by sending a disaster relief team to Almania to help the human population recover and to find a way to repair the injured environment. The thernbees have begun to take desperate measures and are starting to attack other residents to get food. Usually, they eat only small animals and vegetation, but that may be changing.
> Perhaps we can send the same team that went to Honoghr? At the very least they can analyze the environment to find out what ecological agent may be causing their deteriorating physical condition.

While no one has managed to duplicate the thernbees' saliva for any military uses, the New Republic is monitoring the thernbee population against the possibility that they may be exploited.

tin-Tin Dwarfs, a species formally known as the Tintinna, are from Rinn, a little-known and rarely visited primitive world on the Outer Rim. They are a rodentlike species very similar to the Ranats, considered to be distant relatives.

Unlike their cousins, whose incisors emerge from the bottom jaw, the Tintinna have simple, small, rodent incisors that emerge from the top of the mouth. They have black eyes, small round ears, and soft brown fur. They have small, pink paws sporting nimble digits and look, simply, like giant mice. Because of their environment, they often give off a pleasant, wood-chip smell.

Tintinna live in underground burrows that they dig without the benefit of tools. They fleece their subterranean homes with wood chips, leaves, and other natural materials that serve to keep them warm and dry. They chew the wood for this purpose, as well as to wear down their teeth, which otherwise may grow to uncomfortable lengths.

This species has developed a complex, if still primitive, form of government. Most live in tribes ruled jointly by a chieftain and shaman. They toil in their underground world to survive and to create easier ways of living, and have even advanced to the point of developing simple technologies based on steam-powered engines. They have created small cities and towns, burrowed out of mountainsides, and have set up a system of trade between towns and tribes. They engage in an active system of agriculture, as well, having developed a basic means of gathering seeds, plowing, and irrigating crops.

Because their planet is remote, Tin-Tin Dwarfs are rarely seen off their homeworld. Traders and smugglers use Rinn as a backwater hiding place, so

DESIGNATION
> **SENTIENT** <
....
PLANET OF ORIGIN
> **RINN** <
....
HEIGHT OF
AVERAGE ADULT
> **0.9 METERS** <
....

some Tintinna have been known to befriend spacers and hitch rides offworld. They are an easygoing, pleasant, and curious species and are quick learners. When exposed to technology, they begin to understand it almost immediately. Spacers have therefore found them useful as teammates and as lookouts, the latter because of their highly sensitive rodent hearing and eyesight.

Because of their pleasant demeanor and appearance, Tintinna are often underestimated, as this log entry by Shug Ninx, a friend of Han Solo, shows.

> When I first met the little guy, I thought he was adorable, so I took him with me as a pet. I thought he was a dumb animal. He couldn't talk, as far as I could tell,

but he just charmed me to the point that I had to take him with me on the ship.
> Two days later, I realized that this little rodent was no ordinary rat. I returned to my ship and found my tools organized by size, shape, and function. Then I discovered that some of the things I'd intended to fix on the ship had already been repaired.
> Kit, as I called him, waited excitedly for my approval. I was both embarrassed and amused. Now, instead of a pet, I have a partner.

T'landa Til

distant cousins to the Hutts, the t'landa Til inhabit the world Nal Hutta along with their gastropod cousins. Their status in Hutt society, however, is far from equal to their relatives.

T'landa Til are large creatures with two small arms and four tree-trunk-like legs, at the bottom of which are huge, padded feet. Their faces resemble those of Hutts, save for the addition of a single long horn that juts above their nostrils. Their heads are attached to short, humped necks that sit upon massive bodies. Leathery skin covers them, hanging in creases, wrinkles, and loose folds, especially on the almost nonexistent neck. Their skin, like that of the Hutts, shines with oily gleam. Long, whipping tails curl over their backs, and the two undersized arms fold against their chests, half-hidden by folds of neck skin. They have delicate, almost feminine hands, with four long, supple fingers on each.

T'landa Til are considered second-class citizens on their world, living primarily to serve their Hutt cousins. They are, however, as ambitious, greedy, and clever as their relatives and for many years have grown increasingly dissatisfied with their role in Hutt society. However, their drive is motivated by a lust for luxury, as opposed to the Hutts' lust for power. For this reason, the Hutts are more able to exploit them by appealing to their desire for comfort, and it is most likely that the t'landa Til will never be able to effectively remove themselves from the control of their overlords.

Ten years before the Battle of Yavin, the Hutts enlisted the t'landa Til to launch a scheme. A religion was invented based on the t'landa Til ability to emit a frequency resonance that attracts females of their species during mating season. This humming vibration is produced when air flows over the cilia in their neck pouches when they inflate them. This stimulates the female's pleasure centers. They also employ a low-grade empathic ability that allows them to project pleasant feelings toward humanoid creatures. When the two unique abilities are combined, the t'landa Til can render the average humanoid mind pliable for manipulation.

They used these abilities on humanoids in the guise of presenting a religious epiphany luring hapless pilgrims to Ylesia, where they were enslaved in spice purification plants. Bria Tharen, one of the first officers of the Rebel Alliance, fell victim to the cult and later wrote in her journal:

> Whatever the t'landa Til did, I was helpless against their power. Years later I still yearn for the feelings their abilities stirred in me. It was glorious—like embracing love, peace, and the feeling of achievement all at one time, combined with glorious, physical, intimate pleasure.
> When I left it behind, the depression I experienced was colossal. I wanted to end my life, rather than face the misery of living without the euphoria—even though I knew it was all a sham.

DESIGNATION
> SENTIENT <
....
PLANET OF ORIGIN
> UNKNOWN <
(PRESENT RESIDENCE
NAL HUTTA)
....
HEIGHT OF
AVERAGE ADULT
> 2.5 METERS <

Togorian

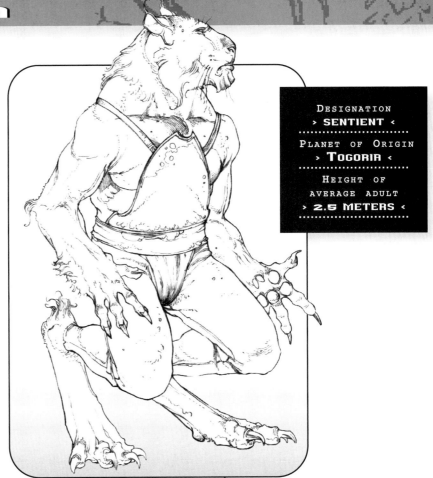

Togorians are tall, feline bipeds that come from Togoria, a world of endless, grassy plains and large forests. They have slender, muscular, fur-covered bodies that are well suited for slinking through forests or running across open plains. Their fingers and toes have long retractable claws, and their feline faces show long, twitching whiskers, triangular eyes with slit pupils, and needle-sharp teeth. Female Togorians are smaller than males, standing between 1.6 and 2.2 meters tall, while the males tower over them at 3 meters. Fur coloration in both sexes varies from gray-white to black, and distinctive stripes and spots are common.

Among this species there is a significant philosophical difference between females and males. This conflict dates back several centuries to when Togorians were primarily nomadic night-hunters preying on herds of native bist and etelo and combating the flying reptiles called liphons. During this period, they befriended another avian reptile species called the mosgoths, also hunted by the liphons, who would invade liphon nests and steal eggs. Because the Togorians saw that these creatures had a common enemy, they started protecting the mosgoth nests. Soon mosgoths were building nests near the Togorian camps, and the camps became more permanent. After several hundred years the Togorians domesticated the mosgoths, using them as riding mounts.

However, the males longed to return to their nomadic ways, while the females preferred the luxury of a permanent home. Neither side yielded their desires, so the society was split along sexual lines. Today, males roam the plains in tribes, hunting, competing in vigorous tests of prowess, and caring for their mounts. Females remain in villages and cities, herding domesticated bist and etelo, studying, and developing a primitive industrial technology based on solar energy.

Despite the fact that the sexes do not cohabitate, Togorians remain monogamous. Once a year the males return to their spouses for several days at a time, during which the couples spend as much time together as possible. The rest of the year the females raise children. When young males reach puberty, they leave with their fathers.

Female Togorians are sophisticated for members of such a primitive society, and they like to visit other worlds for vacations, shopping, and study. While they enjoy luxury, they are industrious, working hard to improve their standard of living. Males, meanwhile, are aloof and suspicious of outsiders. In particular they do not like droids or technological creatures.

Despite their levelheadedness, the females do not ultimately run the government, as Senior Anthropolist Hoole notes in his observations.

> *During my visit to Togoria, I met the Margrave, who, in his hereditary role as male leader, rules the planet and roams with his tribe. It was a special honor to pitch a tent in his camp, or so I was told by the other Togorians who camped with him.*
> *However, as a male, he is thought to be incapable of understanding female concerns. Thus, his closest female relative—either his wife or a blood relative—governs the female population from their ancestral home in Caross.*

Toka [Sharu]

The Toka of the world Rafa V in the Centrality region of the galaxy were, when first encountered by the Old Republic, a primitive people possessing little intelligence. They have the appearance of humanoids, but even from the time of infancy, they look old and in ill health, with white hair, sallow, wrinkled faces, and a bent, discouraged gait. The Empire labeled them subhuman, but in truth their intelligence was hidden.

Being a backwater, primitive world, Rafa V held little interest for anyone other than archaeologists and quack physicians. Archaeologists came to Rafa V to excavate the Sharu ruins, gaudily colored pyramids made of an indestructible plastic resin, stretching upward for kilometers, blocking the sky and dwarfing the human settlements that sprang up between them. The Sharu ruins cover every planet in the Rafa system.

Physicians, meanwhile, came to Rafa V for the life crystals, a jewel-like fruit that sprouts from indigenous silicon-based lifetrees. An orchard of these trees will sap a person's intelligence and vitality. The crystals, however, were rumored to extend life spans when snapped off and worn around the neck as pendants. Many sick, elderly, or paranoid people around the galaxy were willing to pay any price for them.

Lando Calrissian also came to Rafa V, blackmailed by the local governor to look for a legendary artifact called the Mindharp of Sharu, which would control the minds of the Toka natives. Lando succeeded, but when the governor used the Mindharp, instead of placing the Toka under his control, it released them from a mental imprisonment that had been imposed upon them thousands of years in the past. The Toka, it seems, were actually the Sharu of ancient legend—the highly advanced and scientifically superior people who had built the enormous pyramids. Eons ago they had been frightened by an overwhelming alien power that was interested only in dominating intelligent societies. To protect themselves, they hid their society beneath the ubiquitous plastic pyramids, while the lifetree orchards drained away their intelligence. When the Mindharp was activated, the Sharu, alerted that it was safe to return, regained their intelligence, and the cities hidden beneath the pyramids were revealed. In a log entry he filed concerning the event, Lando Calrissian wrote:

> As Vuffi Raa and I escaped the planet, quakes shook the ground, causing the pyramids and other buildings to crumble. The Mindharp's subharmonic emanations were causing a preplanned reversal of the social order in that planetary system. As the pyramids imploded, spires and towers emerged from the ground that were

both strange and marvelous at the same time.

For a time, an interdiction field was used by the Imperial Navy to blockade the system, preventing any visitors from coming to the world. When this field finally was dropped, Rafa V had completely changed. New cities had sprung up, and the Sharu had become aloof and unresponsive to the humans on their world, considering them lesser beings. Despite this, researchers still came to Rafa V. The Sharu allowed them to remain, but did nothing at all to help them in their efforts.

DESIGNATION
> **SENTIENT** <

PLANET OF ORIGIN
> **RAFA V** <

HEIGHT OF AVERAGE ADULT
> **1.7 METERS** <

Toydarian

native to Toydaria in Hutt space, Toydarians are short aliens with blue skin, small wings, and vaguely avian features. They have stubby trunks on their faces that rest above short tusks, and their thin legs end in webbed feet. The males of the species usually show sparse whiskers.

Despite the diminutive size of their wings, Toydarians can fly quite rapidly—their wings beat almost ten times a second. And while they appear pudgy and heavy, the Toydarians are actually very light because their tissues are spongy and filled with gas. Their potbellied stomachs are also gas-filled, functioning much like small balloons. Nonetheless, their flying requires a great deal of energy, and they must eat constantly to maintain their strength.

Like most mammals, Toydarians are born live. They can fly at birth, and they prefer to fly everywhere rather than walk, hence the sky is always filled with buzzing Toydarians. Spaceship traffic is allowed to land and take off only at certain times and in specified areas, in order to prevent a midair collision. There is also very little solid land for space vessel take-offs and landings.

Because of all the air traffic on Toydaria, the use of speeders is prohibited. As a result, the Toydarians have constructed a light-rail system that takes them from city to city. Beyond this, they do not have a technologically advanced society, although they have incorporated some technology from other worlds into their day-to-day lives.

Toydaria is mostly covered with nutrient-rich muck lakes that support a number of predators, including the dangerous grabworms. Toydarians have survived by flying over the muck, landing only on the relative safety of algae mats. They harvest the nutrients found in the lakes and have developed high-end farming techniques to provide food to their populace. But because the amount of food they need is so great, war will break out from time to time between Toydarian confederacies when food supplies are low. During hard times, they form armies and fight bitterly, sometimes to the extent of poisoning the other nation's food supply, under the belief that "If we can't have it, no one can." However, when the supply situation improves, these wars quickly end and life returns to normal. This pattern usually recurs every thirty years, depending on weather cycles.

The Toydarians also exhibit a certain amount of mental strength, as is noted in this personal log of Lord Darth Vader, recovered from his fortress on Vjun.

> These creatures have become such an irritation that every time I see one I want to strike it down with my lightsaber. Be that as it may, I interviewed a Toydarian subject who showed a great amount of resistance to Force suggestion, up to the point that I created physical discomfort. I found that they easily can be intimidated by a demonstration of strength. And it proved relatively simple to cause it to expire, merely by making its existence extremely painful. Ultimately, though it showed a great degree of willpower, it was no match for the power of the Force.

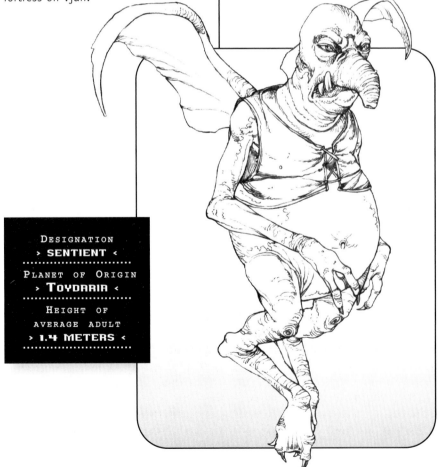

DESIGNATION
> **SENTIENT** <

PLANET OF ORIGIN
> **TOYDARIA** <

HEIGHT OF AVERAGE ADULT
> **1.4 METERS** <

Trandoshan

Trandoshans, who refer to themselves as T'doshok, are large, bipedal reptilians known for their ruthless warrior culture. Like most reptiles, Trandoshans are cold-blooded and possess scaly skin that they shed every year. Their orange, supersensitive eyes can see into the infrared range, and they are able to regenerate limbs until they reach middle age. Each of their limbs has three digits with sharp claws. While these claws are excellent for fighting, they aren't very dexterous, making Trandoshans clumsy in some situations.

This species is extremely violent. Their culture is based on hunting and tracking beings less powerful than themselves. They were one of the first species to ally themselves with the Empire, and they were the ones that suggested the Empire use Wookiees as slave labor. When the Empire took over the Wookiee world Kashyyyk, in the same system as Trandosha, the Trandoshans assisted by hunting down Wookiees that escaped.

In this letter sent to Han Solo's first mate Chewbacca, written during the war with the Empire, the Wookiee's wife Mallatobuck described the situation on Kashyyyk.

> Yesterday, my brother Vargi returned to Kashyyyk. I had long thought him dead, or taken by the troopers. The truth is he was working with the Trandoshans. He was the one who gave them details on how to invade our cities; told them our secret hiding places, our weaknesses.
> He came to see me yesterday and told me he had done it all to prevent wholesale slaughter. He'd learned about the Trandoshan plan early on and felt we could not resist

the Empire, but he wanted to make sure his own family was safe. To lead the Trandoshans away from us, he gave them information on some of the more elusive tribes—so they would have a more "enjoyable hunt." I was horrified and sent him from my house. He is no longer my brother.

Trandoshans worship a female deity known as the Scorekeeper, who awards jagannath points to Trandoshans based on their success or failure in the hunt. Jagannath points, which refer to the spoils of victory won in mortal combat, are accumulated throughout a Trandoshan's life. Those hunters possessing more points enjoy greater status in society and are considered valuable as mates by most females. At death, a Trandoshan presents his points to the mythological Scorekeeper, who determines his place in the afterlife by his merits.

When Trandoshan males have proven themselves successful in the hunt, they return to their homeworld to mate with a convenient "clutch mother." These arranged relationships are not considered binding. Once a couple has mated, the female lays her eggs and watches over them until they hatch. From infancy the males are trained as warriors and are shown many different methods of hunting. As soon as they are old enough, they go on their way into the galaxy to start scoring points for their goddess.

DESIGNATION
> **SENTIENT** <

PLANET OF ORIGIN
> **TRANDOSHA** <
(REFERRED TO AS DOSHA BY TRANDOSHANS)

HEIGHT OF AVERAGE ADULT
> **2 METERS** <

---

an advanced, adventurous feline species, the Trianii inhabit the outermost portion of the Corporate Sector. In many ways they are similar to the Togorians, Cathar, and Catuman Warriors. Unlike these other feline species, however, Trianii have prehensile tails, and their more agile figures are perfect for leaping, jumping, and acrobatics. Like most feline species, Trianii have excellent balance and eyesight. Their sleek fur comes in a wide range of colors and patterns.

Trianii females are generally stronger, faster, and more dexterous than their male counterparts. For this reason, tribunals of females called yu'-nar run their society. Trianii culture is organized around their religious beliefs. Dance, art, music, literature, and even industry and commerce all revolve around spirituality. At one time, the Trianii hosted many diverse religions, but the leaders of these different faiths all agreed upon a specific moral code of conduct and brought together a religious coalition that has lasted for thousands of years. Most Trianii are still active in the traditional faith of their families, though, and all religious figures are held in great regard.

This species is fiercely independent. Trianii are constantly driven to explore, and being technologically advanced, they have established colonies in six systems, including Brochiib, Pypin, Ekibo, and Fibuli. Each of these colonies is organized as a completely independent civilization, founded by Trianii who were seeking a different way of life.

Because of their determination and forbearance, they ferociously resisted Corporate Sector Authority expansion into their territories. Colonists, assisted by Trianii Rangers—an independent space force of Trianii people—pushed the invaders out of their system.

DESIGNATION
> SENTIENT <

PLANET OF ORIGIN
> TRIAN <

HEIGHT OF
AVERAGE ADULT
> 2 METERS <

An example of this fierceness is evident in an account logged by Captain Jiprin Kosh of the Corporate Sector Authority.

> Fifteen Trianii attack vessels set upon us, and they had us completely surrounded. They destroyed most of our fighters and our motivator systems, rendering us helpless in space. Then, despite our offers for surrender, they busted through our shields and boarded the vessel, slaughtering everyone in their path on the way to the bridge.
> When they reached the command staff, they took us as prisoners to their lead ship. There I was forced, on my knees, to explain my presence in the Trianii system and to apologize for our interference there. After this, they set us back on our own ship to limp back to our own system as a warning to others who would test them. I suggested to my superiors that we heed the warning.

Trian remained independent and unhindered throughout the rise and fall of the Empire. The Trianii have indicated no desire to join the New Republic.

tsils are mineral-based life-forms on the planet Nam Chorios that look like green and purple crystal chimney formations. The planet's Oldtimers, descendants of the planet's original settlers, named them after the small ground electrical storms the tsils incite that last five to ten minutes. They also nicknamed them smokies or spook-crystals because of their unusual colors and properties. While Oldtimers remain unaffected by the electrical storms the tsils produce, newcomers are left sick for a day and a half if any of the charges pass through them.

The Tsils are the source of Force-sensitivity inherent to Nam Chorios. By magnifying life and light energy around them, they increase the power of the Force on that world. Even the slightest exercise of Force power on the planet can set off a raging Force storm, as Luke Skywalker discovered.

Tsils communicate telepathically and empathically by implanting images in another being's mind. The Oldtimer religious leaders, especially the prophet Theras, could "hear" these voices. The Tsils warned Theras about the Death Seed plague caused by the insects known as the drochs. The Tsils instructed the prophet to prevent any ship large enough to support powerful shielding from landing or leaving their world. Since the drochs were weakened by the sunlight reflected by the Tsils, they could not be permitted to reach the lightless void of space, where they would be free to spread their contagion.

The Tsils have lived on Nam Chorios since the planet first formed. Nine years after the Battle of Endor, thousands of Tsils were callously mined as minerals and altered so they could be used for various technological purposes. Officially, surveyors used them in the optical equipment that fil-

DESIGNATION
> SENTIENT <

PLANET OF ORIGIN
> NAM CHORIOS <

HEIGHT OF
AVERAGE ADULT
> 0.5 METERS <

ters light for K-class planets, but the Loronar Corporation secretly employed them in Centrally Controlled Independent Replicant (CCIR) technology, remote-controlled "brain" technology used in synthdroids and Needle starfighters.

An engineering specification from Loronar Corporation states how the crystals can be reprogrammed and what that accomplishes.

> The crystals can be tuned to focus solar energy into microscopic beams of light that power all the autonomic responses of the replicant's systems. They do this with the efficiency of nerve cells in a human body. The gray channels in the crystal, which act as power streams, redirect impulses in any manner we

choose, but they must be altered for that purpose. They are, without question, the most pliable and potent means of transferring focused energy that we have found to date.

These atrocities enraged the Tsil population. Despite the reprogrammed state of the Tsils who were removed, they maintained contact with their relatives, often over great distances. When, in a second incident, the remaining Tsil once again helped stop the drochs from escaping Nam Chorios, they asked Luke Skywalker to provide some assurance that the stolen Tsils would be returned, no matter their condition.

New Republic Intelligence quickly announced a galaxywide recall, which has been successful in recovering a majority of the wayward crystals.

DESIGNATION
> SENTIENT <

PLANET OF ORIGIN
> TATOOINE <

HEIGHT OF AVERAGE ADULT
> 1.8 METERS <

t usken Raiders, also called Sand People, are tall, strong, aggressive, nomadic humanoid warriors that live in the desert wastelands of Tatooine. From head to toe, every Tusken is covered in strips of cloth and tattered robes belted together with dewback-hide leather. They view the world through tubelike shields that protect their eyes, and breathe through simple filters that keep them from inhaling the sand particles that constantly swirl through the Tatooine air. Everything in their attire serves to keep moisture trapped near their bodies.

The Tuskens are ruthless fighters, hardened by their harsh environment to the point that they show no mercy to other species. They fear little but can be driven away when they face a strong show of force. They tend to travel in bands of up to twenty or thirty individuals and nearly always ride their bantha mounts in a straight line, one behind the other, in order to hide their numbers from potential enemies. Their weapon of choice is the gaderffii, or gaffi stick, which is basically a double-edge weapon made of cannibalized metal scavenged from abandoned or wrecked vehicles. Some carry blaster rifles, but Tusken blasters are not the most technologically advanced or powerful weapons.

Sand People are inherently angered by the presence of human settlers in their territories, whom they feel encroach upon their rations of water and food. They will often attack moisture farmers and settlers without provocation—simply for the sake of intimidating those they perceive as enemies.

Despite their bullying natures, Tusken Raiders actually shy away from massive Jawa sandcrawler fortresses, heavily protected farmsteads, large cities, and even settlements. They also wisely avoid the vicious krayt dragons. It is evident that they favor situations where they clearly seem to have the upper hand and will take only calculated risks.

Since they are a nomadic people, they maintain no permanent shelters and keep few possessions, which they view as liabilities. Despite their willingness to move constantly, they allow no other changes in their society or culture. They are thoroughly resistant to technologies—even those they steal from hapless patrols, caravans, and moisture farmers. They feel that killing with primitive weapons provides the bravest of victories.

Sand People make no social distinction between males or females, and both are expected to perform to the peak of their abilities.

The language of Tusken Raiders is to most outsiders an unintelligible, angry combination of consonants and growls. They have no written language, so they rely on a long and complex oral tradition to keep track of their lineage and legends. Each tribe has a storyteller, whose duty is to preserve and retell the tribe's history. The storyteller chronicles the coming-of-age stories for each member of the clan. Once he or she tells a tale the first time, not one word is allowed to change from that time forward.

Each storyteller takes an apprentice and begins teaching him the clan history. The apprentice is not allowed to practice the history aloud, as the words may never be spoken incorrectly. If the apprentice makes a mistake, he is killed outright, because such an error is considered blasphemy. Once an apprentice has learned every tale of every lineage perfectly, he becomes the next storyteller, and the teacher wanders into the desert to die.

Because they live such a harsh, warlike existence, coming of age is a process that is very important to them. Children are cared for by adult Tuskens, but they are not considered people until they have endured the ceremonies that make them adults. Babies often die because of the difficult desert life, and Sand People take great pride in knowing that only the strongest survive. To earn the distinction of adulthood, youths must each perform a great feat of skill or prowess, the magnitude of which determines their stations in the tribe. In his notes, Senior Anthropologist Hoole writes:

> A solemn ceremony was held to prepare two Tusken youths for their journey into the wilderness. They were given totems, armaments, and water.

Saying no words, and showing no fear, they mounted their banthas and headed off into the wilderness. The rest of the clan watched until the youths disappeared on the horizon, then returned to their lives as if it were a normal day.
> Several weeks passed, and the Sand People said nothing of the two youngsters who had left them. Since they were not seen as people until they passed their test, no one would acknowledge them.
> Then, one day, a solitary figure on a bantha appeared on the horizon. One youth had returned, carrying on his mount the armor and weapons of four Imperial stormtroopers. Raucous activity erupted among the tribe's membership. A bonfire was lit, food was prepared, and amidst great ceremony, the storyteller added the young Tusken's story of bravery to the tribal history.
> Again, no word was mentioned about the other youth who did not return. It was as if he had never existed.

Twi'lek

twi'leks are tall, thin humanoids indigenous to the Ryloth system in the Outer Rim. Their most notable feature is the tentacle head-tails—called either lekku or tchun-tchin—two of which protrude from the back of each individual's skull, distinguishing them from the multitude of other species found across the known galaxy. These fatty, tapered, prehensile growths serve both sensual and cognitive functions. In conversation, Twi'leks will often refer to their lekku individually: tchin is the right lekku, and tchun is the left lekku. On a few rare instances, Twi'leks are born with more than two head-tails. Such variation affords them status and, in some cases, wealth. The Old Republic Senator Orn Free Taa, for example, was a Rutian Twi'lek with four head-tails.

The Twi'lek's smooth skin comes in many variations of color, spanning the rainbow. Sharp, clawlike nails punctuate their long, flexible fingers. Their orange or yellow eyes are especially good for seeing in the dark.

Ryloth is a dry, rocky world with a peculiar orbit that causes one half of the world to remain a barren, unlivable desert where the sun's rays constantly scorch the surface. The other side is always trapped in frigid darkness. Most of Ryloth's indigenous species inhabit the dark portion of the planet, while Twi'leks live in cities carved out of the mountains in the "twilight" section that borders the light and the dark side of the world—where the temperature is somewhat comfortable.

Theirs is a primitive industrial civilization based on windmills and air-spun turbines that provide power for heat, air circulation, lights, and minor industry within their city complexes. Hot air blows from the sun-based regions; called heat storms, these winds power the turbines and wind-

> **DESIGNATION**
> **> SENTIENT <**
>
> **PLANET OF ORIGIN**
> **> RYLOTH <**
>
> **HEIGHT OF AVERAGE ADULT**
> **> 2 METERS <**

mills. The dry twisters reach temperatures in excess of 300 degrees, with gusts hitting 500 kilometers per hour. Although dangerous, they provide the warmth necessary to sustain life.

Twi'leks are omnivorous. They cultivate edible molds and fungi and raise bovinelike rycrits, which they use for food and clothing. While their ancestors seem to have been hunters who struck out upon the frosty plains to find game for food, present-day Twi'leks have developed a more agrarian society.

The Twi'lek people are intelligent, capable of learning and speaking most galactic languages. Their own language combines verbal sounds and subtle movements for which they use their head-tails to communicate complex concepts. Even the most advanced offworld linguists have difficulty interpreting all the head-tail movements inherent to the Twi'lek language. For this reason, when two Twi'leks converse in public their discussions may remain completely private, unless observed by another Twi'lek or an appropriately programmed protocol droid.

This ability to conduct private communication led to much suspicion on the part of many Imperial humans. However, this fear was unfounded, for the Twi'leks reserve this advantage for much more personal benefits, as revealed in the personal journal of a young female.

> *These Imperials feel that we are treasonous spies, but what they do not realize is that the lekku are, in truth, our "spiritual appendages." In jostling them, we express the movement of our inner divinity. While this is indeed private communication, it is also a communion on the metaphysical level. While its meaning may remain a secret maintained amongst the speakers, it is not duplicitous or deceitful, nor is harm meant to those outside the communication. Without exception, it is truthful and real, and it cannot go against our verbal expression. To speak one thing and sign something entirely different would require extreme concentration, the likes of which may be impossible.*

Contrary to the paranoia expressed by the Imperials, the people of Ryloth remained clear of the Imperial conflict, although if they had been called upon to spy, they would have been quite good at it. They prefer cunning and slyness to physical battle.

Hidden beneath the surface of their world, their city complexes are massive interconnecting networks of catacombs and chambers. Built into the rocky outcroppings, they blend right in with the environment of their world—vivid evidence of this people's subtle nature.

Each of these cities is autonomous and governed by a head clan consisting of five Twi'leks who collectively direct industry and trade. These leaders are born to their position and exercise absolute power. When one member

of the head clan dies, the remaining four are driven out to follow their colleague to the Bright Lands, making room for the next generation. If there is no generation prepared to follow, a set of regents will take over until a new head clan can be selected.

Because Twi'leks possess no spacefaring capability of their own, they have grown dependent on neighboring systems—as well as on pirates, smugglers, and merchants—for much of

their galactic interaction. One of their greatest exports is a mineral called ryll, which is used in many medicines, but also is used as an expensive and addictive recreational drug.

Ryloth has become vulnerable to the seamy side of galaxy life as criminal vessels comb the planet to stock their thriving ryll trades. Smugglers often raid ryll storehouses, and some head clans have actually forced their own people into slavery, surrendering them as protection payment when threatened by the possibility of pillaging on a wider scale.

With the dawn of the New Republic, some head clans on Ryloth banded together to stop the slave trade and protect one another from the retribution of angry smugglers and slave traders. This has created a much safer environment on Ryloth, and more and more legitimate trading organizations have started to bring business to the world.

tynnans are small, intelligent water mammals who spend nearly as much time in the frigid waters of their planet as they do on the land. A thick layer of blubber insulates each of them from the cold and gives them a cute, pudgy, disarming appearance that belies their high intelligence. They have long buckteeth for gnawing wood as their ancient ancestors did when building river dams, but this is something Tynnans have ceased to do. As a result, their teeth are growing shorter with each generation. Their eyesight is poor, but they have substantial strength and stamina. Like most aquatic mammals, they can hold their breath for extended periods.

An unfortunate result of their appearance is that few other species take them seriously. Odumin, the noted Corporate Sector Authority territory administrator, speaks of this in his memoirs.

> My appearance, admittedly, is not one to inspire confidence or awe. So I had to build a mystique around my real name, assume a new identity, and use my appearance to catch my opponents off guard. No one would ever believe the small, gentle Tynnan named Spray was really someone who could figure out their schemes and haul them off to prison. When they did believe, it was too late.
> Therefore, there's really only one way for Tynnans to deal with the misperceptions others perpetuate. Rather than take offense at their short-sightedness, we should use it to our advantage.

Tynna is a world rich with natural resources, so the Tynnans decided to develop its economic structure and infrastructure through the aid of Old Republic conglomerates. However, they were determined to protect their environment, and for the most part it has remained untouched.

The population of Tynna is one of the wealthiest in the galaxy, because the government reinvested the profits from its industries back into the society itself. While not all Tynnans possess great riches, the entire species benefits from an extensive state-run society. Nearly all necessities of life—housing, food, education, and entertainment— are provided to citizens free of charge. Many devote themselves to the arts and sciences. Others travel the galaxy on tours and expeditions.

The Tynnan love of leisure does not, in any way, prove them to be weak-willed, lazy, or shortsighted. Tynnans plan every project, every job, and every undertaking to the minutest detail and execute their plans with incredible enthusiasm and energy. They are a pragmatic people not given to religion or mythology, as these often cause conflict. Leadership is decided by lottery, and those selected serve in a governing legislature. Once they serve their one-year term, they may not serve again for six years. Because any Tynnan could end up leading, citizens take it upon themselves to be informed and knowledgeable about politics and government affairs.

During the rule of the Empire, the Tynnans tried to accommodate the wishes of Palpatine's representatives. However, when the Empire tried a full-scale invasion, the Tynnans had already predicted their movements and had erected an impenetrable planetary shield. Tynna has remained unharmed ever since.

DESIGNATION
> SENTIENT <

PLANET OF ORIGIN
> TYNNA <

HEIGHT OF
AVERAGE ADULT
> 1.4 METERS <

Ugnaught

Ugnaughts are small, porcine humanoids known for their tireless work ethic. They are especially good mine workers, whether for gas or mineral mining. Their short, stocky, muscular bodies are able to withstand long periods of effort under harsh conditions.

This species is native to the planet Gentes in the Anoat system. However, very few—if any—remain on that world. Unfortunately, the Ugnaughts suffered the fate of many other primitive species throughout the galaxy: merchants, smugglers, traders, and other offworlders gathered entire tribes and took them to new worlds to live and work as indentured servants and slaves.

One of the largest populations of these beings can be found at Cloud City on Bespin. When the Corellian eccentric Lord Ecclessis Figg decided to build this floating Tibanna gas mine colony high in Bespin's atmosphere, he knew the project would require cheap manual labor. Using force, Figg rounded up three Ugnaught tribes—the Irden, Botrut, and Isced—and took them to a space station near Bespin to offer them a deal. If they would build his floating city, he would then grant them their freedom. Further, they and their descendants would be allowed to live and work in the colony and share in the company's profits. The Ugnaughts accepted the deal and went right to work on Figg's project. After the city was finished, they began to reap the benefits of their labor.

When Lando Calrissian acquired the city and became the legal administrator of Bespin, he honored the agreement with the Ugnaughts, until he lost control of the facility to the Empire. With the onset of Imperial occupation, the Ugnaughts were enslaved once again and forced to

work longer hours under even harsher conditions. Many were removed from the facility altogether. Lando eventually returned to Bespin, and with the help of Luke Skywalker, Lando's friend Lobot, and the Ugnaughts, he regained control of the city. He later turned the city over to the Ugnaughts' chosen leader of the ruling Terend Council, King Ozz. Today they own the city that they helped build.

In an address to his subjects, King Ozz lent new insight into what freedom means to the Ugnaught tribes.

> We've always wanted a chance te show t' universe what we can do wit' the fruits of our labors. No longer will t' galaxy think us t' be a primitive people. Many outsiders have mistaken us for brainless drones, laborin' to bring d' gas from t' mines of Bespin. No more. We've educated arselves, trained arselves, learned about t' galaxy and all that's in't, to bring arselves otta our primitive way o' life. We are now masters of our own futures, and our futures are now very promisin'.

> Now that Cloud City is ours, we kin set about creatin' regular system o' trade, and makin' strides in supplyin' our friends in t' Alliance with all t' Tibanna gas they can possibly use ta win this war against t' Empire.

> Today we're free. And troo t' perseverance that has always been our greatest asset

we will remain free. By con-
tinuin' to work hard, my
friends, and continuin' to
strive fer better lives, we
will find that, from this day
forward, all things are wit'in
our grasp.

Although now modernized, the Ugnaught people retain the rich oral tradition they have long maintained. Even though they have been transplanted to countless new worlds, they have held on to many of their customs and laws established in the time before their enslavement. Immediately upon their acceptance of Figg's offer, the three tribes reestablished their ruling Terend Council, elected officers, the ufflor, and chose traditional blood professions.

Blood professions are vocations passed down from generation to generation within each family. A miner will teach his children to mine, and a mechanic teaches his children to repair and construct machinery. When Ugnaughts reach the age of twenty, they become candidates for their inherited professions. If the number of new candidates for any given profession exceeds the community's needs, the candidates call a blood duel. Through a series of fights to the death, young Ugnaughts battle for the right to inherit their blood professions.

Despite this brutal tradition, Ugnaughts are a predominantly nonviolent species. They tend to shy away from contact with other species and usually do not learn Basic, except for the ufflor and members of the Terend Council. As a rule, Ugnaughts feel more comfortable when dealing with members of their own tribes.

Of the three tribes on Bespin, the Isced tribe has encountered the most difficulty with outsiders and with the

other tribes. This is because they have a vicious sense of humor and are prone to playing potentially dangerous practical jokes. One such joke led to the death of six mine workers, when an Isced mischievously hid mining tools inside a carbon-freezing chamber. He planned to only lightly spray his coworkers with carbon dust as a prank as they searched for the tools, but all were asphyxiated.

During their indentured servant years, a majority of the Ugnaughts lived in the Bespin mining quarters. Once the city was liberated, they came to inhabit all portions of the facility. However, council meetings, folk-story telling, dances, and blood duels still take place in various arenas located, by tradition, in the mining quarters area. And although the king of the tribes

meets with the Terend Council on the administrative levels of Cloud City, his coronation and all other special government events are held in this same traditional area, as a reminder of the Ugnaughts' proud history as laborers.

Umgullian Blob

Umgullian blobs are grayish green protozoan creatures bred by various species for specific purposes. Large, single-celled organisms with limited intelligence, they feed on nutrients from Umgul's foggy atmosphere and every three years reproduce through the process of mitosis.

While blobs reproduce by natural splitting, blob variations are created through genetic manipulation in a parent blob, which then splits and creates a copy of itself. Wealthy human residents of Umgul keep blobs that have been bred as pets. Physicians train blobs to ooze across patients' backs to enhance joint alignment and perform muscular massage. Some blobs are bred for racing by increasing the creatures' speed and fluidity; racing blobs can move themselves along at speeds nearing 100 kilometers per hour by rolling and flowing forward like viscous bubbles of liquid. The blobs exhibit a certain animal cunning that can be manipulated by their trainers to inspire them to run an obstacle course—or "blobstacle course," as it is called.

Racing blobs are also frequently bred in different colors and are found in hues of vermilion, turquoise, and lime-green. Before they are permitted to race, they must pass strict requirements regarding age, mass, and viscosity. Samples of their physical matter are analyzed for tampering and drugs before and after each race.

Because of their need for certain nutrients unique to Umgul, these creatures do not fare well on other worlds. Their natural environment is costly to simulate on other planets, so the sport of blob racing remains exclusively Umgullian.

While the blobs are an important part of Umgullian culture, they do require skilled handling. In his notes on his visit to Umgul, Senior Anthropologist Hoole notes:

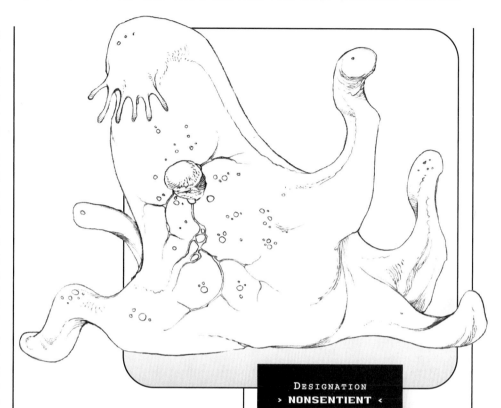

> Two incidents occurred during my trip that revealed how dangerous these seemingly innocuous creatures could be.
> Having been left unsupervised during a massage therapy session, a young patient, Rith Murisson of Krnay, discovered that the treatments had left a series of disfiguring suction marks on her back. The doctor had not taken into account the patient's sensitivity to certain secretions common to the Umgullian blob breed he had used in the procedure.
> Also, a two-year-old child was nearly asphyxiated when his mother left the boy unattended with the family racing blob. The child attempted to give the creature a hug and fell inside of it. The mother quickly summoned medical droids, who managed to extricate the boy just in time to save his life.

DESIGNATION
> NONSENTIENT <

PLANET OF ORIGIN
> UMGUL <

HEIGHT OF AVERAGE ADULT
> 1 METER <

Verpine

Verpine are highly intelligent insectoids that inhabit the Roche asteroid field. Each Verpine has two legs, and their sticklike bodies are covered by plates of flexible, green chitinous shell called carahide, capable of deflecting a glancing blaster bolt or a knife attack. Their two large, black eyes are a superior version of an ordinary insect's compound eyes and can perceive microscopic detail with amazing precision. They have short snouts with toothless mouths, and a single antenna extends from each side of the head. Unlike other insect species, they possess only two arms, each of which ends in three fingers, one being an opposable digit.

The Verpine antennae are sensitive to radio-wave transmissions, and with them, the Verpine can communicate with each other unaided over distances of approximately a hundred kilometers. By passing messages from one individual to another, they can create a natural radio-wave network spanning the entire Roche asteroid field. Some observers have mistaken this ability for telepathy.

Unlike other insectoid species, Verpine are hermaphrodites. When their hive needs additional members, the community asks selected Verpine to reproduce. Some are assigned egg production, and they lay their eggs in the colony's incubator. Others carry out assigned fertilization, then the entire community cares for the resulting hatchlings. At one time in their history, a brood would yield some semisentient drones that would be utilized as menial laborers. As the Verpine evolved, they abandoned the need for drones, and egg-layers began to ingest a special enzyme that ensures that broods yield only intelligent Verpine.

The Verpine are especially good at the arts of compromise and arbitration. Some historians claim that they

DESIGNATION
> SENTIENT <

PLANET OF ORIGIN
> ROCHE <
ASTEROID FIELD

HEIGHT OF
AVERAGE ADULT
> 1.9 METERS <

evolved on a world called Roche, but destroyed it in a civil war. From this disaster sprang their social imperative for consensus, through which they achieve government. They use their radio-signal communication to poll the entire population on any given initiative. Because everyone has a say, everyone considers these decisions thoroughly binding. This system also allows any Verpine to speak with complete authority, so that, in effect, every Verpine is a political leader.

Verpine have an intense curiosity that causes them to take apart, reassemble, modify, and duplicate all devices that fall into their hands. They are experts in every field of technology and have even adapted the asteroids they now inhabit to suit their environmental needs, creating hermetically sealed tunnel colonies. Most house twenty to a hundred inhabi-

tants, while a few larger colonies house up to 1,000. All are self-sufficient, capable of producing energy, food, and air. Repulsor fields envelop the colonized asteroids to prevent collisions with other asteroids.

General Wedge Antilles writes of the Verpine:

> They are some of the finest shipbuilders and technicians in the galaxy. As the inventors of the ship stabilization system, or "gravity gyro," they have placed themselves among the top engineers and technicians. They are prone to making improvements—sometimes unauthorized—on any equipment we assign to them. I suppose there are worse habits a technician could exhibit.

Vors are hollow-boned, winged, reptilian creatures that inhabit the planet Vortex. They are tall, delicate-looking beings with pointed heads and thin bodies. Their leathery wings are sheets of thin flesh stretched between their arms and legs, and using them, the Vors maintain an extraordinary degree of control in flight, even in the severe windstorms that are common on their world.

They are a highly intelligent species, capable of magnificent artistic accomplishment. One of their greatest achievements is the Cathedral of Winds—an immense crystalline structure constructed from an organic blueprint to produce exquisite musical tones when Vortex's wind currents pass over and through it.

This structure is the symbol of—and the center of—Vor civilization. They perform beautiful concerts of ethereal music by covering and uncovering openings in the building with their own bodies. The Vors perform the concert only once a year, and recording a concert is strictly prohibited. Hence, each one is a much heralded event.

Because of the harsh winds that plague their world, Vors live in half-buried dwellings during the stormy season, which is several months long. Seen from above, their homes appear as small mounds arranged in rings in the purple, vermilion, and tan grasses of the plains.

The Vors tend to concentrate on the needs of the majority rather than on those of individuals and are always concerned with the "bigger picture." At first impression, they appear to be completely emotionless. However, they are simply very good at objectifying their feelings and are actually able to strictly contain their emotions, to consider them at a more private time.

This control was exemplified dur-ing a traumatic incident involving the Mon Calamari Admiral Ackbar, who accidentally destroyed the original Cathedral of Winds. His B-wing, which had been tampered with by an Imperial operative, crashed into the crystal structure, shattering it and killing more than 350 Vors. Though Ackbar was devastated by the accident and even resigned his post in the New Republic, the Vors remained completely calm. Rather than seek revenge, Krini-shen, chief council of Vortex, made the following announcement:

> We cannot blame anyone for the Cathedral's destruction.

We understand that it was an accident, and we forgive Admiral Ackbar. While the Cathedral is gone, this is not forever. We will rebuild, and this will be our sole purpose until we can once again play our concert in peace.
> Until that time, let no music sound. No pipe shall be blown, nor voice raised in song. It would be a mockery of our broken sacred place. In silence the Cathedral was first born, so it will be again. Let all heed this command.

DESIGNATION
> SENTIENT <
....
PLANET OF ORIGIN
> VORTEX <
....
HEIGHT OF
AVERAGE ADULT
> 2 METERS <
....

Vornskr

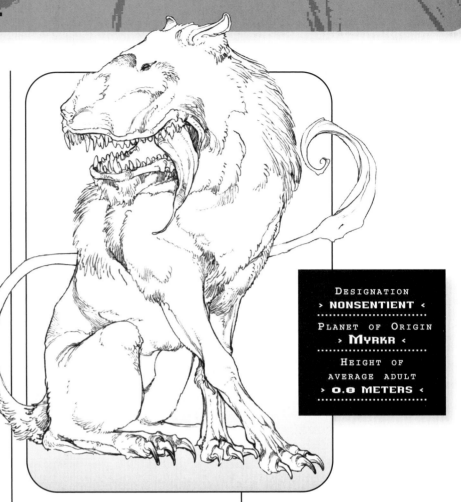

Cunning predators, the vornskrs are vicious canine animals indigenous to the planet Myrkr. They are covered with gray or black fur and have doglike muzzles, red eyes, sharp teeth, and lethal, whiplike tails.

These creatures usually hunt their prey during the night, though they will stalk during the day if they are hungry. They count the reptilian, Force-sensitive ysalamiri among their natural prey. When attacking, they use their tails as efficient attack weapons. Their tails are coated with a mild poison that can stun creatures as large as a human. When their prey is effectively stunned, a vornskr will leap on it and tear it apart.

Vornskrs have been found to be capable of detecting Force-users, and they hunt the ysalamiri through the two species' attunement to the Force. They mistake any Force-users for being their natural prey, and react in hunt-attack mode. They also demonstrate a particular hatred for Jedi. While on Myrkr, Luke Skywalker was attacked by several of the creatures, who did their best to attempt to kill him.

Smuggler Talon Karrde, a friend and former associate of Mara Jade, once domesticated two vornskrs and trained them to serve as his own guard animals. He described some of their traits in this article submitted to *Galactic Zoology Monthly*.

> It's a strange fact about the vornskrs, but if you bob their tails, they lose some of their normal hunting aggression. I've run into these beasts a couple of times in the past, and I discovered this quite by accident when I met one and shot its tail off—purely in self-defense. It was stunned and hurt, of course, and being a softhearted guy, I doctored him up and named him Sturm. He warmed up to me quickly, especially since I was feeding him.

> Later, I encountered another vornskr, pinned in one of our perimeter traps. I tranquilized him and bobbed his tail. This one, whom I named Drang, also trained pretty easily.

> So, as long as you get rid of the tail, feed them, and play with them regularly, they're pretty good company. Just don't invite your Jedi friends over for dinner.

DESIGNATION
> NONSENTIENT <

PLANET OF ORIGIN
> MYRKR <

HEIGHT OF AVERAGE ADULT
> 0.8 METERS <

Vratix

the Vratix, a highly intelligent insectoid species native to the world Thyferra, are the creators of the miraculous healing substance known as bacta. They are tall beings with greenish gray skin and black bulbous eyes, and each stands upright on four slender legs—two long and two short. The long, muscular forelegs propel them forward, while the shorter hind legs provide additional lift when they jump. Two triple-jointed arms extend from their shoulders, ending in long, three-fingered hands. At their elbow joints they have sharp spikes, which are often used in hand-to-hand combat. The two skinny, floppy antennae on their small heads offer unusually acute hearing. A thin, long neck connects the head to their scaly torsos.

A Vratix's entire body is covered by small, thin hairs that excrete a chemical called denin that changes the color of the skin as an expression of emotion. This ability is part of their language, and it accompanies their high-pitched voices, punctuated by clicking sounds. Because of their continuous trade relationship with other species, Vratix can speak and comprehend Basic. They also use the sense of touch in social interactions, because to them, it is the most reliable of the senses. This tradition often makes other species uncomfortable and has led to misunderstandings. Vratix also possess limited telepathic ability, allowing them to share thoughts with other Vratix whom they know well.

There are two different castes within their society, and one caste—the Verachen—makes bacta. All Vratix reproduce asexually, and they live very long lives in their modest rain-forest villages. These villages consist of high towers with circular terraces and arching bridges connecting them. The knytix, who occupy a lower caste, are actually a different, smaller species that scientists believe may be related to the Vratix. They serve as common laborers and servants.

The Vratix once shared their homeworld with humans who ran the bacta-producing cartels and maintained Imperial connections. Competition between cartels was harsh, and the Vratix were often caught in the middle of it, so they formed insurgent groups to fight for reform, sometimes using terrorist methods. Rogue Squadron, under the leadership of Wedge Antilles, helped liberate Thyferra from cartel control. Since then, the Verachen run the cartels and supply the galaxy with bacta. In this report, Antilles describes the way the Vratix would fight.

> One of the insurgent groups who call themselves the Ashern Circle painted themselves black and fought with ruthless desperation and absolutely no remorse. To gain control of the bacta supply, they had no qualms about kidnapping and killing company agents, or even poisoning the company's precious merchandise. They were willing, in fact, to kill their own people to drive off the cartels.

Bacta is a translucent reddish solution of alazhi and kavam bacterial particles. The Vratix have used bacta for thousands of years. Combined with a liquid called ambori, the solution acts like a body's own vital fluids and heals all but the most serious of wounds. Bacterial particles actually seek out the injuries and promote amazingly quick tissue growth without scarring.

DESIGNATION
> SENTIENT <
PLANET OF ORIGIN
> THYFERRA <
HEIGHT OF AVERAGE ADULT
> 1.8 METERS <

Wampa

Wampas are vicious primate creatures that inhabit the ice world Hoth. They stand up to three meters tall and possess razor-sharp claws and fangs. A wampa that has passed puberty usually has on its head sharp, curving horns that continue to grow larger with age.

Because of their acute sense of smell and well-camouflaged coat of thick, white fur, wampas are excellent hunters and are rarely themselves the victims of predators. They wander the icy wastelands of Hoth preying on tauntauns and other unwary creatures. After disabling his prey, the wampa will drag it to his cavernous, icy lair beneath Hoth's surface. Using hot breath to melt the ice, and saliva to moisten portions of the prey's body, the wampa places the prey against the roof of his cave so that it freezes in place, suspended from the ceiling. Wampas will also impale large creatures, such as tauntauns, on ice stalagmites, piercing them through the anklebones. Because wampas prefer fresh meat, they often keep their victims alive until they choose to consume them.

Luke Skywalker, who was once a prisoner of a wampa, described the experience in a report filed after the Rebel Alliance evacuation of Hoth.

> The lair was a foul place. I could smell the blood and entrails in the snow, since the wampa was feasting on my tauntaun nearby. Tauntauns smell even worse dead than alive. The wampa had frozen my feet to the ceiling, so I was hanging upside down. Not to mention the fact that the place was so cold that my nose hairs were freezing. I'm just glad I had the presence of mind to shut out the stink and the cold, or I never would have focused my energies and gotten out of there. Luckily my captor wasn't terribly smart.

Wampas usually hunt alone, but they will occasionally band together to lash out against a threat to the local wampa population, such as a human settlement. In this, they show a rudimentary form of intelligence and cunning, as they will often scout their enemies' location and strength before formulating an attack.

Skywalker has claimed that these creatures do possess long memories. During the routine patrol when he was attacked and captured by a wampa, he escaped its lair by slicing off its arm with his lightsaber. When he returned on a later visit to Hoth, the same one-armed wampa discovered and attacked him, along with his cohort Callista. This time, Skywalker managed to kill the beast with his lightsaber, allowing them to escape.

DESIGNATION
> **SEMISENTIENT** <

PLANET OF ORIGIN
> **HOTH** <

HEIGHT OF AVERAGE ADULT
> **3 METERS** <

Weequay

a strong, rugged people, with countenances weathered by harsh desert winds, the Weequays are a humanoid species from the desert world Sriluur in the system of the same name. Their skin is coarse and gnarled and may be black, gray, brown, or tan in color. The males wear topknots drawn to the top of their otherwise bald heads, while the females usually shave their heads completely.

Often seen as threatening, the Weequays will not usually speak in the presence of a non-Weequay. They will frequently hire a trustworthy non-Weequay to speak for them. In fact, they don't talk much even when around their own people. This is because they possess a type of pheromone-based communication that allows members of the same clan to communicate in complete silence. This type of speaking is as clear as the spoken word, but it works only with clan members.

Theirs is a complex, brutal culture that is centered on the worship of a multitude of gods that symbolize the natural forces and indigenous animals. Their primary god is Quay, the god of the moon, from whom the species' name is derived. To contact their gods they use totems that symbolize the sphere of control of each given deity. Their main totem is a spherical object that they use for obtaining advice from Quay himself. They address the totem as Quay in an effort to please the god.

Senior Anthropologist Hoole describes the use of this object, in the following quote from his notes on the Weequay belief system.

> The Quay totem behaves much like a child's toy. Every Weequay carries one, and they shake it and wait for advice to appear, directing them in every decision they must make. They maintain a great devotion for the totem and will grow violently angry if anyone questions the validity of the answer given.
> The Quay produces its own problems, however, as a Weequay may shake the object for hours seeking the answers he wants to receive. But he will remain patient, assuming that because all Weequays have the totem, the god was probably occupied answering the questions posed by others.

Life in a Weequay clan is completely impersonal, and clan members do not even possess names, since individuality is not a concept they understand. They will take a name only when they leave their homeworld.

The Weequays were originally a nomadic, desert-dwelling people, but eventually established large clan cities in ocean coastal areas. They employ limited technology, though they are known as skilled makers of melee weapons such as force pikes. At the center of their cities are shrines made of black polished stone. The shrines are called *thal*, where followers known as *sant* leave anonymous offerings. Building *thal* offplanet is not allowed, but Weequays who are not on Sriluur may sacrifice a strong animal or adversary to address the gods. Weequays who are offplanet will wear individual topknot braids for each Sriluur year they are not at home. When they return to Sriluur, they will shave off the topknots.

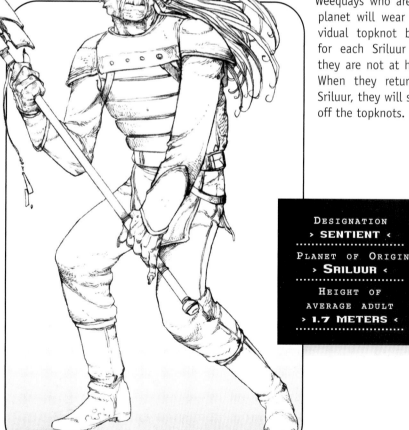

DESIGNATION
> **SENTIENT** <

PLANET OF ORIGIN
> **SRILUUR** <

HEIGHT OF AVERAGE ADULT
> **1.7 METERS** <

Whiphid

Whiphids are tall, bulky bipeds with long, yellow-white or golden fur. They live on the icy planet called Toola, and are characterized by their prominent, hairless faces, with exaggerated cheekbones and forehead. Two tusks protrude from their lower jaws, and their two massive arms end in three-fingered hands with razor-sharp claws.

Because of their cold environment, Whiphid bodies maintain a thick layer of blubber that serves to trap heat in their system. Their fur, which is covered with a natural oil, repels water so they can swim in the frigid seas. In warmer environments they shed several centimeters of fur, burn off much of their fat, and their hollow cheeks widen, creating a broader face that serves to dissipate heat.

Whiphids are carnivorous predators who experience no greater joy than tracking down something to kill. They exhibit pleasant, easygoing personalities, however, and when dealing with offworlders they will take great care to determine who is proper prey and who is not. Their criteria seem to include (1) whether the subject talks back, and (2) whether the subject seems to be good company. Children are always considered off-limits.

In the following journal entry, Senior Anthropologist Hoole writes of a good survival tactic for dealing with Whiphids.

> When I approached the group of Whiphids, I saw the leader leaning toward me and taking several deep breaths. He was sniffing—as if trying to pick up a scent. The others near him held spears as if making ready to throw them in my direction.
> I opened my arms as a gesture of friendship, told the

DESIGNATION
> SENTIENT <
....
PLANET OF ORIGIN
> TOOLA <
....
HEIGHT OF
AVERAGE ADULT
> 2 METERS <
....

leader my name, and explained that I meant no harm. He walked around me, inspecting me, and asked me why I had no weapons.
> "One who comes as a friend for learning should require no weapons," I answered.
> He sniffed again, nodded, then turned to say something to his fellows. They relaxed their spears and approached to greet me.

On Toola, Whiphids live in nomadic tribes consisting of three to ten families. During the warmer months, these tribes build permanent shelters of rocks, skins, and animal bones, to which they return each summer. During winter, the tribes migrate across the snowy steppes, following food and building temporary shelters. They track the native graze animals called mastmots and are strong enough to kill the large creatures with their bare hands and tusks. Most, how-ever, use spears, crude sabers, and clubs, and they transport their kill on sledges. The most successful hunters, called the Spearmasters, become the leaders of these Whiphid tribes. The Spearmaster determines where the tribe camps and what quarry to hunt.

Whiphids entered galactic society when various advanced species from dry, desert worlds came to Toola to harvest its ice. Some Whiphids have left with the ice harvesters to find work across the galaxy as mercenaries and bounty hunters. Others established businesses of their own, having learned the ways of offworlders. One such entrepreneur is Lady Valarian, who made her mark as the owner of the Lucky Despot Hotel and Casino on Tatooine. Valarian renovated a grounded ship and turned it into a thriving business, imbuing it with culinary and decorative themes unique to her native culture.

Womp Rat

Womp rats are members of a carnivorous, ill-tempered, and plentiful rodent species native to the desert world Tatooine. There are a couple of different varieties of these creatures, but for the most part they all exhibit much the same features.

Depending on the breed, womp rats can grow to be upward of three meters long, and they frequently travel in packs to overwhelm their prey—which may include dewbacks and banthas. They often target prey that is old, weak, or sick. They live primarily in the caves of Beggar's Canyon and the Jundland Wastes. Womp rats also like to forage in town garbage dumps.

Like most rodents, womp rats possess keen eyesight, hearing, and sense of smell. Their fur is usually brown, tan, or gray, and their orange eyes refract sunlight. They have sharp claws and teeth that can easily slice through flesh, enabling them to kill and eat just about any creature they encounter. Their medium-long, thickish tails are quite strong and can be used to whip around their prey's legs to drag them off their feet. A ridge of spiky, dark fur forms a line down the length of the spine. They reproduce at an alarming rate, and a single female may produce a brood of sixteen or more at a time.

The most common womp rat is the variety that lives in the Beggar's Canyon region of Tatooine. These usually grow no larger than two meters, but are well known for attacking Jawas and raiding the storehouses of moisture farmers in the region. Beggar's Canyon womp rats are so numerous that local residents go to great lengths to get rid of them, as Luke Skywalker reported.

> Biggs and I celebrated when we heard the government of Anchorhead and the surrounding Affiliated Moisture Farmers passed the bounty ordinance. At ten credits per womp rat, how could we resist running the Canyon to tag as many as we could? All of the local kids competed against each other to see who could bring in the most. Biggs and I banked so many womp rat corpses, we made enough money to upgrade both of our T-16s, and still had enough left to save for our education, which we both hoped would be at the Academy.

Another variety of womp rat, larger than the Beggar's Canyon rodent, is sometimes called the mutant womp rat. Found in the Jundland Wastes, it is known for the long, winglike ears growing from its head. These creatures appeared mysteriously a short time after the Empire came to Tatooine, and rumors persist that they evolved from Beggar's Canyon womp rats that raided caustic substances in Imperial waste dumps. They are not as numerous and do not reproduce as often as the regular Beggar's Canyon womp rats.

DESIGNATION
> NONSENTIENT <
....
PLANET OF ORIGIN
> TATOOINE <
....
HEIGHT OF
AVERAGE ADULT
> 2 METERS <
....

Wookiee

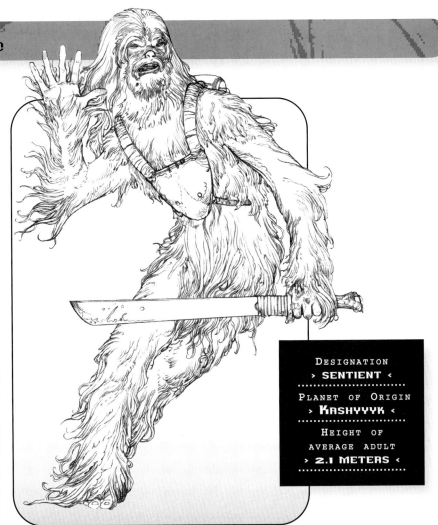

as members of one of the strongest sentient species in the galaxy, Wookiees are intelligent, arboreal creatures from the jungle world Kashyyyk. In addition to possessing many natural strengths and abilities from the day they are born, they show an extraordinary talent for repairing and adapting machines and technology.

With the emergence of Imperial rule, it was the Trandoshans, a species on a world neighboring Kashyyyk, who suggested that the Empire exploit the powerful Wookiees as slave labor. The Empire quickly overwhelmed the generally peaceful Wookiees, taking them to work camps located throughout the galaxy. The prisoners even helped—under duress—to build both of the Death Star battle stations. But the Wookiees did not give in easily, and even those remaining on their home planet maintained an undercurrent of rebellion. The Empire made it nearly impossible for those Wookiees to leave their world, and enlisted Trandoshan hunters to capture any Wookiees who did escape. For this reason there remains to this day quite a bit of animosity between the Wookiees and Trandoshans.

Wookiees are tall, fur-covered humanoids who exhibit varying eye color and fur that ranges in hue from white to light brown and black, often in a blend of different tones. They have retractable claws on their feet and on their hands, which they use only for climbing. To use their claws in hand-to-hand combat is considered dishonorable in their culture and is strictly forbidden.

Wookiees are especially known for loyalty and dedication to honor. They are devoted to friends and family and to those whom they feel they owe a life debt. Life debts are given by an individual to someone who has saved

DESIGNATION
> SENTIENT <

PLANET OF ORIGIN
> KASHYYYK <

HEIGHT OF AVERAGE ADULT
> 2.1 METERS <

his life, or who has given him another, similarly intense cause for loyalty. Wookiees who pledge themselves feel that only the giving of one's life can be adequate repayment for such a gift. One of the most famous life-debt arrangements was the one that existed between Captain Han Solo and his copilot Chewbacca. In his personal log entry, Solo wrote:

> Although initially it was annoying, I'd say right now, it isn't much of a debt really. Now it's a true friendship. When I saved his life, I ruined my promising military career. The last thing I wanted at the time was a walking reminder of my dishonorable discharge following me

around. Even though I'd realized at that point that the Empire wasn't the ideal employer, somehow seeing Chewie all the time was like rubbing salt in an open wound.

> But after a while, I came to depend on him. He was always there, out of some misbegotten duty to me—a man who really didn't deserve it. He was reliable and steadfast, unlike any other friend I'd had. I soon became more indebted to him than he was to me. I needed him. Still do.

Wookiees are also known for having short tempers, especially when honor is at stake, and can fly into berserker rages if they, their families, or their honor families—those with whom they share a life debt—are threatened. They have a reputation for hostility and have been known to smash objects as evidence they are angry. Despite this, they possess capacity for great kindness, sharp wit, and appreciation of the qualities of loyalty, honesty, and friendship.

Though they live in a natural, seemingly primitive environment, they are a mechanically advanced species and have developed much of their own technology, constructing huge cities in the trees of their homeworld Kashyyyk. They have developed high-tech tools unique to their own culture, the most famous of which is the bow-caster, or laser crossbow. They prefer, however, to use simple, homemade implements for accomplishing simple tasks.

Wookiees communicate via a system of grunts, growls, snuffles, barks, and roars, and the structure of their vocal cords and voice boxes won't allow them to speak Basic. For this same reason, humans find their language difficult to reproduce. Their primary dialect, used for trading and dealing with outsiders, is Shyriiwook, "tongue of the tree people." There are various dialects, such as Xaczik, spoken by Wookiees indigenous to the Wartaki Islands. Because Imperials thought all Wookiees were alike, they did not discover these other dialects, so when Wookiees were enslaved, they used Xaczik for delivering secret information to members of their resistance movement.

Theirs is a cultured society, and they exist in harmony with the environment of their world, living in well-developed cities on the seventh level of vegetation on Kashyyyk, high in the wroshyr trees. Though they wander the many levels, they never go any lower

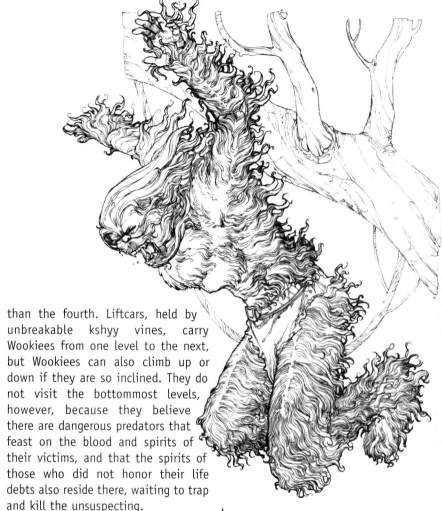

than the fourth. Liftcars, held by unbreakable kshyy vines, carry Wookiees from one level to the next, but Wookiees can also climb up or down if they are so inclined. They do not visit the bottommost levels, however, because they believe there are dangerous predators that feast on the blood and spirits of their victims, and that the spirits of those who did not honor their life debts also reside there, waiting to trap and kill the unsuspecting.

When Wookiees reach adulthood, however, they leave their families to explore the lower levels as a means of proving themselves. One way they do this is by harvesting fibers from the center of the alluring, pheromone-rich syren plant. When the yellow blossom's sensitive, bloodred inner flesh is touched, the petal jaws close over the victim, and he is digested painfully. Usually, a stronger Wookiee will hold the flower open, while a smaller one will scramble up and take the fibers. Wearing these fibers is said to be a symbol of virility and bravery.

Wookiees will hunt the dangerous quillarats that live just under the fifth level. These small, brownish green creatures, standing only a half-meter tall, sport long, needle-sharp quills all over their bodies and can hurl these quills with deadly accuracy. Male Wookiees hunt them for use as an offering that they present when they ask permission to marry a female Wookiee. They must, however, catch the quillarat barehanded and kill it without using a weapon. If the female Wookiee accepts the proposal, she shows her approval by biting into the creature's soft underbelly.

When they marry, Wookiees become mates for life. They bear their young one offspring at a time, and the traditional Wookiee family includes two to three children.

Yaka

Yakas are brutish-looking near-human cyborgs, large, muscular, and almost expressionless. Their large heads are implanted with cyborg brains, transforming them into one of the most intelligent and technically adept species in the galaxy—on par with the Verpine and the Sluissi.

The Yakas were once a simple and primitive people who lived on a planet neighboring Arkania. The scientifically advanced Arkanians took pity on these poor "mindless" people and implanted them with high-tech cyborg brains. While some socially conscious Arkanians protested, the Yakas themselves adapted to their change quite well, taking quickly to their new genius-level mental abilities.

Hence, the Yakas are much smarter than they appear. One unforeseen side effect of the implants, however, is that all Yakas possess a twisted sense of humor. The minds of the Yakas often whirl with accelerated thoughts, and after a while the chaos in their minds becomes boring. They enjoy making sarcastic comments and playing practical jokes and will find sources of humor in most circumstances. They often observe ironies in grim situations when others do not.

Yakas bear children the same way that most humanoid species do. Once the offspring are born, they undergo surgery to add their implants. The cyborg implants grow and develop along with the children. Because of their enhanced intelligence, the Yakas now perform this surgery themselves, desiring their children to inherit the same intelligence they have.

A recent development has shed a new, interesting light on the development of the Yaka cyborg implants. In his notes, Senior Anthropologist Hoole speaks of an interview he had with a state coroner on Coruscant who had

DESIGNATION
> SENTIENT <

PLANET OF ORIGIN
> NAME UNKNOWN <

HEIGHT OF AVERAGE ADULT
> 2 METERS <

noticed something unique about the Yakas' technology.

> Dr. Hira Deboota of the Coruscant State Coroner's office told me about the circumstances whereby he performed an autopsy on a deceased Yaka. Upon studying the implants, he was struck by the similarity to those he'd seen in Ganks often employed by Hutts as hired guns. He had reason to believe that there was a common origin for the circuitry of both the Yakas and the Ganks, and that while the technologies are similar, the Yakas' were more advanced.

> It looked to him as if the Gank circuitry was a beta test for the final implementation on the Yakas. He forwarded his findings to the proper New Republic scientific authorities for further investigation.

Yarkora

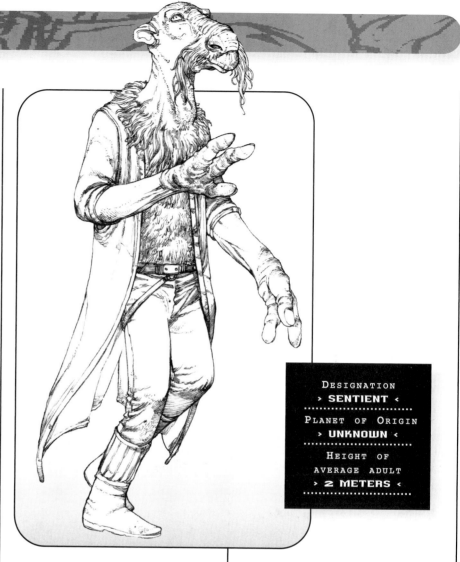

Yarkora are rarely seen, appearing only in the company of the lowest levels of galactic society, particularly in the Outer Rim Territories. They are tall, bipedal creatures, whose huge faces are characterized by two wide-set eyes, a large nose with a pair of unusually large nostrils, and furry whiskers that protrude from each cheek. They have the appearance of an ungulate species, though they do not chew their cud like unintelligent ungulates. They bear thick, heavy, black claws on their three-fingered hands, and these indicate an ancestry that can be traced back to hoofed creatures.

What little scientists have been able to glean about this people indicates that they seem to be obsessed with the gathering and controlling of information for their own gain. A security officer on Corellia notes in one police report:

> The Yarkora named Saelt-Marae is a sly one. He showed up at a gallery show and began to ask all sorts of questions. The art dealer, being a trusting fellow, probably told him a little too much about how secure he has to keep his place. A week later, his place was broken into, and some precious pieces of art were stolen.
> Saelt-Marae is so slick with his questions that this guy didn't even recall that he'd given out any valuable information to anyone until I brought it up myself several times. The dealer's statement was "Oh, yeah, there was this one guy who made me uncomfortable and asked me a lot of questions, but I don't think I gave away anything

very important!" As far as the dealer knew, they'd simply discussed philosophy, politics, and religion.
> Somehow, from that, Saelt-Marae was able to figure out how the guy protected his art. With this Yarkora on the loose, anyone can be a victim.

Though most of the Yarkora seen in the galaxy are known to be con artists or criminals who prey on the gullibility of others, members of the species tend to be rather unassuming. However, sentients who have encountered them have consistently noted that they seem to project an aura that makes others uncomfortable. They also exhibit the ability to intimidate others, either via their size or demeanor. Some scientists theorize that the Yarkora simply use their ability to observe and exploit a victim's own weaknesses, while others feel they may actually possess some sort of projected empathy.

DESIGNATION
> SENTIENT <

PLANET OF ORIGIN
> UNKNOWN <

HEIGHT OF AVERAGE ADULT
> 2 METERS <

Yevetha

the Yevetha are a xenophobic species from the planet N'zoth in the Koornacht Cluster, an isolated collection of about 2,000 stars that has yielded very little intelligent life in its system. They are thin, tall, bony mammalian humanoids, and the males of the species have scarlet facial crests along their cheeks, jaws, and the tops of their heads. These crests swell up when a male is spurred to violence, and their primary head crest engorges when a male is prepared to mate. The females of the species exhibit no such features.

Each Yevetha has wide-set black eyes and retractable dewclaws, one on the inside of each wrist above their six-fingered hands. Yevethan skin incorporates vestigial armor on the back of the neck and down the spine. Their brains are located in their thoraxes behind thick bone braincages, and a line of indentations along their temples contains fine hair cells for auditory sensing.

Yevetha reproduce by laying eggs in birth casks—external wombs—often kept in special rooms. If the children remain in these birth casks past birth, the casks are then referred to as nestings. Unborn children feed on blood, preferably the mother's blood, although the blood of any Yevetha will do. Often, Yevethan leaders will kill underlings and feed their blood to their unborn or nesting children in the casks, and this is considered a great honor for the victim.

This biological need for blood is the central focus of Yevethan culture and religious belief system, making them a violent people. They are a dutiful, attentive, cautious, but fatalistic species shaped by strictly hierarchical culture. Most male Yevetha live day to day with the knowledge that, at any moment, a superior may kill them simply for their blood.

Until their contact with the Empire, the Yevetha believed they were the only intelligent creatures in the universe. Initially they submitted to Imperial rule, but allowed the Empire to become lax in its control, then—without warning—rebelled violently, slaughtering every human stationed on N'zoth. As a result of their experience with the Empire, their ethnocentrism turned to xenophobia, causing them to consider all other intelligent life morally and physically inferior.

Their government is led by a viceroy, often called "the Blessed" because of his role as both religious and political leader. He sits at the head of a complex hierarchy, served by military leaders called primates and administrators called proctors. All of these obey him without question and will eagerly die for him. They are ruthless fighters and are unwilling to surrender, even in the face of certain defeat.

In his notes, Senior Anthropologist Hoole writes of the Yevetha.

> The Yevetha abhor contact with other species. They go to extreme measures to avoid alien contamination and will conduct intense purification rituals, bathing, and disinfecting procedures if they must spend time in close quarters with outsider "vermin." They find the smell of other species distasteful and claim that without bathing or purifying themselves, they can still smell the stink on their own persons.

DESIGNATION
> **SENTIENT** <
....
PLANET OF ORIGIN
> **N'ZOTH** <
....
HEIGHT OF
AVERAGE ADULT
> **1.9 METERS** <
....

Ysalamiri

Salamanderlike, nonsentient creatures native to the planet Myrkr, ysalamiri are most notable for their singular ability to push back the Force.

While the Force usually binds all living things together, these small creatures no bigger than fifty centimeters long exhibit the inherent ability to sever those bonds. In truth, they are little more than smooth-skinned creatures with legs, showing scaly patches on their small bodies. Being even-tempered, sessile creatures, they exhibit personality traits similar to those of a sloth. They live in the branches of Myrkr's trees, and they have claws that actually grow directly into their perch, making it nearly impossible to remove them without killing them.

Each ysalamiri creates a bubble-shaped region in which the Force does not exist. This sphere can extend up to ten meters in radius, and in groups of ysalamiri these bubbles overlap, extending their reach. Scientists believe this unique ability evolved to protect the creatures from the Force-sensitive vornskrs, who hunt the ysalamiri by utilizing their Force-sensing abilities.

These creatures came to light when the fledgling New Republic was battling Grand Admiral Thrawn. Thrawn used ysalamiri to protect his people—as well as himself—from Force-users such as the Jedi.

In this log entry, Captain Gilad Pellaeon wrote about how the ysalamiri were used for this purpose during Thrawn's battle against a dark Jedi.

> Thrawn had the staff lure ysalamiri onto pipe frames that served to support and nourish the tiny creatures once they were safely removed

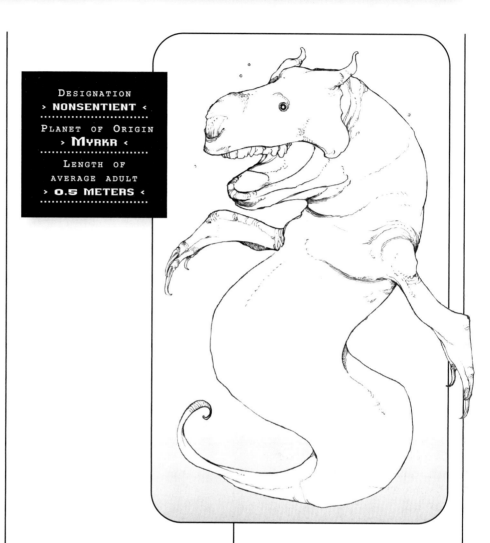

DESIGNATION
> **NONSENTIENT** <

PLANET OF ORIGIN
> **MYRKR** <

LENGTH OF AVERAGE ADULT
> **0.5 METERS** <

from their branches. They were apparently attracted to a specific natural herb that caused them to move just enough so the handlers could place them on the frames. Thrawn had these frames designed so they could be worn on the backs of individuals, providing them with a mobile means of defense against Joruus C'baoth.

Yuuzhan Vong

the Yuuzhan Vong are bipedal, humanoid aliens whose origins lie somewhere outside of the known galaxy. They resemble humans in many ways, but are usually taller, heavier, and have less hair on their heads. Their faces look like lumps of pulsating flesh with droopy eyes underscored by bluish sacks. Their foreheads are sloped, giving them a barbaric appearance that is magnified by ritual tattooing and self-scarring employed by those of lower rank. Individuals of higher rank exhibit ever more grotesque mutilation and reshaping of the features.

This type of disfiguration appears to exemplify a ritualized system expected of each Yuuzhan Vong. The goal is glory: to become close to the gods by remaking oneself in their image. Thus, the disfiguration symbolizes a rise in rank, as the subject makes an additional physical change, ultimately remaking himself. To do this, they may graft other parts onto themselves—limbs from another creature or bioengineered body parts. They never attempt to maim themselves in any way that might permanently hinder their ability to function, but only in ways that change their appearance or improve their abilities. Those whose changing ceremony has failed, and who are functionally maimed, are considered Shamed Ones and demoted to the lowest ranks of the lowest caste.

Everything the Yuuzhan Vong do is for the greater glory of their gods, as they follow their path of conquering and dominating the galaxy, re-creating it—like their own bodies—at the direction of their gods. Along the way, they perform constant sacrifice and penance, because in their mythology, their creator sacrificed pieces of himself through great pain and eventually his own death, to rise to a higher exal-tation. Through this, it is said, he created the lesser gods, who in turn created the Yuuzhan Vong through the mixing and matching of parts from other creatures. Sacrifice, therefore, is required and is considered sacred.

These people are fierce warriors who will not surrender to an enemy under any circumstances, for fear of insulting their gods. Because they worship life, and find anything purely manufactured unacceptable, they use bioengineered weapons, tools, and ships, and they find the use of actual machinery inherently perverse. They particularly hate droids, since to them droids are imitations of life, and thus are totally anathema.

They refer to those not of the Yuuzhan Vong as infidels. An attack on their pride is cause for a death duel, which also can be considered a sacrifice to their gods. To die in battle is among the highest honors they can achieve.

For some unknown reason, the Jedi cannot sense the Yuuzhan Vong through the Force. It is as if the Yuuzhan Vong are completely devoid of the Force.

After the Yuuzhan Vong force swept into the galaxy, advancing inexorably from planet to planet, a Garqi refugee caught up in the fleeing population related her experience with the invaders.

DESIGNATION
> SENTIENT <
....
PLANET OF ORIGIN
> UNKNOWN <
....
HEIGHT OF
AVERAGE ADULT
> 1.8 METERS <
....

The technological creatures of the Yuuzhan Vong are exclusively made up of bioengineered organic life-forms, and thus may be considered alien species in their own right. Only a limited number of these creatures have been encountered, so there is no way to determine whether the gathered data is exemplary of each species.

Amphistaff

DESIGNATION: **NONSENTIENT**
LENGTH: **1.3 METERS** (APPROX.)

an amphistaff is an organic weapon that appears to be a vicious serpent, yet can harden all or part of its body to the consistency of stone, flattening its neck and tail so that it can cut like a razor. It also can become supple and whiplike for use by its Yuuzhan Vong master, remaining rigid at one end and flexible at the snake-head end of its body, allowing it to inflict a venomous bite which causes numbness and paralysis.

The amphistaff can also become a deadly missile weapon, to be used like a spear. In addition, it has the ability to spit forth a stream of venom that arcs across twenty meters with stunning accuracy, blinding opponents instantly and killing them slowly over many agonizing hours, as the poison seeps in through the victim's ducts and wounds.

Coralskipper

DESIGNATION: **NONSENTIENT**
LENGTH: **13 METERS** (APPROX.)

coralskippers are Yuuzhan Vong bioengineered starfighters made of a living substance known as yorik coral. While no two coralskippers look exactly alike, they tend to share some features, such as a tapered nose and an aerodynamic hull. They are roughly triangular in shape, resembling an asteroid. Their canopies resemble natural mica more than transparisteel.

At the front of each skip, as they have come to be called by New Republic pilots, is a dovin basal that propels the coralskipper and creates black holes that absorb an opposing fighter ship's laserfire.

To engage the enemy, a coralskipper draws close to its opponent and a small appendage on the front erupts like a miniature volcano, spewing forth a burst of fire and a single globe of molten rock that can melt through the hull of a spacecraft. In a circle of enemies, the coralskipper spins faster and faster, bending an adversary's laser blasts into a field of gravity. Opponents can't break free and are forced to orbit the coralskipper until they crash together, at which point the gravity well dissipates, and all of the ships, including the coralskipper and its suicidal pilot, go up in a tremendous flash of energy.

The coralskipper needs to gather nourishment in order to continue functioning. To get its required nutrients, and to rearm itself, it simply eats mineral-rich rocks.

Dovin Basal

DESIGNATION: **NONSENTIENT**
DIAMETER: **1-3 METERS**
(DEPENDING ON SIZE OF VESSEL)

dovin basals are bioengineered, spherical organisms that act like gravity-well projectors. They resemble huge, pulsating, dark red hearts with deep blue spikes projecting from them.

This creature can be used to propel a worldship and other Yuuzhan Vong craft through space and even through hyperspace, though it can't chase enemies through a lightspeed jump because it can't hold a lock on ships through such a ride. It can lock on to stationary gravity fields, to the exclusion of all others, even targeting gravity fields millions of kilometers away. The adult, three-meter, spherical dovin basals work like perpetual thrusters. The more they focus their line, the greater the pull. One was used to pull down a moon onto the planet Sernpidal, resulting in the deaths of millions—including Han Solo's close friend Chewbacca.

Blasters have no effect on these creatures, which create gravity fields that function like a black hole, even serving as a shield by containing proton torpedoes and other enemy projectiles. A dovin basal can similarly counter energy shields in opposing spacecraft, though New Republic pilots learned that, by boosting the sphere of the inertial compensator, they could prevent the dovin basals from taking their shields down. Cycling low-power shots through the lasers will also force a dovin-basal-powered coralskipper to expend a lot of energy creating the black-hole shields, thus degrading its maneuvering ability.

Gnullith

DESIGNATION: **NONSENTIENT**
LENGTH: **1 METER**

a bioengineered breathing apparatus for underwater use, the gnullith is a soft, star-shaped creature that latches on to the user's face. The central tendril of the gnullith then snakes down the user's throat. Once in place, it filters water to pull in only oxygen through the tendril. Yuuzhan Vong often use these in conjunction with the ooglith cloaker.

Jacen Solo, who had to use a gnullith to infiltrate a Yuuzhan Vong stronghold, writes in this report:

> *The gnullith was very uncomfortable. It stung as it sealed itself into my pores like burning shards of transparisteel, and it gagged*

me as it slithered down my throat. It worked very well, but I wondered why they had to make so painful something that should be so easy to use. What's the value in that?

Grashal

DESIGNATION: **NONSENTIENT**
HEIGHT/WIDTH: **3 × 16 METERS**
(VARIABLE, DEPENDING ON BUILDING SIZE NEEDED)

a grashal is a bioengineered building. It looks like a huge mollusk shell, easily large enough to house a freighter and to store supplies.

The interior walls and floors of the grashal are smooth and vary in color from dark ivory to a soft pink. Darker gray spots dapple the walls at different points, but in no discernible pattern. The walls also seem fairly luminescent, but that may be due to sunlight filtering through the shell. Although the flooring is smooth, it's not slippery. Just inside the entrance to a grashal, a set of stairs leads

down into the main chamber. A number of tunnels from the main chamber lead to smaller chambers. A lightsaber can easily cut through the grashal's shell.

Ooglith Cloaker

DESIGNATION: **NONSENTIENT**
LENGTH: **2 METERS**
(VARIABLE DEPENDING ON SIZE OF WEARER)

t he ooglith cloaker is an organic environment suit. A variation of the ooglith masquer, the ooglith cloaker has thousands of tiny grappling tendrils that slip into a user's pores. Unlike the masquer, the cloaker's facial mask is transparent. It is paired with a gnullith, a soft, star-shaped creature that latches on to the host's face and allows the user to breathe underwater or in other harsh environments.

Ooglith Masquer

DESIGNATION: **NONSENTIENT**
LENGTH: **0.3 METERS**

t he ooglith masquer serves as a disguise for Yuuzhan Vong agents. Similar to the ooglith cloaker, the ooglith masquer has thousands of tiny grappling tendrils that insert themselves into a Yuuzhan Vong's pores, creating a false outer skin. Each masquer takes on the specific appearance for which it has been grown, and this enables the user to appear human or as any species, depending on the wearer's size and build. Sensitive to touch, it is well trained and can be reused many times. To remove the ooglith masquer, the user opens a seam along his nose and the masquer peels itself from the user, slithering down to the ground in the form of a slurping, sucking puddle.

Villip

DESIGNATION: **NONSENTIENT**

HEIGHT: **0.2 METERS**

Villips are bioengineered organic communication devices, a pair of which are joined in consciousness with each other to communicate remotely across vast distances. There are several different types of villips, and the most common, when inactive, appears to be a ridged lump of membranous tissue. A Yuuzhan Vong strokes his villip to wake it so it will commune with its mate over distances. When the villip wakes, a single break in the membranous tissue—a hole that resembles an eye socket—puckers to life. Unfurling itself from around this puckered aperture, the villip swells and adapts its shape to resemble the head and shoulders of the Yuuzhan Vong with whom the user is speaking, including the voice. A villip also can be launched through space, where it can melt, or morph, through a spacecraft in order to communicate with its occupants.

In the case of the phenomenon known as the villip-choir field, a group of budded villips can be used together to broadcast a panoramic visual image. This affords the Yuuzhan Vong warrior a tremendous advantage in combat.

Yammosk

DESIGNATION: **SENTIENT**

DIAMETER: **16 METERS**

a yammosk is an intelligent, bio-engineered creature that serves the Yuuzhan Vong in a role they refer to as a war coordinator. It has a bulbous head that glows red with energy and excitement, two round black eyes, and many coiled and twitching tentacles that are each around a hundred kilometers long, some thick and some

filament-thin. It possesses one huge central tooth, which can be used with the force of a laser cannon to drill down into a planet. The yammosk secretes a liquid from the tooth to further erode a planet's crust. Like the jellyfish that it resembles, its body is boneless.

The yammosk can belch forth a huge, plasticlike bubble underwater—an air pocket—to encompass a large chamber, enabling its occupants to breathe without the aid of gnulliths or other breathing apparatus.

Telepathy is one of the yammosk's greatest weapons. Its telepathic power is strong enough to facilitate communication throughout a large gathering of Yuuzhan Vong. It can project its thoughts and feelings onto other species, as well, including humans. Following the earliest incursion by the Yuuzhan Vong, a victim of the yammosk's power, Danni Quee, noted in a report:

> It wanted Miko Reglia, a Jedi Knight, to experience uncontrollable despair and fear. It seemed to feed on it, enjoy it—as did all the Yuuzhan Vong who witnessed the torture. Time after time it taunted Miko with his own death, bringing him close to its cavernous mouth and its single, hideous tooth. It pummeled him with telepathic waves of hopelessness, and each time he weakened, its mental hold grew stronger and stronger. It slowly drained him of his will to live.

> It was horrible to witness. This creature that one might assume is mindless, unable to act without the commands of its masters, really does have thoughts of its own—and all of them are evil.

A yammosk will often reproduce quickly and will train its singular offspring immediately through a mental joining, teaching it to perform specific tasks. It has a huge blue pulsating vein that runs between its massive eyes and acts as a point of transference, sending out the signal that allows a Yuuzhan Vong to telepathically join its consciousness.

As a war coordinator, the creature provides the perfect communication and coordination tool that can bring forces of at least three expeditionary worldships into tight focus. It can allow the coralskippers to fly in perfect unison, thus making them many times more efficient than ordinary military craft. But if the enemy can manage to destroy the yammosk, the resulting chaos may bring about complete disaster among the Yuuzhan Vong.

Yuzzem are giant, bipedal, humanoid creatures with long snouts, long arms, thick brown fur, and large black eyes. They are noted for their great strength and volatile, unpredictable temperaments. Like the Wookiees, Yuzzem were an enslaved species taken from their forested home on Ragna III to work at heavy labor projects for the Empire, primarily in mining facilities.

These creatures are incredibly intelligent, and many scientists believe they could be distant relatives to the Wookiees themselves, although no official studies have been done to prove that theory. It is unlikely that Yuzzem would have enough patience to sit through such an investigation, as they prefer to be constantly moving or working.

Like Wookiees, Yuzzem adhere to strict rules regarding honor and the fulfilling of debts. Yuzz, their language, is mostly unpronounceable by humans, although most Yuzzem can easily understand Basic.

They are fierce fighters, and their size makes them difficult to subdue. They follow prey by scent, and their strong arms and long, sharp claws make it possible for one to easily bring down an opponent. They are not readily frightened or intimidated, and are quite stubborn, which—as representatives of the Empire discovered—made them difficult to control as slaves. Reports registered from several mining installations told of Wookiees and Yuzzem teaming up to rebel against their taskmasters.

Based on his own experiences, Luke Skywalker offered his impressions of the creatures.

> After our experiences on Mimban, Leia asked me how I'd managed to learn the Yuzzem language, considering I'd not traveled the galaxy much. The truth is, I knew a Yuzzem back home in Anchorhead. His name was Pok, and he was an indentured servant to a merchant in town. The merchant, a farm equipment dealer, had a relative in the Empire who sent him Pok as a gift. The merchant was against slavery, so he freed Pok and allowed him the opportunity to work. Pok fixed equipment and moved and delivered machinery around the territory. Everyone got to know him, and he proved he was both clever and capable on a regular basis.

> Because I'd been around Pok enough, I decided to study his people a bit to learn about them. I found out some of their language, and started speaking it to him when Uncle Owen and I would come to town for equipment. He took to me quickly, and we became friends.

DESIGNATION
> **SENTIENT** <

PLANET OF ORIGIN
> **RAGNA III** <

HEIGHT OF AVERAGE ADULT
> **2.5 METERS** <

the Yuzzum of Endor's moon are an intelligent yet primitive species with round, fur-covered bodies, long, thin legs, and wide mouths that show protruding teeth. They often travel in groups, hunting down ruggers, rodents that are their primary source of food.

Yuzzum actually vary widely in appearance. Some have sharp fangs, while others have blunt teeth. Some have thick, woolly coats, while others have short fur. Hence, the term *Yuzzum* broadly refers to a class of migratory, fur-bearing mammals on the forest moon of Endor.

Developmentally they are at the same level as their diminutive Ewok neighbors, defending themselves from predators and outsiders with spears and other primitive weapons. Their ability to eat and survive depends upon their large size, which often intimidates predators and even drives them away.

The Yuzzum people communicate in a language made up of musical elements, and it is sung rather than spoken. Their voices retain a gravelly tone, yet many Yuzzum are hailed as excellent singers. Those Yuzzum who have managed to leave Endor—for very few ever do—often end up singing for their suppers.

One such Yuzzum is Joh Yowza, a regular performer on passenger liners throughout the Outer Rim Territories. Rejected by his own herd because of his small size in comparison to other Yuzzum, Yowza, whose real name isn't pronounceable in Basic, was often left alone to fend for himself. One day, while searching for food, he sneaked aboard a smuggler's ship. The smuggler, named Roark Garnet, took to Yowza and gave him the nickname Furball. Yowza showed his friendship by helping with menial tasks on the ship. Later, when Garnet's ship docked at Nar Shaddaa, Yowza followed the sound of music to a seedy bar. He immediately rushed in and burst into song, to the delight of the audience and the surprise of the band. Because the audience enjoyed his performance, the band members, Max Rebo, Droopy McCool, Sy Snootles, and their leader Evar Orbus, took him on as a member. Sy gave him his stage name, and he has become something of a celebrity, although some music critics offer a dim view of his musical talent.

In this music review that appeared on the HoloNet news on Sullust, this Sullustan critic has a very different theory on the voice of the Yuzzum.

> While others in my field discredit the Yuzzum voice, my Sullustan ears hear something unique with Joh Yowza. What a casual (non-Sullustan) listener misses is the entire range of communication that is layered and interwoven in the Yuzzum's singing voice. Yowza is delivering more than lyrics in his entertaining style—he's communicating joy. If I didn't hear it myself with my own ears, I'd swear it was telepathic. But it's not. It's an actual pitch that affects me and makes me happy. Many species I've observed—even if they don't like the sound of the voice—will end up clapping and cheering when Joh Yowza finishes a set.

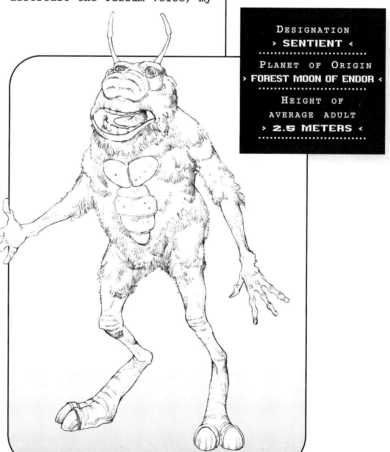

DESIGNATION
> SENTIENT <

PLANET OF ORIGIN
> FOREST MOON OF ENDOR <

HEIGHT OF
AVERAGE ADULT
> 2.5 METERS <

Zeltron

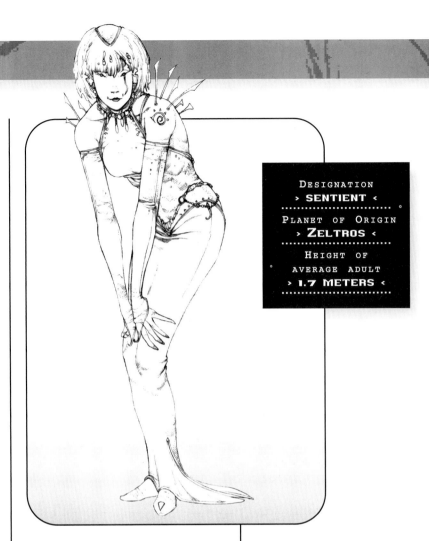

DESIGNATION
> **SENTIENT** <
....
PLANET OF ORIGIN
> **ZELTROS** <
....
HEIGHT OF
AVERAGE ADULT
> **1.7 METERS** <
....

the extraordinarily attractive Zeltrons are near-humans native to the planet Zeltros. Their skin is bright pink, a special pigmentation that develops from a reaction to their sun's radiation. The Zeltron people have the ability to project powerful pheromones. These can be activated at will and can affect a specific individual or entire groups at the same time. Of these pheromones Senior Anthropologist Hoole writes:

> Zeltron pheromones have failed to affect another species only once in recorded history. After the Battle of Endor, King Arno and Queen Leonie apparently hosted a huge celebration for Alliance visitors, and the army of a warrior race known as the Nagai stormed the ballroom. The attending Zeltrons immediately began emitting pheromones to subdue the Nagai, but to no avail. However, when a longtime enemy of the Nagai subsequently invaded, the Nagai joined forces with the Zeltrons and the Alliance to defeat them. In their victory, the Zeltrons found a new reason to throw another two-month-long party—breaking the standing party record.

Zeltrons are also empathic, able to sense the feelings of others as well as project their own emotions. For this reason, love and comfort are extremely important to them. Sharing positive emotions is deemed to everyone's benefit, while sharing negative emotions is shunned, and the Zeltrons' democratic government will go to great lengths to make sure no one on Zeltros is unhappy. Zeltros has experienced few tyrants, because they cannot commit atrocities without feeling another's pain. Zeltros has, however, been invaded twelve times in the past six centuries, but because of the Zeltrons' pheromones, most invaders have given up their hostile intentions and joined in the nonstop planetary festivities. Hence, Zeltrons don't worry about such trivial matters as planetary defenses or military forces. They are able fighters, though, and they stay in peak physical condition at all times.

A noted HoloNet critic once called Zeltros "the ultimate party experience," for Zeltrons hold massive celebrations for practically any event. They are extremely promiscuous and are extremely proud of their sexual prowess. They consider the concept of monogamy quaint, but unrealistic.

Zeltron technology is on par with most space-faring worlds. They possess space travel, advanced agricultural and industrial methods, and excellent knowledge of medicine, particularly antibiotics. Zeltron scientists created much of the technology used in the pleasure domes at Hologram Fun World. Zeltron craftspeople are renowned for their erotic sculptures, paintings, and other works of art. Zeltron courtesans, known as cafarel, fulfill *any* physical desire one may have, without limits. Many crimelords, particularly Hutts, have taken special interest in these Zeltron servants. Because of their popularity, and because they spend their lives pursuing gratification, Zeltrons are quite common across the galaxy, particularly at spaceports, where they can find many prospective mates.

Pronunciation Guide

The pronunciation of a species name will vary depending on the accent inherent to the speaker's home planet. What follows are the most common pronunciations relating to the species included in this book, as well as some key pronunciation symbols used in most standard dictionaries that will guide you in articulating the names of alien species. Note: an apostrophe (') is used after the emphasized syllable in each name.

Vowel Sounds

ă: short *a* sound as in the words *bat* and *act*.

ā: long *a* sound as in the words *age* and *rate*.

ä: open *a* sound used for words like *part, calm,* or *father*. It duplicates the short *o* sound of the word *hot*.

ĕ: short *e* sound used in *edge* or *set*.

ē: long *e* sound used in *equal* or *seat*.

ēr: a vowel sound before *r* that may range from ē through ĭ in different dialects.

ĭ: short *i* sound used in *hit* or *pit*.

ī: long *i* sound used in *bite* or *whine*.

ŏ: short *o* sound used in *hot* and *pot*.

oi: a diphthong vowel sound that is a combination of an ō and an ē, such as in the words *boy* and *toy*.

ō: long *o* sound used in *moan* and *tone*.

o͞o: long *o* sound used in *toot* and *hoot*.

ô: relatively long *o* used in *order* and *border*.

o͝o: short double *o* sound used in *book* and *tour*.

ŭ: short *u* sound used in *up* and *sum*.

ûr: *u* sound used in *turn* and *urge*.

Consonant Sounds

kh: a hard *k* pronounced at the back of one's throat, such as *loch* or *ach*.

hw: a soft *w* sound used in the words *who* and *what*.

Species Names

Amanin (Amanaman): ăm-ăn'-ĭn (ăm-ăn'-ä-măn)
Anzati: än-zä'-tē
Aqualish: äk'-wä-lĭsh
arachnor: är-ăk'-nôr
Arcona: är-kōn'-ä
Arkanian: är-kän'-ē-ăn
Askajian: ăs-kä'-jē-ăn
Assembler (Kud'ar Mub'at): ăs-sĕm'-blûr (ko͞od'-är mo͞o'-bät)
bantha: băn'-thä
Barabel: bär'-ä-bĕl
Bimm: bĭm
Bith: bĭth
Blood Carver: blŭd cär'-vēr
Bothan: bŏ'-thän
Caamasi: kä-ä-mä'-sē
Chadra-Fan: chăd'-rä-făn
Chevin: shĕ'-vĭn
Chiss: chĭss
Codru-Ji: cō-dro͞o-jē'
Coway: cō'-wä
Devaronian: dĕv-ä-rō'-nē-ăn
dewback: do͞o'-băk
dianoga: dī-ä-nō'-gä
dinko: dēn'-kō
Drall: dräll
Dressellian: drĕ-sĕl'-lē-ăn
droch: drŏkh (also drōkh)
Drovian: drō'-vē-ăn
Dug: dŭg
Duros: do͞o-rōs
Elom: ē'-lŏm
Elomin: ē-lō-mĭn'
energy spider: ĕn'-ēr-gē spī'-dēr
Ewok: ē'-wŏk
Falleen: fäl-lēn'
Fia: fē'-ä

Firrerreon: fĭr-rā'-rē-ăn
Gamorrean: gă-mōr'-rē-ăn
Gand: gănd
Gank: gănk
Givin: gĭ'-vĭn
Gotal: gō'-tăl
Gran: grăn
gundark: gŭn'-därk
Gungan: gŭn'-găn
hawk-bat: häwk'-băt
H'nemthe: hĕ-nĕm'-thē
Ho'Din: hō'-dĭn
howlrunner: hŏwl'-rŭn-nēr
hssiss: hĭs-sĭs'
Hutt: hŭt
Ishi Tib: ĭsh'-ē tĭb
Ithorian: ĭ-thō'-rē-ăn
Ixll: ĭx'-ĭl
Jawa: jä'-wä
Jenet: jĕ'-nĕt
Kamarian: kä-mär'-ē-ăn
Khommite: khŏm'-mĭt
Kitonak: kĭt'-ō-näk
Klatooinian: klă-to͞o-ĭn'-ē-ăn
Kowakian monkey-lizard: kō-wä'-kē-ăn mŏn'-kē-lĭ'-zärd
krayt dragon: krāt drä'-gŏn
Kubaz: ko͞o-băz'
Kurtzen: kĕrt'-zĕn
Lorrdian: lôr'-dē-ăn
Massassi: mä-sä'-sē
Melodie: mĕl'-ō-dē
Mimbanite: mĭm'-băn-ĭt
Mon Calamari: mŏn căl-ä-mär'-ē
Mrlssi: mr-lĭs'-sē
Myneyrsh: mĭn-ä-rĭsh'
mynock: mī'-nŏk
Neek: nēk
Neimoidian: nē-ĭ-moi'-dē-ăn
nerf: nûrf
Neti: nĕ'-tē
Nikto: nĭk'-tō
Noghri: nō'-grē
Ortolan: ôr-tō'-lăn
Oswaft: ŏs'-wäft
Pa'lowick: păl'-ō-wĭk
Phindian: fĭn'-dē-ăn
Pho Ph'eahian: fō fä'-ĕn
piranha-beetle: pĕ-rän'-hä-bē'-tĕl

Priapulin: prē-ä-pōō'-lĭn

Psadan: pĕ-sā'-dăn

pterosaur: tĕr'-ō-sär

purella: pŭ'-rĕ-lä

Pydyrian: pē-dē'-rē-ăn

Qom Jha and Qom Qae:
  kōm jä' and kōm kā'

Quarren: kwä'-rĕn

Ranat: ră'-năt

rancor: răn'-kōr

Rishii: rē'-shē

Rodian: rō'-dē-ăn

ronto: rŏn'-tō

Ruurian: rōō'-rē-ăn

Sarlacc: sär'-lăk

Selonian: sĕl-ō'-nē-ăn

Shi'ido: shē-ē'-dō

Shistavanen: shĭst'-ŭ-văn-ĕn

slashrat: slăsh'-răt

Sluissi: slōō-ē'-sē

space slug: spās' slŭg

Ssi-ruuk: sē'-rōōk

Sullustan: sŭl'-lŭs-tăn

Talz: tălz

tauntaun: tän'-tän

taurill: tä'-rĭl

thernbee: thĕrn'-bē

Tin-Tin Dwarf (Tintinna):
  tĭn'-tĭn dwärf (tĭn-tĭn'-ä)

t'landa Til: tĭ-lăn'-dä tĭl

Togorian: tŏg-ō'-rē-ăn

Toka (Sharu): tō'-kä (shā'-rōō)

Toydarian: toi-dăr'-ē-ăn

Trandoshan: trăn-dō'-shăn

Trianii: trē-än'-ē

tsil (spook-crystal): sĭl
  (spōōk-crĭs-täl)

Tusken Raider (Sand People):
  tŭs'-kĕn rā'-dĕr (sănd pē'-pĕl)

Twi'lek: twē'-lĕk (also twĭ'-lĕk)

Tynnan: tĭ'-năn

Ugnaught: ŭg'-nŏt

Umgullian blob: ŭm-gŭl'-ē-ăn blŏb

Verpine: vŭr'-pīn

Vor: vōr

vornskr: vōrn'-skŭr

Vratix: vrā'-tĭx

wampa: wäm'-pä

Weequay: wē'-kwā

Whiphid: hwĭ'-fĭd

womp rat: wŏmp' răt

Wookiee: wōō'-kē

Yaka: yă'-kä

Yarkora: yär-kōr'-ä

Yevetha: yĕ-vē'-thä

ysalamiri: säl-ä-mē'-rē
  (also ē-säl-ä-mē'-rē)

Yuuzhan Vong: yōō'-zän vŏng

Yuzzem: yŭ'-zĕm

Yuzzum: yŭ'-zŭm

Zeltron: zĕl'-trŏn

Appendix 2

Additional Creatures of Note

Senior Anthropologist Mammon Hoole is presently researching the following species. Although his notes are not yet complete, he felt they were worth mentioning at least briefly in this book.

Annoo-dat (Ă'-NOO-DĂT)

DESIGNATION: **SENTIENT**
PLANET OF ORIGIN: **ANNOO**
HEIGHT OF
AVERAGE ADULT: **2 METERS**

The Annoo-dat are a reptilian species with drowsy eyes, flat noses, and spotted faces. They are known for being involved in organized crime and maintain syndicates that rival some Hutt organizations. Jabba the Hutt considered the Annoo-dat group known as the Fromm gang to be such a serious threat to his operation that he hired Boba Fett to capture them for a sizable bounty.

Ball Creature of Duroon (BĂL CRĒ'-TŬR ŬV DŬ-ROON')

DESIGNATION: **NONSENTIENT**
PLANET OF ORIGIN: **DUROON**
DIAMETER OF
AVERAGE ADULT: **0.05 METERS**

Also referred to as a bouncebeast by the native peoples and residents of neighboring worlds, the ball creatures of Duroon are timid, noncarnivorous creatures that resemble smooth spheres. They have pliable skin that varies in color from green to blue to yellow. They are also nocturnal and live in giant herds, which will stampede if startled, bouncing from place to place and rolling at incredible speeds. These creatures have no limbs or sensory organs, but their bodies allow limbs to form as needed. They can even create some specialized organs like mouths and eyestalks.

Bouncebeasts are also known for having keen instincts for detecting danger and are sometimes used as guard animals for Duroon's native peoples.

Bogey (BŌ'-GĒ)

DESIGNATION: **NONSENTIENT**
PLANET OF ORIGIN: **KESSEL**
LENGTH OF
AVERAGE ADULT: **0.05 METERS**

Bogeys are mysterious, formless, luminescent creatures that inhabit the spice mines of Kessel. They are the main diet of the native energy spiders, whose web yields the drug known as glitterstim. Bogeys feed on energy and are drawn to areas of light and activity, hence they are sometimes seen by miners. They speed through the tunnels, making a humming or chittering sound as they go, setting off showers of sparks when they contact the veins of glitterstim in the rock walls. They bound from wall to wall randomly, finally plunging into portions of rock that are clear of glitterstim. Unfortunately the predators that follow them have been known to attack the workers who get in their way.

Bordok (BŌR'-DŎK)

DESIGNATION: **SEMISENTIENT**
PLANET OF ORIGIN:
FOREST MOON OF ENDOR
HEIGHT OF
AVERAGE ADULT: **1 METER**

Bordoks are small horselike creatures used by the Ewoks as beasts of burden.

They have long manes, gentle features, and strong backs. They make strong ties to their owners and are often considered part of the family. Some have been known to show a remarkable amount of intelligence, enough to cause scientists to begin readdressing the level of their sentience.

Defel/Wraith (DĔF'-ĔL/WRĀTH)

DESIGNATION: **SENTIENT**
PLANET OF ORIGIN: **AF'EL**
HEIGHT OF
AVERAGE ADULT: **1.7 METERS**

The Defels, often called Wraiths, are stocky, fur-covered humanoids with protruding snouts and hands with long claws and triple-jointed digits. They can be seen only under ultraviolet light. In standard light, Defels appear to be little more than ghosts—red-eyed shadows that are difficult to detect with the human eye. They have the ability to bend light around their bodies, causing them to blend into their surroundings. Defels live in underground cities on their homeworld, where they are known for their ore-mining facilities and their excellence in metallurgy. Offworld, Defels are often hired as spies and assassins due to their ability to "disappear."

Dragonsnake (DRĀ'-GŎN-SNĀK)

DESIGNATION: **NONSENTIENT**
PLANET OF ORIGIN: **DAGOBAH**
LENGTH OF
AVERAGE ADULT: **7 METERS**

The dragonsnake is a large, reptilian predator that inhabits Dagobah's bodies of water, seeking out victims, rearing up and slashing them with its fangs or razor-sharp fins. Because they are rarely seen above water, they are often mistaken for swamp slugs. They will float along the surface of the murky water like drifting logs, until their prey wanders close by. They will snatch the prey out of the water, or sometimes off land if a creature is walking along the shoreline. If it is land prey, the dragonsnake will hold it underwater until it drowns before devouring it. They are strong enough to kill their natural enemy and competitor for nourishment, the swamp slug. One such creature swallowed Luke Skywalker's astromech R2-D2, but finding him unpalatable, spit him out onto shore.

Dulok (DOO'-LŎK)

DESIGNATION: **SENTIENT**
PLANET OF ORIGIN:
FOREST MOON OF ENDOR
HEIGHT OF
AVERAGE ADULT: **1.5 METERS**

Duloks are bipeds with large ears, green fur, and perpetually snarling faces. Lanky, unkempt, and usually bug-infested, these distant relatives of the Ewoks are extremely ill-tempered and treacherous. Duloks live in the marshlands of Endor's moon in villages that are clusters of rotted logs and swampy caves surrounding altars made from stumps covered with skins and skulls of small animals. Duloks are an extremely covetous species, and the Ewoks have related many stories of how the Duloks have tried to conquer their villages. Many Ewoks, therefore, consider the Duloks their greatest rivals.

Fosh (FŎSH)

DESIGNATION: **SENTIENT**
PLANET OF ORIGIN: **UNKNOWN**
HEIGHT OF
AVERAGE ADULT: **1.3 METERS**

The Fosh are an avian species whose mysterious planet of origin is believed to be located in the Corporate Sector. They are thought to be on the verge of extinction. Fosh have thin torsos with delicate arms and four-fingered hands. Short feathers and two antennae that are twisted in a corkscrewlike manner crown their slightly disproportionate heads. Their faces are concave with slanted eyes and soft whiskers. Their leg joints bend backwards like those of land-based birds, and their flayed-toed feet cause them to move in agile leaps. Their tears have peculiar healing properties.

Gorax (GŌ'-RĂKS)

DESIGNATION: **SEMISENTIENT**
PLANET OF ORIGIN:
FOREST MOON OF ENDOR
HEIGHT OF
AVERAGE ADULT: **30 METERS**

The gorax is a giant primate native to the forest moon of Endor, with long black hair, large tufted ears, and a

piglike snout. It is carnivorous and lives in limestone mounds located beyond the Desert of Salma. Its height allows it to reach the tree villages of the Ewoks and capture them for food. However, gorax are intelligent enough to value companionship, so they will sometimes kidnap Ewoks for pets. They have also been known to attack a boarwolf mother as she is giving birth, killing her and all her pups except for one chosen to act as a pet. Some gorax are also documented as having stored food for later consumption.

Hanadak (HĂN'-Ä-DĂK)

DESIGNATION: **SEMISENTIENT**
PLANET OF ORIGIN:
FOREST MOON OF ENDOR
HEIGHT OF
AVERAGE ADULT: **3 METERS**

Hanadaks are large, carnivorous primates with dark purple fur and colorful facial markings. They inhabit the forest floor of Endor's moon. They use menacing teeth and sharp, dangerous claws to attack their prey. The Ewoks claim that the hanadaks are mysteriously controlled by the gorax, although no scientific evidence has been uncovered to support this claim.

Hoojib (HOO'-JĬB)

DESIGNATION: **SENTIENT**
PLANET OF ORIGIN: **ARBRA**
HEIGHT OF
AVERAGE ADULT: **0.5 METERS**

The Hoojibs are a telepathic rodent species with pastel-colored fur, long antennae, and cute features that often cause other species to underestimate their intelligence. They consume thermal energy, electricity, light, or any other form of energy available to them. Many joined the Alliance after the Rebels saved them from a slivilth, a dangerous predator that had commandeered their underground cave on their homeworld of Arbra. Since that incident, their species has remained an infrequently seen, but steady, member of the New Republic.

Iskalonian (IS'-KÄ-LŌ-NĒ-ĂN)

DESIGNATION: **SENTIENT**
PLANET OF ORIGIN: **UARRIOUS**
(SEE BELOW)
HEIGHT OF AVERAGE ADULT:
0.5–2 METERS
(DEPENDING ON RACE)

Iskalonians are actually a group, or school, of six major aquatic species, with a few stragglers from eleven others. The most well known member faces of the Iskalonian school are the following:

Inleshat, originally from Drexel II, have long, silky hair, three webbed fingers on each hand, wide, pupil-less eyes, and long, pointed ears that allow them to hear underwater.

Chuhkyvi, of Aquaris, a humanoid species, are similar to the Inleshat, with tan skin, yellow eyes, four-fingered hands, and a more pronounced nose.

Frid, of the planet Mackar, are fishlike creatures with green skin, violet bulbous eyes, long skin-flaps on both sides of their mouths, and long scaly tails.

Graygl, of Danalbeth, sport round, fleshy heads with wide mouths of sharp, pointed teeth, flaring nostrils, and red eyes.

Stribers, from Julsujod III, are the rarest of the Iskalonians. They are smooth and finless, with crystal blue skin, large eyes, and thin bodies. They are telepathic.

Nejma, of Eriscot, are also called Honored Ones. They are extremely tall, brown-skinned creatures, with a wild

shock of orange hair and huge red eyes. A long dorsal fin runs the length of their backs.

In general, all the races of the Iskalonian school are peaceful and nonviolent. A primary leader guides the school and, with the support of the races, maintains a separatist position from the rest of the galaxy. As a result, they have not yet joined the New Republic.

Krish (KRĬSH)

DESIGNATION: **SENTIENT**
PLANET OF ORIGIN: **KRISH**
HEIGHT OF
AVERAGE ADULT: **1.7 METERS**

Krish are a humanoid race with supple skin and large, wide heads topped with short, wiry hair. Bony ridges dominate their faces above the eyes and along the nose, and their mouths are filled with rows of tiny, pointed teeth. The Krish are renowned hunters, often engaging themselves in pursuing illegal prey. They enjoy participating in sports of any kind.

Lahsbee/Huhk

(LĂZ'-BĒ/HŬK)
DESIGNATION: **SENTIENT**
PLANET OF ORIGIN: **LAHSBANE**
HEIGHT OF AVERAGE ADULT:
0.5–3 METERS

The Lahsbee are diminutive felinoids who shun technology and modern contrivances, preferring a simpler life of playtime. But this is merely their appearance during childhood, as they have two stages of life. The second stage begins at puberty, whereupon the harmless Lahsbee transform into mindless, ferocious savages called Huhks. Music is the only known nonviolent means of subduing a Huhk.

Marauder (MÄ-RÄ-DÛR)

DESIGNATION: **SENTIENT**
PLANET OF ORIGIN: **UNKNOWN**
HEIGHT OF
AVERAGE ADULT: **2 METERS**

Because their true name is unknown, this species is referred to in scientific circles simply as Marauders. Marauders are tall, barbaric, warlike humanoids known to prey on people weaker than themselves. One of the largest populations of this group was seen on Endor's forest moon, where they harassed and intimidated the local Ewoks. Though they fancy themselves accomplished space pirates, as a culture Marauders have little knowledge of piloting spaceships. In fact, the group found on Endor's moon had crashed there due to their own ignorance of how to control their vessel.

Marauders have scaly, rugged, skull-like faces and wear tattered clothing adorned with scavenged items. Their greasy hair sprouts from the tops of their thick heads, as well as their faces. They tend to inhabit primitive fortresses in desolate areas, from which they can strike out in military force unnoticed.

Nagai (NÄ-GÄ'-Ē)

DESIGNATION: **SENTIENT**
PLANET OF ORIGIN: **NAGI**
HEIGHT OF
AVERAGE ADULT: **1.8 METERS**

The Nagai are a humanoid warrior people whose weapons of choice are daggers and knives. They came upon the galactic scene following the Bakuran incident while fleeing their cruel oppressors, the Tofs. Tall and exceedingly thin, with straight black hair and pale, almost white skin, the Nagai might fool an unaware observer into thinking they are delicate or weak. This is not the case at all, as a Nagai warrior can be extremely formidable. Nagai are known to kill without hesitation if it suits them, particularly if honor demands it, but if there is no honor in killing, or if their foe is weak, they will take no pleasure from the victory. The Nagai once claimed to be from another galaxy, but most believe that their homeworld is in the Unknown Regions and that they spread this misinformation to other species to keep their homeworld a secret.

Nek
(Cyborrean Battle Dog)
(NĔK [CĪ-BŌR'-Ē-ĂN BĂT-ĔL DŎG])

DESIGNATION: **NONSENTIENT**
PLANET OF ORIGIN: **CYBORREA**
LENGTH OF
AVERAGE ADULT: **1.1 METERS**

Bred by the Cyborrean people, neks were originally used as animal-weapons during the wars that spread across their homeworld. They have since become hot commodities on the black market. Genetically altered to function in a heavy-gravity environment, these creatures are extremely aggressive and strong. They are also fitted with armor, attack simulators, and bionic treat-

ments that enhance their combat ability and serve to make them fearless. The dogs usually attack with their multiple rows of sharp teeth, while raking the victim's body with their cybernetic claws. A remote control device used by hunters, warriors, and nek handlers interacts with implants placed in the dog's brain and controls each dog.

Nimbanel (NĬM'-BĂN-ĔL)

DESIGNATION: **SENTIENT**
PLANET OF ORIGIN: **NIMBAN**
HEIGHT OF
AVERAGE ADULT: **1.7 METERS**

The Nimbanese are tall, pale-skinned humanoids who generally work for the Hutts in administrative roles. They are warm-blooded reptiles that place great pride in their intelligence and morals, to the point of arrogance. For this reason, a Nimbanel will prefer contests of will and cleverness to physical combat. They were instrumental in founding the galactic Bureau of Ships and Services, as well as several financial institutions. While they continue to work for these organizations, they still facilitate the needs of their Hutt employers.

Ryn (RĬN)

DESIGNATION: **SENTIENT**
PLANET OF ORIGIN: **UNKNOWN**
HEIGHT OF
AVERAGE ADULT: **1.6 METERS**

The Ryn are a humanoid species exhibiting beaklike noses, slender tails, and soft, smoke-colored hair on their bodies. The males often have white mustaches and thick white hair on their heads, while the shapely, compact females slick back their hair, and their tails look as if they have been dipped in blue paint as a fashion statement. Ryn tails are prehensile—and Ryn can grasp large objects or hang from tree limbs with them. Besides these unique gifts, Ryn mimic sounds by blowing air through their beaks, which have several holes like a wind instrument. By covering and uncovering the holes while blowing air through their beaks, they play music or imitate sounds.

A flamboyant species, Ryn wear wildly colorful clothing and jewelry. They travel in large family or tribal groupings like caravans and make their living from thievery and con games. Many believe they were the originators of the game sabacc, and they often use sabacc cards as a means of divination.

Snogar (SNŌ'-GÄR)

DESIGNATION: **SENTIENT**
PLANET OF ORIGIN: **OTA**
HEIGHT OF
AVERAGE ADULT: **2.5 METERS**

Snogars are tall, furry, snow-dwelling humanoids of limited intelligence who, despite their impressive size, are wary of strangers. Scientists believe the Snogars were once a great, technologically advanced species that devolved to a primitive lifestyle through thousands of years of forgetting how to build advanced technology. The ancestors of the present-day Snogars, called the Old Ones, supposedly developed the heating machines that keep habitable the Snogar living environment on their frozen world. Unfortunately, the Snogar have great difficulty keeping the machines functioning. The Snogars once captured Luke Skywalker and Boba Fett and demanded that they repair the machines for them.

Swamp Slug (SWÄMP SLÜG)

DESIGNATION: **NONSENTIENT**
PLANET OF ORIGIN: **DAGOBAH**
LENGTH OF
AVERAGE ADULT: **8 METERS**

The giant swamp slug is a gastropod that eats nearly anything it can pull into its wide, lipless mouth. It pulverizes its food into digestible pieces by the thousands of tiny grinding teeth that line its throat. It has up to twenty-four pairs of legs that enable it to move along the bottom of swamps, rivers, and lakes; however, only six small legs are visible when it rears out of the water. Its large, orange eyes can see clearly beneath the murky waters, and two antennae on the top of its head

act like sonar, sending signals around the creature's body to determine its distance from the bottom and banks.

Tof (TŎF)

DESIGNATION: **SENTIENT**
PLANET OF ORIGIN: **TOF**
HEIGHT OF
AVERAGE ADULT: **1.8 METERS**

The Tofs are the longtime enemy of the Nagai. Large, rotund humanoids with green skin, they dress in piratelike attire and appear devoid of morals or compassion. Hungering for more power and lusting for battle, the Tofs are cruel despots who conquered the Nagai for 300 years and eventually tried to conquer the Alliance of Free Planets after the Bakuran incident. After their defeat at the hands of the New Republic, the Tofs retreated to their homeworld and have been little seen in the galaxy since that time.

Vodran (VŌD'-RĂN)

DESIGNATION: **SENTIENT**
PLANET OF ORIGIN: **VODRAN**
HEIGHT OF
AVERAGE ADULT: **1.8 METERS**

The Vodrans are two-legged, warm-blooded reptilian beings whose faces are studded with short spikes around the eyes and mouth. Indentured by the Hutts after their battles with Xim the Despot, they—along with the Klatooinians and Nikto—are loyal servants to their Hutt masters. Because their tough skin and limited facial muscles do not allow for emotional displays, Vodrans appear to be expressionless. They do have deep devotion to authority, however, especially as pertaining to their Hutt masters. While they are a generally peaceful species, they strongly resisted the Empire's attempt to rule

their world. As a result, much of their planet's population was decimated. The handful of survivors subsequently became pro–New Republic, not, however, without forgetting their allegiance to the Hutts.

Wandrella (WĂN-DRĔL'-Ä)

DESIGNATION: **NONSENTIENT**
PLANET OF ORIGIN:
CIRCARPOUS V (MIMBAN)
LENGTH OF AVERAGE ADULT:
10–15 METERS

Wandrellas are huge invertebrates, or worms, with pale pink bodies that are covered in brown streaks. A wandrella's blunt head is dotted with multiple eyespots, and its gaping mouth, filled with sharp black teeth, sits underneath the eyes. The wandrella's body has a faint phosphorescent glow, and the suction organs on its underbelly allow it to move across or through the ground. Wandrellas are very sensitive to surface movement when they are burrowing below ground, and are known to burst up through the surface to attack unsuspecting prey.

Whaladon (HWĀL'-Ä-DŎN)

DESIGNATION: **SENTIENT**
PLANET OF ORIGIN:
MON CALAMARI
LENGTH OF
AVERAGE ADULT: **10 METERS**

Whaladon are water mammals native to the oceans of Mon Calamari. These creatures have large bodies, short snouts, and long flippers. Whaladon are intelligent and have developed a society and culture separate from the Mon Calamari and the Quarren. They are ruled by Leviathor, the great white Whaladon. These sentient creatures were hunted cruelly by big-game hunters and remnants of the Empire.

Planet Reference List

This listing indicates where the majority of a species resides. Those that have moved from their worlds of origin have been specially noted.

Alderaan
- nerf

Almania
- thernbee

Alzoc III
- Talz

Ambria
- hssiss
- neek

Ammuud
- pterosaur

Ando
- Aqualish

Antar 4
- Gotal

Anzat
- Anzati

Aralia
- Ranat (planet of origin: Rydar II)

Arkania
- Arkanian
- Yaka (originally from a neighboring planet)

Arzid
- arachnor

Askaj
- Askajian

Bakura
- Kurtzen

Barab I
- Barabel

Batorine
- Blood Carver

Belderone
- Firrerreo (planet of origin: Firrerre)

Bimmiel
- slashrat

Bimmisaari
- Bimm

Bothawui
- Bothan

Chad
- Chadra-Fan

Clak'dor VII
- Bith

Cona
- Arcona

Coruscant
- hawk-bat

Da Soocha V
- Ixll

Devaron
- Devaronian

Drall
- Drall

Dressel
- Dressellian

Duro
- Duros

Elom
- Elom
- Elomin

Endor, forest moon of
- Ewok
- Yuzzum

Falleen
- Falleen

Galantos
- Fia

Gamorr
- Gamorrean (Gamorreans also inhabit a colony on Pzob)

Gand
- Gand

Garban
- Jenet

Gentes
- Ugnaught

H'nemthe
- H'nemthe

Honoghr
- Noghri

Hoth
- tauntaun
- wampa

Ithor
- Ithorian

Kamar
- howlrunner
- Kamarian

Kashyyyk
- Wookiee

Kerilt
- Caamasi (planet of origin: Caamas)

Kessel
- energy spider

Khomm
- Khommite

Kintan
- Nikto

Kinyen
- Gran

Kirdo III
- Kitonak

Klatooine
- Klatooinian

Kowak
- Kowakian monkey-lizard

Kubindi
- Kubaz

Lao-man (Sh'shuun)
- Shi'ido

Lorrd
- Lorrdian

Lowick
- Pa'lowick

Lwhekk
- Ssi-ruuk

Malastare
- Dug
- Gran (planet of origin: Kinyen, colonized Malastare)

Maridun
- Amanin

Mimban (Circarpous V)
- Coway
- Mimbanite

Moltok
- Ho'Din

Mon Calamari
- Mon Calamari
- Quarren

Mrlsst
- Mrlssi

Munto Codru
- Codru-Ji
Myrkr
- vornskr
- ysalamiri
Naboo
- Gungan
Nal Hutta
- Hutt (planet of origin: Varl)
- t'landa Til
Nam Chorios
- droch
- Tsil
Neimoidia
- Neimoidian
(planet of origin: Duro)
Nim Drovis
- Drovian
Nirauan
- Qom Jha and Qom Qae
N'zoth
- Yevetha
Orto
- Ortolan
Phindar
- Phindian
Pho Ph'eah
- Pho Ph'eahian
Pria
- Priapulin
Proxima Dibal
- dinko
Pydyr
- Pydyrian
Rafa V
- Toka (Sharu)
Ragna III
- Yuzzem
Rinn
- Tin-Tin Dwarf
Rishi
- Rishii
Roche asteroid field
- Verpine
Rodia
- Rodian
Ruuria
- Ruurian
Ryloth

- Twi'lek
Ryyk
- Neti
Selonia
- Selonian
Sluis Van
- Sluissi
Sriluur
- Weequay
Sullust
- Sullustan
Tatooine
- dewback
- Jawa
- krayt dragon
- ronto
- Sarlacc
- Tusken Raiders (Sand People)
- womp rat
ThonBoka nebula
- Oswaft
Thyferra
- Vratix
Tibrin
- Ishi Tib
Togoria
- Togorian
Toola
- Whiphid
Toydaria
- Toydarian
Trandosha
- Trandoshan
Trian
- Trianii
Tynna
- Tynnan
Umgul
- Umgullian blob
Uvena Prime
- Shistavanen
Vinsoth
- Chevin
Vodran
- dianoga
Vortex
- Vor
Wayland
- Myneyrsh

- Psadan
Yag'Dhul
- Givin
Yavin 4
- Massassi (originally brought by
the ancient Sith)
- piranha-beetle
Yavin 8
- Melodie
- purella
Zeltros
- Zeltron

Species from Unknown Worlds
Assembler
bantha
Chiss
Gank
gundark
mynock
(popularly attributed to Ord Mynock)
rancor
space slug
taurill
Yarkora
Yuuzhan Vong

Bibliography

The Adventures of Lando Calrissian I: *Lando Calrissian and the Mindharp of Sharu,* L. Neil Smith, Del Rey Books, 1983.

The Adventures of Lando Calrissian III: *Lando Calrissian and the StarCave of ThonBoka,* L. Neil Smith, Del Rey Books, 1983.

Alien Encounters: The Star Wars Aliens Compendium, Paul Sudlow et al., West End Games, 1998.

Anakin Skywalker, one-shot, Timothy Truman et al., Dark Horse Comics, 1999.

The Art of Star Wars Episode I: The Phantom Menace, Jonathan Bresman, Del Rey Books, 1999.

The Black Fleet Crisis Trilogy I: *Before the Storm,* Michael P. Kube-McDowell, Bantam Books, 1996.

The Black Fleet Crisis Trilogy II: *Shield of Lies,* Michael P. Kube-McDowell, Bantam Books, 1996.

The Black Fleet Crisis Trilogy III: *Tyrant's Test,* Michael P. Kube-McDowell, Bantam Books, 1997.

The Bounty Hunter Wars I: *The Mandalorian Armor,* K. W. Jeter, Bantam Books, 1998.

The Bounty Hunter Wars III: *Hard Merchandise,* K. W. Jeter, Bantam Books, 1999.

Children of the Jedi, Barbara Hambly, Bantam Books, 1995.

Classic Star Wars, twenty-issue series, Archie Goodwin and Al Williamson et al., Dark Horse Comics, 1992–1994.

Classic Star Wars: A Long Time Ago, six-issue series, Archie Goodwin et al., Dark Horse Comics, 1999.

Classic Star Wars: The Early Adventures, nine-issue series, Russ Manning, Dark Horse Comics, 1994–1995.

The Corellian Trilogy I: *Ambush at Corellia,* Roger MacBride Allen, Bantam Books, 1995.

The Corellian Trilogy II: *Assault at Selonia,* Roger MacBride Allen, Bantam Books, 1995.

The Corellian Trilogy III: *Showdown at Centerpoint,* Roger MacBride Allen, Bantam Books, 1995.

The Courtship of Princess Leia, Dave Wolverton, Bantam Books, 1994.

The Crystal Star, Vonda N. McIntyre, Bantam Books, 1994.

Dark Empire, six-issue series, Tom Veitch and Cam Kennedy, Dark Horse Comics, 1991–1992.

Dark Empire Sourcebook, Michael Allen Horne, West End Games, 1993.

Dark Force Rising Sourcebook, Bill Slavicsek, West End Games, 1992.

Dark Horse Presents Annual 1999, "Star Wars: Luke Skywalker—Walk-about," Phil Norwood, 1999.

Darksaber, Kevin J. Anderson, Bantam Books, 1995.

Droids, animated television show, thirteen episodes, Nelvana, 1985.

Droids, series and specials, Dark Horse Comics, 1994–1995.

Droids: Rebellion, four-issue series collection (#1–4), Ryder Windham and Ian Gibson, Dark Horse Comics, 1995; collection 1997.

Droids: Rebellion (uncollected), four-issue series (#5–8), Jan Strnad et al., Dark Horse Comics, 1995.

Droids: The Kalarba Adventures, six-issue series collection, Dan Thorsland and Ryder Windham et al., Dark Horse Comics, 1994; collection 1995.

Droids: The Protocol Offensive, Brian Daley, Ryder Wyndham, and Anthony Daniels, Dark Horse Comics, 1997.

Droids Special, Dan Thorsland, Dark Horse Comics, 1995.

Empire's End, two-issue series, Tom Veitch and Jim Baikie, Dark Horse Comics, 1995.

The Essential Guide to Characters, Andy Mangels, Del Rey Books, 1995.

The Essential Guide to Droids, Daniel Wallace, Del Rey Books, 1999.

The Essential Guide to Planets and Moons, Daniel Wallace, Del Rey Books, 1998.

The Essential Guide to Vehicles and Vessels, Bill Smith, Del Rey Books, 1996.

The Ewok Adventure (Caravan of Courage), MGM/UA, 1984.

Ewoks, animated television show, twenty-six episodes, Nelvana, 1985–1987.

Ewoks: The Battle for Endor, MGM/UA, 1985.

"First Contact," Timothy Zahn, *Star Wars Adventure Journal,* number 1, edited by Peter Schweighofer, West End Games, 1994.

Galaxy Guide 2: Yavin and Bespin, Jonatha Caspian and Bill Slavicsek et al., West End Games, 1989.

Galaxy Guide 4: Alien Races, Troy Denning, West End Games, 1989.

Galaxy Guide 12: Aliens: Enemies and Allies, C. Robert Carey et al., edited by Bill Smith, West End Games, 1995.

Galaxy of Fear, volumes one through twelve, John Whitman, Bantam Books, 1997–1998.

The Glove of Darth Vader, Paul Davids and Hollace Davids, Bantam Books, 1992.

The Hand of Thrawn Duology I: *Specter of the Past,* Timothy Zahn, Bantam Books, 1997.

The Hand of Thrawn Duology II: *Vision of the Future,* Timothy Zahn, Bantam Books, 1998.

The Han Solo Adventures I: *Han Solo at Stars' End,* Brian Daley, Del Rey Books, 1979.

The Han Solo Adventures III: *Han Solo and the Lost Legacy,* Brian Daley, Del Rey Books, 1980.

Han Solo and the Corporate Sector Sourcebook, Michael Allen Horne, West End Games, 1993.

The Han Solo Trilogy I: *The Paradise Snare,* A. C. Crispin, Bantam Books, 1997.

The Han Solo Trilogy III: *Rebel Dawn,* A. C. Crispin, Bantam Books, 1998.

Heir to the Empire Sourcebook, Bill Slavicsek, West End Games, 1992.

The Illustrated Star Wars Universe, art by Ralph McQuarrie and text by Kevin J. Anderson, Bantam Books, 1995.

Jedi Academy Sourcebook, Paul Sudlow, West End Games, 1996.

The Jedi Academy Trilogy I: *Jedi Search,* Kevin J. Anderson, Bantam Books, 1994.

The Jedi Academy Trilogy II: *Dark Apprentice,* Kevin J. Anderson, Bantam Books, 1994.

Jedi Apprentice 2: *The Dark Rival,* Jude Watson, Scholastic, 1999.

Jedi Apprentice 3: *The Hidden Past,* Jude Watson, Scholastic, 1999.

Junior Jedi Knights 2: *Lyric's World,* Nancy Richardson, Berkley Books, 1995.

Junior Jedi Knights 5: *Vader's Fortress,* Rebecca Moesta, Berkley Books, 1997.

The Last Command Sourcebook, Eric S. Trautmann, West End Games, 1994.

Monopoly Star Wars, Parker Brothers; CD-ROM, 1996; board game, 1997.

The Movie Trilogy Sourcebook, Greg Farshtey, Bill Smith et al., West End Games, 1993.

The New Jedi Order I: *Vector Prime,* R. A. Salvatore, Del Rey Books, 1999.

The New Jedi Order 2: Dark Tide I: *Onslaught,* Michael A. Stackpole, Del Rey Books, 2000.

The New Jedi Order 4: Agents of Chaos I: *Hero's Trial,* James Luceno, Del Rey Books, 2000.

The New Rebellion, Kristine Kathryn Rusch, Bantam Books, 1996.

Planet of Twilight, Barbara Hambly, Bantam Books, 1997.

Prophets of the Dark Side, Paul Davids and Hollace Davids, Bantam Books, 1993.

Rogue Planet, Greg Bear, Del Rey Books, 2000.

Shadows of the Empire, Steve Perry, Bantam Books, 1996; six-issue comics adaptation, John Wagner et al., Dark Horse Comics, 1996.

Shadows of the Empire Sourcebook, Peter Schweighofer, West End Games, 1996.

Splinter of the Mind's Eye, Alan Dean Foster, Del Rey Books, 1978; four-issue comics adaptation, Terry Austin et al., Dark Horse Comics, 1995–1996.

Star Wars, 107 issues, Marvel Comics, 1977–1986.

Star Wars, National Public Radio dramatizations, thirteen episodes, Brian Daley, 1981; Del Rey Books, 1994.

Star Wars: Return of the Jedi: The Adventures of Teebo: A Tale of Magic and Suspense, Joe Johnston, Random House Books, 1984.

Star Wars: The Roleplaying Game, Second Edition, Bill Smith, West End Games, 1992.

Star Wars Adventure Journal, issues 1–15, edited by Peter Schweighofer, West End Games, 1994–1998.

Star Wars Encyclopedia, Stephen J. Sansweet, Del Rey Books, 1998.

Star Wars Episode I: Insider's Guide, CD-ROM, LucasArts Entertainment Company, 1999.

Star Wars Episode I: The Phantom Menace, film, Twentieth Century Fox, Lucasfilm Ltd., 1999; novelization, Terry Brooks, Del Rey Books, 1999.

Star Wars Episode IV: A New Hope, film, Twentieth Century Fox, 1977; novelization, George Lucas, Del Rey Books, 1976.

Star Wars Episode V: The Empire Strikes Back, film, Twentieth Century Fox, Lucasfilm Ltd., 1980; novelization, Donald F. Glut, Del Rey Books, 1980.

Star Wars Episode V: The Empire Strikes Back, National Public Radio dramatization, ten episodes, Brian Daley, 1983; Del Rey Books, 1995.

Star Wars Episode VI: Return of the Jedi, film, Twentieth Century Fox, Lucasfilm Ltd., 1983; novelization, James Kahn, Del Rey Books, 1983.

Star Wars Sourcebook, Bill Slavicsek and Curtis Smith, West End Games, 1987.

Tales from the Mos Eisley Cantina, edited by Kevin J. Anderson, Bantam Books, 1995.

Tales of the Bounty Hunters, edited by Kevin J. Anderson, Bantam Books, 1996.

Tales of the Jedi (Knights of the Old Republic), five-issue series, Tom Veitch et al., Dark Horse Comics, 1993–1994.

Tales of the Jedi: Dark Lords of the Sith, six-issue series, Tom Veitch and Kevin J. Anderson, Dark Horse Comics, 1994–1995.

Tales of the Jedi: Redemption, five-issue series, Kevin J. Anderson et al., Dark Horse Comics, 1998.

Tales of the Jedi: The Fall of the Sith Empire, five-issue series, Kevin J. Anderson et al., Dark Horse Comics, 1997.

Tales of the Jedi: The Freedon Nadd Uprising, two-issue series, Tom Veitch et al., Dark Horse Comics, 1994.

Tales of the Jedi: The Golden Age of the Sith, six-issue series, Kevin J. Anderson et al., Dark Horse Comics, 1996–1997.

Tales of the Jedi: The Sith War, six-issue series, Kevin J. Anderson et al., Dark Horse Comics, 1995–1996.

Tales of the Jedi Companion, George R. Strayton, West End Games, 1996.

The Thrawn Trilogy I: *Heir to the Empire,* Timothy Zahn, Bantam Books, 1991; six-issue comics adaptation, Mike Baron et al., Dark Horse Comics, 1995–1996.

The Thrawn Trilogy II: *Dark Force Rising,* Timothy Zahn, Bantam Books, 1992.

The Thrawn Trilogy III: *The Last Command,* Timothy Zahn, Bantam Books, 1993; six-issue comics adaptation, Mike Baron et al., Dark Horse Comics, 1997–1998.

The Truce at Bakura, Kathy Tyers, Bantam Books, 1994.

X-Wing 1: *Rogue Squadron,* Michael A. Stackpole, Bantam Books, 1996.

X-Wing 2: *Wedge's Gamble,* Michael A. Stackpole, Bantam Books, 1996.

X-Wing 3: *The Krytos Trap,* Michael A. Stackpole, Bantam Books, 1996.

X-Wing 4: *The Bacta War,* Michael A. Stackpole, Bantam Books, 1997.

X-Wing Rogue Squadron, issues 1–35, Dark Horse Comics, 1995–1998.

Young Jedi Knights 4: *Lightsabers,* Kevin J. Anderson and Rebecca Moesta, Berkley Books, 1996.

About the Author

ann Margaret Lewis began her career writing children's stories, comic stories, and activity books for DC Comics. She has contributed to several media magazines, books, and Web sites. She presently works in Silicon Alley as an Internet content specialist helping Fortune 1000 companies utilize the power of specially targeted language in their Web endeavors. She inhabits a section of our universe known as the Bronx in New York City with her life-mate Joseph Lewis and a member of a feline species whose name is Camille.